OLD JUDGE PRIEST

IRVIN S. COBB

THE WORKS OF
IRVIN S. COBB

OLD JUDGE PRIEST

THE REVIEW OF REVIEWS CORPORATION
Publishers   NEW YORK
PUBLISHED BY ARRANGEMENT WITH GEORGE H. DORAN COMPANY

TO MARGARET MAYO

CONTENTS

OLD JUDGE PRIEST

I

THE LORD PROVIDES

THIS story begins with Judge Priest sitting at his desk at his chambers at the old courthouse. I have a suspicion that it will end with him sitting there. As to that small detail I cannot at this time be quite positive. Man proposes, but facts will have their way.

If so be you have read divers earlier tales of my telling you already know the setting for the opening scene here. You are to picture first the big bare room, high-ceiled and square of shape, its plastering cracked and stained, its wall cases burdened with law books in splotched leather jerkins; and some of the books stand straight and upright, showing themselves to be confident of the rectitude of all statements made therein, and some slant over sideways against their fellows to the right or the left, as though craving confirmatory support for their contents.

Observe also the water bucket on the little shelf in the corner, with the gourd dipper hang-

ing handily by; the art calendar, presented with
the compliments of the Langstock Lumber
Company, tacked against the door; the spittoon
on the floor; the steel engraving of President
Davis and his Cabinet facing you as you enter;
the two wide windows opening upon the west
side of the square; the woodwork, which is of
white poplar, but grained by old Mr. Kane, our
leading house, sign and portrait painter, into
what he reckoned to be a plausible imitation of
the fibrillar eccentricities of black walnut; and
in the middle of all this, hunched down behind
his desk like a rifleman in a pit, is Judge Priest,
in a confusing muddle of broad, stooped shoulders, wrinkled garments and fat short legs.

Summertime would have revealed him clad in
linen, or alpaca, or ample garments of homespun
hemp, but this particular day, being a day in the
latter part of October, Judge Priest's limbs and
body were clothed in woollen coverings. The
first grate fire of the season burned in his grate.
There was a local superstition current to the
effect that our courthouse was heated with
steam. Years before, a bond issue to provide the
requisite funds for this purpose had been voted
after much public discussion pro and con.
Thereafter, for a space, contractors and journey-
men artisans made free of the building, to the
great discomfort of certain families of resident
rats, old settler rats really, that had come to
look upon their cozy habitats behind the
wainscoting as homes for life. Anon iron pipes

emerged at unexpected and jutting angles from the baseboards here and there, to coil in the corners or else to climb the walls, joint upon joint, and festoon themselves kinkily against the ceilings.

Physically the result was satisfying to the eye of the taxpayer; but if the main function of a heating plant be to provide heat, then the innovation might hardly be termed an unqualified success. Official dwellers of the premises maintained that the pipes never got really hot to the touch before along toward the Fourth of July, remaining so until September, when they began perceptibly to cool off again. Down in the cellar the darky janitor might feed the fire box until his spine cracked and the boilers seethed and simmered, but the steam somehow seemed to get lost in transit, manifesting itself on the floors above only in a metallic clanking and clacking, which had been known seriously to annoy lawyers in the act of offering argument to judge and jurors. When warmth was needed to dispel the chill in his own quarters Judge Priest always had a fire kindled in the fireplace.

He had had one made and kindled that morning. All day the red coals had glowed between the chinks in the pot-bellied grate and the friendly flames had hummed up the flue, renewing neighbourly acquaintance with last winter's soot that made fringes on the blackened fire brick, so that now the room was in a glow. Little tiaras of sweat beaded out on the judge's bald forehead as he laboured over the papers in a certain case, and frequently he laid down his pen that he might use both hands, instead of his left only, to reach and rub remote portions of his person. Doing this, he stretched his arms until red strips showed below the ends of his wristbands. At a distance you would have said the judge was wearing coral bracelets.

The sunlight that had streamed in all afternoon through the two windows began to fade, and little shadows that stayed hidden through the day crawled under the door from the hall beyond and crept like timorous mice across the planking, ready to dart back the moment the gas was lit. Judge Priest strained to reach an especially itchy spot between his shoulder blades and addressed words to Jeff Poindexter, coloured, his body servant and house boy.

"They ain't so very purty to look at—red flannels ain't," said the judge. "But, Jeff, I've noticed this—they certainly are mighty lively company till you git used to 'em. I never am the least bit lonely fur the first few days after I put on my heavy underwear."

There was no answer from Jeff except a deep, soft breath. He slept. At a customary hour he had come with Mittie May, the white mare, and the buggy to take Judge Priest home to supper, and had found the judge engaged beyond his normal quitting time. That, however, had not discommoded Jeff. Jeff always knew what to do with his spare moments. Jeff always had a way of spending the long winter evenings. He leaned now against a bookrack, with his elbow on the top shelf, napping lightly. Jeff preferred to sleep lying down or sitting down, but he could sleep upon his feet too—and frequently did.

Having, by brisk scratching movements, assuaged the irritation between his shoulder blades, the judge picked up his pen and shoved it across a sheet of legal cap that already was half covered with his fine, close writing. He never dictated his decisions, but always wrote them out by hand. The pen nib travelled along steadily for awhile. Eventually words in a typewritten petition that rested on the desk at his left caught the judge's eye.

"Huh!" he grunted, and read the quoted phrase, " 'True Believers' Afro-American Church of Zion, sometimes called ——' " Without turning his head he again hailed his slumbering servitor: "Jeff, why do you-all call that there little church-house down by the river Possum Trot?"

Jeff roused and grunted, shaking his head clear of the lingering dregs of drowsiness.

"Suh?" he inquired. "Wuz you speakin' to me, Jedge?"

"Yes, I was. Whut's the reason amongst your people fur callin' that little church down on the river front Possum Trot?"

Jeff chuckled an evasive chuckle before he made answer. For all the close relations that existed between him and his indulgent employer, Jeff had no intention of revealing any of the secrets of the highly secretive breed of humans to which he belonged. His is a race which, upon the surface of things, seems to invite the ridicule of an outer and a higher world, yet dreads that same ridicule above all things. Show me the white man who claims to know intimately the workings of his black servant's mind, who professes to be able to tell anything of any negro's lodge affiliations or social habits or private affairs, and I will show you a born liar.

Mightily well Jeff understood the how and the why and the wherefore of the derisive hate borne by the more orthodox creeds among his people for the strange new sect known as the True Believers. He could have traced out step by step, with circumstantial detail, the progress of the internal feud within the despised congregation that led to the upspringing of rival sets of claimants to the church property, and to the litigation that had thrown the whole tangled business into the courts for final adjudication. But except in company of his own choosing and his own colour, wild horses could not have drawn that knowledge from Jeff, although it would have pained him to think any white person who had a claim upon his friendship suspected him of concealment of any detail whatsoever.

"He-he," chuckled Jeff. "I reckin that's jes' nigger foolishness. Me, I don' know no reason why they sh'd call a church by no sech a name as that. I ain't never had no truck wid 'em ole True Believers, myse'f. I knows some calls 'em the Do-Righters, and some calls 'em the Possum Trotters." His tone subtly altered to one of innocent bewilderment: "Whut you doin', Jedge, pesterin' yo'se'f wid sech low-down trash as them darkies is?"

Further discussion of the affairs of the strange faith that was divided against itself might have ensued but that an interruption came. Steps sounded in the long hallway that split the lower floor of the old courthouse lengthwise, and at a door—not Judge Priest's own door but the door of the closed circuit-court chamber adjoining—a knocking sounded, at first gently, then louder and more insistent.

"See who 'tis out yonder, Jeff," bade Judge Priest. "And ef it's anybody wantin' to see me I ain't got time to see 'em without it's somethin' important. I aim to finish up this job before we go on home."

He bent to his task again. But a sudden draft of air whisked certain loose sheets off his desk, carrying them toward the fireplace, and he swung about to find a woman in his doorway. She was a big, upstanding woman, overfleshed and overdressed, and upon her face she bore the sign of her profession as plainly and indubitably as though it had been branded there in scarlet letters.

The old man's eyes narrowed as he recognised her. But up he got on the instant and bowed

[17]

before her. No being created in the image of a woman ever had reason to complain that in her presence Judge Priest forgot his manners.

"Howdy do, ma'am," he said ceremoniously. "Will you walk in? I'm sort of busy jest at present."

"That's what your nigger boy told me, outside," she said; "but I came right on in anyway."

"Ah-hah, so I observe," stated Judge Priest dryly, but none the less politely; "mout I enquire the purpose of this here call?"

"Yes, sir; I'm a-goin' to tell you what brought me here without wastin' any more words than I can help," said the woman. "No, thank you, Judge," she went on as he motioned her toward a seat; "I guess I can say what I've got to say, standin' up. But you set down, please, Judge."

She advanced to the side of his desk as he settled back in his chair, and rested one broad flat hand upon the desk top. Three or four heavy, bejewelled bangles that were on her arm slipped down her gloved wrist with a clinking sound. Her voice was coarsened and flat; it was more like a man's voice than a woman's, and she spoke with a masculine directness.

"There was a girl died at my house early this mornin'," she told him. "She died about a quarter past four o'clock. She had something like pneumonia. She hadn't been sick but two days; she wasn't very strong to start with anyhow. Viola St. Claire was the name she went

[18]

by here. I don't know what her real name was—
she never told anybody what it was. She wasn't
much of a hand to talk about herself. She must
have been nice people though, because she was
always nice and ladylike, no matter what
happened. From what I gathered off and on,
she came here from some little town down near
Memphis. I certainly liked that girl. She'd
been with me nearly ten months. She wasn't
more than nineteen years old.

"Well, all day yestiddy she was out of her
head with a high fever. But just before she died
she come to and her mind cleared up. The doctor was gone—old Doctor Lake. He'd done all
he could for her and he left for his home about
midnight, leavin' word that he was to be called
if there was any change. Only there wasn't time
to call him; it all came so sudden.

"I was settin' by her when she opened her
eyes and whispered, sort of gaspin', and called
me by my name. Well, you could 'a' knocked
me down with a feather. From the time she
started sinkin' nobody thought she'd ever get
her senses back. She called me, and I leaned
over her and asked her what it was she wanted,
and she told me. She knew she was dyin'. She
told me she'd been raised right, which I knew
already without her tellin' me, and she said
she'd been a Christian girl before she made her
big mistake. And she told me she wanted to be
buried like a Christian, from a regular church,
with a sermon and flowers and music and all

that. She made me promise that I'd see it was done just that way. She made me put my hand in her hand and promise her. She shut her eyes then, like she was satisfied, and in a minute or two after that she died, still holdin' on tight to my hand. There wasn't nobody else there—just me and her—and it was about a quarter past four o'clock in the mornin'."

"Well, ma'am, I'm very sorry for that poor child. I am so," said Judge Priest, and his tone showed he meant it; "yit still I don't understand your purpose in comin' to me, without you need money to bury her." His hand went toward his flank, where he kept his wallet.

"Keep your hand out of your pocket, please, sir," said the woman. "I ain't callin' on anybody for help in a money way. That's all been attended to. I telephoned the undertaker the first thing this mornin'.

"It's something else I wanted to speak with you about. Well, I didn't hardly wait to get my breakfast down before I started off to keep my word to Viola. And I've been on the constant go ever since. I've rid miles on the street cars, and I've walked afoot until the bottoms of my feet both feel like boils right this minute, tryin' to find somebody that was fitten to preach a sermon over that dead girl.

"First I made the rounds of the preachers of all the big churches. Doctor Cavendar was my first choice; from what I've heard said about him he's a mighty good man. But he ain't in town.

His wife told me he'd gone off to district conference, whatever that is. So then I went to all the others, one by one. I even went 'way up on Alabama Street—to that there little mission church in the old Acme rink. The old man that runs the mission—I forget his name—he does a heap of work among poor people and down-and-out people, and I guess he might've said yes, only he's right bad off himself. He's sick in bed."

She laughed mirthlessly.

"Oh, I went everywhere, I went to all of 'em. There was one or two acted like they was afraid I might soil their clothes if I got too close to 'em. They kept me standin' in the doors of their studies so as they could talk back to me from a safe distance. Some of the others, though, asked me inside and treated me decent. But they every last one of 'em said no."

"Do you mean to tell me that not a single minister in this whole city is willin' to hold a service over that dead girl?" Judge Priest shrilled at her with vehement astonishment—and something else—in his voice.

"No, no, not that," the woman made haste to explain. "There wasn't a single one of 'em but said he'd come to my house and conduct the exercises. They was all willin' enough to go to the grave too. But you see that wouldn't do. I explained to 'em, until I almost lost my voice, that it had to be a funeral in a regular church, with flowers and music and all. That poor girl got it into her mind somehow, I think, that she'd have a better chance in the next world if she went out of this one like a Christian should ought to go. I explained all that to 'em, and from explainin' I took to arguin' with 'em, and then to pleadin' and beggin'. I bemeaned myself before them preachers. I was actually ready to go down on my knees before 'em.

"Oh, I told 'em the full circumstances. I told 'em I just had to keep my promise. I'm afraid not to keep it. I've lived my own life in my own way and I guess I've got a lot of things to answer for. I ain't worryin' about that—now. But you don't dare to break a promise that's made to the dyin'. They come back and ha'nt you. I've always heard that and I know it's true.

"One after another I told those preachers just exactly how it was, but still they all said no. Every one of 'em said his board of deacons or elders or trustees, or something like that, wouldn't stand for openin' up their church for Viola. I always thought a preacher could run his church to suit himself, but from what I've heard to-day I know now he takes his orders from somebody else. So finally, when I was about to give up, I thought about you and I come here as straight as I could walk."

"But, ma'am," he said, "I'm not a regular church member myself. I reckin I oughter be, but I ain't. And I still fail to understand why you should think I could serve you, though I don't mind tellin' you I'd be mighty glad to ef I could."

"I'll tell you why. I never spoke to you but once before in my life, but I made up my mind then what kind of a man you was. Maybe you don't remember it, Judge, but two years ago this comin' December that there Law and Order League fixed up to run me out of this town. They didn't succeed, but they did have me indicted by the Grand Jury, and I come up before you and pleaded guilty —they had the evidence on me all right. You fined me, you fined me the limit, and I guess if I hadn't 'a' had the money to pay the fine I'd 'a' gone to jail. But the main point with me was that you treated me like a lady.

"I know what I am good and well, but I don't like to have somebody always throwin' it up to me. I've got feelin's the same as anybody else has. You made that little deputy sheriff quit shovin' me round and you called me Mizzis Cramp to my face, right out in court. I've been Old Mallie Cramp to everybody in this town so long I'd mighty near forgot I ever had a handle on my name, until you reminded me of it. You was polite to me and decent to me, and you acted like you was sorry to see a white woman fetched up in court, even if you didn't say it right out. I ain't forgot that. I ain't ever goin' to forget it. And awhile ago, when I was all beat out and discouraged, I said to myself that if there was one man left in this town who could maybe help me to keep my promise to that dead girl, Judge William Pitman Priest was the man. That's why I'm here."

"I'm sorry, ma'am, sorry fur you and sorry fur that dead child," said Judge Priest slowly. "I wish I could help you. I wish I knew how to advise you. But I reckin those gentlemen were right in whut they said to you to-day. I reckin probably their elders would object to them openin' up their churches, under the circumstances. And I'm mightily afraid I ain't got any influence I could bring to bear in any quarter. Did you go to Father Minor? He's a good friend of mine; we was soldiers together in the war—him and me. Mebbe ——"

"I thought of him," said the woman hopelessly; "but you see, Judge, Viola didn't belong to his church. She was raised a Protestant—she told me so. I guess he couldn't do nothin'."

"Ah-hah, I see," said the judge, and in his perplexity he bent his head and rubbed his broad expanse of pink bald brow fretfully, as though to stimulate thought within by friction without. His left hand fell into the litter of documents upon his desk. Absently his fingers shuffled them back and forth under his eyes. He straightened himself alertly.

"Was it stated—was it specified that a preacher must hold the funeral service over that dead girl?" he inquired.

The woman caught eagerly at the inflection that had come into his voice.

"No, sir," she answered; "all she said was that it must be in a church and with some flowers and some music. But I never heard of anybody preachin' a regular sermon without it was a regular preacher. Did you ever, Judge?" Doubt and renewed disappointment battered at her just-born hopes.

"I reckin mebbe there have been extryordinary occasions where an amateur stepped in and done the best he could," said the judge. "Mebbe some folks here on earth couldn't excuse sech presumption as that, but I reckin they'd understand how it was up yonder."

He stood up, facing her, and spoke as one making a solemn promise:

"Ma'am, you needn't worry yourself any longer. You kin go on back to your home. That dead child is goin' to have whut she asked for. I give you my word on it."

She strove to put a question, but he kept on:

"I ain't prepared to give you the full details yit. You see I don't know myself jest exactly whut they'll be. But inside of an hour from now I'll be seein' Jansen and he'll notify you in regards to the hour and the place and the rest of it. Kin you rest satisfied with that?"

She nodded, trying to utter words and not succeeding. Emotion shook her gross shape until the big gold bands on her arms jangled together.

"So, ef you'll kindly excuse me, I've got quite a number of things to do betwixt now and suppertime. I kind of figger I'm goin' to be right busy."

He stepped to the threshold and called out down the hallway, which by now was a long, dim tunnel of thickening shadows.

"Jeff, oh Jeff, where are you, boy?"

"Comin', Jedge."

The speaker emerged from the gloom that was only a few shades darker than himself.

"Jeff," bade his master, "I want you to show this lady the way out—it's black as pitch in that there hall. And, Jeff, listen here! When you've done that I want you to go and find the sheriff fur me. Ef he's left his office—and I s'pose he has by now—you go on out to his house, or wherever he is, and find him and tell him I want to see him here right away."

He swung his ponderous old body about and bowed with a homely courtesy:

"And now I bid you good night, ma'am."

At the cross sill of the door she halted:

"Judge—about gettin' somebody to carry the coffin in and out—did you think about that? She was such a little thing—she won't be very heavy—but still, at that, I don't know anybody —any men—that would be willin' ——"

"Ma'am," said Judge Priest gravely, "ef I was you I wouldn't worry about who the pall-bearers will be. I reckin the Lord will provide. I've took notice that He always does ef you'll only meet Him halfway."

For a fact the judge was a busy man during

the hour which followed upon all this, the hour
between twilight and night. Over the telephone
he first called up M. Jansen, our leading undertaker; indeed at that time our only one, excusing
the coloured undertaker on Locust Street. He
had converse at length with M. Jansen. Then
he called up Doctor Lake, a most dependable
person in sickness, and when you were in good
health too. Then last of all he called up a certain widow who lived in those days, Mrs. Matilda Weeks by name; and this lady was what is
commonly called a character. In her case the
title was just and justified. Of character she
had more than almost anybody I ever knew.

Mrs. Weeks didn't observe precedents. She
made them. She cared so little for following
after public opinion that public opinion usually
followed after her—when it had recovered from
the shock and reorganised itself. There were
two sides to her tongue: for some a sharp and
acid side, and then again for some a sweet and
gentle side—and mainly these last were the
weak and the erring and the shiftless, those
underfoot and trodden down. Moving through
this life in a calm, deliberative, determined way,
always along paths of her making and her choosing, obeying only the beck of her own mind,
doing good where she might, with a perfect
disregard for what the truly good might think
about it, Mrs. Weeks was daily guilty of acts
that scandalised all proper people. But the
improper ones worshipped the ground her feet

touched as she walked. She was much like that
disciple of Joppa named Tabitha, which by
interpretation is called Dorcas, of whom it is
written that she was full of good works and
almsdeeds which she did. Yes, you might safely
call Mrs. Weeks a character.

With her, back and forth across the telephone
wire, Judge Priest had extended speech. Then
he hung up the receiver and went home alone to
a late and badly burnt supper. Aunt Dilsey
Turner, the titular goddess of his kitchen, was
a queen cook among cooks, but she could keep
victuals hot without scorching them for just so
long and no longer. She took pains to say as
much, standing in the dining-room door with
her knuckles on her hips. But the judge didn't
pay much attention to Aunt Dilsey's vigorous
remarks. He had other things on his mind.

Down our way this present generation has
seen a good many conspicuous and prominent
funerals. Until very recently we rather specialised in funerals. Before moving pictures sprang
up so numerously funerals provided decorous
and melancholy divertisement for many whose
lives, otherwise, were rather aridly devoid of
sources of inexpensive excitement. Among us
were persons—old Mrs. Whitridge was a typical
example—who hadn't missed a funeral of any
consequence for years and years back. Let
some one else provide the remains, and they
would assemble in such number as to furnish a
gathering, satisfying in its size and solemn in its

impressiveness. They took the run of funerals as they came. But there were some funerals which, having taken place, stood forth in the public estimation forever after as events to be remembered. They were mortuary milestones on the highway of community life.

For instance, those who were of suitable age to attend it are never going to forget the burial that the town gave lazy, loud-mouthed Lute Montjoy, he being the negro fireman on the ferryboat who jumped into the river that time, aiming to save the small child of a Hungarian immigrant family bound for somewhere up in the Cumberland on the steamer *Goldenrod*. The baby ran across the boiler deck and went overboard, and the mother screamed, and Lute saw what had happened and he jumped. He was a good swimmer all right, and in half a dozen strokes he reached the strangling mite in the water; but then the current caught him—the June rise was on—and sucked him downstream into the narrow, swirling place between the steamboat's hull and the outside of the upper wharf boat, and he went under and stayed under.

Next morning when the dragnets caught and brought him up, one of his stiffened black arms still encircled the body of the white child, in a grip that could hardly be loosened. White and black, everybody turned out to bury Lute Montjoy. In the services at the church two of the leading clergymen assisted, turn and turn about;

and at the graveside Colonel Horatio Farrell, dean of the local bar and the champion orator of seven counties, delivered an hour-long oration, calling Lute by such names as Lute, lying there cased in mahogany with silver trimmings, had never heard applied to him while he lived. Popular subscription provided the fund that paid for the stone to mark his grave and to perpetuate the memory of his deed. You can see the shaft to this day. It rises white and high among the trees in Elm Grove Cemetery, and the word *Hero* is cut deep in its marble face.

Then there was the funeral of old Mr. Simon Leatheritt, mightiest among local financiers. That, indeed, was a funeral to be cherished in the cranial memory casket of any person so favoured by fortune as to have been present; a funeral that was felt to be a credit alike to deceased and to bereaved; a funeral that by its grandeur would surely have impressed the late and, in a manner of speaking, lamented Leatheritt, even though its cost would have panged him; in short, an epoch-making and an era-breeding funeral.

In the course of a long married career this was the widow's first opportunity to cut loose and spend money without having to account for it by dollar, by dime and by cent to a higher authority, and she certainly did cut loose, sparing absolutely no pains in the effort to do her recent husband honour. At a cost calculated as running into three figures for that one item alone, she imported the prize male tenor of a St. Louis cathedral choir to enrich the proceedings with his glowing measures. This person, who was a person with eyes too large for a man and a mouth too small, rendered Abide With Me in a fashion so magnificent that the words were entirely indistinguishable and could not be followed on account of the genius' fashion of singing them.

By express, floral offerings came from as far away as Cleveland, Ohio, and New Orleans, Louisiana. One creation, sent on from a far distance, which displayed a stuffed white dove hovering, with the aid of wires, in the arc of a green trellis above a bank of white tuberoses, attracted much favourable comment. A subdued murmur of admiration, travelling onward from pew to pew, followed after it as the design was borne up the centre aisle to the chancel rail. As for broken columns and flower pillows with appropriately regretful remarks let into them in purple immortelle letterings, and gates ajar—why, they were evident in a profusion almost past individual recording.

When the officiating minister, reading the burial service, got as far as "Dust to dust," Ashby Corwin, who sat at the back of the church, bent over and whispered in the ear of his nearest neighbour: "Talk about your ruling passions! If that's not old Uncle Sime all over—still grabbing for the dust!" As a rule, repetition of this sally about town was greeted with

the deep hush of silent reproof. Our dead
money-monarch's memory was draped with the
sanctity of wealth. Besides, Ash Corwin, as
many promptly took pains to point out, was a
person of no consequence whatsoever, financial
or otherwise. Mrs. Whitridge's viewpoint, as
voiced by her in the months that followed, was
the commoner one. This is Mrs. Whitridge
speaking:

"I've been going to funerals steady ever since
I was a child. I presume I've helped comfort
more berefts by my presence and seen more dear
departeds fittin'ly laid away than any person in
this whole city. But if you're asking me, I
must say Mr. Leatheritt's was the most fashion-
able funeral I ever saw, or ever hope to see.
Everything that lavishness could do was done
there, and all in such lovely taste, too! Why,
it had style written all over it, especially the
interment."

Oh, we've had funerals and funerals down
our way. But the funeral that took place on an
October day that I have in mind still will be
talked about long after Banker Leatheritt and
the estate he reluctantly left behind him are
but dim recollections. It came as a surprise to
most people, for in the daily papers of that
morning no customary black - bordered announcement had appeared. Others had heard of
it by word of mouth. In dubious quarters, and
in some quarters not quite so dubious, the news
had travelled, although details in advance of the

event were only to be guessed at. Anyhow, the reading and talking public knew this much: That a girl, calling herself Viola St. Claire and aged nineteen, had died. It was an accepted fact, naturally, that even the likes of her must be laid away after some fashion or other. If she were put under ground by stealth, clandestinely as it were, so much the better for the atmosphere of civic morality. That I am sure would have been disclosed as the opinion of a majority, had there been inquiry among those who were presumed to have and who admitted they had the best interests of the community at heart.

So you see a great many people were entirely unprepared against the coming of the pitiably short procession that at eleven o'clock, or thereabout, turned out of the little street running down back of the freight depot into Franklin Street, which was one of our main thoroughfares. First came the hearse, drawn by M. Jansen's pair of dappled white horses and driven by M. Jansen himself, he wearing his official high hat and the span having black plumes in their head stalls, thus betokening a burial ceremony of the top cost. Likewise the hearse was M. Jansen's best hearse—not his third best, nor yet his second best, but the splendid crystal-walled one that he ordered in the Eastern market after the relict of Banker Leatheritt settled the bill.

The coffin, showing through the glass sides, was of white cloth and it looked very small, almost like a coffin for a child. However, it

may have looked so because there was little
of its shape to be seen. It was covered and piled
and banked up with flowers, and these flowers,
strange to say, were not done into shapes of
gates aswing; nor into shafts with their tops
gone; nor into flat, stiff pillows of waxy-white
tuberoses, pale and cold as the faces of the dead.
These were such flowers as, in our kindly climate, grew out of doors until well on into No-
vember: late roses and early chrysanthemums,
marigolds and gladioluses, and such. They lay
there loosely, with their stems upon them, just
as Mrs. Weeks had sheared them, denuding
every plant and shrub and bush that grew in her
garden, so a girl whom Mrs. Weeks had never
seen might go to her grave with an abundance
of the blossoms she had coveted about her.

Behind the hearse came a closed coach. We
used to call them coaches when they figured in
funerals, carriages when used for lodge turnouts,
and plain hacks when they met the trains and
boats. In the coach rode four women. The
world at large had a way of calling them painted
women; but this day their faces were not painted
nor were they garishly clad. For the time they
were merely women—neither painted women
nor fallen women—but just women.

And that was nearly all, but not quite. At
one side of the hearse, opposite the slowly turning front wheels, trudged Judge Priest, carrying
in the crook of one bent arm a book. It wouldn't
be a law book, for they commonly are large

books, bound in buff leather, and this book was
small and flat and black in colour. On the other
side of the hearse, with head very erect and eyes
fixed straight ahead and Sunday's best coat
buttoned tightly about his sparse frame, walked
another old man, Doctor Lake.

And that was all. At least that was all at
first. But as the procession—if you could call
it that—swung into Franklin Street it passed
by The Blue Jug Saloon and Short Order Restaurant. In the doorway here lounged Perry
Broadus, who drank. The night before had been
a hard night upon Perry Broadus, whose nights
always were hard, and it promised to be a hard
day. He shivered at the touch of the clear,
crisp air upon his flushed cheek and slanted for
support against a handy doorpost of the Blue
Jug. The hearse turned the corner, and he
stared at it a moment and understood. He
straightened his slouched shoulders, and the
fog left his eyes and the fumes of staling alcohol
quit his brain. He pulled off his hat, twisted his
wreck of a necktie straight with a hand that
shook and, cold sober, he ran out and caught
step behind Judge Priest. Referring to pall-
bearers, Judge Priest had said the Lord would
provide. But Perry Broadus provided himself.

I forget now who the next volunteer was, but
I think possibly it was Sergeant Jimmy Bagby.
Without waiting to analyse the emotions that
possessed him in the first instant of realisation,
the sergeant went hurrying into the road to fall

in, and never thereafter had cause to rue his
impulse, his one regret being that he had no
warning, else he would have slipped on his old,
grey uniform coat that he reserved for high
occasions. I know that Mr. Napoleon B.
Crump, who was active in church and charities,
broke away from two ladies who were discussing
parish affairs with him upon the sidewalk in
front of his wholesale grocery, and with never a
word of apology to them slipped into line, with
Doctor Lake for his file leader. A moment
later, hearing footfalls at his back, Mr. Crump
looked over his shoulder. Beck Giltner, a man
whom Mr. Crump had twice tried to have driven
out of town and whom he yet hoped to see
driven out of town, was following, two paces
behind him.

I know that Mr. Joe Plumm came, shirt-
sleeved, out of his cooper shop and sought a
place with the others. I know that Major Fairleigh, who had been standing idly at the front
window of his law office, emerged therefrom in
such haste he forgot to bring his hat with him.
Almost immediately the Major became aware
that he was sandwiched in between the fat chief
of the paid fire department and worthless Tip
Murphy, who hadn't been out of the penitentiary a month. I know that old Peter J. Galloway, the lame Irish blacksmith, wore his leather
apron as he limped along, bobbing up on his
good leg and down on his short bent one.

I know that Mr. Herman Felsburg brought

with him four of the clerks of Felsburg Brothers'
Oak Hall Clothing Emporium. One of them
left a customer behind, too, or possibly the
customer also came. On second thought, I
believe he did. I know that some men stood
along the curbstones and stared and that other
men, having first bared their heads, broke away
to tail in at the end of the doubled lines of
marching figures. And I know that of those who
did this there were more than of those who
merely stood and stared. The padding of shoe
soles upon the gravel of the street became a
steadily increasing, steadily rising thump-
thump-thump; the rhythm of it rose above the
creak and the clatter of the hearse wheels and
the hoofs of the horses.

Lengthened and strengthened every few feet
and every few yards by the addition of new
recruits, the procession kept on. It trailed past
shops and stores and jobbers' houses. It travelled by the Y. M. C. A. and by Fraternity
Hall. It threaded its way between rows of
residences. It must have been two hundred
strong when the hearse horses came abreast of
that stately new edifice, with its fine memorial
windows and its tall twin spires, which the
darkies called the Big Rock Church. They
didn't stop here though. Neither did they stop
at the old ivy-covered church farther along
nor at the little red-brick church in the middle
of the next block.

The procession kept on. Growing and still

growing, it kept on. By now you might have
counted in its ranks fit representatives of every
grade and class, every cult and every creed to
be found in the male population of our town.
Old men and young men marched; bachelors
and heads of families; rich men and poor; men
who made public sentiment and men who defied
it; strict churchgoers and avowed sceptics; men
called good and men called bad. You might
have ticked off almost any kind of man in that
line. Possibly the Pharisees were missing and
the Scribes were served only in the person of the
editor of the *Daily Evening News*, who appeared
well up toward the front of one of the files, with
a forgotten cedar lead pencil riding in the crotch
of his right ear. But assuredly the Publican was
there and the Sinner.

Heralded by the sound of its own thumping
tread and leaving in its wake a stupefaction of
astonishment, the procession kept straight on
down Franklin Street, through the clear October
sunshine and under the sentinel maples, which
sifted down gentle showers of red and yellow
leaves upon it. It kept on until it reached the
very foot of the street. There it swung off at
right angles into a dingy, ill-kempt little street
that coursed crookedly along the water front,
with poor houses rising upon one side and the
raw mud banks of the river falling steeply away
upon the other.

It followed this street until the head of it
came opposite a little squat box-and-barn of a

structure, built out of up-and-down planking; unpainted, too, with a slatted belfry, like an overgrown chicken coop, perched midway of the peak of its steeply pitched tin roof. Now this structure, as all knew who remembered the history of contemporary litigation as recorded in the local prints, was the True Believers' Afro-American Church of Zion, sometimes termed in derision Possum Trot, being until recently the place of worship of that newest and most turbulent of local negro sects, but now closed on an injunction secured by one of the warring factions within its membership and temporarily lodged in the custody of the circuit court and in the hands of that court's servant, the high sheriff, pending ultimate determination of the issue by his honour, the circuit judge. Technically it was still closed; legally and officially still in the firm grasp of Sheriff Giles Birdsong. Actually and physically it was at this moment open—wide open. The double doors were drawn back, the windows shone clean, and at the threshold of the swept and garnished interior stood Judge Priest's Jeff, with his broom in his hand and his mop and bucket at his side. Jeff had concluded his share of the labours barely in time.

As M. Jansen steered his dappled span close up alongside the pavement and brought them to a standstill, Judge Priest looked back and with what he saw was well content. He knew that morbid curiosity might account for the presence of some among this multitude who had come following after him, but not for all, and perhaps not for very many. He nodded to himself with the air of one who is amply satisfied by the results of an accomplished experiment.

For the bearers of the dead he selected offhand the eight men who had marched nearest to him. As they lifted the coffin out from the hearse it befell that our most honoured physician should have for his opposite our most consistent drunkard, and that Mr. Crump, who walked in straight and narrow paths, should rub elbows with Beck Giltner, whom upon any day in the year, save only this day, Mr. Crump would have rejoiced to see harried with hounds beyond the corporate limits.

Up the creaking steps and in between the lolling door-halves the chosen eight bore the dead girl, and right reverently they rested their burden on board trestles at the foot of the little box-pulpit, where shafts of sunshine, filtering through one of the small side windows, stencilled a checkered pattern of golden squares upon the white velvet box with its silver handles and its silver name plate. Behind the eight came others, bringing the flowers. It must have been years, I imagine, since the soiled hands of some of these had touched such gracious things as flowers, yet it was to transpire that none among them needed the help of any defter fingers. Upon the coffin and alongside it they laid down their arm loads, so that once more the narrow white box was almost covered under bloom and leaf; and then the yellow pencillings of sunlight made greater glory there than ever.

When the crowd was in and seated—all of it that could get in and get seated—a tall, white-haired woman in a plain black frock came silently and swiftly through a door at the back and sat herself down upon a red plush stool before a golden-oak melodeon. Stool and melodeon being both the property of the fractious True Believers, neglect and poor usage had wrought most grievously with the two of them. The stool stood shakily upon its infirm legs and within the melodeon the works were skewed and jangled. But Mrs. Matilda Weeks' finger ends fell with such sanctifying gentleness upon the warped keys, and as she sang her sweet soprano rose so clearly and yet so softly, filling this place whose walls so often had resounded to the lusty hallelujahs of shouting black converts, that to those who listened now it seemed almost as though a Saint Cecelia had descended from on high to make this music. Mrs. Weeks sang a song that she had sung many a time before—for ailing paupers at the almshouse, for prisoners at the county jail, for the motley congregations that flocked to Sunday afternoon services in the little mission at the old Acme rink. And the name of the song was Rock of Ages.

She finished singing. Judge Priest got up from a front pew where he had been sitting and went and stood alongside the flower-piled coffin, with his back to the little yellow-pine pulpit and his prayer book in his hands, a homely, ungraceful figure, facing an assemblage that packed the darky meeting house until it could hold no more. In sight there were just five women: the good woman at the melodeon and four other women, dwellers beneath a sinful roof, who sat together upon what the pastor of the True Believers would have called the mourners' bench. And all the rest were men. Men sat, row on row, in the pews; men stood in the single narrow aisle and against the walls round three sides of the building; and men appeared at the doorway and on beyond the doorway, upon the porch and the steps.

I deem it to have been characteristic of the old judge that he made no explanation for his presence before them and no apology for his assumption of a rôle so unusual. He opened his black-bound volume at a place where his plump forefinger had been thrust between the leaves to mark the place for him, and in his high, thin voice he read through the service for the dead, with its promise of the divine forgiveness. When he had reached the end of it he put the book aside, and spoke to them in the fair and grammatical English that usually he reserved for his utterances from the bench in open court:

"Our sister who lies here asked with almost her last conscious breath that at her funeral a sermon should be preached. Upon me, who never before attempted such an undertaking, devolves the privilege of speaking a few words above her. I had thought to take for my text the words: 'He that is without sin among you, let him first cast a stone at her.'

"But I have changed my mind. I changed it only a little while ago. For I recalled that once on a time the Master said: 'Suffer little children to come unto Me, and forbid them not: for of such is the kingdom of Heaven.' And I believe, in the scheme of everlasting mercy and everlasting pity, that before the eyes of our common Creator we are all of us as little children whose feet stumble in the dark. So I shall take that saying of the Saviour for my text."

Perhaps it would be unjust to those whose business is the preaching of sermons to call this a sermon. I, for one, never heard any other sermon in any other church that did not last longer than five minutes. And certainly Judge Priest, having made his beginning, did not speak for more than five minutes; the caressing fingers of the sunlight had not perceptibly shifted upon the flower-strewn coffin top when he finished what he had to say and stood with his head bowed. After that, except for a rustle of close-packed body and a clearing of men's huskened throats, there was silence for a little time.

Then Judge Priest's eyes looked about him and three pews away he saw Ashby Corwin. It may have been he remembered that as a young man Ashby Corwin had been destined for holy orders until another thing—some said it was a woman and some said it was whisky, and some said it was first the woman and then the whisky —came into his life and wrecked it so that until the end of his days Ashby Corwin trod the rocky downhill road of the profligate and the waster. Or it may have been the look he read upon the face of the other that moved Judge Priest to say:

"I will ask Mr. Corwin to pray."

At that Ashby Corwin stood up in his place and threw back his prematurely whitened head, and he lifted his face that was all scarified with the blighting flames of dissipation, and he shut his eyes that long since had wearied of looking upon a trivial world, and Ashby Corwin prayed. There are prayers that seem to circle round and round in futile rings, going nowhere; and then again there are prayers that are like sparks struck off from the wheels of the prophet's chariot of fire, coursing their way upward in spiritual splendour to blaze on the sills of the Judgment Seat. This prayer was one of those prayers.

After that Judge Priest bowed his head again and spoke the benediction.

It turns out that I was right a while back when I predicted this chapter of this book might end with Judge Priest sitting at his desk in his room at the old courthouse. On the morning of the day following the day of this funeral he sat there, putting the last words to his decision touching upon the merits of the existing

controversy in the congregation of the True
Believers' Afro-American Church of Zion. The
door opened and in walked Beck Giltner, saloon
keeper, sure-thing gambler, handy-man-with-a-
gun, and, according to the language of a resolution unanimously adopted at a mass meeting of
the Law and Order League, force-for-evil.

Beck Giltner was dressed in his best. He
wore his wide-brimmed, black soft hat, with
its tall crown carefully dented in, north, east,
south and west; his long black coat; his white
turn-down collar; his white lawn tie; and in the
bosom of his plaited shirt of fine white linen his
big diamond pin, that was shaped like an
inverted banjo. This was Beck Giltner's attire
for the street and for occasions of ceremony.
Indoors it was the same, except that sometimes
he took the coat off and turned back his shirt
cuffs.

"Good mornin', Beck," said the judge.
"Well?"

"Judge Priest," said Giltner, "as a rule I
don't come to this courthouse except when I
have to come. But to-day I've come to tell
you something. You made a mistake yesterday!"

"A mistake, suh?" The judge's tone was
sharp and quick.

"Yes, suh, that's what you did," returned
the tall gambler. "I don't mean in regards to
that funeral you held for that dead girl. You
probably don't care what I think one way or

the other, but I want to tell you I was strong
for that, all the way through. But you made a
mistake just the same, Judge; you didn't take
up a collection.

"It had been a good many years since I was
inside of a church, until I walked with you and
the others to that little nigger meetin'-house yesterday—forty-odd years I reckon; not since I
was a kid, anyway. But to the best of my early
recollections they always took a collection for
something or other every time I did go to
church. And yesterday you overlooked that
part altogether.

"So last night I took it on myself to get up a
collection for you. I started it with a bill or so
off my own roll. Then I passed the hat round
at several places where you wouldn't scarcely
care to go yourself. And I didn't run across a
single fellow that failed to contribute. Some of
'em don't move in the best society, and there's
some more of 'em that you'd only know of by
reputation. But every last one of 'em put in
something. There was one man that didn't
have only seven cents to his name—he put that
in. So here it is—four hundred and seventy-
five dollars and forty-two cents, accordin' to
my count."

From one pocket he fetched forth a rumpled
packet of paper money and from the other a
small cloth sack, which gave off metallic clinking
sounds. He put them down together on the
desk in front of Judge Priest.

"I appreciate this, ef I am right in my assumption of the motives which actuated you and the purposes to which you natchally assumed this here money would be applied," said Judge Priest as the other man waited for his response. "But, son, I can't take your money. It ain't needed. Why, I wouldn't know whut to do with it. There ain't no outstandin' bills connected with that there funeral. All the expense entailed was met—privately. So you see——"

"Wait just a minute before you say no!" interrupted Giltner. "Here's my idea and it's the idea of all the others that contributed: We all want you to take this money and keep it—keep it in a safe, or in your pocket, or in the bank to your credit, or anywheres you please, but just keep it. And if any girl that's gone wrong should die and not have any friends to help bury her, they can come to you and get the cash out of this fund to pay for puttin' her away. And if any other girl should want to go back to her people and start in all over again and try to lead a better life, why you can advance her the railroad fare out of that money too. You see, Judge, we are aimin' to make a kind of a trust fund out of it, with you as the trustee. And when the four seventy-five forty-two is all used up, if you'll just let me know I'll guarantee to rustle up a fresh bank roll so you'll always have enough on hand to meet the demands. Now then, Judge, will you take it?"

Judge Priest took it. He stretched out and scooped in currency and coin sack, using therefor his left hand only. The right was engaged in reaching for Beck Giltner's right hand, the purpose being to shake it.

II

A BLENDING OF THE
PARABLES

NEARLY every week—weather permitting—the old judge went to dinner
somewhere. To a considerable extent
he kept up his political fences going to
dinners. Usually it was of a Sunday that he
went.

By ten o'clock almost any fair Sunday morning—spring, summer or early fall—Judge
Priest's Jeff would have the venerable side-bar
buggy washed down, and would be leading forth
from her stall the ancient white lady-sheep, with
the unmowed fetlocks and the intermittent
mane, which the judge, from a spirit of
prideful affection and in the face of all visual
testimony to the contrary, persisted in regarding as an authentic member of the equine
kingdom.

Presently, in their proper combination and
alignment, the trio would be stationed at the
front gate, thus: Jeff in front, bracing the forward section of the mare-creature; and the

buggy behind, its shafts performing a similar office for the other end of this unique quadruped. Down the gravelled walk that led from the house, under the water maples and silver-leaf poplars, which arched over to make a shady green tunnel of it, the judge would come, immaculate but rumply in white linens. The judge's linens had a way of getting themselves all rumpled even before he put them on. You might say they were born rumpled.

Beholding his waddlesome approach out of the tail of her eye, the white animal would whinny a dignified and conservative welcome. She knew her owner almost as well as he knew her. Then, while Jeff held her head—that is to say, held it up—the old man would heave his frame ponderously in and upward between the dished wheels and settle back into the deep nest of the buggy, with a wheeze to which the agonised rear springs wheezed back an anthemlike refrain.

"All right, Jeff!" the judge would say, bestowing his cotton umbrella and his palm-leaf fan in their proper places, and working a pair of wrinkled buckskin gloves on over his chubby hands. "I won't be back, I reckin, till goin' on six o'clock this evenin', and I probably won't want nothin' then fur supper except a cold snack. So if you and Aunt Dilsey both put out from the house fur the day be shore to leave the front-door key under the front-door mat, where I kin find it in case I should git back sooner'n I expect. And you be here in due time yourse'f, to unhitch. Hear me, boy?"

"Yas, suh," Jeff would respond. "I hears you."

"All right, then!" his employer would command as he gathered up the lines. "Let loose of Mittie May."

Conforming with the accepted ritual of the occasion, Jeff would let loose of Mittie May and step ceremoniously yet briskly aside, as though fearing instant annihilation in the first resistless surge of a desperate, untamable beast. Judge Priest would slap the leathers down on Mittie May's fat back; and Mittie May, sensing the master touch on those reins, would gather her four shaggy legs together with apparent intent of bursting into a mad gallop, and then, ungathering them, step out in her characteristic gentle amble, a gait she never varied under any circumstances. Away they would go, then, with the dust splashing up from under Mittie May's flat and deliberative feet, and the loose rear curtain of the buggy flapping and slapping behind like a slatting sail.

Jeff would stand there watching them until they had faded away in the deeper dust where Clay Street merged, without abrupt transition, into a winding country road; and, knowing the judge was definitely on his way, Jeff would be on his way, too, but in a different direction. Of his own volition Jeff never fared countryward on Sundays. Green fields and running brooks

laid no spell of allurement on his nimble fancy.
He infinitely preferred metropolitan haunts and
pastimes—such, for instance, as promenades
along the broken sidewalks of the Plunkett's
Hill section and crap games behind the coloured
undertaker's shop on Locust Street.

The judge's way would be a pleasant way—a
peaceful, easy way, marked only by small dis-
putes at each crossroads junction, Mittie May
desiring always to take the turn that would
bring them back home by the shortest route,
and the judge stubborn in his intention of pushing further on. The superior powers of human
obstinacy having triumphed over four-legged instinct, they would proceed. Now they would
clatter across a wooden bridge spanning a
sluggish amber-coloured stream, where that im-
pertinent bird, the kingfisher, cackled derisive
imitations of the sound given off by the warped
axles of the buggy, and the yonkerpins—which
Yankees, in their ignorance, have called water
lilies—spread their wide green pads and their
white-and-yellow cusps of bloom on the face
of the creek water.

Now they would come to cornfields and
tobacco patches that steamed in the sunshine,
conceding the season to be summer; or else old,
abandoned clearings, grown up rankly in shoe-
make bushes and pawpaw and persimmon and
sassafras. And the pungent scent of the wayside
pennyroyal would rise like an incense, saluting
their nostrils as they passed, and the grassy

furrows of long-harvested grain crops were like the lines of graves on old battlegrounds.

Now they would come into the deep woods; and here the sunlight sifted down through the tree tops, making cathedral aisles among the trunks and dim green cloisters of the thickets; and in small open spaces the yellowing double prongs of the mullein stalks stood up stiff and straightly like two-tined altar candles. Then out of the woods again and along a stretch of blinding hot road, with little grey lizards racing on the decayed fence rails as outriders, and maybe a pair of those old red-head peckerwoods flickering on from snag to snag just ahead, keeping company with the judge, but never quite permitting him to catch up with them.

So, at length, after five miles, or maybe ten, he would come to his destination, which might be a red-brick house set among apple trees on a low hill, or a whitewashed double cabin of logs in a bare place down in the bottoms. Here, at their journey's end, they would halt, with Mittie May heaving her rotund sides in and out in creditable simulation of a thoroughbred finishing a hard race; and Judge Priest would poke his head out from under the buggy hood and utter the customary hail of "Hello the house!" At that, nine times out of ten—from under the house and from round behind it—would boil a black-and-tan ground swell of flap-eared, bugle-voiced hound dogs, all tearing for the gate, with every apparent intention of devouring horse and harness, buggy and driver, without a moment's delay. And behind them, in turn, a shirt-sleeved man would emerge from the shelter of the gallery and hurry down the path toward the fence, berating the belling pack at every step he took:

"You Sounder, you Ring, you Queen—consarn your mangy pelts! Go on back yonder where you belong! You Saucer—come on back here and behave yourse'f! I bet I take a chunk some of these days and knock your fool head off!"

As the living wave of dogs parted before his advance and his threats, and broke up and turned about and vanished with protesting yelps, the shirt-sleeved one, recognising Mittie May and the shape of the buggy, would speak a greeting something after this fashion:

"Well, suh—ef it ain't Jedge Priest! Jedge, suh, I certainly am proud to see you out this way. We was beginnin' to think you'd furgot us—we was, fur a fact!"

Over his shoulder he would single out one of a cluster of children who magically appeared on the gallery steps, and bid Tennessee or Virgil or Dora-Virginia or Albert-Sidney, as the name of the chosen youngster might be, to run and tell their ma that Judge Priest had come to stay for dinner. For the judge never sent any advance notice of his intention to pay a Sunday visit; neither did he wait for a formal invitation. He just dropped in, being assured of a welcome under any rooftree, great or humble, in his entire judicial district.

Shortly thereafter the judge, having been welcomed in due state, and provision made for Mittie May's stabling and sustenance, would be established on the gallery in the rocking-chair of honour, which was fetched out from the parlour for his better comfort. First, a brimming gourd of fresh spring water would be brought, that he might take the edge off his thirst and flush the dust out of his throat and moisten up his palate; and then would follow a certain elaborated rite in conjunction with sundry sprigs of young mint and some powdered sugar and outpourings of the red-brown contents of a wicker demijohn.

Very possibly a barefooted and embarrassed namesake would be propelled forward, by parental direction, to shake hands with the guest; for, except old Doctor Saunders, Judge Priest had more children named for him than anybody in our county. And very probably there would come to his ears from somewhere rearward the frenzied clamour of a mighty barnyard commotion—squawkings and cacklings and flutterings—closely followed by the poignant wails of a pair of doomed pullets, which grew fainter and fainter as the captives were borne to the sacrificial block behind the woodpile—certain signs, all these, that if fried chicken had not been included in the scope and plan of Sunday dinner, fried chicken would now be, most assuredly.

When dinner was over, small messengers

would be sent up the road and down to spread the word; and various oldsters of the vicinity would leave their own places to foregather in the dooryard of the present host and pass the time of day with Judge Priest. Sooner or later, somehow, the talk would work backward to war times. Overhearing what passed to and fro, a stranger might have been pardoned for supposing that it was only the year before, or at most two years before, when the Yankees came through under Grant; while Forrest's Raid was spoken of as though it had taken place within the current month.

Anchored among the ancients the old judge would sit, doing his share of the talking and more than his share of the listening; and late in the afternoon, when the official watermelon, all dripping and cool, had been brought forth from the springhouse, and the shadows were beginning to stretch themselves slantwise across the road, as though tired out completely by a hard day's work in the broiling sun, he and Mittie May would jog back toward town, meeting many an acquaintance on the road, but rarely passing one. And the upshot would be that at the next Democratic primary the opposing candidate for circuit judge—if there was any opposing candidate—got powerfully few votes out of that neighbourhood.

Such Sunday excursions as these and such a Sunday dinner as this typical one formed a regular part of Judge Priest's weekly routine through at least nine months of the year. If unforeseen events conspired to rob him of his trip to the country he felt the week had not rightly rounded itself out; but once a year he attended a dinner beside which all other dinner occasions were, in his estimation, as nothing at all. With regard to this particular affair, he used to say it took him a week to get primed and ready for it, one whole night to properly enjoy it, and another week to recover from the effects of it. I am speaking now of the anniversary banquet of the survivors of Company B—first and foremost of the home companies—which was and still is held always on a given date and at a given place, respectively, to wit: The evening of the twelfth of May and the dining room of the Richland House.

Company B held the first of its annual dinners at the Richland House away back in '66. That time sixty and more men—young men, mostly, in their mid-twenties and their early thirties—sat down together to meat and drink, and no less a personage than General Grider presided—that same Meriwether Grider who, going out in the first year of the war as company commander, came back after the Surrender, bringing with him the skeleton remnants of a battered and a shattered brigade.

General Meriwether Grider has been dead this many a year now. He gave his life for the women and the children when the *Belle of the Bends* burned up at Cottonwood Bar; and that

horror befell so long ago that the present generation down our way knows it only as a thing of
which those garrulous and tiresome creatures,
the older inhabitants, are sometimes moved to
speak. But the rules for the regulation and
conduct of subsequent banquets which were
adopted on that long-ago night, when the general sat at the head of the table, hold good, even
though all else in our town has changed.

Of the ardent and youthful sixty-odd who
dined with him then, a fading and aging and
sorely diminished handful is left. Some in the
restless boom days of the eighties moved away
to other and brisker communities, and some
have marched down the long, lone road that
leads to a far country. Yet it abides as a by-
law and a precedent that only orthodox members of the original company shall have covers
and places provided for them when anniversary
night rolls round. The Richland House—
always—must be the place of dining; this, too,
in spite of the fact that the Richland House
has been gnawed by the tooth of time into a
shabby old shell, hardly worthy to be named in
the same printed page with the smart Hotel
Moderne—strictly European plan; rates, three
dollars a day and upward—which now figures
as our leading hotel.

Near the conclusion of the feast, when the
cloth has been cleared of the dishes and only the
glasses are left, the roll is called by the acting
top-sergeant—cholera having taken off the real

top-sergeant in '75. Those who are present answer for themselves, and for those who are absent some other voice answers. And then at the very last, after the story-telling is done, they all stand and drink to Company B—its men, its memories, its most honourable record, and its most honourable dead.

They tell me that this last May just seven met on the evening of the twelfth to sit beneath the crossed battle-flags in the Richland House dining room, and that everything was over and done with long before eleven o'clock. But the annual dinner which I especially have in mind to describe here took place on a somewhat more remote twelfth of May, when Company B still might muster better than the strength of a corporal's guard. If I remember correctly, eighteen grizzled survivors were known to be alive that year.

In saying that, though, I would not have you infer that there were no more than eighteen veterans in our town. Why, in those times there must have been two hundred easily. Gideon K. Irons Camp could turn out upward of a hundred members in good standing for any large public occasion; but you understand this was a dinner limited to Company B alone, which restriction barred out a lot of otherwise highly desirable individuals.

It barred out Sergeant Jimmy Bagby, for the sergeant had served with King's Hellhounds; and Captain Shelby Woodward, who belonged to the Orphan Brigade, as you would have learned for yourself at first hand had you ever enjoyed as much as five minutes of uninterrupted conversation with the captain; and Mr. Wolfe Hawley, our leading grocer, who was a gunner in Lyon's Battery—and many another it barred out. Indeed, Father Minor got in only by the skin of his teeth. True enough he was a Company B man at the beginning; but he transferred early to another branch of the service and for most of the four years he rode with Morgan's men.

The committee in charge looked for a full attendance. It was felt that this would be one of the most successful dinners of them all. Certainly it would be by long odds the best advertised. It would seem that the Sunday editor of the *Courier-Journal*, while digging through his exchanges, came on a preliminary announcement in the columns of the *Daily Evening News*, which was our home paper; and, sensing a feature story in it, he sent one of his young men down from Louisville to spend two days among us, compiling facts, names and photographs. The young man did a page spread in the Sunday *Courier-Journal*, thereby unconsciously enriching many family scrapbooks in our town.

This was along toward the middle of April. Following it, one of the Eastern syndicates rewrote the piece and mailed it out to its constituent papers over the country. The Asso-

ciated Press saw fit to notice it too; and after
that the tale got into the boiler-plate shops—
which means it got into practically all the
smaller weeklies that use patent insides. It
must have been a strictly non-newspaper-read-
ing community of this nation which did not
hear that spring about the group of old soldiers
who for forty years without a break had held a
dinner once a year with no outsiders present, and
who were now, for the forty-first time, about to
dine again.

Considering this publicity and all, the committee naturally counted on a fairly complete
turnout. To be sure, Magistrate Matt Dallam,
out in the country, could not hope to be present
except in the spirit, he having been bedridden
for years. Garnett Hinton, the youngest enlisted member of Company B, was in feeble
health away off yonder in the Panhandle of
Texas. It was not reasonable to expect him to
make the long trip back home. On the tenth
Mr. Napoleon B. Crump was called to Birmingham, Alabama, where a ne'er-do-well son-in-law
had entangled himself in legal difficulties, arising
out of a transaction involving a dubious check,
with a yet more dubious signature on it. He
might get back in time—and then again he
might not.

On the other hand, Second Lieutenant Charley Garrett wrote up from his plantation down
in Mississippi that he would attend if he had to
walk—a mere pleasantry of speech, inasmuch as

Lieutenant Garrett had money enough to charter for himself a whole railroad train should he feel so inclined. And, from his little farm in Mims County, Chickasaw Reeves sent word he would be there, too, no matter what happened. The boys could count on him, he promised.

Tallying up twenty-four hours or so ahead of the big night, the arrangements committee, consisting of Doctor Lake, Professor Lycurgus Reese and Mr. Herman Felsburg, made certain of fifteen diners, and possibly sixteen, and gave orders accordingly to the proprietor of the Richland House; but Mr. Nap Crump was detained in Birmingham longer than he had expected, and Judge Priest received from Lieutenant Charley Garrett a telegram reading as follows:

"May the Lord be with you!—because I can't. Rheumatism in that game leg of mine, —— —— it!"

The excisions, it developed, were the work of the telegraph company.

Then, right on top of this, another disappointment piled itself—I have reference now to the sudden and painful indisposition of Chickasaw Reeves. Looking remarkably hale and hearty, considering his sixty-eight years, Mr. Reeves arrived in due season on the eleventh, dressed fit to kill in his Sunday best and a turndown celluloid collar and a pair of new shoes of most amazing squeakiness. After visiting, in turn, a considerable number of old friends and sharing, with such as them as were not bigoted, the customary and appropriate libations, he dropped into Sherill's Bar at a late hour of the evening for a nightcap before retiring.

At once his fancy was drawn to a milk punch, the same being a pleasant compound to which he had been introduced an hour or so earlier. This milk punch seemed to call for another, and that one for still another. As the first deep sip of number three creamily saluted his palate, Mr. Reeves' eyes, over the rim of the deep tumbler, fell on the free lunch displayed at the far end of the bar. He was moved to step down that way and investigate.

The milk punches probably would not have mattered—or the cubes of brick cheese, or the young onions, or the pretzels, or the pickled beets and pigs' feet. Mr. Reeves' seasoned and dependable gastric processes were amply competent to triumph over any such commonplace combination of food and drink. Undoubtedly his undoing was directly attributable to a considerable number of little slickery fish, belong ing, I believe, to the pilchard family—that is .o say, they are pilchards while yet they do s im and disport themselves hither and yon in their native element; but when caught and brined and spiced and oiled, and put in cans for the export trade, they take on a different name and become, commercially speaking, something else.

Mr. Reeves did not notice them at first. He had sampled one titbit and then another; finally his glance was arrested by a dish of these small, dainty appearing creatures. A tentative nibble at the lubricated tail of a sample specimen reassured him as to the gastronomic excellence of the novelty. He stayed right there until the dish was practically empty. Then, after one more milk punch, he bade the barkeeper good night and departed.

Not until three o'clock the following afternoon was Mr. Reeves able to receive any callers—except only Doctor Lake, whose visits until that hour had been in a professional rather than in a social capacity. Judge Priest, coming by invitation of the sufferer, found Mr. Reeves' room at the hotel redolent with the atmospheres of bodily distress. On the bed of affliction by the window was stretched the form of Mr. Reeves. He was not exactly pale, but he was as pale as a person of Mr. Reeves' habit of life could be and still retain the breath of life.

"Well, Chickasaw, old feller," said Judge Priest, "how goes it? Feelin' a little bit easier than you was, ain't you?"

The invalid groaned emptily before answering in a wan and wasted-away tone.

"Billy," he said, "ef you could 'a' saw me 'long 'bout half past two this mornin', when she first come on me, you'd know better'n to ask sech a question as that. First, I wus skeered I wus goin' to die. And then after a spell I wus skeered I wusn't. I reckin there ain't nobody nowheres that ever had ez many diff'runt kinds of cramps ez me and lived to tell the tale."

"That's too bad," commiserated the judge. "Was it somethin' you et or somethin' you drunk?"

"I reckin it wus a kind of a mixture of both," admitted Mr. Reeves. "Billy, did you ever make a habit of imbibin' these here milk punches?"

"Well, not lately," said Judge Priest.

"Well, suh," stated Mr. Reeves, "you'd be surprised to know how tasty they kin make jest plain ordinary cow's milk ef they take and put some good red licker and a little sugar in it, and shake it all up together, and then sift a little nutmaig seasonin' onto it—you would so! But, after you've drunk maybe three-four, I claim you have to be sorter careful 'bout whut you put on top of 'cm. I've found that much out.

"I reckin it serves me right, though. A country-jake like me oughter know better'n to come up here out of the sticks and try to gormandise hisse'f on all these here fancy town vittles. It's all right, mebbe, fur you city folks; but my stomach ain't never been educated up to it. Hereafter I'm a-goin' to stick to hawg jowl and cawn pone, and things I know 'bout. You hear me—I'm done! I've been cured.

"And specially I've been cured in reguards to these here little pizenous fishes that look somethin' like sardeens, and yit they ain't sardeens. I don't know what they call 'em by name; but it certainly oughter be ag'inst the law to leave 'em settin' round on a snack counter where folks kin git to 'em. Two or three of 'em would be dangerous, I claim—and I must 'a' et purty nigh a whole school."

Again Mr. Reeves moaned reminiscently.

"Well, from the way you feel now, does it look like you're goin' to be able to come to the blow-out to-night?" inquired Judge Priest. "That's the main point. The boys are all countin' on you, Chickasaw."

"Billy," bemoaned Mr. Reeves, "I hate it mightily; but even ef I wus able to git up— which I ain't—and git my clothes on and git down to the Richland House, I wouldn't be no credit to yore party. From the way I feel now, I don't never ag'in want to look vittles in the face so long ez I live. And, furthermore, ef they should happen to have a mess of them there little greasy minners on the table I know I'd be a disgrace to myse'f right then and there. No, Billy; I reckin I'd better stay right where I am."

Thus it came to pass that, when the members of Company B sat down together in the decorated dining room of the Richland House at eight o'clock that evening, the chair provided for Mr. Chickasaw Reeves made a gap in the line. Judge Priest was installed in the place of honour, where Lieutenant Garrett, by virtue of being ranking surviving officer, would have enthroned himself had it not been for that game leg of his. From his seat at the head, the judge glanced down the table and decided in his own mind that, despite absentees, everything was very much as it should be. At every plate was a little flag showing, on a red background, a blue St. Andrew's cross bearing thirteen stars. At every plate, also, was a tall and aromatic toddy. Cocktails figured not in the dinner plans of Company B; they never had and they never would.

At the far end from him was old Press Harper. Once it had been Judge Priest's most painful duty to sentence Press Harper to serve two years at hard labour in the state prison. To be sure, circumstances, which have been detailed elsewhere, interfered to keep Press Harper from serving all or any part of his punishment; nevertheless, it was the judge who had sentenced him. Now, catching the judge's eye, old Press waved his arm at him in a proud and fond greeting.

Father Minor beamingly faced Squire Futrell, whose Southern Methodism was of the most rigid and unbendable type. Professor Reese, principal of the graded school, touched elbows with Jake Smedley, colour bearer of the Camp, who just could make out to write his own name. Peter J. Galloway, the lame blacksmith, who most emphatically was Irish, had a caressing arm over the stooped shoulder of Mr. Herman Felsburg, who most emphatically was not. Doctor Lake, his own pet crony in a town where everybody, big and little, was his crony in some degree, sat one seat removed from the judge, with the empty chair of the bedfast Chickasaw Reeves in between them and so it went.

Even in the matter of the waiters an ancient and a hallowed sentiment ruled. Behind Judge Priest, and swollen as with a dropsy by pomp of pride and vanity, stood Uncle Zach Mathews, a rosewood-coloured person, whose affection for the Cause that was lost had never been questioned—even though Uncle Zach, after confusing military experiences, emerged from the latter end of the conflict as cook for a mess of Union officers and now drew his regular quarterly pension from a generous Federal Government.

Flanking Uncle Zach, both with napkins draped over their arms, both awaiting the word from him to bring on the first course, were posted—on the right, Tobe Emery, General Grider's one-time body servant; on the left, Uncle Ike Copeland, a fragile, venerable ex-human chattel, who might almost claim to have seen actual service for the Confederacy. No ordinary darkies might come to serve when Company B foregathered at the feast.

Uncle Zach, with large authority, had given the opening order, and at the side tables a pleasing clatter of china had arisen, when Squire Futrell put down his glass and rose, with a startled look on his face.

"Looky here, boys!" he exclaimed. "This won't never do! Did you fellers know there wus thirteen at the table?"

Sure enough, there were!

It has been claimed—perhaps not without colour of plausibility—that Southerners are more superstitious than Northerners. Assuredly the Southerners of a generation that is almost gone now uniformly nursed their private beliefs in charms, omens, spells, hoodoos and portents. As babies many of them were nursed, as boys all of them were played with, by members of the most superstitious race—next to actors—on the face of creation. An actor of Ethiopian descent should by rights be the most superstitious creature that breathes the air of this planet, and doubtlessly is.

No one laughed at Squire Futrell's alarm over his discovery. Possibly excusing Father Minor, it is probable that all present shared it with him. As for Uncle Zach Mathews and his two assistants, they froze with horror where they had halted, their loaded trays poised on their arms. But they did not freeze absolutely solid—they quivered slightly.

"Law-zee!" gasped Uncle Zach, with his eyeballs rolling. "Dinner can't go no fur'der twell we gits somebody else in or meks somebody leave and go 'way—dat's sartain shore! Whee! We kin all thank Our Maker dat dey ain't been nary bite et yit."

"Amen to dat, Brer Zach!" muttered Ike shakily; and dumbly Tobe Emery nodded, stricken beyond power of speech by the nearness of a barely averted catastrophe fraught with disaster, if not with death itself.

Involuntarily Judge Priest had shoved his chair back; most of the others had done the same thing. He got on his feet with alacrity.

"Boys," he said, "the squire is right—there's thirteen of us. Now whut d'ye reckin we're goin' to do 'bout that?"

The natural suggestion would be that they send at once for another person. Three or four offered it together, their voices rising in a babble. Names of individuals who would make congenial table mates were heard. Among others, Sergeant Jimmy Bagby was spoken of; likewise Colonel Cope and Captain Woodward. But Judge Priest shook his head.

"I can't agree with you-all," he set forth. "By the time we sent clean uptown and rousted one of them boys out, the vittles would all be cold."

"Well, Billy," demanded Doctor Lake, "what are you going to do, then? We can't go ahead this way, can we? Of course I don't believe in all this foolishness about signs myself; but"— he added—"but I must admit to a little personal prejudice against thirteen at the table."

"Listen here, you boys!" said Judge Priest. "Ef we're jest obliged and compelled to break a long-standin' rule of this command—and it looks to me like that's whut we've got to do— let's foller after a precedent that was laid down a mighty long time ago. You-all remember— don't you—how the Good Book tells about the Rich Man that give a feast oncet? And at the last minute the guests he'd invited didn't show up at all—none of 'em. So then he sent out into the highways and byways and scraped together some hongry strangers; and by all accounts they had a purty successful time of it there. When in doubt I hold it's a fairly safe plan to jest take a leaf out of them old Gospels and go by it. Let's send out right here in the neighbourhood and find somebody—no matter who 'tis, so long as he's free, white and twenty-one—that looks like he could appreciate a meal of vittles, and present the compliments of Company B to him, and ast him will he come on in and jine with us."

Maybe it was the old judge's way of putting it, but the idea took unanimously. The manager of the Richland House, having been sent for, appeared in person almost immediately. To him the situation was outlined and the remedy for it that had been favoured.

"By gum, gentlemen," said their host, instantly inspired, "I believe I know where I can put my hand on the very candidate you're looking for. There's a kind of seedy-looking, lonely old fellow downstairs, from somewhere the other side of the Ohio River. He's been registered since yes'day morning; seems like to me his name is Watts—something like that, anyhow. He don't seem to have any friends or no business in particular; he's just kind of hanging round. And he knows about this dinner too. He was talking to me about it a while ago, just before supper—said he'd read about it in a newspaper up in his country. He even asked me what the names of some of you gentlemen were. If you think he'll do to fill in I'll go right down and get him. He was sitting by himself in a corner of the lobby not two minutes ago. I judge he's about the right age, too, if age is a consideration. He looks to be about the same age as most of you."

There was no need for Judge Priest to put the question to a vote. It carried, so to speak, by acclamation. Bearing a verbal commission heartily to speak for the entire assemblage, Manager Ritter hurried out and in less than no time was back again, escorting the person he had described. Judge Priest met them at the door and was there introduced to the stranger, whose rather reluctant hand he warmly shook.

"He didn't want to come at first," explained Mr. Ritter; "said he didn't belong up here with you-all; but when I told him the fix you was in he gave in and consented, and here he is."

"You're mighty welcome, suh," said Judge Priest, still holding the other man's hand. "And we're turribly obliged to you fur comin', and to Mr. Ritter fur astin' you to come."

With that, he drew their dragooned guest into the room and, standing beside him, made formal presentation to the expectant company.

"Gentlemen of Company B, allow me to make you acquainted with Mr. Watts, of the State of Illinoy, who has done us the great honour of

agreein' to make fourteen at the table, and to
eat a bite with us at this here little dinner of
ours." A straggling outburst of greeting and
approbation arose from twelve elderly throats.
"Mr. Watts, suh, will you be so good as to take
this cheer here, next to me?" resumed Judge
Priest when the noise abated; and he completed
the ceremonial by indicating the place of the
absent Mr. Reeves.

What the stranger saw as he came slowly
forward—if, indeed, he was able to see anything
with distinctness by reason of the evident confusion that covered him—was a double row of
kindly, cordial, curious faces of old men, all
staring at him. Before the battery of their eyes
he bowed his acknowledgments, but did not
speak them; still without speaking, he slipped
into the seat which Tobe Emery sprang forward
to draw clear of the table for his easier admission
to the group. What the others saw was a tall,
stooped, awkward man of, say, sixty-five, with
sombre eyes, set deep in a whiskered face that
had been burned a leathery red by wind and
weather; a heavy-footed man, who wore a suit
of store clothes—clothes of a homely cut and
none too new, yet neat enough; such a man, one
might guess at a glance, as would have little to
say and would be chary about saying that little
until sure of his footing and his audience. Judg-
ing by appearances and first impressions he did
not promise to be what you might call exciting company, exactly; but he made fourteen

at the table, and that was the main point, anyhow.

Now the dinner got under way with a swing and a clatter. For all the stitches and tucks that time had taken in their leg muscles, the three old negroes flitted about like flickery black shadows, bringing food to all and toddies to several, and just plain ice water to at least three of their white friends. Even Kentuckians have been known to be advocates of temperance. To learn how true a statement this is you must read, not the comic weeklies, but the official returns of local-option elections. Above the medley of commingling voices, some cracked and jangled with age, some still full and sonorous, and one at least as thin and piercing as the bleat of a reed flute—that would be Judge Priest's voice, of course—sounded the rattling of dishes and glasses and plated silverware. Uncle Zach and his two aides may have been good waiters, but they were tolerably noisy ones.

Through it all the extra guest sat very quietly, eating little and drinking nothing. Sitting alongside him, Doctor Lake noticed that he fed himself with his right hand only; his left hand stayed in his lap, being hidden from sight beneath the table. Naturally this set afoot a train of mild professional surmise in the old doctor's mind. The arm itself seemed sound enough; he vaguely wondered whether the Illinois man had a crippled hand or a deformed hand, or what. Judge Priest noticed it too, but subconsciously rather. At the beginning he tried to start a conversation with Watts, feeling it incumbent on him, as chief sponsor for the other's presence, to cure him of his embarrassment if he could, and to make him feel more at home there among them; but his well-meant words appeared to fall on barren soil. The stranger answered in mumbled monosyllables, without once looking Judge Priest straight in the face. He kept his head half averted—a posture the judge ascribed to diffidence; but it was evident he missed nothing at all of the talk that ran up and down the long table and back and forth across it. Under his bushy brows his eyes shifted from face to face as this man or that had his say.

So presently the judge, feeling that he had complied with the requirements of hospitality, abandoned the effort to interest his silent neighbour, and very soon after forgot him altogether for the time being. Under the circumstances it was only to be expected of Judge Priest that he should forget incidental matters; for now, to all these lifelong friends of his, time was swinging backward on a greased hinge. The years that had lined these old faces and bent these old backs were dropping away; the memories of great and storied days were mounting to their brains like the fumes of strong wine, brightening their eyes and loosening their tongues.

From their eager lips dropped names of small country churches, tiny backwoods villages of the Southwest, trivial streams and geographically inconsequential mountains—names that once meant nothing to the world at large, but which, by reason of Americans having fought Americans there and Americans having died by the hundreds and the thousands there, are now printed in the school histories and memorised by the school children—Island Number 10 and Shiloh; Peachtree Creek and Stone River; Kenesaw Mountain and Brice's Crossroads. They had been at these very places, or at most of them —these thirteen old men had. To them the names were more than names. Each one burned in their hearts as a living flame. All the talk, though, was not of battle and skirmish. It dealt with prisons, with hospitals, with camps and marches.

"By George, boys, will you ever forget the day we marched out of this town?" It was Doctor Lake speaking, and his tone was high and exultant. "Flags flying everywhere and our sweethearts crying and cheering us through their tears! And the old town band up front playing Girl I Left Behind Me and Johnnie's Gone for a Soger! And we-all stepping along, feeling so high and mighty and stuck-up in our new uniforms! A little shy on tactics we were, and not enough muskets to go round; but all the boys wore new grey suits, I remember. Our mothers saw to that."

"It was different, though, Lew, the day we came home again," reminded some one else, speaking gently. "No flags flying then and nobody cheering, and no band to play! And half the women were in black—yes, more than half."

"An' dat's de Gawd's truth!" half-whispered black Tobe Emery, carried away for the moment.

"Well," said Press Harper, "I know they run out of muskets 'fore they got round to me. I call to mind that I went off totin' an ole flintlock that my paw had with him down in Mexico when he wus campin' on ole Santy Anny's trail. And that wus all I did have in the way of weepins, 'cept fur a great big bowie knife that a blacksmith out at Massac made fur me out of a rasp-file. I wus mighty proud of that there bowie of mine till we got down yonder to Camp Boone and found a whole company, all with bigger knives than whut mine wus. Called themselves the Blood River Tigers, those boys did, 'cause they came frum up on Blood River, in Calloway."

Squire Futrell took the floor—or the table, rather—for a moment:

"I recollec' one Calloway County feller down at Camp Boone, when we fust got there, that didn't even have a knife. He went round 'lowin' as how he wus goin' to pick him out a likely Yank the fust fight we got into, and lick him with his bare hands ef he stood still and fit, or knock him down with a rock ef he broke and run—and then strip him of his outfit."

"Why, I place that feller, jest ez plain ez if he

wus standin' here now," declared Mr. Harper. "I remember him sayin' he could lick ary Yankee that ever lived with his bare hands."

"I reckin mebbe he could, too—he wus plenty long enough," said the squire with a chuckle; "but the main obstacle wus that the Yankees wouldn't fight with their bare hands. They jest would insist on usin' tools—the contrary rascals! Let's see, now, whut wus that Calloway County feller's name? You remember him, Herman, don't you? A tall, ganglin' jimpy jawed, loose-laiged feller he wus—built like one of these here old blue creek cranes."

Mr. Felsburg shook his head; but Press Harper broke in again:

"I've got him! The boys called him Lengthy fur short; but his real name wus Washburn, same ez——"

He stopped short off there; and, twisting his head away from the disapproving faces, which on the instant had been turned full on him from all along the table, he went through the motion of spitting, as though to rid his mouth of an unsavoury taste. A hot colour climbed to Peter J. Galloway's wrinkled cheeks and he growled under the overhang of his white moustache. Doctor Lake pursed up his lips, shaking his head slowly.

There was one black spot, and just one, on the records of Company B. And, living though he might still be, or dead, as probably he was, the name of one man was taboo when his one-time companions broke bread at their anniversary dinner. Indeed, they went farther than that: neither there nor elsewhere did they speak by name of him who had been their shame and their disgrace. It was a rule. With them it was as though that man had never lived.

Up to this point Mr. Herman Felsburg had had mighty little to say. For all he had lived three-fourths of his life in our town, his command of English remained faulty and broken, betraying by every other word his foreign birth; and his habit of mixing his metaphors was proverbial. He essayed few long speeches before mixed audiences; but now he threw himself into the breach, seeking to bridge over the awkward pause.

"Speaking of roll calls and things such as that," began Mr. Felsburg, seeming to overlook the fact that until now no one had spoken of roll calls—"speaking of those kinds of things, maybe you will perhaps remember how it was along in the winter of '64, when practically we were out of everything—clothes and shoes and blankets and money—*ach*, yes; money especially!—and how the orderly sergeant had no book or papers whatsoever, and so he used to make his report in the morning on a clean shingle, with a piece of lead pencil not so gross as that." He indicated a short and stubby finger end.

" 'Long 'bout then we could 'a' kept all the rations we drew on a clean shingle too—eh,

Herman?" wheezed Judge Priest. "And the shingle wouldn't 'a' been loaded down at that! My, my! Ever' time I think of that winter of '64 I find myse'f gittin' hongry all over agin!" And the judge threw himself back in his chair and laughed his high, thin laugh.

Then, noting the others had not yet rallied back again to the point where the flow of reminiscences had been checked by Press Harper's labial slip-up, he had an inspiration.

"Speakin' of roll calls," he said, unconsciously parroting Mr. Felsburg, "seems to me it's 'bout time we had ours. The vittles end of this here dinner 'pears to be 'bout over. Zach" —throwing the suggestion across his shoulder— "you and your pardners'd better be fetchin' on the coffee and the seegars, I reckin." He faced front again, raising his voice: "Who's callin' the roll to-night?"

"I am," answered Professor Reese; and at once he got on his feet, adjusted his spectacles just so, and drew from an inner breast pocket of his long frock coat a stained and frayed scroll, made of three sheets of tough parchment paper pasted end to end.

He cleared his throat; and, as though the sound had been a command, his fellow members bent forward, with faces composed to earnestness. None observed how the stranger acted; indeed, he had been quite out of the picture and as good as forgotten for the better part of an hour. Certainly nobody was interested in him at this moment when there impended what, to that little group, was a profoundly solemn, highly sentimental thing.

Again Professor Reese cleared his throat, then spoke the name that was written in faded letters at the top of the roll—the name of him who had been their first captain and, at the last, their brigade commander.

"Died the death of a hero in an effort to save others at Cottonwood Bar, June 28, 1871," said Judge Priest; and he saluted, with his finger against his forehead.

One by one the old school-teacher called off the list of commissioned and noncommissioned officers. Squire Futrell, who had attained to the eminence of a second corporal's place, was the only one who answered for himself. For each of the others, including Lieutenant Garrett —he of the game leg and the plantation in Mississippi—somebody else answered, giving the manner and, if he remembered it, the date of that man's death. For, excepting Garrett, they were all dead.

The professor descended to the roster of enlisted men:

"Abner P. Ashbrook!"

"Died in Camp Chase as a prisoner of war."

"G. W. Ayres!"

"Killed at Baker's Creek."

"R. M. Bigger!"

"Moved to Missouri after the war, was elected state senator, and died in '89."

"Reuben Brame!"

"Honourably discharged after being wounded at Corinth, and disappeared. Believed to be dead."

"Robert Burnell!"

"Murdered by bushwhackers in East Tennessee on his way home after the Surrender."

So it went down the long column of names. They were names, many of them, which once stood for something in that community but which would have fallen with an unfamiliar sound upon the ears of the oncoming generation —old family names of the old town. But the old families had died out or had scattered, as is the way with old families, and the names were only pronounced when Company B met or when some idler, dawdling about the cemetery, deciphered the lichen-grown lines on gray and crumbly grave-stones. Only once in a while did a voice respond, "Here!" But always the "Here!" was spoken clearly and loudly and at that, the remaining twelve would hoist their voices in a small cheer.

By common consent certain survivors spoke for certain departed members. For example, when the professor came to one name down among the L's, Peter J. Galloway, who was an incorruptible and unshakable Roman of the party of Jefferson and Jackson, blared out: "Turn't Republikin in '96, and by the same token died that same year!" And when he reached the name of Adolph Ohlmann it was Mr.

Felsburg's place to tell of the honourable fate of his fellow Jew, who fell before Atlanta.

The reader read on and on until his voice took on a huskened note. He had heard "Here!" for the thirteenth time; he had come to the very bottomest lines of his roster. He called one more name—Vilas, it was—and then he rolled up his parchment and put it away.

"The records show that, first and last, Company B had one hundred and seventy-two members, all regularly sworn into the service of the Confederate States of America under our beloved President, Jefferson Davis," stated Professor Reese sonorously. "Of those names, in accordance with the custom of this organisation, I have just called one hundred and seventy-one. The roll call of Company B, of the Old Regiment of mounted infantry serving under General Nathan Bedford Forrest, is completed for the current year." And down he sat.

As Judge Priest, with a little sigh, settled back in his chair, his glance fell on the face of the man next him. Perhaps the old judge's eyes were not as good as once they had been. Perhaps the light was faulty. At any rate, he interpreted the look that was on the other's face as a look of loneliness. Ordinarily the judge was a pretty good hand at reading faces too.

"Looky here, boys!" he called out, with such emphasis as to centre general attention on the upper end of the table. "We oughter be 'shamed of ourselves—carryin' on this way 'mongst ourselves and plum' furgittin' we had an outsider with us ez a special guest. Our new friend here is 'bout the proper age to have seen service in the war his own se'f—mebbe he did see some. Of all the states that fought ag'inst us, none of 'em turned out better soldiers than old Illinoy did. If my guess is right I move we hear frum Mr. Watts, frum Illinoy, on some of his own wartime experiences." His hand dropped, with a heartening thump, on the shoulder of the stranger. "Come on, colonel! We've had a word from ever'body exceptin' you. It's your turn—ain't it, boys?"

Before his question might be answered, Watts had straightened to his feet. He stood rigidly, his hands driven wrist-deep into his coat pockets; his weather-beaten face set in heavy, hard lines; his deep eyes fixed on a spot in the blank wall above their heads.

"You're right—I was a soldier in the war between the States," he said in a thickened, quick voice, which trembled just a little; "but I didn't serve with the Illinois troops. I didn't move to Illinois until after the war. My regiment was as good a regiment, though, and as game a regiment, as fought in that war on either side."

Some six or eight broke generously into a brisk patter of handclapping at this, and from the exuberant Mr. Galloway came:

"Whirroo! That's right—stick up for yer own side always! Go on, me boy; go on!"

The urging was unnecessary. Watts was going on as though he had not been interrupted, as though he had not heard the friendly applause, as though his was a tale which stood in most urgent need of the telling:

"I'm not saying much of my first year as a soldier. I wasn't satisfied—well, I wasn't happily placed; I'll put it that way. I had hopes at the beginning of being an officer; and when the company election was held I lost out. Possibly I was too ambitious for my own good. I came to know that I was not popular with the rest of the company. My captain didn't like me, either, I thought. Maybe I was morbid; maybe I was homesick. I know I was disappointed. You men have all been soldiers—you know how those things go. I did my duty after a fashion— I didn't skulk or hang back from danger—but I didn't do it cheerfully. I moped and I suppose I complained a lot.

"Well, finally I left that company and that regiment. I just quit. I didn't quit under fire; but I quit—in the night. I think I must have been half crazy; I'd been brooding too much. In a day or two I realised that I couldn't go back home—which was where I had started for—and I wouldn't go over to the enemy. Badly as I had behaved, the idea of playing the outright traitor never entered my mind. I want you to know that. So I thought the thing over for a day or two. I had time for thinking it over—alone there in that swamp where I was hiding. I've never spoken of that shameful thing in my life since then—not until to-night. I tried not to think of it—but I always have— every day.

"Well, I came to a decision at last. I closed the book on my old self; I wiped out the past. I changed my name and made up a story to account for myself; but I thank God I didn't change flags and I didn't change sides. I was wearing that new name of mine when I came out of those woods, and under it I enlisted in a regiment that had been recruited in a state two hundred miles away from my own state. I served with it until the end of the war—as a private in the ranks.

"I'm not ashamed of the part I played those last three years. I'm proud of it! As God is my judge, I did my whole duty then. I was commended in general orders once; my name was mentioned in despatches to the War Department once. That time I was offered a commission; but I didn't take it. I bear in my body the marks of three wounds. I've got a chunk of lead as big as your thumb in my shoulder. There's a little scar up here in my scalp, under the hair, where a splinter from a shell gashed me. One of my legs is a little bit shorter than the other. In the very last fight I was in a spent cannon ball came along and broke both the bones in that leg. I've got papers to prove that from '62 to '65 I did my best for my cause and my country. I've got them here with me now—

I carry them with me in the daytime and I sleep at night with them under my pillow."

With his right hand he fumbled in his breast pocket and brought out two time-yellowed slips of paper and held them high aloft, clenched and crumpled up in a quivering fist.

"One of these papers is my honourable discharge. The other is a letter that the old colonel of my regiment wrote to me with his own hand two months before he died."

He halted and his eyes, burning like red coals under the thick brows, ranged the faces that looked up into his. His own face worked. When he spoke again he spoke as a prisoner at the bar might speak, making a last desperate appeal to the jury trying him for his life:

"You men have all been soldiers. I ask you this now, as a soldier standing among soldiers— I ask you if my record of three years of hard service and hard fighting can square me up for the one slip I made when I was hardly more than a boy in years? I ask you that?"

With one voice, then, the jury answered. Its verdict was acquittal—and not alone acquittal but vindication. Had you been listening outside you would have sworn that fifty men and not thirteen were yelling at the tops of their lungs, beating on the table with all the might in their arms.

The old man stood for a minute longer. Then suddenly all the rigidity seemed to go out of him. He fell into his chair and put his face in his two cupped hands. The papers he had brandished over his head slipped out of his fingers and dropped on the tablecloth. One of them—a flat, unfolded slip—settled just in front of Doctor Lake. Governed partly by an instinct operating automatically, partly to hide his own emotions, which had been roused to a considerable degree, Doctor Lake bent and spelled out the first few words. His head came up with a jerk of profound surprise and gratification.

"Why, this is signed by John B. Gordon himself!" he snorted. He twisted about, reaching out for Judge Priest. "Billy! Billy Priest! Why, look here! Why, this man's no Yankee! Not by a dam' sight he's not! Why, he served with a Georgia regiment! Why——"

But Judge Priest never heard a word of what Doctor Lake was saying. His old blue eyes stared at the stranger's left hand. On the back of that hand, standing out upon the corded tendons and the wrinkled brown skin, blazed a red spot, shaped like a dumb-bell, a birthmark of most unusual pattern.

Judge Priest stared and stared; and as he stared a memory that was nearly as old as he was crept out from beneath a neglected convolution in the back part of his brain, and grew and spread until it filled his amazed, startled, scarce-believing mind. So it was no wonder he did not hear Doctor Lake; no wonder he did not see black Tobe Emery stealing up behind him, with popped eyes likewise fixed on that red dumb-bell-shaped mark.

No; Judge Priest did not hear a word. As Doctor Lake faced about the other way to spread his wonderful discovery down the table and across it, the judge bent forward and touched the fourteenth guest on the shoulder very gently.

"Pardner," he asked, apparently apropos of nothing that had happened since the dinner started—"Pardner, when was the first time you heard about this here meetin' of Company B— the first time?"

Through the interlaced fingers of the other the answer came haltingly:

"I read about it—in a Chicago Sunday paper —three weeks ago."

"But you knew before that there was a Company B down here in this town?"

Without raising his head or baring his face, the other nodded. Judge Priest overturned his coffee cup as he got to his feet, but took no heed of the resultant damage to the cloth on the table and the fronts of his white trouser legs.

"Boys," he cried out so shrilly, so eagerly, so joyously, that they all jumped, "when you foller after Holy Writ you can't never go fur wrong. You're liable to breed a miracle. A while ago we took a lesson from the Parable of the Rich Man that give a dinner; and—lo and behold!—another parable and a better parable— yes, the sweetest parable of 'em all—has come to pass and been repeated here 'mongst us without our ever knowin' it or even suspectin' it.

The Prodigal Son didn't enjoy the advantage of havin' a Chicago Sunday paper to read, but in due season he came back home—that other Prodigal did; and it stands written in the text that he was furgiven, and that a feast was made fur him in the house of his fathers."

His tone changed to one of earnest demand:

"Lycurgus Reese, finish the roll call of this company—finish it right now, this minute—the way it oughter be finished!"

"Why, Judge Priest," said Professor Reese, still in the dark and filled with wonderment, "it is already finished!"

As though angered almost beyond control, the judge snapped back:

"It ain't finished, neither. It ain't been rightly finished from the very beginnin' of these dinners. It ain't finished till you call the very last name that's on that list."

"But, Judge——"

"But nothin'! You call that last name, Lycurgus Reese; and you be almighty quick about it!"

There was no need for the old professor, thus roughly bidden, to haul out his manuscript. He knew well enough the name, though wittingly it had not passed his lips for forty years or more. So he spoke it out:

"Sylvester B. Washburn!"

The man they had called Watts raised in his place and dropped his clenched hands to his sides, and threw off the stoop that was in his shoulders. He lifted his wetted eyes to the cracked, stained ceiling above. He peered past plaster and rafter and roof, and through a rift in the skies above he feasted his famished vision on a delectable land which others might not see. And then, beholding on his face that look of one who is confessed and shriven, purified and atoned for, the scales fell away from their own eyes and they marvelled—not that they knew him now, but that they had not known him before now. And for a moment or two there was not a sound to be heard.

"Sylvester B. Washburn!" repeated Professor Reese.

And the prodigal answered:

"Here!"

III

JUDGE PRIEST COMES BACK

FROM time to time persons of an inquiring turn of mind have been moved audibly to speculate—I might even say to ponder—regarding the enigma underlying the continued presence in the halls of our National Congress of the Honourable Dabney Prentiss. All were as one in agreeing that he had a magnificent delivery, but in this same connection it has repeatedly been pointed out that he so rarely had anything to deliver. Some few among this puzzled contingent, knowing, as they did, the habits and customs of the people down in our country, could understand that in a corner of the land where the gift of tongue is still highly revered and the golden chimings of a full-jewelled throat are not yet entirely lost in the click of cash registers and the whir of looms, how the Honourable Dabney within his limitations might have been oratorically conspicuous and politically useful, not alone to himself but to others. But as a constructive statesman sent up to Washington, District of Columbia, and there engaged in shaping loose ends of legislation into the welded and the tempered law, they could not seem to see him at all. It was such a one, an editorial writer upon a metropolitan daily, who once referred to Representative Prentiss as The Human Voice. The title stuck, a fact patently testifying to its aptness. That which follows here in this chapter is an attempt to explain the mystery of this gentleman's elevation to the high places which he recently adorned.

To go back to the very start of things we must first review briefly the case of old Mr. Lysander John Curd, even though he be but an incidental figure in the narrative. He was born to be incidental, I reckon, heredity, breeding and the chance of life all conspiring together to fit him for that inconsequential rôle. He was born to be a background. The one thing he ever did in all his span on earth to bring him for a moment into the front of the picture was that, having reached middle age, he took unto himself a young wife. But since he kept her only long enough to lose her, even this circumstance did not serve to focus the attention of the community upon his uncoloured personality for any considerable period of time.

Considering him in all his aspects—as a volunteer soldier in the Great War, as a district school-teacher, as a merchant in our town, as a bachelor of long standing, as a husband for a fleeting space, and as a grass widower for the rest of his days—I have gleaned that he never did anything ignoble or anything conspicuous. Indeed, I myself, who knew him as a half-grown boy may know a middle-aged man, find it hard after the lapse of years to describe him physically for you. I seem to recall that he was neither tall nor short, neither thick nor thin. He had the customary number of limbs and the customary number of features arranged in the customary way— I know that, of course. It strikes me that his eyes were mild and gentle, that he was, as the saying runs, soft-spoken and that his whiskers were straggly and thin, like young second growth in a new clearing; also that he wore his winter overcoat until the hot suns of springtime scorched it, and that he clung to his summer alpaca and his straw hat until the frosts of autumn came along and nipped them with the sweet-gum and the dogwood. That lets me out. Excusing these things, he abides merely as a blur in my memory.

On a certain morning of a certain year, the month being April, Judge Priest sat at his desk in his chamber, so-called, on the right-hand side of the long hall in the old courthouse, as you came in from the Jefferson Street door. He was shoulders deep down in his big chair, with both his plump legs outstretched and one crossed over the other, and he was reading a paper-bound volume dealing in the main with certain inspiring episodes in the spectacular life of a

Western person known as Trigger Sam. On his way downtown from home that morning he had stopped by Wilcox & Powell's bookstore and purchased this work at the price of five cents; it was the latest production of the facile pen of a popular and indefatigable author of an earlier day than this, the late Ned Buntline. In his hours of leisure and seclusion the judge dearly loved a good nickel library, especially one with a lot of shooting and some thrilling rescues in it. Now he was in the middle of one of the most exciting chapters when there came a mild rap at the outer door. Judge Priest slid the Trigger Sam book into a half-open drawer and called out:

"Come right on in, whoever 'tis."

The door opened and old Mr. Lysander John Curd entered, in his overcoat, with his head upon his chest.

"Good morning, Judge Priest," he said in his gentle halting drawl; "could I speak with you in private a minute? It's sort of a personal matter and I wouldn't care to have anybody maybe overhearing."

"You most certainly could," said Judge Priest. He glanced through into the adjoining room at the back, where Circuit Clerk Milam and Sheriff Giles Birdsong, heads together, were busy over the clerical details of the forthcoming term of circuit court. Arising laboriously from his comfortable place he waddled across and kicked the open door between the two rooms

shut with a thrust of a foot clad in a box-toed,
low-quartered shoe. On his way back to his
desk he brushed an accumulation of old papers
out of a cane-bottomed chair. "Set down here,
Lysandy," he said in that high whiny voice of
his, "and let's hear whut's on your mind. Nice
weather, ain't it?"

An eavesdropper trained, mayhap, in the
psychology of tone and gesture might have
divined from these small acts and this small
utterance that Judge Priest had reasons for sus-
pecting what was on his caller's mind; as though
this visit was not entirely unexpected, even
though he had had no warning of it. There was
in the judge's words an intangible inflection of
understanding, say, or sympathy; no, call it
compassion—that would be nearer to it. The
two old men—neither of them would ever see
sixty-five again—lowered themselves into the
two chairs and sat facing each other across the
top of the judge's piled and dusty desk.
Through his steel-rimmed glasses the judge
fixed a pair of kindly, but none-the-less keen,
blue eyes on Mr. Lysander Curd's sagged and
slumped figure. There was despondency and
there was embarrassment in all the drooping
lines of that elderly frame. Judge Priest's lips
drew up tightly, and unconsciously he nodded—
the brief nod that a surgeon might employ on
privately confirming a private diagnosis.

The other did not detect these things—neither
the puckering of the lips nor the small forward

bend of the judge's head. His own chin was in his collar and his own averted eyes were on the floor. One of his hands—a gnarly, rather withered hand it must have been—reached forth absently and fumbled at a week-old copy of the *Daily Evening News* that rested upon a corner of the desk. The twining fingers tore a little strip loose from the margin of a page and rolled it up into a tiny wad.

For perhaps half a minute there was nothing said. Then Judge Priest bent forward suddenly and touched the nearermost sleeve of Mr. Curd with a gentle little half-pat.

"Well, Lysandy?" he prompted.

"Well, Judge." The words were the first the visitor had uttered since his opening speech, and they came from him reluctantly. "Well, sir, it would seem like I hardly know how to start. This is a mighty personal matter that I've come to see you in regards to—and it's just a little bit hard to speak about it even to somebody that I've known most of my life, same as I've always known you. But things in my home have finally come to a head, and before the issue reaches you in an official capacity as the judge on the bench I sort of felt like it might help some—might make the whole thing pass off easier for all concerned—if I could have a few words with you privately, as a friend and as a former comrade in arms on the field of battle."

"Yes, Lysandy, go ahead. I'm listenin'," stated Judge Priest, as the other halted.

Old Mr. Curd raised his face and in his faded eyes there was at once a bewildered appeal and a fixed and definite resolution. He spoke on very slowly and carefully, choosing his words as he went, but without faltering:

"I don't know as you know about it, Judge Priest—the chances are you naturally wouldn't —but in a domestic way things haven't been going very smoothly with me—with us, I should say—for quite a spell back. I reckon after all it's a mistake on the part of a man after he's reached middle age and got set in his ways to be taking a young wife, more especially if he can't take care of her in the way she's been used to, or anyhow in the way she'd like to be taken care of. I suppose it's only human nature for a young woman to hanker after considerable many things that a man like me can't always give her— jewelry and pretty things, and social life, and running round and seeing people, and such as that. And Luella—well, Luella really ain't much more than a girl herself yet, is she?"

The question remained unanswered. It was plain, too, that Mr. Curd had expected no answer to it, for he went straight on:

"So I feel as if the blame for what's happened is most of it mine. I reckon I was too old to be thinking about getting married in the first place. And I wasn't very well off then either—not well enough off to have the money I should've had if I expected to make Luella contented. Still, all that part of it's got nothing to do with the matter as it stands—I'm just telling it to you, Judge, as a friend."

"I understand, Lysandy," said Judge Priest almost in the tone which he might have used to an unhappy child. "This is all a strict confidence between us two and this is all the further it'll ever go, so fur ez I'm concerned, without you authorise me to speak of it."

He waited for what would come next. It came in slow, steady sentences, with the regularity of a statement painfully rehearsed beforehand:

"Judge Priest, I've never been a believer in divorce as a general thing. It seemed to me there was too much of that sort of thing going on round this country. That's always been my own private doctrine, more or less. But in my own case I've changed my mind. We've been talking it over back and forth and we've decided— Luella and me have—that under the circumstances a divorce is the best thing for both of us; in fact we've decided that it's the only thing. I want that Luella should be happy and I think maybe I'll feel easier in my own mind when it's all over and done with and settled up according to the law. I'm aiming to do what's best for both parties—and I want that Luella should be happy. I want that she should be free to live her own life in her own way without me hampering her. She's young and she's got her whole life before her—that's what I'm thinking of."

He paused and with his tongue he moistened his lips, which seemed dry.

"I don't mind telling you I didn't feel this way about it first-off. It was a pretty tolerably hard jolt to me—the way the proposition first came up. I've spent a good many sleepless nights thinking it over. At least I couldn't sleep very much for thinking of it," he amended with the literal impulse of a literal mind to state things exactly and without exaggeration. "And then finally I saw my way clear to come to this decision. And so——"

"Lysandy Curd," broke in Judge Priest, "I don't aim to give you any advice. In the first place, you ain't asked fur it; and in the second place, even ef you had asked, I'd hesitate a monstrous long time before I'd undertake to advise any man about his own private family affairs. But I jest want to ask you one thing right here: It wasn't you, was it, that first proposed the idea of this here divorce?"

"Well, no, Judge, I don't believe 'twas," confessed the old man whose misery-reddened eyes looked into Judge Priest's from across the littered desk. "I can't say as it was me that first suggested it. But that's neither here nor there. The point I'm trying to get at is just this:

"The papers have all been drawn up and they'll be bringing them in here sometime to-day to be filed—the lawyers in the case will, Bigger & Quigley. Naturally, with me and Luella agreeing as to everything, there's not going to be any fight made in your court. And after it's all over I'm aiming to sell out my feed store—

it seems like I haven't been able to make it pay these last few months, the same as it used to pay, and debts have sort of piled up on me some way. I reckon the fellow that said two could live as cheap as one didn't figure on one of them being a young woman—pretty herself and wanting pretty things to wear and have round the house. But I shouldn't say that—I've come to see how it's mainly my fault, and I'm figuring on how to spare Luella in every way that it's possible to spare her. So as I was saying, I'm figuring, when it's all over, on selling out my interests here, such as they are, and going back to live on that little farm I own out yonder in the Lone Elm district. It's got a mortgage on it that I put on it here some months back, but I judge I can lift that and get the place clear again, if I'm given a fair amount of time to do it in.

"And now that everything's been made clear to you, I want to ask you, Judge, to do all in your power to make things as easy as you can for Luella. I'd a heap rather there wouldn't be any fuss made over this case in the newspapers. It's just a straight, simple divorce suit, and after all it's just between me and my present wife, and it's more our business than 'tis anybody else's. So, seeing as the case is not going to be defended, I'd take it as a mighty big favour on your part if you'd shove it up on the docket for the coming term of court, starting next Monday, so as we could get it done and over with just as soon as possible. That's my personal wish, and I know it's Luella's wish too. In fact she's right anxious on that particular point. And here's one more thing: I reckon that young Rawlings boy, that's taken a job reporting news items for the *Daily Evening News*, will be round here in the course of the day, won't he?"

"He likely will," said Judge Priest; "he comes every day—purty near it. Why?"

"Well," said Mr. Curd, "I don't know him myself except by sight, and I don't feel as if I was in a position to be asking him to do anything for me. But I thought, maybe, if you spoke to him yourself when he came, and put it on the grounds of a favour to you, maybe he'd not put any more than just a little short piece in the paper saying suit had been filed—Curd against Curd—for a plain divorce, or maybe he might leave it out of his paper altogether. I'd like to see Luella shielded from any newspaper talk. It's not as if there was a scandal in it or a fight was going to be made." He bent forward in his eagerness. "Do you reckon you could do that much for me, Judge Priest—for old times' sake?"

"Ah-hah," assented Judge Priest. "I reckin part of it kin be arranged anyway. I kin have Lishy Milam set the case forward on the docket at the head of the list of uncontested actions. And I'll mention the matter to that there young Rawlings ef you want me to. Speaking personally, I should think jest a line or two ought to satisfy the readers of the *Daily Evenin' News*.

Of course him bein' a reporter and all that, he'll probably want to know whut the facts are ez set forth in your petition—whut allegations are made in——"

He stopped in mid-speech, seeing how the other had flinched at this last. Mr. Curd parted his lips to interrupt, but the old judge, having no wish to flick wounds already raw, hurried on:

"Don't you worry, Lysandy, I'll be glad to speak to young Rawlings. I jedge you've got no call to feel uneasy about whut's goin' to be said in print. You was sayin' jest now that the papers would be filed sometime to-day?"

"They'll be filed to-day sure."

"And no defence is to be made?" continued Judge Priest, tallying off the points on his fingers. "And you've retained Bigger & Quigley to represent you—that's right, ain't it?"

"Hold on a minute, Judge," Mr. Curd was shaking his whity-grey head in dissent. "I've taken up a lot of your valuable time already, and still it would seem like I haven't succeeded in getting this affair all straight in your mind. Bigger & Quigley are not going to represent me. They're going to represent Luella."

He spoke as one stating an accepted and easily understood fact, yet at the words Judge Priest reared back as far as his chair would let him go and his ruddy cheeks swelled out with the breath of amazement.

"Do you mean to tell me," he demanded, "that you ain't the plaintiff here?"

"Why, Judge Priest," answered Mr. Curd, "you didn't think for a minute, did you, that I'd come into court seeking to blacken my wife's good name? She's been thoughtless, maybe, but I know she don't mean any harm by it, and besides look how young she is. It's her, of course, that's asking for this divorce—I thought you understood about that from the beginning."

Still in his posture of astonishment, Judge Priest put another question and put it briskly: "Might it be proper fur me to ask on what grounds this lady is suin' you fur a divorce?"

A wave of dull red ran up old Mr. Curd's throat and flooded his shamed face to the hair line.

"On two grounds," he said—"non-support and drunkenness."

"Non-support?"

"Yes; I haven't been able to take care of her lately as I should like to, on account of my business difficulties and all."

"But look here at me, Lysandy Curd—you ain't no drunkard. You never was one. Don't tell me that!"

"Well, now, Judge Priest," argued Mr. Curd, "you don't know about my private habits, and even if I haven't been drinking in public up to now, that's no sign I'm not fixing to start in doing so. Besides which my keeping silent shows that I admit to everything, don't it? Well, then?" He stood up. "Well, I reckon that's all. I won't be detaining you any longer.

I'm much obliged to you, Judge, and I wish you good-day, sir."

For once Judge Priest forgot his manners. He uttered not a syllable, but only stared through his spectacles in stunned and stricken silence while Mr. Curd passed out into the hallway, gently closing the door behind him. Then Judge Priest vented his emotions in a series of snorts.

In modern drama what is technically known as the stage aside has gone out of vogue; it is called old-fashioned. Had a latter-day play-wright been there then, he would have resented the judge's thoughtlessness in addressing empty space. Nevertheless that was exactly what the judge did.

"Under the strict letter of the law I ought to throw that case out of court, I s'pose. But I'm teetotally dam' ef I do any sech thing! . . . That old man's heart is broke now, and there ain't no earthly reason that I kin think of why that she-devil should be allowed to tromp on the pieces. And that's jest exactly whut she'll do, shore ez shootin', unless she's let free mighty soon to go her own gait. . . . Their feet take hold on hell. . . . I'll bet in the King-dom there'll be many a man that was called a simple-minded fool on this earth that'll wear the biggest, shiniest halo old Peter kin find in stock."

He reached for the Trigger Sam book, but put it back again in the drawer. He reached into a gaping side pocket of his coat for his corncob pipe, but forgot to charge the fire-blackened bowl from the tobacco cannister that stood handily upon his desk. Chewing hard upon the discoloured cane stem of his pipe, he projected himself toward the back room and opened the door, to find Mr. Milam, the circuit clerk, and Mr. Birdsong, the sheriff, still engaged together in official duties there.

"Lishy," he said from the doorway, "young Rawlings generally gits round here about two o'clock in the evenin', don't he?"

"Generally about two or two-thirty," said Mr. Milam.

"I thought so. Well, to-day when he comes tell him, please, I want to see him a minute in my chambers."

"What if you're not here? Couldn't I give him the message?"

"I'll be here," promised the judge. "And there's one thing more: Bigger & Quigley will file a divorce petition to-day—Curd versus Curd is the title of the suit. Put it at the head of the list of undefended actions, please, Lishy, ez near the top of the docket ez you kin."

"Curd? Is it the Lysander Curds, Judge?" asked Mr. Milam.

"You guessed right the very first pop—it's the Lysandy Curds," said Judge Priest grimly.

"Well, for one I'm not surprised," said Mr. Milam. "If poor old Lysander hadn't stayed blind for about two years after the rest of this town got its eyes wide open this suit would have been filed long before now."

But Judge Priest didn't hear him. He had closed the door.

Mr. Milam looked meaningly at Mr. Birdsong. Mr. Birdsong felt in his pocket for his plug and helped himself to a copious chew, meanwhile looking meaningly back at Mr. Milam. With the cud properly bestowed in his right jaw Mr. Birdsong gave vent to what for him was a speech of considerable length:

"'Jedge said Bigger & Quigley, didn't he? Well, they're a good smart team of lawyers, but ef I was in Lysander John Curd's shoes I think I'd intrust my interests in this matter to a different firm than them."

"Who's that?" inquired Mr. Milam.

"It's a Yankee firm up North," answered Mr. Birdsong, masticating slowly. "One named Smith and the other'n named Wesson."

It will be noted that our worthy sheriff fell plump into the same error over which Judge Priest's feet had stumbled a few minutes earlier —he assumed offhand, Sheriff Birdsong did, that in this cause of Curd against Curd the husband was to play the rôle of the party aggrieved. Indeed, we may feel safe in assuming that at first blush almost anybody in our town would have been guilty of that same mistake. The real truth in this regard, coming out, as it very shortly did—before sunset of that day, in fact —gave the community a profound shock. From

house to house, from street to street and from
civic ward to civic ward the tale travelled,
growing as it went. The *Daily Evening News*
carried merely the barest of bare statements,
coupled with the style of the action and the
names of the attorneys for the plaintiff; but
with spicy added details, pieced out from surmise and common rumour, the amazing tidings
percolated across narrow roads and through the
panels of partition fences with a rapidity which
went far toward proving that the tongue is
mightier than the printed line, or at least is
speedier.

When you see a woman hasten forth from her
house with eyes that burn and hear her hail her
neighbour next door; when you see their two
heads meet above the intervening pickets and
observe that one is doing the talking and the
other is doing the listening, sucking her breath
in, gaspingly, at frequent intervals; and when
on top of this you take note that, having
presently parted company with the first, the second woman speeds hot-foot to call her neighbour
upon the other side, all men may know by these
things alone that a really delectable scandal has
been loosed upon the air. Not once but many
times this scene was enacted in our town that
night, between the going-down of the sun and the
coming-up of the moon. Also that magnificent
adjunct of modern civilisation, the telephone,
helped out tremendously in spreading the word.

Hard upon the heels of the first jolting disclosure correlated incidents eventuated, and these, as the saying goes, supplied fuel to the flames. Just before supper-time old Mr. Lysander Curd went with dragging feet and downcast head to Mrs. Teenie Morrill's boarding house, carrying in one hand a rusty valise, and from Mrs. Morrill he straightway engaged board and lodging for an indefinite period. And in the early dusk of the evening Mrs. Lysander Curd drove out in the smart top-phaeton that her husband had given her on her most recent birthday—she sitting very erect and handling the ribbons on her little spirited bay mare very prettily, and seemingly all oblivious to the hostile eyes which stared at her from sidewalks and porch fronts. About dark she halted at the corner of Clay and Contest, where a row of maples, new fledged with young leaves, made a thick shadow across the road.

Exactly there, as it so chanced, State Senator Horace K. Maydew happened to be loitering about, enjoying the cooling breezes of the spring night, and he lifted his somewhat bulky but athletic forty-year-old form into the phaeton alongside of the lady. In close conversation they were seen to drive out Contest and to turn into the Towhead Road; and—if we may believe what that willing witness, old Mrs. Whitridge, who lived at the corner of Clay and Contest, had to say upon the subject—it was ten minutes of eleven o'clock before they got back again to that corner. Mrs. Whitridge knew the exact

hour, because she stayed up in her front room
to watch, with one eye out of the bay window
and the other on the mantel clock. To be sure,
this had happened probably a hundred times
before—this meeting of the pair in the shadows
of the water maples, this riding in company
over quiet country roads until all hours—but by
reason of the day's sensational developments it
now took on an enhanced significance. Mrs.
Whitridge could hardly wait until morning to
call up, one by one, the members of her circle
of intimate friends. I judge the telephone company never made much money off of Mrs.
Whitridge even in ordinary times; she rented
her telephone by the month and she used it by
the hour.

As we are following the course of things with
some regard for their chronological sequence,
perhaps I should state here that on the next day
but one the Lysander John Curd hay and feed
store was closed on executions sworn out by a
coterie of panic-stricken creditors. It is a mistake, I think, to assume that rats always leave
a sinking ship. It has been my limited observa-
tion that, if they are commercial rats, they stay
aboard and nibble more holes in the hull. However, that is neither here nor there.

In less than no time at all following this—in
less than two weeks thereafter, to be exact—the
coils which united Mr. Lysander Curd and
Luella his wife in the bonds of matrimony were
by due process of the statutory law unloosed

and slackened off. Being free, the ex-husband promptly gathered together such meagre belongings as he might call his own and betook himself to that little mortgage-covered farm of his out Lone Elm way. Being free also, the ex-wife with equal celerity became the bride of State Senator Horace K. Maydew, with a handy justice of the peace to officiate at the ceremony. It was characteristic of State Senator Maydew that he should move briskly in consummating this, the paramount romance of his life. For he was certainly an up-and-coming man.

There was no holding him down, it seemed. Undoubtedly he was a rising light, and the lady who now bore his name was bound and determined that she rise with him. She might have made one matrimonial mistake, but this time she had hitched her wagon to a star—a star which soared amain and cast its radiance afar. Soon she was driving her own car—and a seven-passenger car at that. They sent to Chicago for an architect to design their new home on Flournoy Boulevard and to Louisville for a decorator to decorate it. It wasn't the largest house in town, but it was by long odds the smartest.

The Senator willed that she should have the best of everything, and she had it. For himself he likewise desired much. His was an uneasy ambition, which ate into him like a canker and gave him no peace. Indeed, peace was not of his craving. He watered his desire with the waters of self-appreciation and mulched it with con-

stant energy, and behold it grew like the gourd
and bourgeoned like the bay. He had been
mayor; at this time he was state senator; presently it was to transpire that he would admire
to be more than that.

Always his handclasp had been ardent and
clinging. Now the inner flames that burned its
owner made it feverish to the touch. His smile
was as warming as a grate fire and almost as
wide. Shoulders were made for him to slap, and
children had been created into the world to the
end that he might inquire regarding their general health and well doing. Wherefore parents—
and particularly young parents—were greatly
drawn to him. If there was a lodge he joined it;
if there was a church fair he went to it; if there
was an oration to be made he made it. His
figure broadened and took on a genial dignity.
Likewise in the accumulation of worldly goods
he waxed amazingly well. His manner was
paternal where it was not fraternal. His eye,
though, remained as before—a sharp, greedy,
appraising eye. There is no alibi for a bad eye.
Still, a lot of people never look as high as the
eyes. They stop at the diamond in the scarfpin.

When a vacancy occurred in the district
chairmanship it seemed quite in keeping with
the trend of the political impulses of the times
that Senator Maydew should slip into the hole.
Always a clever organiser, he excelled his past
record in building up and strengthening the
district organisation. It wasn't long before he

had his fences as they should be—hog-tight, horse-high and bull-strong.

Yet in the midst of manifold activities he found time to be an attentive and indulgent husband. If the new Mrs. Maydew did not enjoy the aloof society of those whom we fondly call down our way The Old Families, at least she had her fine new home, and her seven-passenger car, and her generous and loving husband. And she was content; you could tell that by her air and her expression at all times. Some thought there was just a trace of defiance in her bearing.

It was just about a year after her marriage to him that the Senator, in response to the demands of a host of friends and admirers—so ran the language of his column-long paid-for card in the *Daily Evening News* and other papers—announced himself as a candidate for the Democratic nomination for congressman. Considering conditions and everything, the occasion appeared to be propitious for such action on his part. The incumbent, old Major J. C. C. Guest, had been congressman a long, long time—entirely too long a time, some were beginning to say. He had never been a particularly exciting personage, even back yonder in those remote dim days of his entry into public life. At the beginning his principal asset and his heaviest claim upon the support of his fellow-citizens had been an empty trouser-leg.

In eighty-four, a cross-roads wag had said he

didn't believe Major Guest ever lost that leg in
battle—it was his private opinion that the Maje
wore it off running for office. At the time this
quip was thought almost to border upon the
sacrilegious, and nobody had laughed at it
except the utterer thereof. But fully sixteen
lagging years had dragged by since then; and for
the old-soldier element the times were out of
joint. Maybe that was because there weren't so
very many of the old soldier element left. A
mouse-coloured sleeve without an arm inside of
it, no longer had the appeal upon the popular
fancy that once it had, and the same was
true of the one-time sentimental and vote-
catching combination of a pair of hickory
crutches and an amputation at the hip joint.

Nevertheless, Major Guest was by no means
ready to give up and quit. With those who considered him ripe for retirement he disagreed
violently. As between resting on his laurels and
dying in the harness he infinitely preferred the
chafe of the leather to the questionable softness
of the laurel-bed. So the campaign shaped
itself to be a regular campaign. Except for these
two—Maydew and Guest—there were no openly
avowed candidates, though Dabney Prentiss,
who dearly loved a flirtation with reluctant Des-
tiny, was known to have his ear to the ground,
ready to qualify as the dark horse in the event a
deadlock should develop and a cry go forth for a
compromise nominee. Possibly it was because
Dabney Prentiss generally kept his ear to the

ground that he had several times been most painfully trampled upon. From head to foot he was one big mental bruise.

Since he held the levers of the district machinery in the hollows of his two itching hands, Senator Maydew very naturally and very properly elected to direct his own canvass. Judge Priest, quitting the bench temporarily, came forth to act as manager for his friend, Major Guest. At this there was rejoicing in the camp of the clan of Maydew. To Maydew and his lieutenants it appeared that providence had dealt the good cards into their laps. Undeniably the judge was old and, moreover, he was avowedly old-fashioned. It stood to reason he would conduct the affairs of his candidate along old-fashioned lines. To be sure, he had his following; so much was admitted. Nobody could beat Judge Priest for his own job; at least nobody ever had. But controlling his own job and his own county was one thing. Engineering a district-wide canvass in behalf of an aging and uninspiring incumbent was another. And if over the bent shoulders of Major Guest they might strike a blow at Judge Priest, why, so much the better for Maydew now, and so much the worse for Priest hereafter. Thus to their own satisfaction the Maydew men figured it out.

The campaign went forward briskly and not without some passing show of bitterness. In a measure, Judge Priest justified the predictions of the other side by employing certain time-

hallowed expedients for enlisting the votes of
his fellow Democrats for Major Guest. He
appealed, as it were, to the musty traditions of a
still mustier past. He sent the Major over the
district to make speeches. He organised schoolhouse rallies and brush-arbour ratifications. He
himself was mighty in argument and opulent in
the use of homely oratory.

Very different was the way of State Senator
Maydew. The speeches that he made were few
as to number and brief as to their length, but
they were not bad speeches. He was a ready
and a frequent purchaser of newspaper space;
and he shook hands and slapped shoulders and
inquired after babies without cessation. But
most of all he kept both of his eyes and all of his
ten nimble fingers upon the machine, triggering
it and thimbling it and pulling at secret wires by
day and by night. It was, perhaps, a tribute to
his talents in this direction that the method that
he inaugurated was beginning to be called Maydewism—by the opposition, of course—before
the canvass was a month old. In an unusually
vociferous outburst of indignation at a meeting
in the Independent Order of Odd Fellows' hall at
Settleville, Major Guest referred to it as "the
fell blight of Maydewism." When a physician
discovers a new and especially malignant disease
his school of practice compliments him by
naming the malady after him; when a political
leader develops a political system of his own, his
opponents, although actuated by different mo-

tives, do the same thing, which may be taken as an absolute sign that the person in question has made some sincere enemies at least. But if Maydew made enemies he made friends too; at any rate he made followers. As the campaign drew near to its crackling finish it was plain that he would carry most of the towns; Major Guest's strength apparently was in the country—among the farmers and the dwellers in small villages.

County conventions to name delegates to the district conventions which, in turn, would name the congressional nominee were held simultaneously in the nine counties composing the district at two P. M. of the first Tuesday after the first Monday in August. A week before, Senator Maydew, having cannily provided that his successor should be a man after his own heart, resigned as district chairman. Although he had thrown overboard most of the party precedents, it seemed to him hardly ethical that he should call to order and conduct the preliminary proceedings of the body that he counted upon to nominate him as its standard bearer—standard bearer being the somewhat ornamental phrase customarily used among us on these occasions. He was entirely confident of the final outcome. The cheering reports of his aides in the field made him feel quite sure that the main convention would take but one ballot. They allowed, one and all, it would be a walk-over.

Howsoever, these optimists, as it developed, had reckoned without one factor: they had

[117]

reckoned without a certain undercurrent of dis-
favour for Maydew which, though it remained for
the most part inarticulate during the campaign,
was to manifest itself in the county conventions.
Personalities, strictly speaking, had not been
imported into the fight. Neither candidate had
seen fit to attack the private life of his opponent,
but at the last moment there came to the surface
an unexpected and, in the main, a silent antago-
nism against the Senator which could hardly be
accounted for on the ground of any act of his
official and public career.

So, late in the afternoon of the first Tuesday
after the first Monday, when the smoke cleared
away and the shouting and the tumult died, the
complete returns showed that of the nine counties, totalling one hundred and twenty delegate
votes, Maydew had four counties and fifty-seven
votes. Guest had carried four counties also,
with fifty-one votes, while Bryce County, the
lowermost county of the district, had failed to
instruct its twelve delegates for either Maydew
or Guest, which, to anybody who knew anything
at all about politics, was proof positive that in
the main convention Bryce County would hold
the balance of power. It wouldn't be a walk-
over; that much was certain, anyhow. Maydew's jaunty smile lost some of its jauntiness,
and anxious puckers made little seams at the
corners of those greedy eyes of his, when the
news from Bryce County came. As for Judge
Priest, he displayed every outward sign of being

well content as he ran over the completed figures. Bryce was an old-fashioned county,
mainly populated by a people who clung to old-
fashioned notions. Old soldiers were notably
thick in Bryce, too. There was a good chance
yet for his man. It all depended on those
twelve votes of Bryce County.

To Marshallville, second largest town in the
district, befell the honour that year of having the
district convention held in its hospitable midst;
and, as the *Daily Evening News* smartly phrased
it, to Marshallville on a Thursday All Roads
Ran. In accordance with the rote of fifty years
it had been ordained that the convention should
meet in the Marshallville courthouse, but in
the week previous a fire of mysterious origin
destroyed a large segment of the shingled roof of
that historic structure. A darky was on trial
for hog stealing upon the day of the fire, and it
may have been that sparks from the fiery oratory of the prosecuting attorney, as he pleaded
with the jury for a conviction, went upward and
lodged among the rafters. As to that I am not
in a position to say. I only know this explanation for the catastrophe was advanced by divers
ribald-minded individuals who attended the
trial.

In this emergency the local committee on
arrangements secured for the convention the
use of the new Marshallville opera house, which
was the pride of Marshallville—a compact but
ornate structure having on its first floor no less

than one hundred and fifty of those regular
theatre chairs magnificently upholstered in hot
red plush, and above, at the back, a balcony,
and to crown all, two orthodox stage boxes of
stucco, liberally embossed with gold paint,
which clung, like gilded mud-daubers' nests, at
either side of the proscenium arch, overhanging
the stage below.

In one of these boxes, as the delegates gathered that very warm August afternoon, a lady
sat in solitary state. To the delegates were
assigned the plush-enveloped grandeurs of the
main floor. The spectators, including a large
number of the male citizens of Marshallville
with a sprinkling of their women-folk, packed
the balcony to the stifling point, but this lady
had a whole box to herself. She seemed fairly
well pleased with herself as she sat there. Certainly she had no cause to complain of a lack of
public interest in her and her costume. To begin
with, there was a much beplumed hat, indubitably a thing of great cost and of augmented size,
which effectively shaded and set off her plump
face. No such hat had been seen in Marshallville before that day.

The gown she wore was likewise of a fashion
new to the dazzled gaze of her more plainly
habited sisters in the balcony. I believe in the
favoured land where they originated they call
them princesse gowns. Be its name what it may,
this garment ran in long, well-nigh unwrinkled
lines from the throat of its wearer to her ankles.

It was of some clinging white stuff, modelled seemingly with an intent to expose rather than to hide the curves of the rounded figure which it covered. It was close at the neck, snug at the bust, snugger still at the hips, and from there it flowed on tightly yet smoothly to where it ended, above a pair of high-heeled, big-buckled slippers of an amazing shininess. The uninitiated might well have marvelled how the lady ever got in her gown unless she had been melted and poured into it; but there was no mystery concerning the manner in which she had fastened it, once she was inside of it, for, when she turned away from the audience, a wondrously decorative finishing touch was to be seen: straight down the middle of her back coursed a close row of big, shiny black jet buttons, and when she shifted her shoulders these buttons undulated glisteningly along the line of her spinal column. The effect was snaky but striking.

The lady, plainly, was not exactly displeased with herself. Even a rear view of her revealed this. There was assurance in the poise of her head; assuredly there was a beaming as of confidence in her eyes. Indeed, she had reasons other than the satisfaction inspired by the possession of a modish and becoming garb for feeling happy. Things promised to go well with her and what was hers that afternoon. Perhaps I should have stated sooner that the lady in question was Mrs. Senator Maydew, present to witness and to glorify the triumph of her distinguished husband.

For a fact, triumph did seem near at hand now —nearer than it had been any time these past forty-eight hours. A quarter of an hour earlier an exultant messenger had come from her husband to bring to her most splendid and auspicious tidings. Luck had swung his way, and no mistake about it: of the doubtful delegates from Bryce County only two had arrived. The other ten had not arrived. Moreover there was no apparent possibility that they would arrive before the following day, and by then, if the Senator's new-born scheme succeeded, it would be all over but the shouting. A Heaven-sent freshet in Little River was the cause. Sitting there now in her stage box, Mrs. Senator Maydew silently blessed the name of Little River.

Ordinarily Little River is a stream not calculated to attract the attention of historians or geographers—a torpid, saffron-coloured thread of water meandering between flat yellow banks, and owing its chief distinction to the fact that it cuts off three-quarters of Bryce County from the remaining quarter and from the adjoining counties on the north. But it has its moods and its passions. It is temperamental, that river. Suddenly and enormously swollen by torrential summer rains in the hills where it has its rise, it went, the night before, on a rampage, over-flooding its banks, washing away fences and doing all manner of minor damage in the low grounds.

At dawn the big bridge which spanned the river at the gravel road had gone out, and at breakfast time Ferris' Ford, a safe enough crossing place in times of low water, was fifteen feet deep under a hissing brown flood. Two of Bryce County's delegates, who chanced to live in the upper corner of the county, had driven through hub-deep mud to the junction and there caught the train for Marshallville; but their ten compatriots were even now somewhere on the far bank, cut off absolutely from all prospect of attending the convention until the roiled and angry waters should subside.

Senator Maydew, always fertile in expedient, meant to ride to victory, as it were, on the providential high tide in Little River. Immediately on hearing what had happened, he divined how the mishap of the washed-out bridge and the flooded ford might be made to serve his ends and better his fortunes. He was keeping the plan secret for the moment; for it was a very precious plan. And this, in effect, was the word that his emissary brought to his wife just before the convention met. He could not bring it himself; custom forbade that a candidate show himself upon the floor in the early stages, but she was told to wait and watch for what would presently ensue, and meanwhile be of good cheer. Which, verily, she was.

She did not have so very long to wait. The

convention assembled on the hour—a block of
ten vacant seats in the second aisle showing
where the missing ten of Bryce should have been
—and was called to order by the new district
chairman. Up rose Judge Priest from his place
in the middle of the house, flanking the centre
aisle, and addressed the chair. He had just
learned, he stated, that a considerable quota of
the number of duly chosen delegates had not yet
reached Marshallville. It appeared that the
elements were in conspiracy against the extreme
lower end of the district. In justice to the sovereign voters of the sovereign County of Bryce
he moved that a recess of twenty-four hours be
taken. The situation which had arisen was
unforeseen and extraordinary, and time should
be granted for considering it in all its aspects.
And so on and so forth for five minutes or more,
in Judge Priest's best ungrammatical style.
The chairman, who, as will be recalled, was
Maydew's man, ruled the motion out of
order.

I shall pass over as briefly as possible the proceedings of the next half hour. To go fully into
those details would be to burden this narrative
with technicalities and tiresomeness. For our
purposes it is sufficient, I think, to say that the
Maydew machine, operating after the fashion
of a well-lubricated, well-steered and high-pow-
ered steam roller, ran over all obstacles with
the utmost despatch. These painful crunching
operations began early and continued briskly.

On the first roll call of the counties, as the County of Bryce—second on our list after Bland—was reached, one of those two lone delegates from the upper side of Little River stood up and, holding aloft his own credentials and the credentials of his team-mate, demanded the right to cast the votes of the whole Bryce County delegation—twelve in all.

The district chairman, acting with a promptness that bespoke priming beforehand for just such a contingency, held that the matter should be referred to the committee on credentials. As floor leader and spokesman for the Guest faction, old Judge Priest appealed from the ruling of the chair. A vote was taken. The chairman was sustained by fifty-seven to fifty-one, the two indignant delegates from Bryce not being permitted, under a ruling from the chair, to cast any votes whatsoever, seeing as their own status in the convention was the question at issue. Disorder ensued; in the absence of a sergeant-at-arms the services of volunteer peacemakers were required to separate a Maydew delegate from Bland County and a Guest delegate from Mims County.

Dripping with perspiration, his broad old face one big pinky-red flare, his nasal whine rising to heights of incredible whininess under the stress of his earnestness, the judge led the fight for the minority. The steam roller went out of its way to flatten him. Not once, but twice and thrice it jounced over him, each time leaving him figuratively squashed but entirely undismayed. He was fighting a losing but a valiant fight for time.

A committee on resolutions was named and went forth to an ante-room to draw up a platform. Nobody cared much about that. A set of resolutions pointing with pride to everything that was Democratic and viewing with alarm everything even remotely Republican in aspect would be presently forthcoming, as was customary. It was the committee on credentials upon which everything depended. Being chosen, it likewise retired, returning in a miraculously short space of time with its completed report.

And this in brief was what the majority of the committee on credentials—all reliable Maydew men—had to report:

There being no contests, it was recommended that the sitting delegates from the eight counties fully represented upon the floor be recognised as properly accredited delegates. But in respect to the ninth county, namely Bryce, an unprecedented situation had arisen. Two of Bryce's delegates were present, bearing credentials properly attested by their county chairman; unfortunately ten others were absent, through no fault of their own or of the convention. As a majority of the credentials committee viewed the matter, it would be a manifest injustice to deprive these two delegates of their right to take a hand in the deliberations; on the other hand, the committee held it to be equally unfair that those two should be permitted to cast the ballots of their ten associates, inasmuch as they could have no way of knowing what the personal preferences of the absentees might be. However, to meet the peculiar condition the committee now made the following recommendation, to wit as follows: That the secretary of the convention be instructed to prepare an alphabetical list of such delegates as were present in person, and that only such delegates as answered to their own names upon roll call—and no others whatsoever—be permitted to vote upon any question or questions subsequently arising in this convention. Respectfully submitted.

For a period of time to be measured by split seconds there was silence. Then a whirlwind of sound whipped round and round that packed little martin-box of an opera house and, spiraling upward, threatened the integrity of its tin roof. Senator Maydew had delivered his king-stroke, and the purport of it stood clearly betrayed to the understanding of all. With Bryce's voting strength reduced from twelve votes to two, and with all possibility of voting by proxy removed, the senator was bound to win the nomination on the first ballot. The Maydew men foresaw the incvitable result, once the recommendation of the committee had prevailed and they reared up in their places and threw their hats aloft and yelled. The Guest forces saw it, and they howled their disapprobation until they were hoarse.

The tumult stilled down to a ground breeze of mutterings as Judge Priest got upon his feet. To him in this dire emergency the Guest forces, now neck-deep in the last ditch, looked hopefully for a counterfire that might yet save them from the defeat looming so imminent. There and then, for once in his life the judge failed to justify the hopes and the faith of his followers. He seemed strangely unable to find language in which effectively to combat the proposition before the house. He floundered about, making no headway, pushing no points home. He practically admitted he knew of nothing in party usage or in parliamentary law that might serve as a bar to the adoption of the proposed rule. He proposed to vote against it, he said, but in the event that it be adopted he now moved that immediately thereafter the convention take an adjournment, thus giving the secretary time and opportunity in which to prepare the alphabetical list. With that he broke off suddenly and quit and sat down; and then the heart went out of the collective body of the Guest adherents and they quit, too, waiting in sullen, bewildered, disappointed silence for the inevitable.

After this it was felt that any further opposition to the Maydew programme would be but perfunctory opposition. The majority report of the committee on credentials was adopted by fifty-seven to fifty-three, the two Bryce delegates voting in the negative, as was to be expected. Even so, Maydew had a lead of four votes, which was not very many—but enough. To the accompaniment of a few scattering and spiritless *Nays* the convention took a recess of one hour. This meant a mighty busy hour for the secretary, but Maydew, from his temporary abiding place in the wings, sent orders to his floor managers to permit no more than an hour's delay at most. He was famishing for the taste of his accomplished triumph. Besides, there was no trusting so mercurial a stream as Little River. It might go down with the same rapidity that had marked its coming up. So an hour it was.

The delegates flowed out of the Marshallville opera house into the public square of Marshallville, and half of them, or a little more than half, were openly jubilant; and half of them, or a little less than half, were downcast, wearing the look upon their faces of men who were licked and who knew it, good and well. Moving along through the crowded aisle, a despondent delegate from Mims, a distant kinsman of Major Guest, found himself touching shoulders with Sergeant Jimmy Bagby, who was a delegate from our own county.

The Mims County man, with a contemptuous flirt of his thumb, indicated the broad back of Judge Priest as the judge ambled deliberately along toward the door.

"I knowed it," he said in the tones of bitter recapitulation; "I knowed it frum the start and I told 'em so; but no, they wouldn't listen to me. I knowed old Priest yonder was too old to be tryin' to run a campaign ag'inst a smart feller like Maydew, dern his slick hide! When the real test come, whut did your Jedge Priest do? Why, he jest natchelly curled up and laid flat down—that's whut he done. I reckin they'll listen to me next time."

For once in his life, and once only, Sergeant Jimmy Bagby teetered just the least bit in his unquestioning allegiance to his life-long friend.

"Well, I don't know," he said, shaking his head; "I don't know. You might be right in what you say, and then ag'in you might be wrong. It shore did look like he slipped a little, awhile ago, but you can't jest always tell whut's on Jedge Priest's mind," he added, pluckily renewing his loyalty.

The Mims County man grunted his disgust.

"Don't be foolin' yourself," he stated morosely. "You take it frum me—when old men start goin' they don't never come back. And your old Jedge is plumb gone. A baby could 'a' seen that frum the way he acted jest now."

The object of this criticism ploughed his slow way outdoors, all the while shaking his head with the air of one who has abandoned hope. In the street he gently but firmly disengaged himself from those who would have speech with him, and with obvious gloom in his manner made a way across the square to the Mansard House, where he and Major Guest had adjoining rooms on the second floor. His gait briskened, though, as soon as he had passed through the lobby of the Mansard House and was hidden from the eyes of friend and enemy alike.

From the privacy of his room he sent out for certain men. With Cap'n Buck Owings, a small, greyish, resolute gentleman, and with Sheriff Giles Birdsong, a large, reddish, equally resolute gentleman, he was closeted perhaps ten minutes. They went away saying nothing to any one, for the gift of silence was an attribute that these two shared in common. Then the judge had brief audience with Major Guest, who emerged from the conference a crushed and diminished figure. Finally he asked to speak with Sergeant Bagby. The sergeant found him sitting in his shirt-sleeves, with his feet on a window ledge, looking out into the square and gently agitating a palm-leaf fan.

"Jimmy," he said, "I want you to run an errand fur me. Will you go find Dabney Prentiss—I seen him down there on the street a minute ago—and tell him I say to git a speech ready?"

"Whut kind of a speech?" inquired Sergeant Bagby.

"Jimmy Bagby," reproved Judge Priest, "ain't you knowed Dab Prentiss long enough to know that you don't have to tell him whut kind of a speech he's to make? He's got all kinds of speeches in stock at all times. I'll confide this much to you though—it'll be the kind of a speech that he would 'specially prefer to make. Jest tell him I say be ready to speak out and

utter a few burnin' words when the proper time
comes, ef it does come, which I certainly hope
and trust it may."

Not greatly informed in his mind by this
somewhat cryptic explanation, the Sergeant
withdrew, and Judge Priest, getting up on his
feet, actually began humming a little wordless,
tuneless tune which was a favourite of his.
However, a thought of the melancholy interview
that he had just had with Major Guest must
have recurred to him almost immediately, for
when he appeared in the open a bit later on his
return to the opera house his head was bent
and his form was shrunken and his gait was
slow. He seemed a man weighed down with
vain repinings and vainer regrets.

It would appear that the secretary in the
interim had completed his appointed task, for
no sooner had the convention reassembled than
the chairman mounted to the stage and took
his place alongside a small table behind the
footlights and announced that nominations
would now be in order; which statement was a
cue for Attorney-at-Law Augustus Tate, of the
County of Emmett, to get gracefully upon his
feet and toss back his imposing sable mane and
address the assemblage.

Attorney Tate was an orator of parts, as he
now proceeded to prove beyond the slightest
peradventure of a doubt. He was known as the
Black Eagle of Emmett, for it had been said of
him that he had an eye like that noble bird, the

eagle. He had a chin like one, too; but that, of course, had no bearing upon his talents as displayed upon the stump, on the platform and in the forum, and in truth only a few malicious detractors had ever felt called upon to direct attention to the fact. In flowing and sonorous periods he placed in nomination the name of the Honourable Horace K. Maydew, concluding in a burst of verbal pin wheels and metaphorical skyrockets, whereat there was a great display of enthusiasm from floor and balcony.

When quiet had been restored Judge Priest got slowly up from where he sat and took an action which was not entirely unexpected, inasmuch as rumours of it had been in active circulation for half an hour or more. In twenty words he withdrew the name of the Honourable J. C. C. Guest as a candidate before the convention.

Only a rustle of bodies succeeded this announcement—that and an exhalation of breath from a few delegations, which attained to the volume of a deep joint sigh.

The chairman glanced over the house with a brightening eye. It was almost time to begin the jubilation. As a matter of fact several ardent souls among the Maydewites could hardly hold themselves in until the few remaining formalities had been complied with. They poised themselves upon the edges of their chairs, with throats tuned to lead in the yelling.

"Are there any other nominations?" asked the chairman, turning this way and that. He asked it as a matter of form merely. "If not, the nominations will be closed and the secretary will——"

"Mister Cheerman, one minute, ef you please."

The interrupting voice was the high-piped voice of Judge Priest, and the chairman straightened on his heels to find Judge Priest still upon his feet.

"The chair recognises Judge Priest again," said the chairman blandly. He assumed the judge meant to accept his beating gracefully and, in the interest of party harmony, to move the nomination of Maydew by acclamation. On his part that would have been a fair enough presumption, but the first utterances that came now from the old judge jerked open the eyes and gaped the mouth of the presiding officer. However, he was not alone there; nearly everybody was stunned.

"It was my painful duty a minute ago to withdraw the candidate that I had been privileged to foller in this campaign," said Judge Priest in his weedy notes. "It is now my pleasure to offer in his stead the name of another man as a suitable and a fittin' representative of this district in the National Halls of Congress." He glanced about him as though enjoying the surprised hush that had fallen upon the place, and for just a fraction of a second his eyes focused upon the lone occupant of the right-hand stage box, almost above his head. Then he went on, deliberately prolonging his syllables:

"The man whom I would nominate has never so fur as I know been active in politics. So fur as I know he has never aspired to or sought fur public office at the hands of his feller-citizens; in fact, he does not now seek this office. In presentin' his name for your consideration I am doin' so solely upon my own responsibility and without consultin' any one on this earth.

"My present candidate is not an orator. He is not a mixer or an organiser. I am constrained to admit that, measured by the standards of commerce, he is not even a successful man. He is poor in this world's goods. He is leadin' at this moment a life of retirement upon a little barren hillside farm, where the gulleys furrow his tobacco patch and the sassafras sprouts are takin' his cornfield, and the shadder of a mortgage rests heavy upon his lonely roof tree.

"But he is an honest man and a God-fearin' man. Ez a soldier under the stars and bars he done his duty to the sorrowful end. Ez a citizen he has never wilfully harmed his feller-man. He never invaded the sanctity of any man's home, and he never brought sorrow to any hearthstone. Ef he has his faults—and who amongst us is without them?—he has been the sole sufferer by them. I believe it has been charged that he drank some, but I never seen him under the influence of licker, and I don't believe anybody else ever did either.

"I nominate——" His voice took on the shrillness of a fife and his right fist, pudgy and clenched, came up at arm's length above his head—"I nominate—and on that nomination, in accordance with a rule but newly framed by this body, I call here and now fur an alphabetical roll call of each and every delegate—I offer as a candidate fur Congress ag'inst the Honourable Horace K. Maydew the name of my friend, my neighbour and my former comrade, Lysandy John Curd, of the voting precinct of Lone Ellum and the County of Red Gravel."

There was no applause. Not a ripple of approbation went up, nor a ripple of hostility either. But a gasp went up—a mighty gasp, deep and sincere and tremendously significant.

Of those upon the stage it was the chairman, I think, who got his wits back first. He was naturally quick-witted, else his sponsor would never have chosen him for chairman. In a mute plea for guidance he turned his head toward the wing of the stage where he knew that sponsor should be, and abruptly, at a distance from him to be measured by inches rather than by feet, his gaze encountered the hypnotising stare of Cap'n Buck Owings, who had magically materialised from nowhere in particular and was now at his elbow.

"Stay right where you are," counselled Cap'n Buck in a half whisper. "We've had plenty of these here recesses—these proceedin's are goin' right on."

Daunted and bewildered, the chairman hesitated, his gavel trembling in his temporarily palsied hand. In that same moment Sheriff Giles Birdsong had got upon the stage, too; only he deemed his proper place to be directly alongside the desk of the secretary, and into the startled ear of the secretary he now spoke.

"Start your roll call, buddy," was what Mr. Birdsong said, saying it softly, in lullaby tones, yet imparting a profound meaning to his crooning and gentle accents. "And be shore to call off the names in alphabetical order—don't furgit that part!"

Inward voices of prudence dictated the value of prompt obedience in the brain of that secretary. Quaveringly he called the first name on the list of the first county, and the county was Bland and the name was Homer H. Agnew.

Down in the Bland County delegation, seated directly in front of the stage, an old man stood up—the Rev. Homer H. Agnew, an itinerant Baptist preacher.

"My county convention," he explained, "instructed us for Maydew. But under the law of this convention I vote now as an individual. As between the two candidates presented I can vote only one way. I vote for Curd."

Having voted, he remained standing. There were no cheers and no hisses. Everybody waited. In a silence so heavy that it hurt, they waited. And the secretary was constrained to call the second name on the Bland County list: "Patrick J. Burke!"

Now Patrick J. Burke, as one might guess

from his name, belonged to a race that has been called sentimental and emotional. Likewise he was a communicant of a faith which long ago set its face like a flint against the practice of divorce.

"I vote for Curd," said Patrick J. Burke, and likewise he stood up, a belligerent, defiant, stumpy, red-haired man.

"Rufus Burnett!"

This was the first convention Rufus Burnett had ever attended in an official capacity. In order that she might see how well he acquitted himself, he had brought his wife with him and put her in the balcony. We may figure Mrs. Burnett as a strong-minded lady, for before he answered to his name Mr. Burnett, as though seeking higher guidance, cocked a pestered eye aloft to where the lady sat, and she, saying nothing, merely pointed a finger toward the spot where old Judge Priest was stationed. Rufus knew.

"Curd," he said clearly and distinctly. Somebody yelled then, and other voices took up the yell.

There were eleven names on the Bland County list. The secretary had reached the eighth and had heard eight voices speak the same word, when an interruption occurred—perhaps I should say two interruptions occurred.

The Black Eagle of Emmett darted out from the wings, bounded over the footlights and split a path for himself to the seat of Judge Priest. For once he forgot to be oratorical. "We'll quit,

Judge," he panted, "we're ready to quit. May-dew will withdraw—I've just come from him. He can't stand for this to go on; he'll withdraw if you'll take Curd's name down too. Any compromise candidate will do. Only, for heaven's sake, withdraw Curd before this goes any farther!"

"All right, son," said Judge Priest, raising his voice to be heard, for by now the secretary had called the ninth name and the cheering was increasing in volume; "that suits me first rate. But you withdraw your man first, and then I'll tell you who the nominee of this here convention is goin' to be."

Turning, he put a hand upon Sergeant Bagby's arm and shook him until the sergeant broke a whoop in two and hearkened.

"Jimmy," said Judge Priest with a little chuckle, "step down the aisle, will you, and tell Dabney Prentiss to uncork himse'f and git his speech of acceptance all ready. He don't know it yit, but he's goin' to move up to Washington, D. C., after the next general election."

Just as the sergeant started on his mission the other interruption occurred. A lady fainted. She was conspicuously established in the stage box on the right-hand side, and under the circumstances and with so many harshly appraisive eyes fixed upon her there was really nothing else for her to do, as a lady, except faint. She slipped out of her chair and fell backward upon the floor. It must have been a genuine faint, for certainly no person who was even partly conscious, let alone a tenderly nurtured lady, could have endured to lie flat upon the hard planks, as this lady did, with all those big, knobby jet buttons grinding right into her spine.

Although I may have wandered far from the main path and taken the patient reader into devious byways, I feel I have accomplished what I set out to do in the beginning: I have explained how Dabney Prentiss came to be our representative in the Lower House of the National Congress. The task is done, yet I feel that I should not conclude the chapter until I have repeated a short passage of words between Sergeant Jimmy Bagby and that delegate from Mims County who was a distant kinsman of Major Guest. It happened just after the convention, having finished its work, had adjourned, and while the delegates and the spectators were emerging from the Marshallville opera house.

All jubilant and excited now, the Mims County man came charging up and slapped Sergeant Bagby upon the shoulder.

"Well, suh," he clarioned, "the old Jedge did come back, didn't he?"

"Buddy," said Sergeant Bagby, "you was wrong before and you're wrong ag'in. He didn't have to come back, because he ain't never been gone nowheres."

IV

A CHAPTER FROM THE LIFE
OF AN ANT

SOMEONE said once—the rest of us subsequently repeating it on occasion—that this world is but an ant hill, populated by many millions of ants, which run about aimlessly or aimfully as the case may be. All of which is true enough. Seek you out some lofty eminence, such as the top floor of a skyscraper or the top of a hill, and from it, looking down, consider a crowded city street at noon time or a county fairground on the day of the grand balloon ascension. Inevitably the simile will recur to the contemplative mind.

The trouble, though, with the original coiner of the comparison was that he did not go far enough. He should have said the world was populated by ants—and by anteaters. For so surely as we find ants, there, too, do we find the anteaters. You behold the ants bustling about, making themselves leaner trying to make themselves fatter; terrifically busied with their small affairs; hiving up sustenance against the hard winter; gnawing, digging and delving; climbing, crawling, building and breeding—in short, deporting themselves with that energy, that restless industry which so stirred the admiration of the Prophet of old that, on his heavenward pilgrimage, he tarried long enough to tell the sluggard—name of the sluggard not given in the chronicles—to go to the ant and consider of her.

The anteater for the moment may not actually be in sight, but be assured he is waiting. He is waiting around the corner until the ant has propagated in numbers amounting to an excess; or, in other words, until the class that is born every second, singly—and sometimes as twins— has grown plentiful enough to furnish a feasting. Forth he comes then, gobbling up Brer Ant, along with his fullness and his richness, his heirs and his assigns, his substance and his stock in trade.

To make the illustration concrete, we might say that were there no ants there would be no Wall Street; and by the same token were there no anteaters there would be no Wall Street either. Without anteaters the ants would multiply and replenish the earth beyond computation. Without ants the anteaters would have to live upon each other—which would be bad for them but better for the rest of creation. War is the greatest of the anteaters—it feeds upon the bodies of the ants. Kings upon their

thrones, devisers of false doctrines, crooked
politicians, grafters, con men, card sharks,
thimbleriggers—all these are anteaters batten-
ing on the substance of simple-hearted, earnest-
minded ants. The ant believes what you tell
him; the greedsome anteater thrives upon this
credulity. Roughly, then, for purposes of
classification, one may divide the world at large
into two groups—in this larger group here the
ants, in that smaller group there the anteaters.

So much, for purposes of argument, being
conceded, we may safely figure Emanuel Moon
as belonging in the category of the ants, pure
and simple—reasonably pure and undeniably
simple. However, at the time whereof I write
I doubt whether it had ever occurred to anyone to liken him to an ant. His mother had
called him Mannie, his employers called him
plain Moon, and to practically everybody else
he was just little Mr. Moon, who worked in the
Commonwealth Bank. He had started there,
in the bank, as office boy; by dint of years of
untiring fidelity to the interests of that institution he had worked up to the place of assistant
cashier, salary seventy-five dollars a month.
Privately he nursed an ambition to become, in
time, cashier, with a cashier's full powers. It
might be added that in this desire he stood
practically alone.

Emanuel Moon was a little man, rising of
thirty-five, who believed that the Whale swal-
lowed Jonah, that if you swore a certain form of

oath you were certain of hell-fire, and that Mr.
Hiram Blair, president of the Commonwealth
Bank, hung the Big Dipper. If the Bible had
put it the other way round he would have believed as sincerely that it was Jonah who swal-
lowed the Whale. He had a wistful, bashful
little smile, an air of being perpetually busy,
and a round, mild eye the colour of a boiled
oyster. He also had a most gentle manner and
the long, prehensile upper lip that is found only
in the South American tapir and the confirmed
clarinet player. Emanuel Moon had one be-
setting sin, and only one—he just would play the
clarinet.

On an average of three nights a week he withdrew himself from the company assembled
about the base-burner stove in the parlour
if it were winter, or upon the front porch
of Mrs. Teenie Morrill's boarding house if
it were seasonable weather, and went up to
his room on the third floor and played the
clarinet. Some said he played it and some that
he merely played at it. He knew Annie Laurie
off by heart and for a term of years had been
satisfied in that knowledge. Now he was
learning another air—The Last Rose of Summer.

He prosecuted his musical education on what
he called his off evenings. Wednesday night
he went to prayer meeting and Sunday night
to the regular church service. Tuesday night
he always spent at his lodge; and perhaps once
in a fortnight he called upon Miss Katie Rouser,

who taught in the High School and for whom he was believed to entertain sentiments that did him credit, even though he had never found words in which to voice them.

At the lodge he served on the committees which did the hard work; that, as a general proposition, meant also the thankless work. If things went well someone else took the credit; if they went ill Emanuel and his colabourers shared the blame. The conditions had always been so—when he was a small boy and when he was a youth, growing up. In his adolescence, if there was a picnic in contemplation or a straw ride or a barn dance, Mannie had been graciously permitted by common consent of all concerned to arrange with the livery-stable man for the teams, to hire the coloured string band, to bargain with the owner of the picnic grounds or the barn, to see to ice for the ice-water barrel and lemons for the lemonade bucket.

While he thus busied himself the other youths made dates for the occasion with all the desirable girls. Hence it was that on the festal date Emanuel went partnerless to the party; and this was just as well, too, seeing that right up until the time of starting he would be completely occupied with last-moment details, and, after that, what with apologising for any slipups that might have occurred, and being scolded and ordered about on errands and called upon to explain this or that, would have small time to play the squire to any young person of the opposite sex, even had there been one convenient.

It was so at the bank, where he did more work than anybody and got less pay than anybody. It was so, as I have just stated, at the lodge. In a word, Emanuel had no faculty as an executive, but an enormous capacity for executing. The earth is full of him. Wherever five or more are gathered together there is present at least one of the Emanuel Moons of this world.

It had been a hot, long summer, even for a climate where the summers are always long and nearly always hot; and at the fag end of it Emanuel inclined strongly toward a desire for a short rest. Diffidently he managed to voice his mood and his need to Mr. Blair. That worthy gentleman had but just returned home, a giant refreshed, after a month spent in the North Carolina mountains. He felt so fit, so fine, so robust, he took it as a personal grievance that any about him should not likewise be feeling fit. He cut Emanuel off pretty short. Vacations, he intimated, were for those whose years and whose services in behalf of humanity entitled them to vacations; young men who expected to get along in business had best rid their thoughts of all such pampered hankerings.

Emanuel took the rebuke in good grace, as was his way; but that evening at the supper table he created some excitement among his fellow boarders by quietly and unostentatiously fainting, face forward, into a saucer of pear preserves that was mostly juice. He was removed to his room and put to bed, and attended by Doctor Lake. The next morning he was not able to go to the bank. On being apprised of the situation Mr. Blair very thoughtfully abated of his previous resolution and sent Emanuel word that he might have a week or even ten days off—at his own expense—wherein to recuperate.

Some thirty-six hours later, therefore, Emanuel might have been found on board the fast train bound for Louisville, looking a trifle pulled down and shaky, but filled with a great yearning. In Louisville, at a certain establishment doing a large mail-order business, was to be had for thirty-eight dollars, list price, fifteen and five off for cash, a clarinet that was to his present infirm and leaky clarinet as minted gold is to pot metal.

To be sure, this delectable instrument might. be purchased, sight unseen, but with privilege of examination, through the handy medium of the parcel post; the house handling it was in all respects reliable and lived up to the printed promise of the catalogue, but to Emanuel half the pride and pleasure of becoming its proprietor lay in going into the place and asking to see such and such a clarinet, and fingering it and testing its tone, and finally putting down the money and carrying it off with him under his arm. He meant, first of all, to buy his new clarinet; for the rest his plans were hazy. He might stay on in Louisville a few days or he might go elsewhere. He might even return home and spend the remainder of his vacation perfecting himself in his still faulty rendition of The Last Rose of Summer.

For an hour or so after boarding the train he viewed the passing scenery as it revealed itself through the day-coach window and speculated regarding the personalities of his fellow passengers. After that hour or so he began to nod. Presently he slumbered, with his head bobbing against the seat-back and one arm dangling in the aisle. A sense of being touched half roused him; a moment later he opened his eyes with the feeling that he had lost his hat or was about to lose it. Alongside him stood a well-dressed man of, say, thirty-eight or forty, who regarded him cordially and who held between the long, slender fingers of his right hand a little rectangle of blue cardboard, having punch marks in it.

"Excuse me, friend," said this man, "but didn't this fall out of your hat? I picked it up here on the floor alongside you."

"I reckon maybe it did," said Emanuel, removing his hat and noticing that the customary decoration conferred by the conductor was absent from its band. "I'm certainly much obliged to you, sir."

"Don't mention it," said the stranger. "Better stick it in good and tight this time. They might try to collect a second fare from you if you couldn't show your credentials. Remember, don't you, the story about the calf that ate up his express tag and what the old nigger man said about it?"

The stranger's accent stamped him as a Northerner; his manner revealed him indubitably as a man of the world—withal it was a genial manner. He bestowed a suit case alongside in the aisle and slipped into the seat facing Emanuel. Emanuel vaguely felt flattered. It had promised to be rather a lonely journey.

"You don't mind my sitting here a bit, do you?" added the man after he was seated.

"Not at all—glad to have you," said Emanuel, meaning it. "Nice weather—if it wasn't so warm," he continued, making conversation.

It started with the weather; but you know how talk runs along. At the end of perhaps ten minutes it had somehow worked around to amusements—checkers and chess and cards.

"Speaking of cards now," said the stranger, "I like a little game once in a while myself. Helps the time to pass away when nothing else will. Fact is, I usually carry a deck along with me just for that purpose. Fact is, I've got a new deck with me now, I think." He fumbled in the breast pocket of his light flannel coat and glanced about him. "Tell you what—suppose we play a few hands of poker—show-down, you know—for ten cents a corner, say, or a quarter? We could use my suit case for a card

table by resting it on our knees between us."
He reached out into the aisle.

"I'm much obliged," said Emanuel with an
indefinable sense of pain at having to decline
so friendly an invitation; "but, to tell you the
truth, I make it a point never to touch cards at
all. It wouldn't do—in my position. You
see, I'm in a bank at home."

With newly quickened alertness the stranger's
eyes narrowed. He put the cards back into
his pocket and straightened up attentively.
"Oh, yes," he said, "I see. Well, that being
the case, I don't blame you." Plainly he had
not been hurt by Emanuel's refusal to join in so
innocent a pastime as dealing show-down hands
at ten cents a side. On the contrary he warmed
visibly. "A young man in a bank can't be too
careful—especially if it's a small town, where
everybody knows everybody else's business.
You let a young fellow that works in a bank in a
small town, or even a medium-sized town, play
a few hands of poker and, first thing you know,
it's all over the place that he's gambling and
they've got an expert on his books. Let's see
now—where was it you said you lived?"

Emanuel told him.

"Well, now, that's a funny thing! I used
to know a man in your town. Let's see—what
was his name? Parker? Parsons?" He paused.

Emanuel shook his head.

"Perkins? Perkins? Could it have been
Perkins?" essayed the other tentatively, his

THE LIFE OF AN ANT

eyes fixed keenly on the ingenuous countenance
of his opposite; and then, as Emanuel's head
nodded forward affirmatively: "Why, that's
the name—Perkins," proclaimed the stranger
with a little smile of triumph.

"Probably J. W. Perkins," said Emanuel.
"Mr. J. W. Perkins is our leading hardware
merchant. He banks with us; I see him every
day—pretty near it."

"No; not J. W. Perkins," instantly confessed his companion. "That's the name all
right enough, but not the initials. Didn't this
Mr. Perkins have a brother, or a cousin or something, who died?"

"Oh, I know who you mean, now," said Emanuel, glad to be able to help with the identifica-
tion. "Altred Perkins—he died two years ago
this coming October."

"How old was he?" The Northerner had the
air about him of being determined to make sure.

"About fifty, I judge—maybe fifty-two or
three."

"And didn't they use to call him Al for
short?"

"Yes; nearly everybody did—Mr. Al Perkins."

"That's the party," agreed the other. "Al
Perkins! I knew him well. Strange, now, that
I can't think where it was I met him—I move
round so much in my business, being on the
road as a travelling man, it's hard keeping track
of people; but I know we spent a week or two

together somewhere or other. Speaking of
names, mine is Caruthers—John P. Caruthers.
Sorry I haven't got a card with me—I ran out
of cards yesterday."

"Mine," said our townsman, "is Emanuel
Moon."

"Glad to know you, Mr. Moon," said Mr.
Caruthers as he sought Emanuel's right hand
and shook it heartily.

"Very glad indeed. You don't meet many
people of your name—— Oh, by Jove, that's
another funny thing!"

"What?" said Emanuel.

"Why," said Mr. Caruthers, "I used to have
a pal—a good friend—with your name; Robert
Moon it was. He lived in Detroit, Michigan.
Fine fellow, Bob was. I wonder could old Bob
Moon have been your cousin?"

"No," said Emanuel almost regretfully; "I'm
afraid not. All my people live South, so far
as I know."

"Well, anyhow, you'd enjoy knowing old
Bob," went on the companionable Mr. Caruthers. "Have a smoke?"

He produced both cigars and cigarettes.
Emanuel said he never smoked, so Mr. Caruthers lighted a cigar.

Up to this point the conversation had been
more or less general. Now, somehow, it took a
rather personal and direct trend. Mr. Caruthers
proved to be an excellent listener, although he
asked quite a number of leading questions as

they went along.   He evinced a kindly curiosity regarding Emanuel's connection with the
bank.   He was interested in banks, it seemed;
his uncle, now deceased, had been, he said, a
very prominent banker in Springfield, Mas-
sachusetts.

Emanuel had a rôle that was new to him; a
pleasing rôle though.   Nearly always in company he had to play audience; now he held the
centre of the stage, with another listening to
what he might say, and, what was more, listening with every sign of deep attention.   He
spoke at length, Emanuel did, of the bank, its
size, its resources, its liabilities, its physical
appearance and its personnel, leading off with
its president and scaling down to its black
janitor.   He referred to Mr. Blair's crustiness
of manner toward persons of lesser authority,
which manner, he hastened to explain, was quite
all right if you only understood Mr. Blair's
little ways.

He mentioned in passing that Herb Kivil,
the cashier, was addicted to tennis, and that on
Tuesdays and Fridays, when Herb left early
to play tennis, he, Moon, closed up the vault
and took over certain other duties which ordinarily fell to Herb.   From the bank he progressed by natural stages to Mrs. Morrill's
boarding house and from there to his own individual tastes and likings.   In this connection
it was inevitable that the subject of clarinet
playing should obtrude.   Continuing along this

strain Emanuel felt moved to disclose his principal object in journeying to Louisville at this particular time.

"There's a store there that carries a clarinet that I'm sort of interested in," he stated—but got no farther, for here Mr. Caruthers broke in on him.

"Well, sir, it's a mighty little world after all," he exclaimed. "First you drop your punch check out of your hat and I come along and pick it up, and I sit down here and we get acquainted. Then I find out that I used to know a man in your town—Abner Perkins."

"Alfred," corrected Mr. Moon gently.

"Sure—Alfred Perkins. That's what I meant to say but my tongue slipped. Then you tell me your name, and it turns out I've got a good friend that, if he's not your own cousin, ought to be on account of the name being the same. One coincidence right after another! And then, on top of all that, you tell me you want to buy a new clarinet. And that's the most curious part of it all, because—— Say, Moon, you must have heard of Gatling & Moore, of Boston, New York, and Paris, France."

"I can't say as I ever did. I don't seem to place them," admitted Emanuel.

"If you're interested in a clarinet you ought to know about them, because Gatling & Moore are just the biggest wholesale dealers in musical instruments in the United States; that's all— just the whole United States. And I—the

same fellow that's sitting right here facing you—
I travel this territory for Gatling & Moore.
Didn't I say this was a small world?"

A small world indeed—and a cozily comfortable one as well, seeing that by its very
compactness one was thrown into contact with
so pleasing a personality as this Mr. John
Caruthers betrayed. This was the thought
that exhilarated Mr. Emanuel Moon as he
answered:

"You sell clarinets? Then you can tell me
exactly what I ought to pay——"

"No; don't get me wrong," Mr. Caruthers
hastened to explain. "I said I travelled for
Gatling & Moore. You see, they sell everything, nearly—musical instruments is just one
of their lines. I handle—er—sporting goods—
playing cards, poker chips, guns, pistols, athletic
supplies; all like that, you understand. That's
my branch of the business; musical goods is
another branch.

"But what I was going to suggest was this:
Izzy Gottlieb, who's the head of the musical
department in the New York office, is one of
the best friends I've got on this earth. If I was
to walk in and say to Izzy—yes, even if I was
to write in to him and tell him I had a friend
who was figuring on buying a clarinet—I know
exactly what old Izzy would do. Izzy would
just naturally turn the whole shop upside down
until he found the niftiest little old clarinet
there was in stock, and as a favour to me he'd

let us have it at just exactly cost. That's what good old Izzy would do in a blooming minute. Altogether it ought to come to about half what you'd pay for the identical same article out of a retail place down in this country."

"But could you, sir—would you be willing to do that much for a stranger?" Stress of emotion made Emanuel's voice husky.

"If you don't believe I would do just that very thing, why, a dime'll win you a trip to the Holy Land!" answered back the engaging Caruthers beamingly and enthusiastically.

Then his tone grew earnest: "Listen here, Moon: no man that I take a liking to is a stranger to me—not any more. And I've got to own up to it—I like you. You're my kind of a man —frank, open, on the level; and yet not anybody's easy mark either. I'll bet you're a pretty good hand at sizing up people offhand yourself. Oh, I knew you'd do, the minute I laid eyes on you."

"Thank you; much obliged," murmured Emanuel. To all intents he was overcome.

"Now, then," continued his new-found friend warmly, "let me suggest this: You go ahead and look at the clarinet that this piking Louisville concern's got for sale if you want to, but don't buy. Just look—there's no harm in that. But don't invest.

"I'm on my way back to New York now to—to lay in my new lines for the trade. I'll see old Izzy the first thing after I blow in and I'll get

the niftiest clarinet that ever played a tune—
get it at actual cost, mind you! I'll stick it
down into one of my trunks and bring it back
with me down this way.

"Let's see"—he consulted a small memo-
randum book—"I ought to strike this territory
again in about ten days or two weeks. We'll
make it two weeks, to be sure. Um—this is
Wednesday. I'll hit your town on Tuesday,
the twenty-ninth—that's two weeks from yesterday. I ought to get in from Memphis sometime during the afternoon. I'll come to your
bank to find you. You're always there on
Tuesdays, ain't you?"

"Oh, yes," said Emanuel. "Don't you remember my telling you that on Tuesdays Herb
Kivil always left early to play tennis and I
closed up?"

"So you did," confirmed Mr. Caruthers.
"I'd forgotten your telling me that."

"For that matter," supplemented Emanuel,
"I'm there every day till three anyhow, and
sometimes later; so if——"

"We'll make it Tuesday, the twenty-ninth,
to be sure," said Mr. Caruthers with an air of
finality.

"If you should want the money now——"
began Emanuel; and he started to haul out the
little flat leather purse with the patent clasp
wherein he carried his carefully saved cash assets.

With a large, generous gesture the other
checked him.

"Hold on!" counselled Caruthers. "You needn't be in such a hurry, old boy. I don't even know what the thing is going to cost yet. Izzy'll charge it to me on the books and then you can settle with me when I bring it to you, if that's satisfactory."

He stood up, carefully flicking some cigar ashes off the trailing ends of his four-in-hand tie, and glanced at a watch.

"Well, it's nearly six o'clock. Time flies when a fellow is in good company, don't it? We'll be in Louisville in less than an hour, won't we?— if we're on time. I've got to quit you there; I'm going on to Cincy to-night. Tell you what —let's slip into the diner and have a bite and a little nip of something together first—I want to see as much of you as I can. You take a little drink once in a while, don't you?"

"I drink a glass of light beer occasionally," admitted Emanuel.

Probably in his whole life he had consumed as much as five commercial quarts of that liquid, half a pint at a time.

"Fine business!" said Caruthers. "Beer happens to be my regular stand-by too. Come on, then." And he led the way forward for the transported Emanuel.

They said at the bank and at the boarding house that Moon looked better for his week's lay-off, none of them knowing, of course, what had come into the little man's dun-coloured life.

On the twenty-eighth of the month he was so abstracted that Mr. Blair, desiring his presence for the moment in the president's office, had to call him twice, a thing which so annoyed Mr. Blair that the second time he fairly shouted Emanuel's name; and when Emanuel came hurrying into his presence inquired somewhat acidly whether Emanuel was suffering from any auricular affection. On the morning of the twenty-ninth Emanuel was in quite a little fever of anticipation. The morning passed; the noon or dinner hour arrived and passed.

It was one-thirty. The street drowsed in the early autumnal sunshine, and in front of his bookstore, in a tilted-back chair, old Mr. Wilcox for a spell slumbered audibly. There is a kind of dog—not so numerous since automobiles have come into such general and fatal use—that sought always the middle of the road as a suitable spot to take a nap in, arousing with a yelp when wheels or hoofs seemed directly over him and, having escaped annihilation by an eighth of an inch, moving over perhaps ten feet and lying down again in the perilous pathway of traffic. One of this breed slept now, undisturbed except by flies, at the corner of Front and Franklin. For the time being he was absolutely safe. Emanuel had been to his dinner and had returned. He was beginning to worry. About two-thirty, just after the cashier had taken his tennis racket and gone for the day, Emanuel answered a ring at the telephone.

Over the wire there came to him the well-remembered sound of the blithe Carutherian voice:

"That you, old man?" spake Mr. Caruthers jovially. "Well, I'm here, according to promise. Just got in from down the road."

"Did—you—bring—it?" inquired Emanuel, almost tremulously.

"The clarinet? You bet your life I brought it —and she's a bird too."

"I'm ever so much obliged," said Emanuel. "I don't know how I can ever thank you— going to all that trouble on my account. Are you at the hotel? I'll be over there just as soon as I can close up—I can't leave here till three."

"Stay right where you are," bade his friend. "I'll be over to see you inside of fifteen or twenty minutes."

He was as good as his word. At ten minutes before three he walked in, the mould of city fashion in all his outward aspects; and when Emanuel had disposed of Mr. Herman Felsburg, who dropped in to ask what Felsburg Brothers' balance was, and when Mr. Felsburg had gone, Caruthers' right hand and Emanuel's met in an affectionate clasp across the little shelf of the cashier's window. Followed then an exchange of inquiries and assurances touching on the state of health and well-being of each gentleman.

"I'd like mightily to ask you inside," said Emanuel next, anxious to extend all possible hospitalities; "but it's strictly against the rules.

Take a chair there, won't you, and wait for me—
I'll be only a few minutes or so."

Instead of taking one of the row of chairs
that stood in the front of the old-fashioned bank,
Mr. Caruthers paused before the wicket, firing
metropolitan pleasantries across at the little
man, who bustled about inside the railed-off
inclosure, putting books and papers in their
proper places.

"Everybody's gone but me, as it happens,"
he explained, proud to exhibit to Mr. Caruthers
the extent and scope of his present responsi-
bilities.

"Nobody on deck but you, eh?" said
Caruthers, looking about him.

"Nobody but me," answered back Emanuel;
"and in about a minute and a half I'll be
through too."

The cash was counted. He carried it into
the depths of the ancient and cumbersome vault,
which blocked off a section of the wall behind
the cashier's desk, and in their appointed niches
bestowed, also, certain large ledgerlike tomes.
He closed and locked the inner steel door and was
in the act of swinging to the heavy outer door.

"Look here a minute!" came sharply from
Mr. Caruthers.

It was like a command. Obeying involuntarily, Emanuel faced about. From under his
coat, where it had been hidden against his left
side, Mr. Caruthers, still standing at the wicket,
was drawing forth something long and black

and slim, and of a most exceeding shininess—
something with silver trimmings on it and a
bell mouth—a clarinet that was all a clarinet
should be, and yet a half brother to a saxophone.

"I sort of thought you'd be wanting to get
a flash at it right away," said Mr. Caruthers,
holding the magnificent instrument up in plain
sight. "So I brought it along—for a surprise."

With joy Emanuel Moon's round eyes widened and moistened. After the fashion of a
rabbit suddenly confronted with lettuce his
lower face twitched. His overhanging upper
lip quivered to wrap itself about that virgin
mouthpiece, as his fingers itched to fondle that
slender polished fountain of potential sweet
melodies. And he forgot other things.

He came out from behind the counter and
almost with reverence took the splendid thing
from the smiling Mr. Caruthers. He did remember to lock the street door as they issued
to the sidewalk; but from that juncture on,
until he discovered himself with Caruthers in
Caruthers' room on the third floor of the hotel,
diagonally across the street and down the block
from the bank, and was testing the instrument
with soft, tentative toots and finding to his
extreme gratification that this clarinet bleated,
not in sheeplike bleats, as his old one did, but
rather mooed in a deep bass voice suggestive
of cows, all that passed was to Mr. Moon but
a confused blur of unalloyed joyousness.

Indeed, from that point thenceforward he

was not quite sure of anything except that, over his protests, Mr. Caruthers declined to accept any reimbursement whatsoever for the cost of the new clarinet, he explaining that, thanks to the generosity of that kindly soul, Izzy Gottlieb, the requisite outlay had amounted to so trifling a sum as not to be worthy of the time required for further discussion; and that, following this, he played Annie Laurie all the way through, and essayed the first bars of The Last Rose of Summer, while Mr. Caruthers sat by listening and smoking, and seemingly gratified to the utmost at having been the means of bringing this pleasure to Mr. Moon.

If Mr. Caruthers was moved, in chance intervals, to ask certain questions touching upon the banking business, with particular reference to the methods employed in conducting and safeguarding the Commonwealth Bank, over the way, Emanuel doubtlessly answered him full and truthfully, even though his thoughts for the moment were otherwise engaged.

In less than no time at all—so it appeared to Emanuel—six o'clock arrived, which in our town used to mean the hour for hot supper, except on Sunday, when it meant the hour for cold supper; and Emanuel reluctantly got up to go. But Caruthers would not listen to any suggestions of their parting for yet a while. Exigencies of business would carry him on his lonesome way the next morning; he had just stopped over to see Emanuel, anyway, and naturally he wished to enjoy as much of his society as was possible during a sojourn so brief.

"Moon," he ordered, "you stay right where you are. We'll have something to eat together here. I'll call a waiter and we'll have it served up here in this room, so's we can be sort of private and sociable, and afterward you can play your clarinet some more. How does that little programme strike you?"

It struck Emanuel agreeably hard. It was rarely that he dined out, and to dine under such circumstances as these, in the company of so fascinating and so kindly a gentleman as Mr. John P. Caruthers, of the North—well, his cup was simply overflowing, that's all.

"I'd be glad to stay," he said, "if you don't think I'm imposing on your kindness. I was thinking of asking you to go to Mrs. Morrill's with me for supper—if you would."

"We can have a better time here," said Caruthers. He stepped over to the wall telephone. "Have a cocktail first? No? Then neither will I. But a couple of bottles of beer won't hurt us—will it?"

Emanuel was going to say a small glass of beer was as much as he ever imbibed at a sitting, but before he could frame the statement Caruthers was giving the order.

It was at the close of a most agreeable meal when Emanuel, following Mr. Caruthers' invitation and example, had emptied his second glass of beer and was in the act of putting down the tumbler, that a sudden sensation of drowsiness assailed his senses. He bent back in his chair, shaking his head to clear it of the mounting dizziness, and started to say he believed he would step to the window for a breath of fresh air. But, because he felt so very comfortable, he changed his mind. His head lolled over on one side and his lids closed down on his heavy eyes. Thereafter a blank ensued.

When Emanuel awoke there was a flood of sunshine about him. For a moment he regarded an unfamiliar pattern of wall paper, the figures of which added to their unfamiliarity by running together curiously; he was in a strange bed, fully dressed, and as he moved his head on the rumpled pillow he realised that he had a splitting headache and that a nasty dryish taste was in his mouth. He remembered then where he was and what had happened, and sat up with a jerk, uttering a little remorseful moan.

The disordered room was empty. Caruthers was gone and Caruthers' suit case was gone too. Something rustled, and a folded sheet of hotel note paper slid off the bed cover and fell upon the floor. With trembling fingers he reclaimed the paper, and, opening it, he read what was scrawled on it in pencil:

"*Dear Old Scout:* I'm sorry! I didn't suppose one bottle of beer would put you down and out. When you took the count all of a sudden,

I figured the best thing to do was to let you sleep it off; so I got you into the bed. You've been right there all night and nobody's any the wiser for it except me. Sorry I couldn't wait until you woke up, but I have to catch the up train; so I've paid my bill and I'm beating it as soon as I write this. Your clarinet is with you. Think of me sometimes when you tootle on it. I'll let you hear from me one of these days.

Yours in haste,

J. P. C.

"P. S. If I were you I'd stay off the beer in future."

The up train? Why, that left at eight-forty-five! Surely it could not be that late! Emanuel got out his old silver watch, a legacy from a long-dead sire, and took one look at its two hands; and then in a quiver of haste, with no thought of breakfast or of his present state of unwashed untidiness, with no thought of anything except his precious clarinet, which he tucked under his coat, he let himself out of the door, leaving the key in the lock, and slipping through the deserted hallway he hastened down two flights of stairs; and taking a short cut that saved crossing the lobby, where inquisitive eyes might behold him in all his unkemptness and distress, he emerged from the side door of the Hôtel Moderne.

Emanuel had proper cause to hurry. Never in all his years of service for the Commonwealth Bank had he failed to be on hand at eight o'clock to sort out the mail; and if his watch was to be believed here it was a quarter of nine! As he padded across the street on shaky legs a new apprehension that he had come away the day before without locking the combination of the vault smote him. Suppose—suppose something was wrong!

The street door of the Commonwealth stood open, and though the interior seemed deserted he realised, with a sinking of the heart, that someone had arrived before him. He darted inside, dropped the clarinet out of sight in a cuddy under his desk, and fairly threw himself at the vault.

The outer door was closed and locked, as it should be. Nevertheless, his hands shook so that he could hardly work the mechanism. Finally, the tumblers obeyed him, and he swung open the thick twin slabs, unlocked the inner door with the key which he carried along with other keys on his key ring—and then fetched a sigh of relief that was half a sob. Everything was as it should be—cash, paper money, books, files and securities. As he backed out of the vault the door of the president's office opened and Mr. Blair stood there in the opening, confronting him with an accusing glare.

"Young man," said Mr. Blair, "you're late!"

"Yes, sir," said Emanuel. "I'm very sorry, sir. I must have overslept."

"So I judge!" Mr. Blair's accents were ominous. "So I judge, young man—but where?"

"W-where?" Emanuel, burning with shame, stammered the word.

"Yes, sir; that's what I said—where? Twenty minutes ago I telephoned to Mrs. Morrill's to find out what was keeping you from your duties, and they told me you hadn't been in all night—that your bed hadn't been slept in."

"Yes, sir; I slept out."

"I gathered as much." Mr. Blair's long white chin whiskers quivered as Mr. Blair's condemning eyes comprehended the shrinking figure before him from head to foot—the rumpled hair; the bloodshot eyes; the wrinkled clothes; the soiled collar; the skewed necktie; the fluttering hands. "Look here, young man; have you been drinking?"

"No, sir—yes, sir; that is, I—I had a little beer last night," owned Emanuel miserably.

"A little beer, huh?"

Mr. Blair, being popularly reputed to keep a private quart flask in his coat closet and at intervals to refresh himself therefrom behind the cover of the closet door, had a righteous contempt for wantons who publicly plied themselves with potables, whether of a malt, a spirituous or a vinous nature.

"A little beer, huh?" He put tons of menace into the repetition of the words. "Forever and a day traipsing off on vacations seems to breed bad habits in you, Moon. Now, look here! This is the first time this ever happened —so far as I know. I am inclined to excuse it this once. But see to it that it doesn't happen again—ever!"

"No, sir," said Emanuel gratefully. "It won't."

And it did not.

So shaken was Emanuel as to his nerves that three whole nights elapsed before he felt equal to practicing on his new clarinet. After that, though, in all his spare moments at the boarding house he played assiduously.

For the purposes of this narrative the passage of the ensuing fortnight is of no consequence. It passed, and that brings us to a Friday afternoon in mid-October. On the Friday afternoon in question the paymaster of the Great Western Crosstie Company deposited in the Commonwealth Bank, for overnight safeguarding, the funds to meet his semimonthly pay roll due to contractors, subcontractors, towboat owners and extra labourers, the total amounting to a goodly sum.

Next morning, when Herb Kivil opened the vault, he took one look and uttered one strangled cry. As Emanuel straightened up from the mail he was sorting, and as Mr. Blair stepped in off the street, out from between the iron doors staggered Herb Kivil, white as a sheet and making funny sounds with his mouth. The vault was empty—stripped of cash on hand; stripped of the Great Western Company's big deposit; stripped of every scrap of paper money; stripped of everything except the bank books and certain securities—in a word, stripped of between eighteen and nineteen thousand dollars, specie and currency. For the thief, whoever he might be, there was one thing to be said—he had an instinct for thoroughness in his make-up.

To say that the news, spreading with a most miraculous rapidity, made the town hum like a startled hive, is to state the case in the mildest of descriptive phrases. On the first alarm, the chief of police, accompanied by a good half of the day force, came at a dogtrot. Having severely questioned the frightened negro janitor, and examined all the doors and windows for those mysterious things known as clews, the chief gave it as his deliberate opinion that the robbery had been committed by some one who had means of access to the bank and its vault.

Inasmuch as there was about the place no evidence of forcible entry, and inasmuch as the face of the vault was not so much as scratched, and inasmuch, finally, as the combination was in perfect order, the population at large felt constrained to agree that Chief Henley had deduced aright. He took charge of the premises for the time being, Mr. Blair having already wired to a St. Louis detective agency beseeching the immediate presence and aid of an expert investigator.

It came out afterward that privily Mr. Blair

suggested an immediate arrest, and gave to Henley the name of the person he desired to see taken into custody. But the chief, who was good-hearted—too good-hearted for his own good, some people thought—demurred. He stood in a deep and abiding awe of Mr. Blair. But he did not want to make any mistakes, he said. Anyhow, a big-city sleuth was due before night. Would not Mr. Blair consent to wait until the detective had arrived and made his investigation? For his part, he would guarantee that the individual under suspicion did not get away. To his postponement of the decisive step Mr. Blair finally agreed.

On the afternoon train over the Short Line the expert appeared, an inscrutable gentleman named Fogarty with a drooping red moustache and a brow heavily wrinkled. This Mr. Fogarty first conferred briefly with Mr. Blair and with Chief Henley. Then, accompanied by these two and trailed by a distracted group of directors of the bank, he made a careful survey of the premises from the cellar coal hole to the roof scuttle, uttering not a single word the while. His manner was portentous. Following this he asked for a word in private with the head of the rifled institution.

Leaving the others clustered in a group outside, he and Mr. Blair entered Mr. Blair's office. Mr. Fogarty closed the door and faced Mr. Blair.

"This here," said Mr. Fogarty, "was what

we call an inside job. Somebody here in this town—somebody who knew all there was to know about your bank—done it. Now, who do you suspicion?"

Lowering his voice, Mr. Blair told him, adding that only a deep sense of his obligations to himself and to his bank inspired him now to detail certain significant circumstances that had come to his personal attention within the past three weeks—or, to be exact, on a certain Wednesday morning in the latter part of September.

In his earlier movements Mr. Fogarty might have been deliberate; but once he made up his mind to a definite course of conduct he acted promptly. He came out of Mr. Blair's presence, walked straight up to Emanuel Moon, where Emanuel sat at his desk, and, putting his hand on Emanuel's shrinking shoulder, uttered the words:

"Young man, you re wanted! Put on your hat."

Then Mr. Fogarty silently turned and beckoned to Chief Henley, invoking the latter's official co-operation and assistance.

Between the imported detective and the chief of police, Emanuel Moon, a silent, pitifully shrunken figure, walked round the corner to the City Hall, a crowd following along behind, and was locked up in a cell in the basement calaboose downstairs. Lingering about the hall after the suspect had been taken inside,

divers citizens ventured the opinion that if the
fellow wasn't guilty he certainly looked it.
Well, so far as that goes, if a face as pale as
putty and downcast eyes brimming with a
numbed misery betokened guilt Emanuel had
not a leg left to stand on.

However, looks alone are not commonly
accepted as competent testimony under our
laws, and Emanuel did not abide for very long
as a prisoner. The Grand Jury declined to
indict him on such dubious proof as the bank
people and Mr. Fogarty could offer for its consideration. Undoubtedly the Grand Jury was
inspired in its refusal by the attitude the Commonwealth's attorney maintained, an attitude
in which the circuit judge concurred.

It was known that Mr. Blair went to Commonwealth's Attorney Flournoy, practically demanding that Emanuel be held for trial, and,
failing in that quarter, visited Judge Priest
with the same object in view. But perversely
the judge would not agree with Mr. Blair that
the evidence in hand justified such a course;
would not on any account concede that Emanuel Moon was the only person, really, who
might properly be suspected.

On that head he was as one with Prosecutor
Flournoy. They held—these two—that possession of a costly musical instrument, regarding which the present owner would admit
nothing except that it was a gift from an unknown friend, coupled with that individual's

stubborn refusal to tell where he had spent a
certain night and in whose company, did not
constitute a fair presumption that he had made
away with nearly nineteen thousand dollars.

"But look here, Judge Priest," hotly argued
Mr. Blair upon the occasion of his call upon
His Honour, "it stands to reason Moon is the
thief. Why, it couldn't have been anybody
else! And I want the facts brought out."

"Whut facts have you got, Hiram?" asked
the judge.

"Moon knew the combination of the safe,
didn't he? He carried the keys for the inside
door of the safe, didn't he? And a key to the
door of the building, too, didn't he?"

"Hiram," countered Judge Priest, looking
Mr. Blair straight in the eye, "ef you expect the
authorities to go ahead on that kind of evidence
I reckin we'd have to lock you up too."

Mr. Blair started as though a physical blow
had been aimed at his head.

"Why—why—— What do you mean by
that, Judge?" he demanded, gripping the arms
of his chair until his knuckles showed white
through the skin.

"You carry the keys of the bank yourself,
don't you? And you know the combination of
the safe, don't you? And so does Herbie Kivil."

"Do you mean to insinuate——"

"Hiram, I don't mean to insinuate nothin'.
Insinuations don't make the best of evidence
in court, though I will admit they sometimes

count for a good deal outside of court. No, Hiram; I reckin you and your detective friend from St. Louis will have to dig up somethin' besides your personal beliefs before you kin expect the Grand Jury of this county to lay a charge aginst a man who's always enjoyed a fair standin' in this here community. That's all I've got to say to you on the subject."

Taking the hint, Mr. Blair, red-faced and agitated, took his departure. After he was gone Judge Priest remained immersed in reflection for several hours.

So Emanuel went free. But he might almost as well have stayed in jail, for the smell of it seemed to cling to his garments—garments that grew shabbier as the weeks passed, for naturally he did not go back to the bank and just as naturally no one cared to offer employment to one who had been accused by his late employer of a crime. He fell behind with his board at Mrs. Morrill's. He walked the streets with drooping shoulders and face averted, shunning people and shunned by them. And, though he kept to his room in the evening, he no longer played on his clarinet. And the looting of the Commonwealth Bank's vault continued, as the *Daily Evening News* more than once remarked, to be "shrouded in impenetrable mystery."

One evening at dusk, as Judge Priest was going home alone from the courthouse, on a back street he came face to face with Emanuel.

The younger man would have passed by him without speaking, but the old man thrust his broad shape directly in the little man's course.

"Son," he said, putting a hand on the other's arm, "I want to have a little talk with you— ez a friend. Jest you furgit all about me bein' a judge. I wisht, ef you ain't got anythin' else to do, you'd come up to my house to-night after you've had your supper. Will you, son?"

Emanuel, his eyes filling up, said he would come, and he did; and in the judge's old sitting-room they spent half an hour together. Father Minor always said that when it came to hearing confessions the only opposition he had in town came from a nonprofessional, meaning by that Judge Priest. It was one of Father Minor's little jokes.

"And now, Judge Priest," said Emanuel, at the latter end of the talk, "you know every-thing—why I wouldn't tell 'em how I got my new clarinet and where I spent that night. If I had to die for it I wouldn't bring suspicion on an innocent party. I haven't told anybody but you—you are the only one that knows."

"You're shore this here friend of yourn— Caruthers—is an innocent party?" suggested the judge.

"Why, Judge, he's bound to be—he's just naturally bound to be. If he'd been a thief he'd have robbed the bank that night when I was asleep in his room at the hotel. I had the keys to the bank on me and he knew it."

"Then why didn't you come out and say so, son?"

"Because, as I just told you, it would be bringing suspicion on an innocent party. He holds a responsible position with that big New York firm I was telling you about and it might have got him into trouble. Besides"—and Emanuel hung his head—"besides, I hated so to have people know that I was ever under the influence of liquor. I'm a church member, Judge, as you know. I never drank—to excess —before that night, and I don't ever aim to touch another drop as long as I live. I'd almost as lief be called a drunkard as a thief. They're calling me a thief—I don't aim to have them calling me the other thing too."

Judge Priest cloaked an involuntary smile behind a pudgy hand.

"Well, Emanuel," he said, "jest to be on the safe side, did it ever occur to you to make inquiry amongst the merchants here as to whether a travelling gent named Caruthers sold goods to any of 'em?"

"No, Judge; I never thought of that."

"Did you look up Gatling & Moore—I believe that's the name—in Bradstreet's or Dun's to see ef there was sech a firm?"

"Judge, I never thought of that either."

"Son," said the old man, "it sorter looks to me like you ain't been doin' much thinkin' lately." Then his tone changed and became warmly consoling. "But I reckin ef I was in the trouble you're in I wouldn't do much thinkin' neither. Son, you kin rest easy in your mind—I ain't a-goin' to betray your confidences. But ef you don't mind I aim to do a little inquirin' round on my own account. This here robbery interests me powerfully, someway. I've been frettin' a heap about it lately.

"And—oh, yes—there's another thing that I was purty nigh furgittin'," continued Judge Priest. "I ain't purposin' to pry into your personal affairs—but tell me, son, how are you off fur ready money these days?"

"Judge, to tell you the truth, I'm just about out of money," confessed Emanuel desperately. "I owe Mrs. Morrill for three weeks' board now. I hate to keep putting her off—her being a widow lady and dependent for her living on what she takes in. I'd pack up and go somewhere else—to some other town—and try to get work, only I can't bear to go away with this cloud hanging over my good name. It would look like I was running away; and anyway I guess the tale would follow me."

The judge dug into his right-hand trousers pocket. He exhumed a small wad of bills and began counting them off.

"Son," he said, "I know you won't mind my makin' you a temporary loan to help you along till things git brighter with you. By the way, how would you like to go to work in the circuit clerk's office?"

"Me, Judge! Me?" Fresh-kindled hope

blazed an instant in Emanuel Moon's voice; then the spark died.

"I reckon nobody would hire me," he finished despondently.

'Don't you be so shore. 'Lishy Milam come to me only yistiddy sayin' he needed a reliable and experienced man to help him with his books, and askin' me ef I could suggest anybody. He ain't had a capable deputy sense little Clint Coombs died on him. I sort of figger that ef he gave you a job on my say-so it'd go a mighty long way toward convincin' this town that we both regarded you ez an honest citizen. I'll speak to 'Lishy Milam the very first thing in the mornin'—ef you're agreeable to the notion."

"Judge," exclaimed Emanuel, up on his feet, "I can't thank you—I can't tell you what this means——"

"Son, don't try," bade the old judge. "Anyhow, that ain't whut I want to hear frum you now. Set down there agin and tell me all you kin remember about this here friend of yourn—Caruthers; where you met up with him and whut he said and how he said it, and the way he looked and walked and talked. And how much beer you drunk up that night and how much he drunk up, and how you felt when you woke up, and whut Hiram Blair said to you when you showed up at the bank—the whole thing all over agin from start to finish. I'm interested in this here Mr. Caruthers. It strikes me he must 'a' been a mighty likely feller."

When Emanuel Moon walked out of Judge Priest's front door that night he was pumped dry. Also, for the first time in weeks, he walked with head erect and gaze straightforward.

In the morning, true to his promise, Judge Priest made recommendations to Circuit Clerk Milam. This done, he left the courthouse and, going down Legal Row, dropped in at the law office of Fairleigh & Fairleigh, to find young Jere Fairleigh, junior member of the firm, sitting by the grate fire in the front room.

"Jere," asked Judge Priest, directly the young man had made him welcome, "whutever become of them three post-office robbers that hired you to defend 'em—still over in the Marshallville jail, ain't they?"

"Two of them are," said young Fairleigh. "The one they call the Waco Baby got out on bail and skipped. But the other two—Frisco Slim and Montreal Red—are in jail over there awaiting trial at the next term of United States Court."

Judge Priest smiled softly.

"Young man," he said, "it certainly looks to me like you're climbin' mighty fast in your chosen profession. All your clients 'pear to have prominent cities named after 'em. Tell me," he went on, "whut kind of persons are the two that are still lingerin' in Marshallville?"

"Well," said the young lawyer, "there's a world of difference between 'em. Frisco is the glum, morose kind; but Montreal Red—his real name is Mooney, he tells me, though he's got half a dozen other names—he's certainly a wise individual. Just associating with him in my capacity as his counsel has been a liberal education to me in the ways of the underworld. I firmly believe he knows every professional crook in the country."

"Aha! I see," said Judge Priest. "I figger Mister Montreal is the party I want to meet. I'm thinkin' of runnin' down to Marshallville on business right after dinner to-day. I reckin you wouldn't mind—in strict confidence— givin' me a little note of introduction to your client, tellin' him I seek his advice on a private matter, and sayin' that I kin be trusted?"

"I'll be mighty glad to," said Fairleigh, Junior, reaching across his desk for pen and paper. "I'll write it right now. Turning detective, Judge?"

"Well, son," conceded Judge Priest, "you mout call it that and not make sech an awful big mistake."

"Sort of a Sherlock Holmes, eh?"

The judge made a gesture of modest disclaimer.

"No; I reckin Sherlock would be out of my class. By all accounts Sherlock knowed purty nigh ever'thing wuth knowin'. If he'd struck two different trails, both seemin'ly p'intin' in the same direction, he'd know right off which one of 'em to take. That's where he'd be one pawpaw above my tallest persimmon. Sometimes I git to thinkin' I'm a poor purblind old idiot that can't see a thing when it's shoved right up under my nose. No; I ain't aspirin' none to qualify ez a Sherlock. I'm only endeavourin' to walk ez an humble disciple in the hallowed footsteps of Old Cap Collier."

"What do you know about Old Cap Collier?" demanded Fairleigh, astonished. "I thought I was the only grown man in town that still read nickel libraries—on the sly."

"Boy," said Judge Priest, "you and me have got a secret bond between us. Wasn't that there last one that come out a jim-dandy?— the one called Old Cap Collier and the Great Diamond Robbery.

"It was so," stated Fairleigh. "I read it last night in bed."

Three o'clock of that same day disclosed Judge Priest perched on the side of a bunk in a cell in the Marshallville jail, close up alongside a blocky person of unkempt appearance whom we, for convenience, may call Montreal Red, more especially as this happens to be the title to which he commonly answered within the fraternity of which he was a distinguished member. They made a picture sitting there together —the old man, nursing his soft black hat between his hands, with the half light bringing out in relief his bald round skull, his chubby pink face and his tuft of white beard; the captive yeggman in his shirt sleeves, with no collar on and no shoes on, holding Mr. Fairleigh's note in his hand and, with the look upon his face of one who feels a just pride in his professional knowledge, hearkening while the Judge minutely described for him a certain individual. Before the Judge was done, Montreal Red interrupted him.

"Sufficiency, bo," he said lightly; "you've said enough. I know the gun you're talkin' about without you goin' any farther—it's Shang Conklin, the Solitary Kid."

"But this here gentleman went by the name of Caruthers!" demurred the Judge.

"Wot else did you figure he'd be doin'?" countered Montreal Red. "He might 'a' called himself Crowley, or Lord Copeleigh, or half a dozen other things. He might 'a' called himself the King of Bavaria—yes, and got away with it, too, because he's there with the swell front and the education. The Solitary Kid's got a different monniker for every day in the week and two for Sundays. It couldn't be nobody else but him; you've called the turn on him same as if you'd mugged him for the Gallery."

"You know him personally, then?" asked Judge Priest.

"Who don't know him?" said Montreal Red. "Everybody that knows anybody knows Solitary. And I'll tell you why! You take 'most any ordinary gun and he's got just one regular line—he's a stick-up, or he's a moll

buzzer, or a peterman, or a con man; or he
belongs to the hard-boiled people, the same as
me. But Shang he doubles in brass; it's B.
and O. for him. Bein' there with the front,
he's worked the wire; and before that he worked
the bat. Knowin' all there is to know about the
pasteboard papes, he'd done deep-sea fishin'
in his time—playin' for rich guys on the big
liners, you know.

"And when it comes to openin' boxes—bo,
since old Jimmy Hope quit the game and
sneezed in, I guess Shang Conklin's the wisest
boxman that ever unbuttoned a combination
crib with his bare hands. He's sure the real
McCoy there—not no common yegg, you understand, with a steel drill and a gat in his kicks
and a rubber bottle full of soup tied under his
coat; but doin' the real fancy stuff, with nothin'
to help him but the old ten fingers and the
educated ear. And he never works with a mob
neither. Any time you make Shang he'll be
playin' the lone hand—providin' his own nut
and goin' south with all the clean-up. No
splittin' with anybody for Shang—it's against
his business principles. That's why he's labelled
the Solitary Kid."

Most of this was as pure Greek to Judge
Priest, who, I may say, knew no Greek, pure
or otherwise. Suddenly aware of the bewilderment revealed in the countenance of his inter-
viewer, Montreal Red checked up and took a
new track.

"Say, bo, you ain't makin' me, are you? Well, then, maybe I'd better spiel it out slow. Know wot a peterman is?"

The judge shook his head.

"Well, you know wot a box is, don't you?"

"I'm skeered that I don't, though I believe I'm beginnin' to git a faint idea," said Judge Priest.

As though deploring such ignorance Montreal Red shook his flame-coloured head.

"I'll frame it for you different—in sucker language," he said.

And accordingly he did, most painstakingly.

"Now then," he said at the end of five minutes of laborious translation, "do you get me?"

"I git you," said Judge Priest. "And I'm mighty much obliged. Now, then, ef it ain't too much trouble, I'd like to git in touch with this here Mister Conklin, et cetery. Do you, by any chance, know his present whereabouts?"

Before replying to this the Montreal Red communed with himself for a brief space.

"Old-timer," he said finally, "if I thought you was playin' in with the dicks I'd see you in Belgium before I tipped you off to anything. But this here mouthpiece of mine"—he indicated the note from young Mr. Fairleigh— "says you're on the level. I judge he wouldn't take my good fall-money and then cross me this way. I take it you ain't tryin' to slip one over on Shang? All right, then; I'll tell you where he is—he's in Atlanta, Georgia."

"And whut is his address there?" pursued Judge Priest.

"The Federal prison—that's all," said Montreal Red. He smiled softly. "If I don't beat this little case of mine I'm liable to meet him down there along toward spring, or maybe even sooner. The bulls nailed him at Chattanooga, Tennessee, about a month ago for a little national-bank job, and right quick he taken a plea and got off with a short bit in Uncle Sammy's big house. I was readin' about it in the papers. You wouldn't have no trouble findin' him at Atlanta—he'll be in to callers for the next five years."

"Bein' an amateur Old Cap Collier certainly calls fur a lot of travellin' round," murmured Judge Priest, half to himself, and he sighed a small sigh of resignation as he arose.

"Wot's that? I don't make you?" asked Montreal Red.

"Nothin'," said Judge Priest; "nothin' a-tall. I was jest thinkin' out loud; it's a sort of failin' of mine ez I git older. You said, didn't you, that these here sleepin' potions which you was mentionin' a minute ago are mostly administered in beer?"

"Mostly in beer," said Montreal Red. "The little old knock-out seems to work best in the lather stuff. I don't know why, but it does. It's like this: You take the beer——"

"Oh, I wasn't figgerin' on usin' it myself," explained Judge Priest hastily. "Much obliged to you all the same, young man."

A night in a sleeping car brought Judge Priest to Atlanta. A ride in a trolley car brought him to the warden's office of a large reformatory institution beyond the suburbs of that progressive city. A ten-minute chat with the warden and the display of divers credentials brought him the privilege of an interview, in private, with a person who, having so many names to pick from, was yet at this time designated by a simple number. Even in convict garb, which is cut on chastely plain lines and which rarely fits perfectly the form of its wearer, this gentleman continued somehow to bespeak the accomplished metropolitan in his physical outlines and in his demeanour as well, maintaining himself, as you might say, jauntily.

In the first few moments of his meeting with Judge Priest there was about him a bearing of reserve—almost of outright suspicion. But half a dozen explanatory sentences from the judge served speedily to establish an atmosphere of mutual understanding. I believe I stated earlier in my tale that Judge Priest had a little knack for winning people's confidences. Perhaps I should also explain that at a suitable time in the introductory stages of the conversation he produced a line in the characteristic handwriting of Mr. Montreal Red. Being thereby still further enlightened as to the disinterestedness of the venerable stranger's motives, the Solitary Kid proved frankness itself. Preliminarily, though, he listened intently while Judge Priest recited in full a story that had mainly to do with the existing plight of Emanuel Moon.

"Now then, suh," said Judge Priest at the conclusion of his narrative, "I've laid all the cyards that I hold on the table right in front of you. Ef I'm correct in my guess that you're the party of the second part in this here transaction I don't need to go on, because you know a sight more about the rest of it than whut I do. The way I figger it, a decent, honest little man is in serious trouble, mainly on your account. Ef you're so minded I calculate that you kin help him without hurtin' yourself any. Now then, presumin' sech to be the case, is there anythin' you'd like to say to me—ez his friend?"

Conklin, alias Caruthers, alias Crowley, and so on, put a question of his own now:

"You say the president of that bank is the one that tried to fasten this job on Moon, eh? Well, then, before we go any further, suppose you tell me what that president looks like?"

Judge Priest sketched a quick word picture of Mr. Hiram Blair—accurate and fair, therefore not particularly complimentary.

"That's enough," said the convict grimly;

"that'll do. Why, the long-whiskered old dog! Now then, Judge—you said you were a judge, didn't you?—I'm going to spill a funny yarn for you. Never mind what my reasons for coming through are. Maybe I want to get even with somebody that handed me a large disappointment. Maybe I don't want to see that little Moon suffer for something he didn't do. Figure it out for yourself afterward, but first listen to me."

"I'm listenin', son," said Judge Priest.

"Good!" said Conklin, lowering his voice cautiously, though he knew already they were alone in the warden's room.

"Up to a certain point you've got the thing figured out just as it came off. That day on the train going into Louisville I started to take the little man at cards. I was going to deal him the big mitt and then clean him for what he had; but when he told me he worked in a bank—a nice, fat little country bank—I switched the play, of course. I saw thousands of dollars where I'd seen lunch money before. Inside of an hour I knew everything there was to know about that bank—what he knew and what I could figure from what he told me. All I had to do was to turn the spigot once in a while and let him run on. And then, when he began to spill his cravings for a new clarinet, I almost laughed in his face. The whole thing looked like a pipe.

"The dope was working lovely when I hit

that town of yours two weeks later. At the right minute I flashed the clarinet on him and made him forget to throw the combination of the vault. So far, so good. Then, when I got him where I wanted him—over in my room— I slipped the drops into his beer; not enough to hurt him but enough to start him pounding his ear right away. That was easy too—so easy I almost hated to do it.

"Then I waited until about two o'clock in the morning, him lying there all the time on my bed, dead to the world. So I took his keys off him and dropped across the street without being seen by anybody—the main street of your town is nice and quiet after midnight— I'll say that much for it anyway—and walked into the bank the same as if I owned it—in fact, I did own it—and made myself at home. I opened up the vault and went through it, with a pocket flash to furnish light; and then after a little I locked her up again, good and tight, leaving everything just like I'd found it, and went back to the hotel and put the keys in the little man's pocket, and laid down alongside of him and took a nap myself. D'ye see my drift?"

"I reckin I don't altogether understand— yit," said Judge Priest.

"You naturally wouldn't," said Conklin with the air of a teacher instructing an attentive but very ignorant pupil. "Here's what happened: When I took a good look at

the inside door of that vault and tried the
tumblers of the outside door I knew I could
open her any time I wanted to—in five minutes
or less. Besides, I wouldn't need the keys any
more, seeing as I could make impressions of
'em in wax, which I did as soon as I got back
inside of my room at the hotel. So I was
sure of having duplicates whenever I needed
'em."

"I'm feared that I'm still in the dark," said
Judge Priest. "You see it's only here right
recently that I took up your callin' in life—ez
a study."

"Well, figure it out for yourself," said Conklin. "If I made my clean-up and my getaway
that night it was a cinch that they'd connect
up Moon with his strange friend from New
York; even a hick bull would be wise enough
to do that. And inside of twenty-four hours
they'd be combing the country for a gun answering to my general plans and specifications. At
the beginning I was willing to take that chance;
but after I had a look at that combination I
switched my play. Besides, there wasn't enough
coin in the box that night to suit me. I always
play for the big dough when I can, and I remembered what the little man told me about
that lumber company—you know the one I
mean: that big crosstie concern—depositing
its pay roll every other Friday night. So why
wouldn't I hold off?"

"I begin to see," said Judge Priest. "You're

"I don't need to," answered the Solitary Kid. "You did that yourself just a little bit ago. If you're going back home any time soon I suggest that you ask the old pappy-guy with the long white whiskers what he was doing coming out of his own bank at half past one o'clock on the morning of October the sixteenth, with a long overcoat on, and his hat pulled down over his eyes, and a heavy sackful of dough hid under his coat. I didn't exactly see the sack, but he had it, all right—I'll gamble on that. You needn't tell him where you got your information, but just ask him."

"Son," avered Judge Priest, "I shorely will do that very thing; in fact, I came mighty nigh practically doin' so several weeks ago when I didn't know nigh ez much ez I do now —thanks to you and much obliged."

But Judge Priest was spared the trouble— for the time being, at least. What transpired later in a legal way in his courtroom has nothing whatever to do with this narration. It is true that he left Atlanta without loss of time, heading homeward as straight and as speedily as the steam cars could bear him.

Even so, he arrived too late to carry out his promise to the Solitary Kid. For that very day, while he was on his way back, in a city several hundred miles distant—in the city of Chicago, to be precise—the police saw fit to raid an establishment called vulgarly a bucket shop; and finding among the papers and books, which they coincidentally seized, entries tending to show that our Mr. Hiram Blair had, during the preceding months, gone short on wheat to a disastrous extent, the police inconsiderately betrayed those records of a prolonged and unfortunate speculation to one of the Chicago afternoon papers, which in turn wired its local correspondent down our way to call upon the gentleman and ask him pointblank how about it.

But the correspondent, who happened also to be the city staff of the *Daily Evening News*, a young man by the name of Rawlings, was unsuccessful in his attempts to see Mr. Blair, either at his place of business in the bank or at his residence. From what he was able to glean, the reporter divined that Mr. Blair had gone out of town suddenly. Putting two and two together the young man promptly reached the conclusion that Mr. Blair might possibly have had also some word from Chicago. Developments, rapidly ensuing, proved the youth correct in his hypothesis.

Two days later Mr. Blair was halted by a person in civilian garb, but wearing a badge of authority under his coat, as Mr. Blair was about to cross the boundary line near Buffalo into the adjacent Dominion of Canada. Mr. Blair insisted at first that it was not him. In truth it did not look like him. Somewhere en route he had lost his distinguished chin whiskers and his commanding manner, acquiring in lieu of these a name which did not in the least resemble Hiram Blair.

Nevertheless, being peremptorily, forcibly and over his protests detained—in fact, locked up—he was presently constrained to make a complete statement, amounting to a confession. Indeed, Mr. Blair went so far in his disclosures that the *Daily Evening News*, in an extra issued at high noon, carried across its front page, in box-car letters, a headline reading: Fugitive, in Durance Vile, Tells All!

Old Judge Priest was passing Mrs. Teenie Morrill's boarding house one night on his way home from Soule's drug store, where he had spent the evening in the congenial company of Mr. Soule, Sergeant Jimmy Bagby and Squire Roundtree. This was perhaps a week after his return from a flying trip to Atlanta, Georgia, the results of which, as the saying goes, still were locked within his breast.

As he came opposite Mrs. Morrill's front gate a blast of harmonious sound, floating out into the night, saluted his ears. He looked upward. Behind a front window on the top floor, with his upper lip overlapping the mouthpiece of a handsome clarinet and his fingers flitting upon the polished shaft of the instrument, sat little Emanuel Moon, now, by virtue of appointment, Deputy Circuit Clerk Emanuel Moon, playing The Last Rose of Summer with the fervour inspired of a happy heart, a rehabilitated reputation, a lucrative and honourable employment in the public service, and a newly acquired mastery of the melodic intricacies of the air in question—four things calculated, you will allow, to make anyone blithe of the spirit.

The old judge halted and smiled up at the window. Then, as he moved onward, he uttered the very word—a small coincidence, this —which I chose for the opening text of this chapter out of the life and the times of our town.

"Poor little ant!" said Judge Priest to himself; and then, as an afterthought: "But a dag-gone clever little feller!"

V

SERGEANT JIMMY BAGBY'S FEET

SERGEANT JIMMY BAGBY sat on the front porch of the First Presbyterian parsonage with an arched framing of green vines above his head. His broad form reposed in a yet broader porch chair—his bare feet in a foot-tub of cold water.

The sergeant wore his reunion regalia, consisting, in the main, of an ancient fatigue jacket with an absurdly high collar and an even more absurdly short and peaked tail. About his generous middle was girthed a venerable leather belt that snaffled at the front with a broad buckle of age-darkened brass and supported an old cartridge box, which perched jauntily upon a fold of the wearer's plump hip like a birdbox on a crotch. Badges of resplendent new satin, striped in alternate bars of red and white, flowed down over his foreshortened bosom, partly obscuring the scraps of rotted and faded braid and the big round ball buttons of dulled brass, which adhered intermittently to the decayed

front of his uniform coat. Against a veranda
post leaned the sergeant's rusted rifle, the same
he had carried to the war and through the war
and home again after the war, and now reserved
for occasions of high state, such as the present one.

The sergeant's trousers were turned high up
on his shanks; his shoes reposed side by side
alongside him on the floor, each with a white
yarn sock crammed into and overflowing it.
They were new shoes, but excessively dusty and
seamed with young wrinkles; and they bore that
look of total disrepute which anything new in
leather always bears after its first wearing. With
his elbows on his thighs and his hands clasped
loosely between his knees, Sergeant Bagby
bent forward, looking first up the wide street
and then down it. Looking this way he saw
four old men, three of them dressed in grey
and one in black, straggle limpingly across
the road; and one of them carried at a droopy
angle a flag upon which were white-scrolled
letters to tell the world that here was Lyon's
Battery, or what might be left of it. Looking that way he saw a group of ten or fifteen
grey heads riding through a cross street upon
bay horses; and at a glance he knew them for a
detachment of Forrest's men, who always came
mounted to reunions. Once they rode like
centaurs; now, with one or two exceptions, they
rode like sacks or racks. It depended on
whether, with age, the rider had grown stout or
stayed thin.

Having looked both ways, the sergeant addressed himself to a sight nearer home. He considered his feet. Viewed through sundry magnifying and misleading inches of water they seemed pinky white; but when, groaning gently, he lifted one foot clear it showed an angry chafed red upon toe and heel, with large blistery patches running across the instep. With a plop he lowered it back into the laving depths. Then, bending over sideways, he picked up one of his shoes, shaking the crumpled sock out of it and peering down its white-lined gullet to read the maker's tag:

"Fall River, Mass.," the sergeant spelled out the stamped letters—"Reliance Shoe Company, Fall River, Mass."

He dropped the shoe and in tones of reluctant admiration addressed empty space:

"Well, now, ain't them Yankees the persistent devils! Waitin' forty-odd years fur a chance to cripple me up! But they done it!"

Judge Priest turned in at the front gate and came up the yard walk. He was in white linens, severely and comfortably civilian in cut, but with a commandant's badge upon his lapel and a short, bobby, black ostrich feather in the brim of his hat. He advanced slowly, with a slight outward skew to his short, round legs.

"Aha!" he said understandingly. "Whut did I tell you, Jimmy Bagby, about tryin' to parade in new shoes? But no, you wouldn't listen— you would be one of these here young dudes!"

"Judge," pleaded the sergeant, "don't rub it in! I'm about ruint—I'm ruint for life with these here feet of mine."

Still at a somewhat stiff and straddle-legged gait, the judge mounted the porch, and after a quick appraisal of all the chairs in sight eased his frame into one that had a cushioned seat. A small involuntary moan escaped him. It was the sergeant's time to gloat.

"I'm wearin' my blisters on my feet," he exulted, "and you're wearin' yourn—elsewhere. That's whut you git at your age fur tryin' to ride a strange horse in a strange town."

"Jimmy," protested the judge, "age ain't got nothin' a'tall to do with it; but that certainly was a mighty hard-rackin' animal they conferred on me. I feel like I've been straddlin' a hip roof durin' an earthquake. How did you make out to git back here?"

"That last half mile or so I shore did think I was trampin' along on red-hot ploughshears. If there'd been one more mile to walk I reckin I'd 'a' been listed amongst the wounded and missin'. I jest did about manage to hobble in. And Mizz Grundy fetched me this here piggin of cold water out on the porch, so's I could favour my feet and watch the boys passin' at the same time."

Judge Priest undertook to cross one leg over the other, but uncrossed it again with a wince of sudden concern on his pink face.

"How do you aim, then, to git to the big

doin's this evenin'?" he asked, and shifted his
position slightly where he sat.

"I ain't aimin' to git there," said Sergeant
Bagby. "I aim to stay right here and take
my ease. Besides, ef I don't git these feet of
mine shrunk down some by milkin' time, I'm
shore goin' to have to pull my pants off over
my head this night."

"Well, now, ain't that too bad!" commiserated his friend and commander. "I wouldn't
miss hearin' Gen'l Gracey's speech fur a purty."

"Don't you worry about me," the sergeant
was prompt to tell him. "You and Lew Lake
and Hector Woodward and the other boys kin
represent Gideon K. Irons Camp without me fur
oncet anyway. And say, listen, Judge," he
added with malice aforethought, "you'd better
borrow a goosehair cushion, or a feather tick,
or somethin' soft, to set on out yonder. Them
plain pine benches are liable to make a purty
hard roostin' place, even fur an old seasoned
cavalryman."

Judge Priest's retort, if he had one in stock,
remained unbroached, because just then their
hostess bustled out to announce dinner was on
the table. It was to be an early dinner and a
hurried one, because, of course, everybody
wanted to start early, to be sure of getting good
seats for the speaking. The sergeant ate his
right where he was, his feet in his tub, like a
Foot-washing Baptist.

There were servants aplenty within, but the

younger Miss Grundy elected to serve him; a pretty girl, all in snowy white except for touches of red at her throat and her slender belted waist, and upon one wrist was a bracelet of black velvet with old soldiers' buttons strung thickly upon it. On a tray, daintily tricked out, she brought the sergeant fried chicken and corn pudding and butter beans, and the like, with corn pones hot-buttered in the kitchen; and finally a slice carved from the blushing red heart of the first home-grown watermelon of the season. Disdaining the false conventions of knife and fork the sergeant bit into this, full face.

Upon the tub bottom his inflamed toes overlapped and waggled in a gentle ecstasy; and between bites, while black seeds trickled from the corners of his lips, he related to the younger Miss Grundy the beginning of his story of that memorable passage of words upon a certain memorable occasion, between General John C. Breckinridge and General Simon Bolivar Buckner. The young lady had already heard this same beginning thrice, the sergeant having been a guest under the parental roof since noon of the day before, but, until interruption came, she listened with unabated interest and laughed at exactly the right places, whereupon the gratified narrator mentally catalogued her as about the smartest young lady, as well as the prettiest, he had met in a coon's age.

All good things must have an end, however— even a watermelon dessert and the first part of shadows had appreciably lengthened upon the grass before a voice, lifted in a hail, roused him up. Over the low hedge that separated the parsonage yard from the yard adjoining on the left a man was looking at him—a man somewhere near his own age, he judged, in an instantaneous appraisal.

"Cumrud," said this person, "howdy-do?"

"Which?" inquired Sergeant Bagby.

"I said, Cumrud, howdy?" repeated the other.

"No," said the sergeant; "my name is Bagby."

"I taken it fur granted that you was to home all alone, "said the man beyond the hedge. "Be you?"

"At this time of speakin'," said the sergeant, "there's nobody at home exceptin' me and a crop of blisters. Better come over," he added hospitably.

"Well," said the stranger, as though he had been considering the advisability of such a move for quite a period of time, "I mout."

With no further urging he wriggled through a gap in the hedge and stood at the foot of the steps, revealing himself as a small, wiry, rust-coloured man. Anybody with an eye to see could tell that in his youth he must have been as red-headed as a pochard drake. Despite abundant streakings of grey in his hair he was still red-headed, with plentiful whiskers to match, and on his nose a pair of steel-rimmed spectacles, and on his face and neck a close sowing of the biggest, intensest freckles Sergeant Bagby had ever beheld. They spangled his skin as with red asterisks, and the gnarled hand he extended in greeting as he mounted the porch looked as though in its time it had mixed at least one million bran mashes.

Achieving a somewhat wabbly standing posture in his keeler, the sergeant welcomed him in due form.

"I don't live here myself," he explained, "but I reckin you might say I'm in full charge, seein' cz I crippled myself up this mornin' and had to stay behind this evenin'. Come in and take a cheer and rest yourself."

"Thanky!" said the freckly one. "I mout do that too." He did. His voice had a nasal smack to it which struck the sergeant as being alien. "I didn't ketch the name," he said. "Mine's Bloomfield—Christian name, Ezra H."

"Mine's Bagby," stated the sergeant—"late of King's Hell Hounds. You've probably heard of that command—purty nigh everybody in these parts has."

"Veteran myself," said Mr. Bloomfield briskly. "Served four years and two months. Enlisted at fust call for volunteers."

"Started in kind of early myself," said the sergeant, mechanically catching for the moment the other's quality of quick, clipped speech. "But say, look here, pardner," he added, resuming his own natural tone, "whut's the reason

"Pardner," he announced, "I'm right glad I didn't kill you when I had all them chances."

"Cumrud," replied Mr. Bloomfield, "on the whole and considerin' of everything, I don't regret now that I spared you."

If Sergeant Bagby had but worn a Confederate goatee, which he didn't, being smooth-shaved; and if he hadn't been standing mid-shin-deep in a foot-tub; and if only Mr. Bloomfield's left shirtsleeve, instead of being comfortably full of freckled arm, had been empty and pinned to the bosom of his waistcoat—they might have posed just as they stood then for the popular picture entitled *North and South United* which you will find on the outer cover of the Memorial Day edition of every well-conducted Sunday newspaper in the land. But that is ever the way with real life—it so often departs from its traditional aspects. After a bit the sergeant spoke.

"I was jest thinkin'," he said dreamily.

"So was I," assented Mr. Bloomfield. "I wonder now if it could be so that we both of us had our minds on the same pleasin' subject?"

"I was jest thinkin'," repeated the sergeant, "that merely because the Bloody Chasm is bridged over ain't no fittin' reason why it shouldn't be slightly irrigated frum time to time."

"My idee to a jot," agreed Mr. Bloomfield heartily. "Seems as if the dust of conflict has been a-floatin' round loose long enough to stand a little dampin' down."

"Ef only I was at home now," continued Sergeant Bagby, "I'd be able to put my hand on somethin' handy for moistenin' purposes; but, seein' as I'm a visitor here, I ain't in no position to extend the hospitalities suitable to the occasion."

"Sho, now! Don't let that fret you," soothed Mr. Bloomfield—"not with me livin' next door." He nimbly descended the steps, but halted at the bottom: "Cumrud, how do you take yours —straight or toddy?"

"Sugar and water don't hurt none— in moderation," replied the sergeant. "But look here, pardner, this here is a preacher's front porch. We don't want to be puttin' any scandal on him."

"I'd already figured that out too," said the provident Mr. Bloomfield. "I'll bring her over in a couple of chiny teacups."

The smile which, starting from the centre, spread over the sergeant's face like ripples over a pond had not entirely faded away when in a miraculously short time Mr. Bloomfield returned, a precious votive offering poised accurately in either hand. "Bagby," he said, "that's somethin' extry prime in the line of York-state rye!"

"Is it?" said the sergeant. "Well, I reckin the sugar comes frum Newerleans and that oughter take the curse off. Bloomfield, here's lookin' toward you!"

"Same to you, Bagby!"

China clicked pleasantly on china as teacup bottom touched teacup brim, this sound being succeeded instantly by a series of soft sipping sounds. Sitting thus, his eyes beaming softly over the bulge of his upturned cup and his lips drawing in the last lingering drops of sirupy sweetness, the sergeant became aware of a man clumping noisily along the sidewalk—an old man in a collarless hickory shirt, with a mouse-grey coat dangling over one arm and mouse-grey trousers upheld by home-made braces. He was a tall, sparse, sinewy old man, slightly withered, yet erect, of a build to remind one of a blasted pine; his brow was very stormy and he talked to himself as he walked. His voice but not his words came to the sergeant in a rolling, thundery mutter.

"Hey, pardner!" called Sergeant Bagby, holding his emptied cup breast-high. "Goin' somewheres or jest travellin' round?"

The passer-by halted and regarded him gloomily over the low palings of the Reverend Doctor Grundy's fence.

"Well," he made slow answer, "I don't know ez it's anybody's business; but, since you ast me, I ain't headin' fur no place in particular—I'm tryin' to walk a mad off."

"Come right on in here then," advised the sergeant, "we've got the cure fur that complaint." He glanced sideways toward his companion. "Bloomfield, this here love feast looks mighty like she might grow a little. Do you reckin you've got another one of them teacups over at your place, right where you could put your hands on it easy?"

"That's a chore which won't be no trouble whatsoever," agreed Mr. Bloomfield; and he made as if to go on the errand, but stopped at the porch edge just inside the vines as the lone pedestrian, having opened the gate, came slowly toward them. The newcomer put his feet down hard on the bricks; slashes of angry colour like red flares burned under the skin over his high and narrow cheekbones.

"Gabe Ezell—Cherokee Rifles," he said abruptly as he mounted the steps; "that's my name and my command."

"I'm Sergeant Bagby, of King's Hell Hounds, and monstrous glad to make your acquaintance," vouchsafed, for his part, the sergeant. "This gentleman here is my friend, Major Bloomfield. Take a cheer and set down, pardner, and rest your face and hands a spell. You look like you might be a little bit put out about something?"

The stranger uttered a grunt that might mean anything at all or nothing at all. He lowered himself into a chair and tugged at the collarless band of his shirt as though it choked him. The sergeant, pleasingly warmed to the core of his being, was not to be daunted. He put another question:

"Whut's the reason you ain't out to the speakin'? I'm sort of lamed up myse'f—made the fatal mistake of tryin' to break in a pair of

Dam-Yankee shoes on a couple of Southern-Rights feet. I'm purty well reconciled, I reckin; but my feet appear to be still unreconstructed, frum what I kin gather." Chuckling, he glanced downward at the stubborn members. "But there don't seem to be nothin' wrong with you—without it's your feelin's."

"I was figgerin' some on goin' out there," began the tall old man, "but I couldn't git there on time—I've been at the calaboose." He finished the confession in a sort of defiant blurt.

"You don't say so!" said the sergeant wonderingly, and commiseratingly too; and from where he stood on the top step the newly brevetted major evidenced his sympathy in a series of deprecatory clucks. The third man glared from one to the other of them.

"Oh, I ain't ashamed of it none," he went on stormily. "Ef I had it to do over agin I'd do it agin the very same way. I may not be so young ez I was oncet, but anybody that insults the late Southern Confederacy to my face is breedin' trouble for hisse'f—I don't care ef he's as big as a mountain!"

From the depths of the foot-tub came small splashing sounds, and little wavelets rose over its sides and plopped upon the porch floor.

"I reckin sech a thing as that might pester me a little bit my own se'f," stated the sergeant softly. "Yes, suh; you might safely venture that under them circumstances I would become kind of irritated myse'f. Who done it?"

"I'll tell you," said Mr. Ezell, "and let you boys be the jedges of whether I done the right thing. After the parade was through with this mornin' me and some of the other boys from down my way was knockin' round. I got separated from the rest of 'em someway and down yond' on that main street—I'm a stranger in this town and I don't rightly recall its name, but it's the main street, whar all them stores is —well, anyway, down there I come past whar one of these here movin'-picture to-dos was located. It had a lot of war pictures stuck up out in front of it and a big sign that said on it: At the Cannon's Mouth! So, not havin' nothin' else to do, I paid my ten cents to a young lady at the door and went on in. They gimme a seat right down in frontlike, and purty soon after that they started throwin' them pictures on a big white sheet—a screen, I think they calls it.

"Well, suhs, at the fust go-off it was purty good. I got consider'bly interested—I did so. There was a house come on the sheet that looked powerful like several places that I knows of down in Middle Georgia, whar I come frum; and there was several young ladies dressed up like they used to dress up back in the old days when we was all young fellows together. Right off, though, one of the young ladies—the purtiest one of the lot and the spryest-actin'—she fell in love with a Yankee officer. That jarred me up a little; yet, after all, it mout 'a' happened and, besides, he wasn't sech a bad young fellow—

fur a Yankee. He saved the young lady's brother when the brother come home frum the army to see his sick baby and was about to be ketched fur a spy. Yes, suhs; I've got to admit that there Yankee behaved very decently in the matter.

"Well, purty soon after the lovin' part was over they come to the fightin' part, and a string band began to play war pieces. I must say I got right smartly worked up 'long about there. Them fellows that was dressed up ez soldiers looked too tony and slick to be real natchel—there didn't seem to be nary one of 'em wearin' a shirt that needed searchin', the way it was when we-all was out soldierin'—but ef you'd shet your eyes 'bout halfway you could mighty nigh imagine it was the real thing agin. A battery of our boys went into action on the aidge of a ploughed field and you could see the smoke bustin' out of the muzzles of the pieces, and you could hear the pieces go off, kerboom!—I don't know how they worked that part of it, but they did; and 'way over yond' in a piece of woods you could see the Yankees jest a-droppin'. I seem to recollect standin' up long about there and givin' a yell or two myself; but in a minute or so a whole lot more Yankees come chargin' out of the timber, and they begin to drive our boys back.

"That didn't seem right to me—that didn't seem no way to have it. I reckin, though, I might 'a' stood that, only in less'n no time a-tall

our boys was throwin' away their guns and some
of 'em was runnin' away, and some of 'em was
throwin' up their hands and surrenderin'! And
the Yankees was chargin' in amongst 'em, a-cut-
tin' and slashin' and shootin', and takin' prisoners right and left. It was a scandalous thing
—and a lie besides! It couldn't never 'a' happened noway."

His voice, deep and grumbling before, became
sharply edged with mounting emotion. Mr.
Bloomfield looked away to avoid exposing a
happy grin, new-born among his whiskers. It
was Sergeant Bagby who spoke, the intention
on his part being to soothe rather than to
inflame.

"Pardner," he said, "you've got to remember
it wasn't nothin' but jest play-actin'—jest hired
hands makin' believe that it was so."

"I don't care none ef it was," snapped Mr.
Ezell. "And, besides, whut's that got to do
with it—with the principle of the thing? It
was a deliberate insult flung right in the face
of the late Southern Confederacy—that and
nothin' short of it. Well, I stood it jest as long
as I natchelly could—and that wasn't very long,
neither, lemme tell you, gentlemen."

"Then whut?" inquired Sergeant Bagby,
bending forward in his seat.

"Then I up with my cheer and chunked it
right through their dad-burned, lyin' sheet—
that's whut I done! I busted a big hole in her
right whar there was a smart-alecky Yankee

colonel sailin' acrost on a horse. I says: 'Here's a few reinforcements frum the free state of Georgia!' And I let him have it with the cheer, kerblim! That there battle broke up right then and there. And that's how I come to go to the calaboose."

Mr. Bloomfield, now rigidly erect, and with no grin on his face, opened his lips to say something; but Sergeant Bagby beat him to it.

"Pardner," he asked incredulously, "did they lock you up jest fur doin' that?"

"No," said the heated Mr. Ezell, "they didn't really lock me up a-tall. But the secont I throwed that cheer there was a lot of yellin' and scrabblin' round, and the lights went up, and the string band quit playin' its piece and here come a-runnin' an uppidy-lookin' man—he was the one that run the show, I take it— bleatin' out somethin' about me havin' broke up his show and him wantin' damages. He made the mistake of grabbin' holt of me and callin' me a name that I don't purpose to have nobody usin' on me. He wanted damages. Well, right there he got 'em!"

He raised a bony fist, on which the knuckles were all barked and raw, and gazed at it fondly, as though these were most honourable scars.

"So then, after that, a couple of them other show people they drug him away frum whar he was layin' on the floor a-yellin'," he went on, "and a town policeman come in and taken me off to the calaboose in a hack, with a crowd followin' 'long behind. But when we got there the gentleman that was runnin' the place—he wore blue clothes and I jedge from his costume and deportment he must 'a' been the town marshal—he listened to whut we-all had to say, and he taken a look at that there showman's busted jaw and sort of grinned to hisse'f; then he said that, seein' as all us old soldiers had the freedom of the city for the time bein', he 'lowed he'd let the whole matter drop right whar it was providin' I'd give him my solemn promise not to go projectin' round no more movin'-picture places endurin' of my stay in their midst. Well, ef they're all like the one I seen to-day it's goin' to be a powerful easy promise fur me to keep— I know that! But that's how I come to miss the doin's this evenin'—I missed my dinner too —and that's how I come to be walkin' way out here all by myse'f."

In the pause that followed Mr. Bloomfield saw his chance. Mr. Bloomfield's voice had a crackling tone in it, like fire running through broom-sedge.

"Lookyhere, my friend!" he demanded crisply. "Ain't you been kind of flyin' in the face of history as well as the movin'-picture industry? Seems to me I recall that you pleg-taked Rebs got a blamed good lickin' about ever' once in so often, or even more frequently than that. If my memory serves me right it seems to me you did indeed!"

Mr. Ezell swung in his chair and the spots in

his cheeks spread until his whole face burned a brick-dust red. Sergeant Jimmy Bagby threw himself into the breach. Figuratively speaking, he had both arms full of heartsease and rosemary.

"In reguards to the major here"—he indicated Mr. Bloomfield with a gracious gesture of amity—"I furgot to tell you that he taken a rather prominent part—on the other side frum us."

As Mr. Ezell's choler rose his brows came down and lowered.

"Huh!" said Mr. Ezell with deadly slowness. "Whut's a Yankee doin' down here in this country?"

"Doin' fairly well," answered Mr. Bloomfield. "F'r instance, he's payin' taxes on that there house next door." He flirted his whiskered chin over his left shoulder. "F'r instance, also, he's runnin' the leadin' tannery and saddle-works of this city, employin' sixteen hands regular. Also, he was elected a justice of the peace a week ago last We'nesday by his fellow citizens, regardless of politics or religion— thanky for askin'!

"Also," he went on, his freckles now standing out beautifully against a mounting pink background—"Also and furthermore, he remembers distinctly having been present on a number of occasions when he helped to lick you Seceshers good and proper. And if you think, my friend, that I'm goin' to abate one jot or tittle from that statement you're barkin' up the wrong tree, I tell you!"

Now behold in the rôle of peacemaker Sergeant Jimmy Bagby rising grandly erect to his full height, but keeping his feet and ankles in the foot-tub.

"Say, listen here, Major," he pleaded, "ef you kin kindly see your way clear to abatin' a few jots on behalf of Indiana I'll bet you I kin induce Georgia to throw off every blamed tittle he's got in stock. And then ef Indiana kin dig up another of them delightful teacups of his'n I believe I kin guarantee that Kintucky and Georgia will join him in pourin' a small but nourishin' libation upon the altar of friendship, not to mention the thresholds of a reunited country. Ain't I got the right notion, boys? Of course I have! And then, as soon as we-all git settled down agin comfortable I'm goin' to tell you two boys something mighty interestin' that come up oncet when I was on hand and heared the whole thing. Did I mention to you before that I belonged to King's Hell Hounds?"

Diplomacy surely lost an able advocate in the spring of 1865 when Sergeant Bagby laid down the sword to take up retail groceries. As soothing oil upon roiled waters his words fell; they fell even as sweet unguents upon raw wounds. And, besides, just then Mr. Ezell caught a whiff of a most delectable and appealing aroma as the sergeant, on concluding his remarks with a broad-armed gesture, swished his teacup directly under Mr. Ezell's nose.

Probably not more than ten or twelve minutes had pleasantly elapsed—it usually took the sergeant twenty to tell in all its wealth of detail the story of what General Breckinridge said to General Buckner, and what General Buckner said in reply to General Breckinridge, and he was nowhere near the delectable climax yet— when an interruption came. Into the ken of these three old men, seated in a row upon the parsonage porch, there came up the street a pair whose gait and general air of flurriment and haste instantly caught and held their attention. Side by side sped a young woman and a young man—a girl and a boy rather, for she looked to be not more than eighteen or, say, nineteen, and he at the most not more than twenty-one or so. Here they came, getting nearer, half-running, panting hard, the girl with her hands to her breast, and both of them casting quick, darting glances backward over their shoulders as though fearing pursuit.

"Well," said Mr. Bloomfield, "all the excitement appears to be happenin' round here this afternoon. I wonder now what ails them two young people?" He squinted through his glasses at the nearing couple. "Why, the gal is that pore little Sally Fannie Gibson that lives over here on the next street. Do tell now!"

He rose; so, a moment later, did his companions, for the youth had jerked Doctor Grundy's gate open and both of them were scudding up the walk toward them. Doubtless because of their agitation the approaching two seemed to notice nothing unusual in the fact that these three elderly men, rising at their coming, should each be holding in his right hand a large china teacup, and that one, the central figure of the three, and the largest of bulk, should be planted ankle-deep and better in a small green tub, rising from it at an interested angle, like some new kind of plump, round potted plant.

"Oh! Oh!" gasped the girl; she clung to the lowermost post of the step-rail. "Where is Doctor Grundy, please? We must see Doctor Grundy right away—right this minute!"

"We want him to marry us!" exclaimed the youth, blurting it out.

"We've got the license," the girl said. "Harvey's got it in his pocket."

"And here it is!" said the youth, producing the document and holding it outspread in a shaking hand. It appeared crumpled, but valid.

It was but proper that Sergeant Bagby, in his capacity as host pro tem, should do the necessary explaining.

"Well now, young lady and young gentleman," he said, "I'm sorry to have to disappoint you—monstrous sorry—but, to tell you the truth, the Reverend Doctor Grundy ain't here; in fact, we ain't lookin' fur him back fur quite some time yit."

"He is reunionisin' at the Pastime Skating Rink," volunteered Mr. Bloomfield. "You'll have to wait a while, Sally Fannie."

"Oh," cried the girl, "we can't wait—we just can't wait! We were counting on him. And now—— Oh, what shall we do, Harvey?"

Shrinking up against the railing she wrung her hands. The sergeant observed that she was a pretty little thing—small and shabby, but undeniably pretty, even in her present state of fright. There were tears in her eyes. The boy was trembling.

"You'd both better come in and take a cheer and ca'm yourselves," said the sergeant. "Let's talk it over and see whut we-all kin do."

"I tell you we can't wait!" gulped the girl, beginning to sob in earnest. "My stepfather is liable to come any minute! I'm as 'fraid as death of him. He's found out about the license —he's looking for us now to stop us. Oh, Harvey! Harvey! And this was our only chance!" She turned to her sweetheart and he put both his arms round her protectingly.

"I know that stepfather of yours," put in Mr. Bloomfield, in a tone which indicated that he did not know much about him that was good or wholesome. "What's his main objection to you and this young fellow gittin' married? Ain't you both of age?"

"Yes, we are—both of us; but he don't want me to marry at all," burst from the girl. "He just wants me to stay at home and slave and slave and slave! And he don't like Harvey— he hates him! Harvey hasn't been living here very long, and he pretends he don't know anything about Har-rr-r-vey."

She stretched the last word out in a pitiful, long-drawn quaver.

"He don't like Harvey, eh?" repeated Mr. Bloomfield. "Well, that's one thing in Harvey's favour anyway. Young man," he demanded briskly, "kin you support a wife?"

"Yes, sir," spoke up Harvey; "I can. I've got a good job and I'm making good pay—I'm in the engineering crew that came down from Chicago last month to survey the new short line over to Knoxville."

"Oh, what are we wasting all this time for?" broke in the desperate Sally Fannie. "Don't you-all know—didn't I tell you that he's right close behind us? And he'll kill Harvey! I know he will—and then I'll die too! Oh, don't be standing there talking! Tell us what to do, somebody—or show us where to hide!"

Mr. Bloomfield's dappled hand waggled his brindled whiskers agitatedly. Mr. Ezell tugged at his hickory neckband; very possibly his thoughts were upon that similar situation of a Northern wooer and a Southern maid as depicted in the lately interrupted film drama entitled At the Cannon's Mouth. Like a tethered pachyderm, Sergeant Bagby swayed his form upon his stationary underpinning.

"Little gal, I most certainly do wisht there was something I could do!" began Mr. Bloomfield, the spirit of romance all aglow within his elderly and doubtless freckled bosom.

"Well, there is, Major!" shouted the sergeant suddenly. "Shore as gun's iron, there's somethin' you kin do! Didn't you tell us boys not half an hour ago you was a jestice of the peace?"

"Yes, I did!"

"Then marry 'em yourself!" It wasn't a request—it was a command, whoopingly, triumphantly given.

"Cumrud," said Mr. Bloomfield, "I hadn't thought of it—why, so I could!"

"Oh, could you?" Sally Fannie's head came up and her cry had hope in it now. "And would you do it—right quick?"

Unexpected stage fright overwhelmed Mr. Bloomfield.

"I've took the oath of office, tubby sure—but I ain't never performed no marriage ceremony—I don't even remember how it starts," he confessed.

"Think it up as you go 'long," advised Sergeant Bagby.

"Whutever you say is bindin' on all parties concerned—I know that much law." It was the first time since the runaways arrived that Mr. Ezell had broken silence, but his words had potency and pith.

"But there has got to be witnesses—two witnesses," parried Mr. Bloomfield, still filled with the buck-ague qualms of the amateur.

"Whut's the matter with me and him fur witnesses?" cried Sergeant Bagby, pointing toward Mr. Ezell. He wrestled a thin gold band off over a stubborn fingerjoint. "Here's even a weddin' ring!"

The boy, who had been peering down the silent street, with a tremulous hand cupped over his anxious eyes, gave a little gasp of despair and plucked at the girl's sleeve. She turned—and saw then what he had already seen.

"Oh, it's too late! It's too late!" she quavered, cowering down. "There he comes yonder!"

"'Tain't no sech of a thing!" snapped Sergeant Bagby, actively in command of the situation. "You two young ones come right up here on this porch and git behind me and take hands. Indiana, perceed with your ceremony! Georgia and Kintucky, stand guard!" With big spread-eagle gestures he shepherded the elopers into the shelter of his own wide bulk.

A man with a red, passionate face and mean, squinty eyes, who ran along the nearer sidewalk, looking this way and that, saw indistinctly through the vines the pair he sought, and, clearing the low fence at a bound, he came tearing across the grassplot, his heels tearing deep gouges in the turf. His voice gurgled hoarsely

in his throat as he tried to utter—all at once—
commands and protests, threats and curses.

From somewhere behind Sergeant Bagby's
broad back came the last feebly technical objection of the officiating functionary:

"But, cumruds, somebody's got to give the
bride away!"

"I give the bride away, dad-gum you!"
blared Sergeant Bagby at the top of his vocal
register. "King's Hell Hounds give the bride
away!"

Thus, over his shoulder, did Sergeant Bagby
give the bride away; and then he faced front,
with chest expanded and the light of battle in
his eyes.

Vociferating, blasphemous, furious, Sally Fannie's tyrant charged the steps and then recoiled
at their foot. A lean, sinewy old man in a hickory shirt barred his way, and just beyond this
barrier a stout old man with his feet in a foot-
tub loomed both large and formidable. For
the moment baffled, he gave voice to vain and
profane foolishness.

"Stop them two!" he yelled, his rage making
him almost inarticulate. "She ain't of age—
and even ef she is I ain't agoin' to have this!"

"Say, ain't you got no politeness a'tall!"
inquired Mr. Ezell, of Georgia. "Don't you
see you're interruptin' the holy rites of matrimony—carryin' on thataway?"

"That's whut I aim to do, blame you!"
howled the other, now sensing for the first time

the full import of the situation. "I'll matrimony her, the little——" He spat out the foulest word our language yields for fouler tongues to use. "That ain't all—I'll cut the heart out of the man that interferes!"

Driving his right hand into his right trousers pocket he cleared the three lower steps at a bound and teetered upon his toes on the very edge of the fourth one.

In the act of making his hand into a fist Mr. Ezell discovered he could not do so by reason of his fingers being twined in the handle of a large, extra-heavy ironstone-china teacup. So he did the next best thing—he threw the cup with all his might, which was considerable. At close range this missile took the enemy squarely in the chest and staggered him back. And as he staggered back, clutching to regain his balance, Mr. Bloomfield, standing somewhat in the rear and improvising as fast as his tongue could wag, uttered the concluding, fast-binding words:

"Therefore I pernounce you man and wife; and, whatever you do, don't never let nobody come betwixt you, asunderin' you apart!"

With a lightning-fast dab of his whiskers he kissed the bride—he had a flashing intuition that this was required by the ritual—shoved the pair inside Doctor Grundy's front hall, slammed the door behind them, snatched up Sergeant Bagby's rusted rifle from where it leaned against Doctor Grundy's porch post, and sprang forward in a posture combining defence and offense. All in a second or two Mr. Bloomfield did this.

Even so, his armed services were no longer required; for Sergeant Jimmy Bagby stepped nimbly out of his tub, picked it up in both hands and turned it neatly yet crashingly upside down upon the head of the bride's step-parent—so that its contents, which had been cold and were still coolish, cascaded in swishing gallons down over his person, effectually chilling the last warlike impulse of his drenched and dripping bosom, and rendering him in one breath whipped, choked and tamed.

"With the compliments of the Southern Confederacy!" said Sergeant Bagby, so doing.

The shadows on the grass lay lank and attenuated when the folks came back from the Pastime Rink. Sergeant Bagby sat alone upon Doctor Grundy's porch. There were puddles of spilt water on porch and step and the walk below, and a green foot-tub, now empty, stood on its side against the railings. The sergeant was drawing his white yarn socks on over his water-bleached shanks.

"Well, suh, Jimmy," said Judge Priest as he came up under the vines, "you certainly missed it this evenin'. That was the best speech Gen'l Tige Gracey ever made in his whole life. It certainly was a wonder and a jo-darter!"

"Whut was the subject, cumrud?" asked Sergeant Bagby.

"Fraternal Strife and Brotherly Love," replied the judge. "He jest natchelly dug up the hatchet and then he reburied her ag'in—reburied her miles deep under Cherokee roses and magnolia blossoms. But how's your feet? I reckon you've had a purty toler'ble lonesome time settin' here, ain't you?"

"I see—love and war! War and love," commented the sergeant softly.

Before answering further, he raised his head and glanced over the top of the intervening hedge toward the house next door. From its open door issued confused sounds of which he alone knew the secret—it was Georgia trying to teach Indiana the words and music of the song entitled Old Virginny Never Tire!

"Oh, my feet are mighty nigh cured," said he; "and I ain't had such a terrible lonesome time as you might think fur either—cumrud."

"That's the second time you've called me that," said Judge Priest suspiciously. "Whut does it mean?"

"Oh, that? That's a fureign word I picked up to-day." And Sergeant Bagby smiled gently. "It's a pet name the Yankees use when they mean pardner!"

VI

ACCORDING TO THE CODE

THE most important thing about Quintus Q. Montjoy, Esquire, occurred a good many years before he was born. It was his grandfather.

In the natural course of things practically all of us have, or have had, grandfathers. The science of eugenics, which is comparatively new, and the rule of species, which is somewhat older, both teach us that without grandfathers there can be no grandchildren. But only one in a million is blessed even unto the third generation by having had such a grandfather as Quintus Q. Montjoy had. That, indeed, was a fragrant inheritance and by day and by night the legatee inhaled of its perfumes. I refer to his grandfather on his father's side, the late Braxton Montjoy.

The grandfather on the maternal side must have been a person of abundant consequence too, else he would never have begat him a daughter worthy to be mated with the progeny of that other illustrious man; but of him you heard little or nothing. Being long deceased, his memory was eclipsed in the umbra of a more compelling personality. It would seem that in all things, in all that he did and said in this life, Braxton Montjoy was exactly what the proud grandsire of a justly proud grandscion should be. He was a gentleman of the Old School in case that conveys anything to your understanding; and a first family of Virginia. He was a captain of volunteers in the War of Eighteen-Twelve. He was a colonel in the Mexican war; that though was after he emigrated out over the Wilderness Trail to the newer and cruder commonwealth of Kentucky. He was one of the founders of our town and its first mayor in that far-distant time when it emerged from the muddied cocoon of a wood-landing on the river bank and became a corporation with a charter and a board of trustees and all. Later along, in the early fifties, he served our district in the upper branch of the State Legislature. In the Civil war he would undoubtedly have been a general—his descendant gainsaying as much—except for the unfortunate circumstance of his having passed away at an advanced age some years prior to the beginning of that direful conflict. Wherefore the descendant in question, being determined that his grandfather should not be cheated of his due military meed by death, conferred an honourary brevet upon him, anyway.

Nor was that all that might be said of this most magnificent of ancestors—by no means was it all. Ever and always was he a person of lofty ideals and mountainous principles. He never drank his dram in a groggery nor discussed the affairs of the day upon the public highway. Spurning such new-fangled and effetely-luxurious modes of transportation as carriages, he went horseback whenever he went, and wheresoever. In the summer time when the family made the annual pilgrimage back across the mountains to Old White Sulphur he rode the entire distance, both going and coming, upon a white stallion named *Fairfax*. To the day of his death he chewed his provender with his own teeth and looked upon the world-at-large through eyes, unlensed.

Yet he might have owned a hundred sets of teeth or five hundred pairs of spectacles, had he been so minded, for to him appertained eighty slaves and four thousand acres of the fattest farm lands to be found in the rich bottoms of our county. War and Lincoln's Proclamation freed the slaves but the lands remained, intact and unmortgaged, to make easier the pathways of those favoured beings of his blood who might come after him. Finally, he was a duellist of a great and fearsome repute; an authority recognised and quoted, in the ceremonials of the code. In four historic meetings upon the field of honour he figured as a principal; and in at least three more as a second. Under his right shoulder blade, a cousin of President Thomas Jefferson carried to his grave a lump of lead which had been deposited there by this great man one fair fine morning in the Valley of Virginia, during the adjudication, with pistols, of a dispute which grew out of a difference of opinion touching upon the proper way of curing a Smithfield ham.

We did not know of these things at first hand. Only a few elderly inhabitants remembered Braxton Montjoy as he had appeared in the flesh. To the rest of our people he was a tradition, yet a living one, and this largely through virtue of the conversational activities of Quintus Q. Montjoy, the grandson aforesaid, aided and abetted by Mrs. Marcella Quistenbury. I should be depriving an estimable lady of a share of the credit due her did I omit some passing mention of Mrs. Quistenbury from this narrative. She was one who specialised in genealogy. There is one such as she in every Southern town and in most New England ones. Give her but a single name, a lone and solitary distant kinsman to start off with, and for you she would create, out of the rich stores of her mind, an entire family tree, complete from its roots, deeply implanted in the soil of native aristocracy, to the uttermost tip of its far-spreading and ramifying branches. In the delicate matter of superior breeding she liberally accorded the Montjoy connection first place among the old families of our end of the state. So, too, with equal freedom, did the last of the Montjoys, which made it practically unanimous and left the honour of the lineage in competent hands.

For Quintus Q.—alas and alackaday—was the last of his glorious line. Having neither sisters nor brothers and being unmarried he abode alone beneath the ancestral roof tree. It was not exactly the ancestral roof tree, if you wish me to come right down to facts. The original homestead burned down long years before, but the present structure stood upon its site and was in all essential regards a faithful copy of its predecessor.

It might be said of our fellow-townsman—and it was—that he lived and breathed and had his being in the shadow of his grandfather. Among the ribald and the irreverent stories circulated was one to the effect that he talked of him in his sleep. He talked of him pretty assiduously when awake; there wasn't any doubt of that. As you entered his home you were confronted in the main hall by a large oil portrait of an elderly gentleman of austere mien, wearing a swallow-fork coat and a neck muffler and with his hair brushed straight back from the forehead in a sweep, just as Andrew Jackson brushed his back. You were bound to notice this picture, the very first thing. If by any chance you didn't notice it, Quintus Q. found a way of directing your attention to it. Then you observed the family resemblance.

Quintus Q., standing there alongside, held his hand on his hip after exactly the same fashion that his grandfather held *his* hand on *his* hip in the pictured pose. It was startling really— the reproduction of this trait by hereditary impulse. Quintus Q. thought there was something about the expression of the eyes, too.

If during the evening some one mentioned horses—and what assemblage of male Kentuckians ever bided together for any length of time without some one mentioning horses?— the host's memory was instantly quickened in regard to the white stallion named *Fairfax*. *Fairfax* achieved immortality beyond other horses of his period through Quintus Q. Some went so far as to intimate that Mr. Montjoy made a habit of serving hams upon his table for a certain and especial purpose. You had but to refer in complimentary terms to the flavour of the curly shavings-thin slice which he had deposited upon your plate.

"Speaking of hams," he would say—"speaking of hams, I am reminded of my grandfather, the old General—General Braxton Montjoy, you remember. The General fought one of his duels—he fought four, you know, and acted as second in three others—over a ham. Or perhaps I should say over the process of smoking a ham with hickory wood. His antagonist was no less a person than a cousin of President Thomas Jefferson. The General thought his veracity had been impugned and he called the

other gentleman out and shot him through the
shoulder. Afterwards I believe they became
great friends. Ah, sir, those were the good old
days when a Southern gentleman had a proper
jealousy of his honour. If one gentleman
doubted another gentleman's word there was
no exchange of vulgar billingsgate, no un-
seemly brawling upon the street. The Code
offered a remedy. One gentleman called the
other gentleman out. Sometimes I wish that
I might have lived in those good old days."

Sometimes others wished that he might have,
too, but I state that fact in parenthesis.

Then he would excuse himself and leave the
table and enter the library for a moment,
returning with a polished rosewood case borne
reverently in his two hands and he would put
the case down and dust it with a handkerchief
and unlock it with a brass key which he carried
upon his watch chain and from their bed of
faded velveteen within, bring forth two old
duelling pistols with long barrels, and carved
scrolls on their butts and hammers that stood
up high like the ears of a startled colt. And he
would bid you to decipher for yourself the name
of his grandfather inscribed upon the brass
trigger guards. You were given to understand
that in a day of big men, Braxton Montjoy
towered as a giant amongst them.

Aside from following the profession of being
a grandson, Quintus Q. had no regular business.
There was a sign reading *Real Estate and Loans*

upon the glass door of his one-room suite in the Planters' Bank building, but he didn't keep regular hours there. With the help of an agent, he looked after the collecting of the rents for his town property and the letting upon shares or leaseholds of his river-bottom farms; but otherwise you might say his chief occupation was that of being a sincere and conscientious descendant of a creditable forebear.

So much for the grandfather. So much, at this moment, for the grandson. Now we are going to get through the rind into the meat of our tale:

As may be recalled, State Senator Horace K. Maydew, of our town and county, being a leader of men and of issues, once upon a time hankered mightily to serve the district in Congress and in the moment that he could almost taste of triumph accomplished had the cup dashed from his lips through the instrumentality of one who, locally, was fancied as being rather better than a dabster at politics, himself. During the months which succeeded this defeat, the mortified Maydew nursed a sharpened grudge toward the enemy, keeping it barbed and fletched against the time when he might let fly with it. Presently an opportunity for reprisals befell. Maydew's term as State Senator neared its close. For personal reasons, which he found good and sufficient, the incumbent did not offer as a candidate to succeed himself. But quite naturally, and perhaps quite properly, he desired to name his successor. Privily he began casting about him for a likely and a suitable candidate, which to the senator's understanding meant one who would be biddable, tractable and docile. Before he had quite agreed with himself upon a choice, young Tobias Houser came out into the open as an aspirant for the Democratic nomination, and when he heard the news Senator Maydew re-honed his hate to a razor-edge. For young Tobe Houser, who had been a farmer-boy and then a country school teacher and who now had moved to town and gone into business, was something else besides: He was the nephew of Judge Priest, the only son of the judge's dead sister. It was the judge's money that had helped the young man through the State university. Undoubtedly—so Maydew read the signs of the times—it was the judge's influence which now brought the youngster forth as an aspirant for public office. In the Houser candidacy Maydew saw, or thought he saw, another attack upon his fiefship on the party organisation and the party machinery.

On an evening of the same week in which Tobe Houser inserted his modestly-worded announcement card in the *Daily Evening News*, Senator Maydew called to conference—or to concurrence—two lieutenants who likewise had cause to be stalwart supporters of his policies. The meeting took place in the living room of the Maydew home. When the drinks had been sampled and the cigars had been lighted Senator Maydew came straight to the business in hand:

"Well, gentlemen," he said, "I've got a candidate—a man none of us ever thought of before. How does the name of Quintus Q. Montjoy seem to strike you?"

Mr. Barnhill looked at Mr. Bonnin, and Mr. Bonnin looked back at Mr. Barnhill. Then both of them looked at Maydew.

"Montjoy, eh?" said Barnhill, doubtfully, seeming not to have heard aright.

"Quintus Q. Montjoy you said, didn't you?" asked Bonnin as though there had been any number of Montjoys to choose from. He spoke without enthusiasm.

"Certainly," answered Maydew briskly, "Quintus Q. Montjoy, Esquire. Any objections to him that you can think of, off-hand?"

"Well," said Mr. Barnhill, who was large of person and slow of speech, "he ain't never done anything."

"If I'm any judge he never will do anything —much," supplemented Mr. Bonnin, who was by way of being small and nervous.

"You've said it—both of you," stated their leader, catching them up with a snap. "He never has done anything. That gives him a clean record to run on. He never will do anything—on his own hook, I mean. That'll make him a safe, sound, reliable man to have representing this district up yonder at Frank-

fort. Last session they licked the Stickney
warehouse bill for us. This season it'll come up
again for passage. I guarantee here and now
that Quint Montjoy will vote right on that
proposition and all other propositions that'll
come up. He'll vote right because we'll tell him
how to vote. I know him from the skin out."

"He's so powerfully pompious and bumpious
—so kind of cocksure and high-an'-mighty,"
said Mr. Barnhill. "D'ye reckin, Hod, as how
he'll stand without hitchin'?"

"I'll guarantee that, too," said Senator Maydew, with his left eyelid flickering down over
his left eye in the ghost of a wink. "He don't
know yet that he's going to be our candidate.
Nobody knows it yet but you and me. But
when he finds out from us that he's going to
have a chance to rattle round in the same seat
that his revered granddaddy once ornamented
—well, just you watch him arise and shine.
There's another little thing that you've overlooked. He's got money,—plenty of it; as
much money as any man in this town has got.
He's not exactly what I'd call a profligate or a
spendthrift. You may have noticed that except when he was spending it on himself he's
very easy to control in money matters. But
when we touch a match to his ambition and it
flares up, he'll dig down deep and produce
freely—or I miss my guess. For once we'll
have a campaign fund with some real money
behind it."

His tone changed and began to drip rancour:

"By Judas, I'll put up some of my own money! This is one time when I'm not counting the cost. I'm going to beat that young lummox of a Houser, if it's the last thing I do. I'm going to rub his nose in the mud. You two know without my telling you why I'd rather see Houser licked than any other man on earth—except one. And you know who that one is. We can't get at Priest yet—that chance will come later. But we can get his precious nephew, and I'm the man' that's going to get him. And Quint Montjoy is the man I'm going to get him with."

"Well, Hod, jest ez you say," assented Mr. Barnhill dutifully. "I was only jest askin', that's all. You sort of tuck me off my feet at fust, but the way you put it now, it makes ever'thing look mighty promisin'. How about you, Wilbur?" and he turned to Mr. Bonnin.

"Oh, I'm agreeable," chimed Mr. Bonnin. "Only don't make any mistake about one thing—Houser's got a-plenty friends. He'll give us a fight all right. It won't be any walk-over."

"I want it to be a fight, and I don't want it to be a walk-over, either," said Senator Maydew. "The licking we give him will be all the sweeter, then."

He got up and started for the telephone on the wall.

"I'll just call up and see if our man is at

home. If he is, we'll all three step over there right now and break the news to him, that the voice of the people has been lifted in an irresistible and clamorous demand for him to become their public servant at his own expense."

The Senator was in a good humour again.

"And say, Hod, whilst I'm thinkin' of it," put in Mr. Barnhill sapiently, "ef he should be at home and ef we should go over there, tell him for Goddle Midey's sake not to drag in that late lamentable grandpaw of his'n, more'n a million times durin' the course of the campaign. It's all right mebbe to appeal to the old famblies. I ain't bearin' ary grudge ag'inst old famblies, 'though I ain't never found the time to belong to one of 'em myself. But there's a right smart chance of middle-aged famblies and even a few toler'ble new famblies in this here community. And them's the kind that does the large bulk of the votin' in primary elections."

. . . . . .

We've had campaigns and campaigns and then more and yet other campaigns in our county. We had them every year—and we still do. Being what they were and true to their breeding the early settlers started running for office, almost before the Indians had cleared out of the young settlements. Politics is breath to the nostrils and strong meat to the bellies of grown men down our way. Found among us are persons who are office-seekers by instinct and office-holders by profession. Whole families, from one generation to another, from father to son and from that son to his son and his son's son become candidates almost as soon as they have become voters. You expect it of them and are not disappointed. Indeed, this same is true of our whole state. Times change, party lines veer and snarl, new issues come up and flourish for awhile and then are cut down again to make room for newer crops of newer issues still, but the Breckinridges and Clays, the Hardins and Helms, the Breathitts and Trimbles, the Crittendons and Wickliffes, go on forever and ever asking the support of their fellow-Kentuckians at the polls and frequently are vouchsafed it. But always the winner has cause to know, after winning, that he had a fight.

As goes the state at large, so goes the district and the precinct and the ward. As I was saying just now, we have had warm campaigns before now; but rarely do I recall a campaign of which the early stages showed so feverishly high a temperature as this campaign between Quintus Q. Montjoy and young Tobias Houser for the Democratic nomination for State Senator. You see, beneath the surface of things, a woman's personality ran in the undercurrents, roiling the waters and soiling the channel. Her name of course, was not spoken on the hustings or printed in the paper, but her influence was manifest, nevertheless.

There was one woman—and perhaps only one in all that community—who felt she had abundant cause to dislike Judge Priest and all that pertained to him by ties of blood, marriage, affection or a common interest. And this person was the present wife of the Hon. Horace K. Maydew, and by that same token the former wife of old Mr. Lysander John Curd. Every time she saw Congressman Dabney Prentiss passing by, grand and glorious in his long-tailed coat and his broad black hat and his white tie, which is ever the mark of a statesman who is working at the trade, she harked back to that day when Judge Priest had obtruded his obstinate bulk between her husband and her husband's dearest ambition; and she remembered that, except for him, she might now be Mrs. Congressman Maydew, going to White House receptions and giving dinners for senators and foreign diplomats and cabinet officers and such. And her thoughts grew bitter as aloes; and with rancour and rage the blood throbbed in her wrists until her bracelets hurt her. Being minded to have a part and a parcel in the undoing of the Priest plans, she meddled in this fight, giving to Mr. Montjoy the benefit of her counsel and her open, active advocacy.

Perhaps it was because he inclined a flattered ear to the lady's admonitions rather than to her husband's subtler chidings that Mr. Montjoy confirmed the astute Mr. Barnhill's forebodings

and refused to stand without hitching. He
backed and he filled; he kicked over the traces
and got tangled in the gears. He was, as it
turned out, neither bridle-wise nor harness-
broken. In short he was an amateur in politics,
with an amateur's faults. He took the stump
early, which was all well and good, because· in
Red Gravel county if a candidate can't talk to
the voter, and won't try, he might just as well
fold up his tents like the Arab and take his
doll rags and go on about his business, if he has
any business. But against the guidance and
the best judgment of the man who had led him
forth as a candidate, he accepted a challenge
from young Houser for a series of joint debates;
and whilst Mr. Barnhill and Mr. Bonnin wagged
their respective heads in silent disapproval,
he repeatedly and persistently made proclamation in public places and with a loud voice, of
the obligation which the community still owed
his illustrious grandparent, the inference being
that he had inherited the debt and expected
to collect it at the polls.

It is likewise possible that Candidate Montjoy listened over-much to the well meant words
of Mr. Calhoun Tabscott. This Mr. Calhoun
Tabscott esteemed himself a master hand at
things political. He should have been, at that.
One time or another he had been on opposite
sides of every political fence; other times he
bestraddled it. He had been a Greenbacker,
a Granger, and a Populist and once, almost

but not quite, a Republican. Occasions were when, in rapid succession, he flirted with the Single Taxers, and then, with the coy reluctance of one who is half-converted, harkened to the blandishments of the Socialists. Had he been old enough he would have been either a Know-Nothing or a Whig—either or perhaps both. In 1896 he quit the Silver Democrats cold, they having obtusely refrained from sending him as a delegate to their national convention. Six weeks later he abandoned the Gold Democrats to their fate because they failed to nominate the right man for president. It was commonly believed he voted the straight Prohibition ticket that year—for spite.

In the matter of his religious convictions, Mr. Tabscott displayed the same elasticity and liberality of choice. In the rival fields of theology he had ranged far, grazing lightly as he went. When the Cumberland Presbyterians put chime bells in their spire, thereby interfering with his Sunday morning's rest, for he lived just across the street, he took his letter out of the church and thereafter for a period teetered on the verge of agnosticism, even going so far as to buy the works of Voltaire, Paine and Ingersol combined and complete in six large volumes. He worshipped a spell with the Episcopalians and once during a space of months, the Baptists had hopes of him. Rumour had it that he finally went over to the Methodists, because old Mr. Leatheritt, of the Traders

National Bank, who was a Baptist, called one of his loans.

Now, having been twice with Judge Priest in his races for the Circuit Judgeship and twice against him, Mr. Tabscott espoused the Montjoy candidacy and sat in Mr. Montjoy's amen corner, which, indeed, was altogether natural and consistent, since the Tabscotts, as an old family, dated back almost as far and soared almost as high as the Montjoys. There had been a Tabscott who nearly fought a duel himself, once. He sent the challenge and the preliminaries were arranged but at the eleventh hour, a magnanimous impulse triumphed over his lust for blood, and for the sake of his adversary's wife and helpless children, he decided to spare him. Mr. Tabscott felt that as between him and Mr. Montjoy a sentimental bond existed. Mr. Montjoy felt it, too; and they confabbed much together regarding ways, means and measures somewhat to the annoyance of Senator Maydew who held fast to the principle that if a master have but one man, the man should have but one master.

The first of the joint debates took place, following a barbecue, at Gum Spring Schoolhouse in the northermost corner of the county and the second took place three days later at the Old Market House in town, a large crowd attending. Acrimony tinctured Mr. Montjoy's utterances from the outset. Recrimination seemed his forte—that and the claims of

honourable antiquity as expressed in the person
of its posterity upon a grateful and remembering
constituency. He bore heavily upon the fact
—or rather the allegation—that Judge Priest
was the head and the front of an office-holding
oligarchy, who thought they owned the county
and the county offices, who took what spoils
of office and patronage they coveted for themselves, and sought to parcel the remainder out
among their henchmen and their relatives. This
political tyranny, this nepotism, must end, he
said, and he, Quintus Q. Montjoy, was the instrument chosen and ordained to end it. "Nominate Montjoy and break up the County ring,"
was the slogan he carried on his printed card.
Therein, in especial, might be divined the under-
mining and capable hand of Senator Maydew.
But when at the second meeting between the
candidates Mr. Montjoy went still further and
touched directly upon alleged personal failings
of Judge Priest, one who knew the inner workings of the speaker's mind might have hazarded
a guess that here a certain lady's suggestions,
privately conveyed, found deliverance in the
spoken word.

The issue being thus, by premeditated intent
of one of the two gentlemen most interested,
so clearly and so acutely defined, the electors
took sides promptly, becoming not merely
partisans but militant and aggressive partisans.
Indeed, citizens who seldom concerned themselves in fights within the party, but were

mainly content to vote the straight party ticket after the fighting was over, came out into the open and declared themselves. Perhaps the most typical exemplar of this conservative class, now turning radical, was offered in the person of Mr. Herman Felsburg. Until this time Mr. Felsburg had held to the view that needless interference in primary elections jibed but poorly with the purveying of clothing to the masses. Former patrons who differed with one politically were apt to go a-buying elsewhere. No matter what your own leanings might be, Mr. Felsburg, facing you across a showcase or a counter, without ever committing himself absolutely, nevertheless managed to convey the impression that, barring that showcase or that counter, there was nothing between him and you, the customer—that in all things you twain were as one and would so continue. Such had been his attitude until now.

When Mr. Montjoy speared at Judge Priest, Judge Priest remained outwardly quite calm and indifferent, but not so Mr. Felsburg. If he did not take the stump in defence of his old friend at least he frequented its base, in and out of business hours, and in the fervour of his championship he chopped his English finer and twisted his metaphors worse than ever he had done before, which was saying a good deal.

One afternoon, when he returned to the store, after a two-hours' absence spent in sidewalk argument down by the Square, his brother,

Mr. Ike Felsburg, who was associated in the firm, ventured to remonstrate with him, concerning his activities in the curbstone forum, putting the objections on the grounds of commercial expediency. At that he struck an attitude remotely suggestive of a plump and elderly Israelitish Ajax defying the lightning.

"Listen here, you Ike," he stated. "Thirty years I have been building up this here Oak Hall Clothing Emporium, and also hats, caps and gents' furnishings goods. You—you can run around with your lodge meetings and your benevolence societies, and all this time I work here, sweating like rats in a trap, and never is a word said by me to you, vicer or verser. I ask you as brother to brother, ain't that so, or ain't it? It is," continued Mr. Herman, answering his own question.

"But, Hermy," interjected Mr. Ike, put on the defensive by the turn which the argument had taken, "but, Hermy, all what I have said to you is that maybe somebody who likes Montjoy would get mad at you for your words and take their custom up the street."

"Let 'em!" proclaimed Mr. Herman with a defiant gesture which almost upset a glass case containing elastic garters and rubber armbands, "let 'em. Anybody which would be a sucker enough to vote for Montjoy against a fine young fellow like this here Houser would also be a sucker enough to let Strauss, Coleman & Levy sell him strictly guaranteed all-wool suitings made out of cotton shoddy, and I wouldn't want his custom under any circumstances whatsoever!"

"But, Hermy!" The protest was growing weaker.

"You wait," shouted Mr. Herman. "You have had your say, and now I would have mine, if you please. I would prefer to get one little word in sideways, if you will be so good. You have just now seen me coming in out of the hot sun hoarse as a tiger from trying to convince a few idiots which they never had any more sense than a dog's hind leg and never will have any, neither. And so you stand there—my own brother—and tell me I am going too far. Going too far? Believe me, Mister Ike Felsburg, I ain't started yet."

He swung on his heel and glared into the depths of his establishment. "Adolph," he commanded, "come here!" Adolph came, he being head salesman in the clothing department, while Mr. Ike quivered in dumb apprehension, dreading the worst and not knowing what dire form it would assume.

"Adolph," said Mr. Herman with a baleful side-glance at his offending kinsman. "To-day we are forming here the Oak Hall and Tobias J. Houser Campaign and Marching Club, made up of proprietors, clerks, other employees and well wishers of this here store, of which club I am the president therefrom and you are the secretary. So you will please open up a list right away and tell all the boys they are already members in good standing."

"Well, now, Mr. Herman," said Adolph, "I've always been good friends with Quintus Q. Montjoy and besides which, we are neighbours. No longer ago than only day before yesterday I practically as good as promised him my vote. I thought if you was coming out for Houser, some of us here in. the store should be the other way and so——"

Mr. Herman Felsburg stilled him with a look and removed his hat in order to speak with greater emphasis.

"Adolph Dreifus," he said with a deadly solemnity, "you been here in this store a good many years. I would assume you like your job here pretty well. I would consider that you have always been well treated here. Am I right, or am I wrong? I am right! I would assume you would prefer to continue here as before. Yes? No? Yes! You remember the time you wrote with a piece of chalk white marks on the floor so that that poor near-sighted Leopold Meyer, who is now dead and gone, would think it was scraps of paper and go round all day trying to pick those chalk marks up? With my own eyes I saw you do so and I said nothing. You remember the time you induced me to buy for our trade that order of strictly non-selling Ascot neckties because your own cousin from Cincinnati was the salesman handling the line which, from that day to this, we are still carrying those dam' Ascot ties in stock? Did I say anything to you then? No! Not a word did I say. All those things is years past and I have never spoken with you regarding them until to-day. But now, Adolph, I must say I am ashamed for you that you should pick on that poor Leopold Meyer, who was blind like a barn-door. I am ashamed for you that you should boost up that cousin of yours from Cincinnati and his bum lines. If I should get more ashamed for you than what already I now am, there is no telling what I should do. Adolph, you will please be so good as to remember that all persons that work in this here Oak Hall Clothing Emporium are for Tobe Houser for State Senator and no one else, whatsoever. Otherwise, pretty soon, I am afraid there will be some new faces selling garments around here. Do I make myself plain? I do!

"My brother—the junior partner here"—he dwelt heavily upon the word *junior*, making of it a most disqualifying adjective—"he also thinks in this matter the same way as I do. If you don't believe me, ask him for yourself. There he stands like a dumb engraved image—ask him."

And Mr. Ike, making craven surrender, raised both hands in token of his capitulation and weakly murmured, "Yes."

.   .   .   .   .

The third of the joint debates, which, as it

turned out, was to be the last one of the series, began according to schedule and announcement at the boat store corner in the presence of an assemblage mustering up in the hundreds. In fact the *Daily Evening News* reporter, in the introductory paragraph of his account, referred to it, I believe, as "a sea of upturned faces." Mr. Montjoy led off first. He had his say, for the better part of an hour, speaking with much fluency from a small board platform that was built up against the side of the old boat store and occasionally, with a fretful shake of his head, raising his voice so it might be heard above the rumbling objurgations of the first mate of the *Cumberland Queen* who, thirty yards down the old gravel levee, was urging his black rousters to greater speed as they rolled the last of a consignment of tobacco hogsheads across the lower wharf boat and aboard the *Queen's* boiler deck. Mr. Montjoy concluded with a neat verbal flourish and sat down, mopping his moistened brow with a square of fine cambric. Mr. Montjoy never permitted himself to sweat and in public, at least, he perspired but seldom; but there were times when he did diffuse a perceptible glow.

His rival arose to answer him. He started off—Houser did—by stating that he was not running on his family record for this office. He was running on his own record, such as it was. Briefly, but vigorously, he defended his uncle; a thing he had done before. Continuing, he would say Mr. Montjoy had accused him of being young. He wished to plead guilty to that charge. If it were a defect, to be counted against him, time would probably cure him of it and he thought the Senate Chamber at Frankfort, this state, provided a very suitable spot for the aging process. (Laughter and applause.) He had a rather whimsical drawl and a straightforward, commonplace manner of delivery.

He continued, and I quote:

"Some of you may have heard somewhere—casually—that my opponent had a grandfather. Stories to that general effect have been in circulation for quite some little time in this vicinity. I gather from various avenues of information that my opponent is not exactly ashamed of his grandfather. I don't blame him for that. A person without many prospects so far as the future is concerned is not to be blamed for dwelling rather heavily upon the past. But, fellow citizens, doesn't it strike you that in this campaign we are having altogether too much grandfather and not enough grandson? (Renewed laughter from the Houser adherents and Mr. Montjoy's face turning a violent red.) It strikes me that the stock is sort of petering out. It strikes me that the whale has bred a minnow.

"And so, in light of these things, I want to make this proposition here and now: I want every man in this county whose grandfather

owned eighty slaves and four thousand acres
of bottom lands to vote for Mr. Montjoy.
And all I ask for myself is that every man whose
grandfather didn't own eighty slaves and four
thousand acres, should cast his vote for me."
(A voice, "My grandpop never owned nary
nigger, Toby,—I reckin you git my vote without a struggle, boy.")

Along this strain Mr. Houser continued
some minutes. It was a line he had not taken
in either of his previous arguments with his
opponent. He branched away from it to tell
what he meant to do for the people of the district in the event of his nomination and election but presently he came back again to the
other theme, while Judge Priest grinned up at
him from his place in the edge of the crowd
and Mr. Montjoy fidgeted and fumed and
wriggled as though the chair upon which he sat
had been the top of a moderately hot stove.
From these and from yet other signs it might
have been noted that Mr. Montjoy, under
the nagging semihumorous goadings of young
Houser, was rapidly losing his temper, which,
by our awkward Anglo-Saxon mode of speech,
is but another way of saying he was not losing
his temper at all but, instead, finding out that
he had one.

The *Cumberland Queen* blew her whistle for
departure and as the roar died away Mr.
Houser might be heard in the act of finishing
a sentence touching with gentle irony upon

the topic which seemed so to irk and irritate Mr. Montjoy. He never finished it.

Up, from his chair, sprang Mr. Montjoy, and shook a knotted fist beneath Mr. Houser's nose.

"How dare you?" he demanded. "How dare you indulge in your cheap sarcasm—your low scurrilities—regarding one of the grandest men the Southland ever produced?"

His voice turned falsetto and soared to a slate-pencilly screech:

"I repeat it, sir—how dare you—you un-derbred ignoramus—you who never knew what it was to have a noble grandfather! Nobody knows who your grandfather was. I doubt whether anybody knows who your father——"

Perhaps it was what Mr. Montjoy appeared to be on the point of asserting. Perhaps it was that his knuckles, as he brandished his fist in Mr. Houser's face, grazed Mr. Houser's cheek.

Mr. Houser stretched forth a solid arm and gripped a handful of sinewy fingers in the lapels of Mr. Montjoy's coat. He didn't strike Mr. Montjoy, but he took him and he shook him— oh, how he shook him. He shook him up and down, and back and forth and to and fro and forward and rearward; shook him until his collar came undone and his nose glasses flew off into space; shook him until his hair came down in his eyes and his teeth rattled in his jaw; shook him into limp, breathless, voiceless helplessness, and then holding him, dangling and flopping for a moment, slapped him once very gently, almost as a mother might slap an erring child of exceedingly tender years; and dropped the limp form, and stepped over it and climbed down off the platform into the midst of the excited crowd. The third of the series of the joint debates was ended; also the series itself.

Judge Priest instantly shoved forward, his size and his impetuosity clearing the path for him through a press of lesser and less determined bodies. He thrust a firm hand into the crook of his nephew's arm and led him off up the street clear of those who might have sought either to compliment or to reprehend the young man. As they went away linked together thus, it was observed that the judge wore upon his broad face a look of sore distress and it was overheard that he grievously lamented the most regrettable occurrence which had just transpired and that openly he reproached young House for his elemental response to the verbal attacks of Mr. Montjoy and, in view of the profound physical and spiritual shock to Mr. Montjoy's well-known pride and dignity, that he expressed a deep concern for the possible outcome. Upon this last head, he was particularly and shrilly emphatic.

In such a fashion, with the nephew striving vainly to speak in his own defence and with the uncle as constantly interrupting to reprimand him and to warn him of the peril he had brought

upon his head, and all in so loud a voice as to
be clearly audible to any persons hovering
nearby, the pair continued upon their journey
until they reached Soule's Drug Store. There,
with a final sorrowful nod of the judge's head
and a final shake of his admonishing forefinger,
they parted. The younger man departed,
presumably for his home to meditate upon his
foolhardy conduct and the older went inside
the store and retired to Mr. Soule's little box
of an office at the rear, hard by the prescrip-
tion case. Carefully closing the door after
him to insure privacy, he remained there for
upwards of an hour, engaged undoubtedly in
melancholy reflections touching upon the out-
break of his most culpable kinsman and upon
the conceivable consequences. He must have
done some writing, too, for when at length he
emerged he was holding in one hand a sealed
envelope. Summoning to him Logan Eaker,
Mr. Soule's coloured errand boy, he entrusted
the note to Logan, along with a quarter of a
dollar for messenger hire, and sent the black boy
away. From this circumstance several persons
who chanced to be in Soule's, hypothesised
that very probably the judge had taken it upon
himself to write Mr. Montjoy a note of apology
in the name of his nephew and of himself.
However, this upon the part of the onlookers
was but a supposition. They merely were engaged in the old practice, so hallowed among
bystanders, of putting two and two together,

by such process sometimes attaining a total of four, and sometimes not.

As regards, on the other hand, Quintus Q. Montjoy, he retained no distinct recollection of the passage homeward, following his mishandling by Tobias J. Houser. For the time a seething confusion ruled his being. Mingled emotions of chagrin, rage and shame—but most of all rage—boiled in his brain until the top of his skull threatened to come right off. Since he was a schoolboy until now, none had laid so much as an impious finger upon him. For the first time in his life he felt the warm strong desire to shed human blood, to see it spatter and pour forth in red streams. The spirit of his grandfather waked and walked within him; anyway it is but fair to assume that it did so.

Somebody must have rebuttoned Mr. Montjoy's collar for him and readjusted his necktie. Somebody else of equally uncertain identity must have salvaged his glasses and restored them to their customary place on the bridge of his slender nose. True, he preserved no memory of these details. But when, half an hour after the encounter, a hired hack deposited him at his yard gate and when Mr. Barnhill, who it would appear dimly and almost as a figment from a troubled dream, accompanied him on the ride, had dismounted and had volunteered to help him alight from the vehicle, meanwhile offering words intended to be sympathetic, Mr. Montjoy found collar, necktie and glasses all properly bestowed.

Within the sanctified and solitary precincts of his library, beneath the grim, limned eyes of his ancestor, Mr. Montjoy re-attained a measure of outward calm and of consecutive thought; coincidently with these a tremendous resolution began to harden inside of him. Presently as he walked the floor, alternately clenching and unclenching his hands, the telephone bell sounded. Answering the call, he heard coming across the line the familiar voice of one, who, in the temporary absence of her husband from the city, now undertook to offer advice. It would seem that Mrs. Maydew had but heard of the brutal assault perpetrated upon her friend; she was properly indignant and more than properly desirous that a just vengeance be exacted. It would seem in this connection she had certain vigorous suggestions to offer. And finally it would seem she had just seen the evening paper and desired to know whether Mr. Montjoy had seen his copy?

Mr. Montjoy had not. After a short interchange of views, when, from intensity of feeling, the lady fairly made the wire sibilate and sing as her words sped over it, she rang off and Mr. Montjoy summoned his butler. His was the only roof in town which harboured a butler beneath it. Other families had male servants—of colour—who performed duties similar to those performed by Mr. Montjoy's man but they didn't call these functionaries butlers and Mr. Montjoy did. He sent the butler out into the yard to get the paper, which a boy had flung over the fence palings in a twisted wisp. And when the butler brought it to him he opened, to read, not the *Daily Evening News'* highly impartial account of the affair at the boat store corner—that could come later—but to read first off a card signed *Veritas* which was printed at the bottom of the second column of the second inside page, immediately following the editorial comment of the day. It was this card to which young Mrs. Maydew had particularly directed his attention.

He bent his head and he read. The individual who chose to hide behind the nom de plume of *Veritas* wrote briefly and to the point. At the outset he confessed himself as one who harboured old-fashioned ideals. Therefore he abhorred the personal altercations which in these latter and degenerate days so often marred the course of public discussions between gentlemen entertaining opposite views upon public problems or private matters. And still more did he deplore the common street brawls, not unmarked by the use of lethal weapons and sometimes by tragically fatal results to one or the other of the parties engaged, which had been known before now to eventuate from the giving and taking of the offensive word, or blow. Hardly need the writer add that he had in mind the unfortunate affray of even date in a certain populous quarter of our city. Without mentioning names, he, *Veritas*, took that deplorable occurrence for his present text. It had inspired him to utter these words of protest against the vulgarity, the coarseness and the crassness of the methods employed for the appeasing of individual and personal wrongs. How much more dignified, how much more in keeping with the traditions of the soil, and the very history of this proud old commonwealth, was the system formerly in vogue among gentlemen for the adjudication of their private misunderstandings! Truly enough the law no longer sanctioned the employment of the *code duello;* indeed for the matter of that, the law of the land had never openly sanctioned it; but once upon a time a jealous regard for his own outraged honour had been deemed sufficient to lift a Southern gentleman to extremes above the mere written letter of the statutes. *"O tempora, O mores!* Oh, for the good old days!" And then came the signature.

Barely had Mr. Montjoy concluded the reading and the re-reading of this, when Mr. Calhoun Tabscott was announced and promptly entered to proffer his hand and something more, besides. Mr. Tabscott carried with him a copy of the *Daily Evening News* opened at the inside page. His nostrils expanded with emotion, his form shook with it.

challenge to fight a duel with him, me to name
the weapons, the time and the place! That's
what I've got to tell you."

His uncle's eyes opened innocently wide.

"Boy, you don't tell me?" he said. "And
whut did you do then?"

"Well, suh, I came within an ace of just
hauling off and mashing that blamed idiot in
the mouth—coming to my door with a challenge for a duel! But I remembered what you
told me yesterday about keeping my temper
and I didn't do it. Then I started to tear up
that fool note and throw the pieces in his face."

"You didn't do that neither, did you?" demanded the judge quickly, with alarm in his
voice. "You kept it?"

"I didn't do that either and I kept the note,"
replied the younger man, answering both questions at once. "I shut the door in Tabscott's
face and left him on the doorstep and then I
went and put on my hat and came right on over
here to see you. Here's the note—I brought it
along with me."

His uncle took from him the single sheet of
note paper and adjusted his specks. He gazed
admiringly for a moment at the embossed
family crest at the top and read its contents
through slowly.

"Ah hah," he said; "seems to be regular
in every respect, don't it?—polite, too. To
the best of my remembrances I never seen one
of these challenges before, but I should judge

this here one is got up strictly accordin' to the Code. Son, our ancestors certainly were the great hands for goin' accordin' to the codes, weren't they? If it wasn't one Code, it was another, with them old fellers. Quintus Q. Montjoy writes a nice hand, don't he?"

With great care, he folded the note along its original crease, handling it as though it had been a fragile document of immense value and meanwhile humming a little tuneless tune abstractedly. Still humming, he put the paper in an ancient letter wallet, wrapped a leather string about the wallet, and returned wallet and string to the breast pocket of his black seersucker coat.

"Son," he said when all this had been accomplished, "I reckin you done the right thing in comin' straight to me. I must compliment you."

"Yes, suh, much obliged," said young Houser, "but, Uncle Billy, what would you advise my doing now?"

He rubbed his forehead in perplexity.

"Why, nothin'—nothin' a'tall," bade his uncle, as though surprised at any suggestion of uncertainty upon the nephew's part. "You ain't got a thing to do, but jest to go on back home and finish up your breakfast. It ain't wise to start the day on an empty stomach, ever. After that, ef I was you, I would put in the remainder of the day remainin' perfectly ca'm and collected and whilst so engaged I wouldn't say nothin' to nobody about havin' received a challenge to fight a duel." He re-gripped his mallet. "Son, watch me make this shot." He stopped and squinted along the imaginary line from his ball to the wicket.

"But, Uncle Billy, I——"

"Son, please don't interrupt me ag'in. Jimmy Bagby is comin' over this evenin' to play off a tie match with me, and I aim to be in shape fur him when he does come. Now run along on back home like I told you to and keep your mouth shet."

The judge whacked his ball and made an effective shot—or rather an effective miss—and Tobe Houser betook himself away wagging his puzzled head in a vain effort to fathom the enigma of his relative's cryptic behaviour.

Approximately thirty-six hours passed without public developments which might be con-strued as relating to the matter chiefly in hand and then—in the early afternoon—young Houser returned to the house of his uncle, this time, finding its owner stretched out for his after-dinner nap upon an old and squashy leather couch in the big old-timey sitting-room. The judge wasn't quite asleep yet. He roused as his nephew entered.

"Uncle Billy," began young Houser, with-out preamble, "you told me yesterday not to do anything and I've obeyed your orders al-though I didn't understand what you were driving at, exactly, but now I must do something if I aim to keep my self-respect or to stay in this race—either one, or both. Unless I take up the dare he's laid down in front of me, Montjoy's going to brand me on the stump as a coward. Yes, suh, that's his intention—Oh, it came to me straight. It seems Mrs. Horace K. Maydew told old Mrs. Whitridge this morning in strict confidence and Mrs. Whitridge just took her foot in hand and put out to tell Aunt Puss Lockfoot and Aunt Puss didn't lose any time getting through the alley gate into my back yard to tell my wife.

"Yes, suh, if I keep silent and don't take any notice of his challenge, Montjoy's going to get up before this whole town at a mass meeting and denounce me as a coward,—he's going to say I'm willing enough to take advantage of being younger and stronger than he is to attack him with my bare hands, but that I'm afraid to back up my act where it puts my hide in danger. I know mighty good and well who's behind him, egging him on—I can see her finger in it plain enough. She hopes to see me humiliated and she hopes to see your chances hurt in your next race. She aims to strike at you through me and ruin us both, if she can.

"But, Uncle Billy, all that being so, doesn't alter the situation so far as I'm concerned. The man doesn't live that can stand up and brand me as a sneaking quitting coward and not have to answer for it. One way or another, it will come to a pass where there's bound to be shooting. I've just got to do something and do it quick."

"Well, son," said Judge Priest, still flat on his back, "I sort of figgered it out that things might be takin' some sech a turn as this. I've heard a few of the rumours that're beginnin' to creep round, myse'f. I reckin, after all, you will have to answer Mister Montjoy. In fact, I taken the trouble this mornin' to wrop up your answer and have it all ready to be sent over to Mister Montjoy's place of residence by the hands of my boy Jeff."

"You wrapped it up?" queried Houser, bewildered again.

"That's whut I said—I wropped it up," answered the judge. He heaved himself upright and crossed the room to his old writing table that stood alongside one of the low front windows and from the desk took up a large squarish object, securely tied up in white paper with an address written upon one of its flat surfaces.

"Jeff!" he called, "oh, you Jeff."

"Why, Uncle Billy, that looks like a book to me," said Mr. Houser. Assuredly, this was a most mystified young man.

"It ain't no box of sugar kisses—you kin be shore of that much, anyway," stated that inscrutable uncle of his. "You're still willin', ain't you, son, to set quiet and be guided by me in this matter?"

"Yes, suh, I am. That is, I'm perfectly

willing to take your advice up to a certain point but——"

"Then set right still and do so," commanded Judge Priest. "I'm goin' to take you into my confidences jest as soon as I see how my way of doin' the thing works out. We oughter git some definite results before dark this evenin'. And listen here, son, a minute—when all's said and done even Quintus Q. Montjoy, Esquire, ain't no more of a stickler for foller-ing after the Code than whut I am. I'm jest ez full of time-hallowed precedents ez he is—and maybe even more so."

"Callin' me, Jedge?" The speaker was Jefferson Poindexter, who appeared at the door leading into the hall.

"Yes, I was—been callin' you fur a half hour—more or less," stated his master. "Jeff, you take this here parcel over to Mister Quintus Q. Montjoy's and present it with the com-pliments of Mister Houser. You needn't wait fur an answer—jest come on back. I reckin there won't be no answer fur some little time."

He turned again to his nephew with the air of a man who, having disposed of all immediate and pressing business affairs, is bent now upon pleasurable relaxation.

"Son, ef you ain't got nothin' better to do this evenin' I wish't you'd stay here and keep score fur the tournament. Playing crokay, I licked the pants off'en that poor old Jimmy Bagby yis'tiddy, and now he wants to git even."

The judge spoke vaingloriously. "He's skeered
to tackle me again single-handed, I reckin.
So him and Father Tom Minor are comin'
over here to play me and Herman Felsburg a
match game fur the crokay champeenship of
Clay Street and adjacent thoroughfares. They
oughter be here almost any minute now—I
was jest layin' here, waitin' fur 'em and sort
of souplin' up my muscles."

Playing magnificently as partners, Father
Minor and Sergeant Bagby achieved a signal
victory—score three to one—over the Felsburg-
Priest team. The players, with the official
referee who maintained a somewhat abstracted,
not to say a pestered, air, were sitting in the
little summer house, cooling off after the ardours
of the sport. Jeff Poindexter had been dis-
patched indoors, to the dining-room sideboard,
to mix and fetch the customary refreshments.
The editor of the *Daily Evening News*, who was
by way also of being chief newsgatherer of that
dependable and popular journal, came up the
street from the corner below and halted outside
the fence.

"Howdy, gentlemen!" over the paling he
greeted them generally. "I've got some news
for you-all. I came out of my way, going back
to the office, to tell you." He singled out the
judge from the group. "Oh, you *Veritas!*"
he called, jovially.

"Sh-h-h, Henry, don't be a-callin' me that,"

spoke up Judge Priest with a warning glance about him and a heavy wink at the editor. "Somebody that's not in the family might hear you and git a false and a misleadin' notion about the presidin' circuit judge of this district. Whut's your news?"

"Well," said Mr. Tompkins, "it's sort of unprofessional to be revealing the facts before they're put in type but I reckon it's no great breach of ethics to tell a secret to an occasional contributor of signed communications—" he indicated Judge Priest, archly—"and the contributor's close friends and relatives. Anyhow, you'd all know it anyhow as soon as the paper comes out. Quintus Q. Montjoy is withdrawing from the race for State Senator."

"What?" several voices spoke the word in chorus, only Sergeant Bagby pronounced it *Whut* and Mr. Felsburg sounded the *W* with the sound of *V* as in *Vocal*.

"Montjoy quits. I've got his card of withdrawal right here in my pocket now. Tobe, allow me to congratulate you on your prospect of getting the nomination without any opposition at the polls."

"Quits, does he?" echoed Judge Priest. "Well, do you boys know, I ain't surprised. I've been lookin' fur him to do somethin' of that nature fur the last two hours. I wonder whut delayed him?" He addressed the query to space.

"He gives some reasons—maybe, yes?" asked Mr. Felsburg, releasing Mr. Houser's hand which he had been shaking with an explosive warmth.

"Oh, yes," said Editor Tompkins, "I suppose he felt as if he had to do that. The principal reason he gives is that he finds he cannot spare the time from his business interests for making an extended canvass—and also his repugnance to engaging further in a controversy with a man who so far forgets himself as to resort to physical violence in the course of a joint debate upon the issues of the day. That's a nice little farewell side-slap at you, Houser.

"But I gleaned from what I picked up after I got over to Montjoy's in answer to his telephone message asking me to call that there may have been other reasons which are not set forth in his card of withdrawal," continued Mr. Tompkins. "In fact, about the time I got over there—to his house—Hod Maydew arrived in a free state of perspiration and excitement—Hod's been up in Louisville on business, you know, and didn't get in until the two-thirty train came—and I rather gathered from what he said a little bit ago to Quintus Q., in the privacy of the dining room while I was waiting in the library, that he was considerably put out about something. His voice sounded peeved—especially when he was calling Montjoy's attention to the fact that even if he should win the race now, he wouldn't be able to take the oath of office. Anyhow, I think that's what he was saying.

"Say, Judge, just for curiosity's sake now and strictly between ourselves—just what was the message, or whatever it was, that you sent over to Montjoy's right after dinner? I overheard something about that too."

"Oh, that?" said the judge, as all eyes turned in his direction. "That was jest a spare copy of the Code that I happened to have 'round the house—with a page in it marked and turned down."

"The Code—what Code?" Mr. Tompkins pressed the point like the alert collector of news that he was.

"The Code and the Statutes—with the accent on the Code," answered the old judge, simply. "Although, speakin' pussonally, I pay more attention to the Statutes than some folks do. In fact it would seem like some persons who are reasonably well informed on most subjects— ancestors fur instance—ain't never took the time to peruse them old Statutes of ourn with the care they should give to 'em ef they're aimin' to engage in the job of bein' a statesman." He faced his nephew. "Tobe, my son, this oughter be a great lesson to you—it's a work that'll bear consid'able study frum time to time. I'm afeared you ain't ez well posted on the subject ez you should be. Well, this is a mighty good time to begin. You kin take your first lesson right now."

He stooped and lifted the lid of the croquet box, beneath the bench upon which they had been sitting, and fetched forth a large, heavy volume, bound in splotchy law calf. "I put my other copy here jest a little while ago, thinkin' somebody might be interested later on in its contents," he explained as he ran through the leaves until he came to a certain page. Upon that page, with a blunt forefinger, he indicated a certain paragraph as he handed the tome over to his nephew.

"There, Tobe," he ordered, "you've got a good strong voice. Read this here section— aloud."

So then, while the others listened, with slowly widening grins of comprehension upon their several faces, and while Judge Priest stood alongside, smiling softly, young Tobe read. And what he read was this:

"OATH TO BE TAKEN BY ALL OFFICERS— FORM OF. Members of the General Assembly and all officers, before they enter upon the execution of the duties of their respective offices, and all members of the bar, before they enter upon the practice of their profession, shall take the following oath or affirmation: I do solemnly swear (or affirm, as the case may be) that I will support the Constitution of the United States and the Constitution of this Commonwealth, and be faithful and true to the Commonwealth of Kentucky so long as I continue a citizen thereof, and that I will faithfully execute, to the best of my ability, the office of————————————according to law; and I do solemnly swear (or affirm) that since the adoption of the present Constitution, I, being a citizen of this State, have not fought a duel with deadly weapons within this State, nor out of it, nor have I sent or accepted a challenge to fight a duel with deadly weapons, nor have I acted as second in carrying a challenge, nor aided or assisted any person thus offending, so help me God."

Having read it aloud, young House now re-read it silently to himself. He was rather a slow-thinking and direct-minded person. Perhaps time was needed for the full force and effect of the subject-matter to soak into him. It was Mr. Tompkins who spoke next.

"Judge Priest," he said, "what do you suppose those two fellows over yonder at Montjoy's are thinking about you right now?"

"Henry," said Judge Priest, "fur thinkin' whut they do about me, I reckin both of them boys could be churched."

VII

FORREST'S LAST CHARGE

TOWARD morning, after a spell of unusually even-tempered and moderate weather, it blew up cold, snowed hard for two or three hours, and turned off to be clear and freezing. The sun, coming up at seven-thirty-five, according to his curtailed December schedule, peeped out on a universe that was clothed all in white, whereas when he retired the night before in his west bedroom he left it wearing a motley of faded yellows and seasoned greens. Swinging in the east as a pale coppery disk, he blinked his astonishment through a ragged grey veil of the last of the storm clouds.

Others beside the sun were taken by surprise. It was the first snowfall of the year and a good, hard, heavy one. Down our way, some winters, we had hardly any snows at all; then, again, some winters we had a plenty; but scarcely ever did we have them before Christmas. This one came as a profound and an annoying visitation, taking the community at large unawares and unprepared, and making a great nuisance of itself from the start. Practically without exception, doorstep hydrants had tight colds in the head that morning. On being treated with lavings of hot water they dripped catarrhally from their cast-iron noses for a little while and then developed the added symptoms of icicles.

Cooks were hours late coming to cook breakfast, and when they did come uttered despairing moans to find range boilers frozen up and kitchen taps utterly unresponsive to first-aid measures. At some houses it was nearly eight o'clock before the milkman got round, with wooden runners under his milk wagon in place of wheels and rosaries of rusted sleigh bells on the necks of his smoking team. Last year's rubber boots came out of the closet and any old year's toy sled came out of the attic.

The old negro man who did whitewashing in the spring, picked blackberries for his summertime living, and in the fall peddled corn-shuck doormats and scaly-bark hickory nuts, made the circuit of his regular patrons, equipped with a shovel over his shoulder and his venerable feet done up in burlaps, to shovel footpaths for a price. Where the wind piled the snow in little drifts he left a wake behind him as though a baby elephant had floundered through there.

In the back yard Sir Rooster squawked his loud disgust as his naked legs sank shank-deep into the feathery mass. His harem, a row of still and huddled shapes on the roosts, clamped their chilled toes all the tighter to their perch and stared out through the chicken-house door at a transformed and unfamiliar world. With them — except for their eyes — rigor mortis seemed far advanced. Small boys, rabbit dogs, plumbers and the few persons in town who owned sleighs rejoiced. Housewives, house cats and thin-blooded old ladies and gentlemen were acutely miserable—and showed it.

There were tramps about in numbers. It took a sudden cold snap, with snow accompaniments such as this one, to fetch the tramps forth from their sleeping places near the tracks, and make the citizen realise how many of these south-bound soldiers of misfortune the town harboured on any given date between Thanksgiving Day and New Year's. Judge Priest did not know it —and probably would not have much cared if he had known it—but on the right-hand-side post of his front gate, just below the wooden letter box, was scratched the talismanic sign which, to an initiated nation-wide brotherhood, signified that here, at this place, was to be had free and abundant provender, with no stove wood to chop afterward and no heavy buckets of coal to pack in.

Wherefore and hence, throughout the rising hour and well on into the forenoon, a succession of ragged and shivering travellers tracked a straggling path up his walk and round to the back door, coming, with noses a frostbitten red and hands a frostbitten blue, to beg for sustenance. It was part and parcel of the judge's creed of hospitality to turn no stranger away from his door unfed.

"Jedge!" Aunt Dilsey Turner bulged into the old sitting room, where her master sat with his feet close to the grate toasting his shoesoles. "Jedge, they's 'nother one of 'em miz'ble wuthless w'ite trash out yere axin' fur vittles. Tha's de fo'th one inside er hour. Whut you reckin I best do wid 'im?"

"Well, Aunt Dilsey," the old man answered, "ef vittles is what he asts fur, I believe, under the circumstances, I'd give him some."

"Whar we goin' git vittles fur 'im?" she demanded.

"Wasn't there anything left over frum breakfast?" He risked the inquiry mildly—almost timidly.

"Breakfus'!" She sniffed her contempt for masculine ignorance. "Breakfus'? How long does you think one li'l' batch of breakfus' is goin' last round yere? I ain't never tek much fur myse'f—jes' swallers a mossil of hot coffee to stay my stomach, but you's suttinly a mighty stiddy feeder; and ez fur 'at nigger Jeff of yourn —huh!—he acks lak he wuz holler cl'ar down to his insteps. Ef dat nigger had de right name, de name would be Famine! 'Sides, ain't I done tole you they's been three of dem trafflin', no- 'count vagroms here already dis mawnin', a-eatin' us plum' out of house and home? Naw, suh; dey ain't nary grain of breakfus' lef'—de platters is done lick' clean!"

"Well, Aunt Dilsey, ez a special favour to me, I'd be mighty much obliged to you ef you'd cook up a little somethin' fur the pore feller."

"Po' feller! Po', you sez? Jedge, dat ole tramp out yonder at my kitchen do' is mighty nigh ez fat ez whut you is. Still, you's de cap'n. Ef you sez feed 'im, feed 'im I does. Only don't you come round blamin' me w'en we-all lands in de po'house—tha's all I asts you."

And out the black tyrant flounced, leaving the judge grinning to himself. Aunt Dilsey's bark was worse than her bite and there was no record of her having bitten anybody. Nevertheless, in order to make sure that no breakfast applicant departed hungry, he lingered on past his usual time for starting the day's work. It was cozily warm in his sitting room. Court was not in session either, having adjourned over for the holidays. It was getting well on toward ten o'clock when, with Jeff Poindexter's aid, he struggled into his ancient caped overcoat and buckled his huge red-lined galoshes on over his shoes, and started downtown.

Midway of the next block a snowball sailed out and over from behind a hedge fence and knocked his old black slouch hat half off his head. Showing surprising agility for one of his years and bulk, he ran down the fleeing sharp-shooter who had fired on him; and, while with one hand he held the struggling youngster fast, with the other he vigorously washed his captive's face in loose snow until the captive bawled for mercy. Then the judge gave him a dime to console him for his punishment and went on his way with a pleasant tingling in his blood and a ruby tip on his already well-ruddied nose.

His way took him to Soule's Drug Store, the gathering place of his set in fair weather and in foul. He was almost there before he heard of the trouble. It was Dave Baum who brought the first word of it. Seeing him pass, Dave came running, bareheaded, out of his notions store.

"Judge Priest, did you know what's just happened?" Dave was highly excited. "Why, Beaver Yancy's been cut all to pieces with a dirk knife by one of those Dagos that was brought on here to work on the new extension —that's what just happened! It happened just a little bit ago, down there where they've got those Dagos a-keepin' 'em. Beave, he must've said somethin' out of the way to him, and he just up with his dirk knife and cut Beave to ribbons."

Really it required much less time for little Mr. Baum to make this statement than it has taken for me to transcribe it or for you to read it. In his haste he ran the syllables together. Dan Settle came up behind them in time to catch the last words and he pieced out the narrative:

"They toted poor old Beaver into Doctor Lake's office—I just came from there—there's a big crowd waitin' to hear how he comes out. They don't think he's goin' to live but a little while. They ain't got the one that did the cuttin'—yet. There's quite a lot of feelin' already."

"That's what the railroad gets for bringin' all those foreigners down here." Mr. Baum, who was born in Bavaria, spoke with bitterness. "Judge, what do you think ought to be done about this business?"

"Well, son," said Judge Priest, "to begin with, ef I was you I'd run back inside of my store and put my hat on before I ketched a bad cold. And ef I was the chief of police of this city I'd find the accused party and lock him up good and tight. And ef I was everybody else I'd remain ez ca'm ez I could till I'd heared both sides of the case. There's nearly always two sides to every case, and sometimes there's likely to be three or four sides. I expect to impanel a new grand jury along in January and I wouldn't be surprised ef they looked into the matter purty thoroughly. They ginerally do.

"It's too bad, though, about Beaver Yancy!" added the judge; "I certainly trust he pulls through. Maybe he will—he's powerful husky. There's one consolation—he hasn't got any family, has he?"

And, with that, Judge Priest left them and went on down the snow-piled street and turned

in at Mr. Soule's door. What with reading a
Louisville paper and playing a long game of
checkers with Squire Rountree behind the pre-
scription case, and telephoning to the adjutant
regarding that night's meeting of Gideon K.
Irons Camp, and at noontime eating a cove
oyster stew which a darky brought him from
Sherill's short-order restaurant, two doors below,
and doing one thing and another, he spent the
biggest part of the day inside of Soule's and so
missed his chance to observe the growing and
the mounting of popular indignation.

It would seem Beaver Yancy had more friends
than any unprejudiced observer would have
credited him with having. Mainly they were
the type of friends who would not have lent him
so much as fifty cents under any conceivable
circumstance, but stood ready to shed human
blood on his account. Likewise, as the day wore
on, and the snow, under the melting influence of
the sun, began to run off the eaves and turn to
slush in the streets, a strong prejudice against
the presence of alien day labourers developed
with marvellous and sinister rapidity.

Yet, had those who cavilled but stopped long
enough to take stock of things, they might have
read this importation as merely one of the mani-
festations of the change that was coming over
our neck of the woods—the same change that
had been coming for years, and the same that
inevitably would continue coming through years
to follow.

Take for example, Legal Row
street of stubby little brick buildi
the lawyers and some of the doct
offices. Summer after summer,
long afternoons, the tenants had
cane-bottomed chairs tilted back
housefronts, swapping gossip and
dog fight or a watermelon cutting
monotony. But Legal Row was g
lawyers did not sit out on the si
more; it was not dignified. They
most of them, on the upper floor
sky-scraping Planters' Bank buildi
Easterners would not have rated
scraper; but in our country the skies
friendly skies, and a structure of e
piled one on the other, with a fanc
top off with, rears mightily high a
when about it, for contrast, are on
three and four story buildings.

Kettler's wagon yard, where the f
to bring their tobacco for overnight
where they slept on hay beds in the
with homemade bedquilts wrapped r
had been turned into a garage and s
of gasoline, oils and money transacti
brick market house stood on the sit
wooden one. A Great White Way
seven blocks long made the busin
almost as bright as day after dark
not quite. There was talk of establis
centre, with a regular plaza, and a

in at Mr. Soule's door. What with reading a
Louisville paper and playing a long game of
checkers with Squire Rountree behind the pre-
scription case, and telephoning to the adjutant
regarding that night's meeting of Gideon K.
Irons Camp, and at noontime eating a cove
oyster stew which a darky brought him from
Sherill's short-order restaurant, two doors below,
and doing one thing and another, he spent the
biggest part of the day inside of Soule's and so
missed his chance to observe the growing and
the mounting of popular indignation.

It would seem Beaver Yancy had more friends
than any unprejudiced observer would have
credited him with having. Mainly they were
the type of friends who would not have lent him
so much as fifty cents under any conceivable
circumstance, but stood ready to shed human
blood on his account. Likewise, as the day wore
on, and the snow, under the melting influence of
the sun, began to run off the eaves and turn to
slush in the streets, a strong prejudice against
the presence of alien day labourers developed
with marvellous and sinister rapidity.

Yet, had those who cavilled but stopped long
enough to take stock of things, they might have
read this importation as merely one of the mani-
festations of the change that was coming over
our neck of the woods—the same change that
had been coming for years, and the same that
inevitably would continue coming through years
to follow.

Take for example, Legal Row—that short street of stubby little brick buildings where all the lawyers and some of the doctors had their offices. Summer after summer, through the long afternoons, the tenants had sat there in cane-bottomed chairs tilted back against the housefronts, swapping gossip and waiting for a dog fight or a watermelon cutting to break the monotony. But Legal Row was gone now and lawyers did not sit out on the sidewalks any more; it was not dignified. They were housed, most of them, on the upper floor levels of the sky-scraping Planters' Bank building. Perhaps Easterners would not have rated it as a sky-scraper; but in our country the skies are low and friendly skies, and a structure of eight stories, piled one on the other, with a fancy cornice to top off with, rears mightily high and imposing when about it, for contrast, are only two and three and four story buildings.

Kettler's wagon yard, where the farmers used to bring their tobacco for overnight storage, and where they slept on hay beds in the back stalls, with homemade bedquilts wrapped round them, had been turned into a garage and smelled now of gasoline, oils and money transactions. A new brick market house stood on the site of the old wooden one. A Great White Way that was seven blocks long made the business district almost as bright as day after dark—almost, but not quite. There was talk of establishing a civic centre, with a regular plaza, and a fountain in

the middle of the plaza. There was talk of trying the commission form of government. There
was talk of adopting a town slogan; talk of an
automobile club and of a country club. And
now white labour, in place of black, worked on
a construction job.

When, after many false alarms, the P. A. &
O. V. got its Boaz Ridge Extension under way
the contractors started with negro hands; but
the gang bosses came from up North, whence
the capital had likewise come, and they did not
understand the negroes and the negroes did not
understand them, and there was trouble from
the go-off. If the bosses fraternised with the
darkies the darkies loafed; if, taking the opposite tack, the bosses tried to drive the gangs
under them with hard words the gangs grew
sullen and insolent.

There was a middle ground, but the perplexed
whites could not find it. A Southern-born over-
seer or a Southern-born steamboat mate could
have harried the crews with loud profanity, with
dire threats of mutilation and violent death, and
they would have grinned back at him cheerfully
and kept right on at their digging and their
shovelling. But when a grading expert named
Flaherty, from Chicago, Illinois, shook a freckled
fist under the nose of one Dink Bailey, coloured,
for whom, just the night before, he had bought
drinks in a groggery, the aforesaid Dink Bailey
tried to disarticulate him with a razor and made
very fair headway toward the completion of the

undertaking, considering he was so soon interrupted.

Having a time limit ever before their pestered eyes, it sorely irked the contractors that, whereas five hundred black, brown and yellow men might drop their tools Saturday night at six o'clock, a scant two hundred or so answered when the seven-o'clock whistle blew on Monday morning. The others came straggling back on Tuesday or Wednesday, or even on Thursday, depending on how long their wages held out.

"Whut I wants to go to work fur, Mist' W'ite Man? I got 'most two dollars lef'. Come round to see me w'en all dat's done spent and mebbe we kin talk bus'ness 'en."

The above statement, made by a truant grading hand to an inquiring grading boss, was typical of a fairly common point of view on the side of Labour. And this one, below, which sprang from the exasperated soul of a visiting contractor, was just as typical, for it was the cry of outraged Capital:

"It takes two white men, standing over every black man, to make the black man work—and then he won't! I never was a Southern sympathiser before, but I am now—you bet!"

The camel's back broke entirely at the end of the third week. It was a green paymaster from the Chicago offices who furnished the last straw. He tried to pay off with paper money. Since those early postbellum days, when the black brother, being newly freed from servitude

and innocently devoid of the commercial instinct, thought the white man's money, whether
stamped on metal disks or printed on parchment rectangulars, was always good money,
and so accepted much Confederate currency, to
his sorrow at the time and to his subsequent
enlightenment, he has nourished a deep suspicion of all cash except the kind that jingles;
in fact, it is rarely that he will accept any other
sort.

Give him the hard round silver and he is well-
content. That is good money—money fit to
buy things with. He knows it is, because it
rattles in the pocket and it rings on the bar;
but for him no greenbacks, if you please. So
when this poor ignorant paymaster opened up
his satchel and spread out his ones and his twos,
his fives and his tens, his treasury certificates
and his national bank notes, there was a riot.

Then the contractors just fired the whole outfit bodily; and they suspended operations, leaving the fills half-filled and the cuts half-dug
until they could fetch new shifts of labourers
from the North. They fetched them—a train-
load of overalled Latins, and some of these were
tall and swarthy men, and more were short,
fair men; but all were capable of doing a full
day's work.

Speedily enough, the town lost its first curious
interest in the newcomers. Indeed, there was
about them nothing calculated to hold the public
interest long. They played no guitars, wore no

handkerchief headdresses, offered to kidnap no small children, and were in no respect a picturesque race of beings. They talked their own outlandish language, dined on their own mysterious messes, slept in their bunks in the long barracks the company knocked together for them in the hollow down by the Old Fort, hived their savings, dealt with their employers through a paid translator, and beautifully minded their own business, which was the putting through of the Boaz Ridge Extension. Sundays a few came clunking in their brogans to early mass in Father Minor's church; the rest of the time they spent at the doing of their daily stint or in camp at their own peculiar devices.

Tony Palassi, who ran the biggest fruit stand in town, paid them one brief visit—and one only—and came away, spitting his disgust on the earth. It appeared that they were not his kind of people at all, these being but despised Sicilians and he by birth a haughty Roman, and by virtue of naturalisation processes a stalwart American; but everybody knew already, without being told, that there was a difference, and a big difference. A blind man could see it.

Tony, now, was a good fellow—one with sporting blood in his veins. Tony was a member of the Elks and of the Knights of Columbus. He owned and he drove one of the smartest trotting horses in the county. He played a brisk game of poker. Once a month he sent a barrel of apples or a bunch of bananas or a box of oranges,

as a freewill offering, to the children out at the
Home for the Friendless—in short, Tony belonged. Nobody ever thought of calling Tony
a Dago, and nobody ever had—more than once;
but these other fellows, plainly, were Dagos and
to be regarded as such. For upward of a month
now their presence in the community had meant
little or nothing to the community, one way or
the other, until one of them so far forgot himself
as to carve up Beaver Yancy.

The railroad made a big mistake when it hired
Northern bosses to handle black natives; it made
another when it continued to retain Beaver
Yancy, of our town, in its employ after the Sicilians came, he being a person long of the arm and
short of the temper. Even so, things might
have gone forward to a conclusion without mis-
adventure had it not been that on the day
before the snow fell the official padrone of the
force, who was likewise the official interpreter,
went North on some private business of his own,
leaving his countrymen without an intermediary
during his absence. It came to pass, therefore,
that on the December morning when this account
properly begins, Beaver Yancy found himself
in sole command of a battalion whose tongue he
did not speak and whose ways he did not know.

At starting time he ploughed his way through
the drifts to the long plank shanty in the bottoms and threw open a door. Instead of being
up and stirring, his charges lay in their bunks
against the walls, all of them stretched out

comfortably there, except a half dozen or so who brewed garlicky mixtures on the big stoves that stood at intervals in a row down the middle of the barracks. Employing the only language he knew, which was a profanely emphatic language, he ordered them to get up, get out and get to work. By shakes of the head, by words of smiling dissent and by gestures they made it plain to his understanding that for this one day at least they meant to do no labour in the open.

One more tolerant than Beaver Yancy, or perhaps one more skilled at translating signs, would have divined their reasons readily enough. They had come South expecting temperate weather. They did not like snow. They were not clad for exposure to snow. Their garments were thin and their shoes leaked. Therefore would they abide where they were until the snow had melted and the cold had moderated. Then they would work twice as hard to make up for this holiday.

The burly, big, overbearing man in the doorway was of a different frame of mind. In the absence of his superior officers and the padrone, his duty was to see that they pushed that job to a conclusion. He'd show 'em! He would make an example of one and the others would heed the lesson. He laid violent grasp on a little man who appeared to be a leader of opinion among his fellows and, with a big, mittened hand in the neckband of the other's shirt, dragged him, sputtering and expostulating, across the threshold and, with hard kicks of a heavy foot, heavily booted, propelled him out into the open.

The little man fell face forward into the snow. He bounced up like a chunk of new rubber. He had been wounded most grievously in his honour, bruised most painfully and ignominiously elsewhere. He jumped for the man who had mishandled him, his knifeblade licking out like a snake's tongue. He jabbed three times, hard and quick—then fled back indoors; and for a while, until help came in the guise of two children of a shanty-boater's family on their way to the railroad yards to pick up bits of coal, Beaver Yancy lay in the snow where he had dropped, bleeding like a stuck pig. He was not exactly cut to ribbons. First accounts had been exaggerated as first accounts so frequently are. But he had two holes in his right lung and one in the right side of his neck, and it was strongly presumptive that he would never again kick a Sicilian day labourer—or, for that matter, anybody else.

Judge Priest, speaking dispassionately from the aloof heights of the judicial temperament, had said it would be carrying out an excellent and timely idea if the chief of police found the knife-using individual and confined him in a place that was safe and sound; which, on being apprised of the occurrence, was exactly what the chief of police undertook to do. Accompanied by two dependable members of his day shift, he very promptly set out to make an arrest and an investigation; but serious obstacles confronted him.

To begin with, he had not the faintest notion of the criminal's identity or the criminal's appearance. The man he wanted was one among two hundred; but which one was he? Beaver Yancy, having been treated in Doctor Lake's office, was now at the city hospital in no condition to tell the name of his assailant even had he known it, or to describe him either, seeing that loss of blood, pain, shock and drugs had put him beyond the power of coherent speech. Nevertheless, the chief felt it a duty incumbent on him to lose no time in visiting what the *Daily Evening News*, with a touch of originality, called "the scene of the crime." This he did.

Everything was quiet on the flatlands below the Old Fort when he got there, an hour after the stabbing. Midway between the bluff that marked the rim of the hollow and the fringe of willows along the river, stood the long plank barracks of the imported hands. Smoke rose from the stovepipes that broke the expanse of its snow-covered roof; about one door was a maze of tracks and crosstracks; at a certain place, which was, say, seventy-five feet from the door, the snow was wallowed and flurried as though a heavy oxhide had been dragged across its surface; and right there a dark spot showed reddish brown against the white background.

However, no figures moved and no faces showed at the small windows as the chief and his men, having floundered down the hill, cautiously approached the silent building; and when he knocked on the door with the end of his hickory walking stick, and knocked and knocked again, meantime demanding admittance in the name of the law, no one answered his knock or his hail. Losing patience, he put his shoulder to the fastened door and, with a heave, broke it away from its hinges and its hasp, so that it fell inward.

Through the opening he took a look, then felt in his overcoat pocket for his gun, making ready to check a rush with revolver shots if needs be; but there was no rush. Within the place two hundred frightened, desperate men silently confronted him. Some who had pistols were wearing them now in plain sight. Others had knives and had produced them. All had picks and shovels—dangerous enough weapons at close quarters in the hands of men skilled in the use of them.

Had the big-hatted chief been wise in the ways of these men, he might peacefully have attained his object by opening his topcoat and showing his blue uniform, his brass buttons and his gold star; but naturally he did not think of that, and as he stood there before them, demanding of them, in a language they did not know, to surrender the guilty one, he was ulstered, like any civilian, from his throat to the tops of his rubber boots.

In him the foreigners, bewildered by the sudden turn in events, saw only a menacing enemy coming, with no outward show of authority about him, to threaten them. They went right on at their task of barricading the windows with strips of planking torn from their bunks. They had food and they had fuel, and they had arms. They would stand a siege, and if they were attacked they would fight back. In all they did, in all their movements, in their steadfast stare, he read their intent plainly enough.

Gabriel Henley was no coward, else he would not have been serving his second term as our chief of police; but likewise and furthermore he was no fool. He remembered just then that the town line ended at the bluff behind him. Technically, at least, the assault on Beaver Yancy had been committed outside his jurisdiction; constructively this job was not a job for the city, but for the county officials. He backed away, and as he retired sundry strong brown hands replaced the broken door and began making it fast with props and improvised bars. The chief left his two men behind to keep watch—an entirely unnecessary precaution, since none of the beleaguered two hundred, as it turned out, had the slightest intention of quitting his present shelter; and he hurried back uptown, pondering the situation as he went.

On his way to the sheriff's office he stopped by Palassi's fruit store. As the only man in town who could deal with Sicilians in their own tongue, Tony might help out tremendously; but Tony wasn't in. Mrs. Palassi, née Callahan, regretted to inform him that Tony had departed for Memphis on the early train to see about certain delayed Christmas shipments of oranges and bananas. To the youth of our town oranges and bananas were almost as necessary as firecrackers in the proper celebration of the Christmas. And when he got to the courthouse the chief found the sheriff was not in town either. He had started at daylight for Hopkinsburg to deliver an insane woman at the state asylum there; one of his deputies had gone with him. There was a second deputy, to be sure; but he was an elderly man and a chronic rheumatic, who mainly handled the clerical affairs of the office—he never had tried to arrest anyone in his whole life, and he expressed doubt that the present opportunity was auspicious for an opening experiment in that direction.

Under the circumstances, with the padrone away, with Tony Palassi away, with the sheriff away, and with the refuge of the culprit under close watch, Chief of Police Henley decided just to sit down and wait—wait for developments; wait for guidance; perhaps wait for popular sentiment to crystallize and, in process of its crystallization, give him a hint as to the steps proper to be taken next. So he sat him down at his roll-top desk in the old City Hall, with his feet on the stove, and he waited.

Had our efficient chief divined the trend of opinion as it was to be expressed during the day by divers persons in divers parts of the town, it is possible he might have done something, though just what that something might have been, I for one confess I do not know—and I do not think the chief knew either. There was a passion of anger abroad. This anger was to rise and spread when word circulated—as it very shortly did—that those other Dagos were harbouring and protecting the particular Dago who had done the cutting.

Such being the case, did not that make them outlaws too—accessories after the fact, comalefactors? The question was asked a good many times in a good many places and generally the answer was the same. And how about letting these murderous, dirk-toting pauper labourers come pouring down from the slums of the great cities to take the bread right out of the mouths of poor, hard-working darkies? With the sudden hostility to the white stranger rose an equally sudden sympathy for the lot of the black neighbour whose place he had usurped. Besides, who ever saw one of the blamed Dagos spending a cent at a grocery, or a notions store, or a saloon—or anywhere? Money earned in the community ought to be spent in the community. What did the railroad mean by it anyway?

Toward the middle of the afternoon somebody told somebody else—who, in turn, told everybody he met—that poor old Beaver was sinking fast; the surgeons agreed that he could not live the night out. Despite the rutted snow underfoot and the chill temperature, now rapidly dropping again to the freezing point and below it, knots of men began to gather on the streets discussing one topic—and one only.

Standing at the Richland House corner and addressing an entirely congenial gathering of fifteen or so who had just emerged from the Richland House bar, wiping their mouths and their moustaches, a self-appointed spokesman ventured the suggestion that it had been a long time between lynchings. Maybe if people just turned in and mobbed a few of these blood-thirsty Dagos it would give the rest of them a little respect for law and order? What if they didn't get the one that did the cutting? They could get a few of his friends, couldn't they—and chase all the others out of the country, and out of the state? Well, then, what more could a fair-minded citizen ask? And if the police force could not or would not do its duty in the prem-ises, was it not up to the people themselves to act?—or words to that general effect. In the act of going back inside for another round of drinks the audience agreed with the orator unani-mously, and invited him to join them; which he did.

Serenely unaware of these things, Judge Priest spent his day at Soule's Drug Store, beat Squire Roundtree at checkers, went trudging home at dusk for supper and, when supper was eaten, came trudging back downtown again, still hap-pily ignorant of the feeling that was in the icy air. Eight o'clock found him in the seat of honour on the platform at Kamleiter's Hall, presiding over the regular semi-monthly meeting of Gideon K. Irons Camp.

Considering weather conditions, the judge, as commandant, felt a throb of pride at the size of the attendance. Twenty-two elderly gentlemen answered to their names when the adjutant, old Professor Reese, of the graded school, called the roll. Two or three more straggled in, bundled up out of all their proper proportions, in time to take part in the subsequent discussion of new business. Under that elastic heading the Camp agreed to co-operate with the Daughters in a campaign to raise funds for a monument to the memory of General Meriwether Grider, dead these many years; voted fifty dollars out of the Camp treasury for the relief of a dead comrade's widow; and listened to a reminiscence of the retreat from Atlanta by Sergeant Jimmy Bagby.

One overhearing might have gathered from the tenor of the sergeant's remarks that, if King's Hell Hounds had been given but the proper support in that campaign, the story of Sherman's March to the Sea would have a vastly different ending from the one set forth in the schoolbooks and the histories. In conclusion, and by way of a diversion from the main topic, Sergeant Bagby was launching on a circumstantial recital of a certain never-to-be-forgotten passage of words between General Buckner and

General Breckenridge on a certain momentous and historic occasion, when an interruption occurred, causing him to break off in the middle of his opening sentence.

Old Press Harper, from three miles out in the county, was sitting well back toward the rear of the little hall. It is possible that his attention wandered from the subject in hand. He chanced to glance over his shoulder and, through the frosted panes of a back window, he caught a suffused reflection. Instantly he was on his feet.

"Hey, boys!" called out Mr. Harper. "Somethin's on fire—looky yander!"

He ran to the window. With his sleeve he rubbed a patch clear on the sweated pane and peered out. Others followed him. Sashes were hoist, and through each of the three window openings in the back wall protruded a cluster of heads—heads that were pinky-bald, grey-grizzled or cottony-white, as the case might be.

"You bet there's a fire, and a good hot one! See them blazes shootin' up."

"Must be down by the Old Fort. D'ye reckin it could be the old plough factory burnin' up?"

"Couldn't be that far away, could it, Bony? Looks closer'n that to me."

"Fires always seem closer than what they really are—that's been my experience."

"Listen, boys, for the engines—they ought to be startin' now in a minute."

They listened; but, though the fire bell in the City Hall tower, two blocks away, was sounding in measured beats, no clatter of hoofs, no clamour of fast-turning wheels, rose in the street below or in any neighbouring street. Only the red flare widened across the northern horizon, deepening and brightening, and shot through in its centre with lacings of flame.

"That's funny! I don't hear 'em. Well, anyway, I'm a-goin'."

"Me, too, Press."

The windows were abandoned. There was a rush for the corner where overcoats had been swung on hooks and overshoes had been kicked back against the baseboard. Various elderly gentlemen began adjusting earmuffs and mufflers, and spearing with their arms at elusive sleeve openings. The meeting stood adjourned without having been adjourned.

"Coming, Billy?" inquired Mr. Nap. B. Crump in the act of hastily winding two yards of red knitted worsted about his throat.

"No; I reckin not," said Judge Priest. "It's a mighty bitter night fur folks to be driv' out of their homes in this weather. I'm sorry fur 'em, whoever they are—but I reckin I couldn't do no good ef I went. You young fellers jest go ahead without me—I'm sort of gittin' along too fur in years to be runnin' to other people's fires. I've got one of my own to go to—out there in my old settin' room on Clay Street."

He rose slowly from his chair and stepped round from behind the table, then halted, canting his head to one side.

"Listen, boys! Ain't that somebody runnin' up the steps?"

It surely was. There was a thud of booted feet on the creaking boards. Somebody was coming three stairs at a jump. The door flew open and Circuit Clerk Elisha Milam staggered in, gasping for breath. They assailed him with questions.

"Hey, Lisha, where's the fire?"

"It's that construction camp down below town burning up," he answered between pants.

"How did it get started?"

"It didn't get started—somebody started it. Gentlemen, there's trouble beginning down yonder. Where's Judge Priest? . . . Oh, yes, there he is!"

He made for Judge Priest where the judge still stood on the little platform, and all the rest trailed behind him, scrouging up to form a close circle about those two, with hands stirruped behind faulty ears and necks craned forward to hear what Mr. Milam had to say. His story wasn't long, the blurting way he told it, but it carried an abundant thrill. Acting apparently in concert with others, divers unknown persons, creeping up behind the barracks of the construction crew, had fired the building and fled safely away without being detected by its dwellers or by the half-frozen watchers of the police force on the hillock above. At least that was the presumption in Mr. Milam's mind, based on what he had just heard.

The fire, spreading fast, had driven the Sicilians forth, and they were now massed under the bluff with their weapons. The police force—eight men, all told, constituted the night shift—hesitated to act, inasmuch as the site of the burning camp lay fifty yards over the town line, outside of town limits. The fire department was helpless. Notice had been served at both the engine houses, in the first moment of the alarm, that if the firemen unreeled so much as a single foot of hose it would be cut with knives—a vain threat, since all the water plugs were frozen up hard and fast anyhow. The sheriff and his only able-bodied deputy were in Hopkinsburg, eighty miles away; and an armed mob of hundreds was reported as being on the way from its rendezvous in the abandoned plough factory to attack the foreigners.

Mr. Milam, essentially a man of peace, had learned these things at first hand, or at second, and had hastened hotfoot to Kamleiter's Hall for the one man to whom, in times of emergency, he always looked—his circuit-court judge. He didn't know what Judge Priest could do or would do in the face of a situation so grave; but at least he had done his duty—he had borne the word. In a dozen hasty gulping sentences he told his tale and finished it; and then, by way of final punctuation, a chorus of exclamatory sounds—whistled, grunted and wheezed—rose from his auditors.

As for Judge Priest, he, for a space of seconds

after Mr. Milam had concluded, said nothing at all. The rapping of his knuckled fist on the tabletop alongside him broke in sharply on the clamour. They faced him then and he faced them; and it is possible that, even in the excitement of the time, some among them marked how his plump jaws had socketed themselves into a hard, square-mortise shape, and how his tuft of white chin beard bristled out at them, and how his old blue eyes blazed into their eyes. And then Judge Priest made a speech to them—a short, quick speech, but the best speech, so his audience afterward agreed, that ever they heard him make.

"Boys," he cried, lifting his high, shrill voice yet higher and yet shriller, "I'm about to put a motion to you and I want a vote on it purty dam' quick! They've been sayin' in this town that us old soldiers was gittin' too old to take an active hand in the affairs of this community any longer; and at the last election, ez you all know, they tried fur to prove it by retirin' most of the veterans that offered themselves ez candidates fur re-election back to private life.

"I ain't sayin' they wasn't partly right neither; fur here we've been sittin' this night, like a passel of old moo-cows, chewin' the cud of things that happened forty-odd year' ago, and never suspicionin' nothin' of what was goin' on, whilst all round us men, carried away by passion and race prejudice, have been plottin' to break the laws and shed blood and bring an everlastin' disgrace on the reppitation fur peace and good order of this fair little city of ourn. But maybe it ain't too late yit fur us to do our duty ez citizens and ez veterans. Oncet on a time—a mighty long while ago—we turned out to pertect our people ag'inst an armed invader. Let's show 'em we ain't too old or too feeble to turn out oncet more to pertect them ag'inst themselves."

He reared back, and visibly, before their eyes, his short fat figure seemed to lengthen by cubits.

"I move that Gideon K. Irons Camp of United Confederate Veterans, here assembled, march in a body right now to save—ef we can— these poor Eyetalians who are strangers in a strange and a hosstil land from bein' mistreated, and to save—ef we can—our misguided fellow townsmen from sufferin' the consequences of their own folly and their own foolishness. Do I hear a second to that motion?"

Did he hear a second to his motion? He heard twenty-five seconds to it, all heaved at him together, with all the blaring strength of twenty-five pairs of elderly lungs. Sergeant Jimmy Bagby forgot parliamentary usage.

"Will we go?" whooped Sergeant Bagby, waving his pudgy arms aloft so that his mittened hands described whizzing red circles in the air. "You betcher sweet life we'll go! We'll go through hell and high water—with you as our commandin' officer, Billy Priest."

"You betcher! That's the ticket!" A whoop
of approval went up.

"Well, then, ef that's the way you feel about
it—come on!" their leader bade them; and they
rushed for the door, sweeping the circuit clerk
aside. "No; wait jest a minute!" He singled
out the jostled Mr. Milam. "Lishy, you've got
the youngest, spriest legs of anybody here. Run
on ahead—won't you?—and find Father Minor.
He'll be at the priest house back of his church.
Tell him to jine up with us as quick as ever the
Lord'll let him. We'll head down Harrison
Street."

Mr. Milam vanished. With a wave of his
arm, the judge comprehended those who remained.

"Nearly everybody here served one time or
another under old Nathan Bedford Forrest.
The rest would 'a' liked to. I reckin this here is
goin' to be the last raid and the last charge that
Forrest's Cavalry, mounted or dismounted, ever
will make! Let's do it regular—open up that
there wardrobe-chist yonder, some of you, and
git what's inside!"

Hurried old hands fumbled at the catches of
a weather-beaten oaken cabinet on the platform
and plucked forth the treasured possessions of
the Camp—the dented bugle; the drum; the
slender, shiny, little fife; the silken flag, on its
short polished staff.

"Fall in—by twos!" commanded Judge
Priest. "Forward—march!"

Half a minute later the gasjets that lighted Kamleiter's Hall lighted only emptiness —an empty chest in a corner; empty chairs, some overturned on their sides, some upright on their legs; an empty hall doorway opening on an empty patch of darkness; and one of Judge Priest's flannel-lined galoshes, gaping emptily where it had been forgotten.

From the street below rose a measured thud of feet on the hard-packed snow. Forrest's Cavalry was on the march!

With bent backs straightening to the call of a high, strong impulse; with gimpy, gnarled legs rising and falling in brisk unison; with heads held high and chests puffed out; with their leader in front of them and their flag going before them—Forrest's Cavalry went forward. Once and once only the double line stopped as it traversed the town, lying snug and for the most part still under its blanketing of snow.

As the little column of old men swung round the first corner below Kamleiter's Hall, the lights coming through the windows of Tony Palassi's fruit shop made bright yellow patches on the white path they trod.

"Halt!" ordered Judge Priest suddenly; and he quit his place in the lead and made for the doorway.

"If you're looking for Tony to go along and translate you're wasting time, Judge," sang out Mr. Crump. "He's out of town."

"Is he?" said Judge Priest. "Well, that's too bad!"

As though to make sure, he peered in through the glassed upper half of the fruitshop door. Within might be seen Mrs. Delia Callahan Palassi, wife of the proprietor, putting the place to rights before locking it up for the night; and at her skirts tagged Master Antonio Wolfe Tone Palassi, aged seven, only son and sole heir of the same, a round-bellied, red-cheeked little Italian-Irish-American. The judge put his hand on the latch and jiggled it.

"I tell you Tony's not there," repeated Mr. Crump impatiently.

If the judge heard him he paid no heed. He went through that door, leaving his command outside, as one might go who knew exactly what he was about. Little Tony Wolfe Tone recognised an old friend and came, gurgling a welcome, to greet him. Most of the children in town knew Judge Priest intimately, but little Tony Wolfe Tone was a particular favourite of his; and by the same token he was a particular favourite of Tony's.

Whatever Judge Priest said to Mrs. Palassi didn't take long for the saying of it; yet it must have been an argument powerfully persuading and powerfully potent. It is possible—mind you, I don't make the positive assertion, but it is possible—he reminded her that the blood of a race of fighting kings ran in her veins; for in less than no time at all, when Judge Priest

reissued from the fruit shop, there rode pack-
fashion on his back a little figure so well bundled
up against the cold that only a pair of big
brown Italian eyes and a small, tiptilted Irish
nose showed themselves, to prove that Judge
Priest's burden was not a woolly Teddy-bear,
but a veritable small boy. No; I'm wrong there.
One other thing proved it—a woman standing
in the doorway, wringing her apron in her hands,
her face ablaze with mother love and mother
pride and mother fear, watching the hurrying
procession as it moved down the wintry street,
straight into the red glare on ahead.

The flimsy framework of resiny pine burned
fast, considering that much snow had lain on
the roof and much snow had melted and run
down the sides all day, to freeze again with the
coming of nighttime. One end of the barracks
had fallen into a muddle of black-charred ruina-
tion. The fire ate its way along steadily, purring
and crackling and spitting as its red teeth bit
into the wetted boards. Above, the whole sky
was aglare with its wavering red reflections. The
outlines of the bowl-shaped flat stood forth distinctly revealed in the glow of that great wooden
brazier, and the snow that covered the earth
was channelled across with red streaks, like spilt
blood.
Here, against the nearermost bank, the foreigners were clumped in a tight, compact black
huddle, all scared, but not so badly scared that

they would not fight. Yonder, across the snow, through the gap where a side street debouched at a gentle slope into the hollow, the mob advanced—men and half-grown boys—to the number of perhaps four hundred, coming to get the man who had stabbed Beaver Yancy and string him up on the spot—and maybe to get a few of his friends and string them up as an added warning to all Dagos. They came on and came on until a space of not more than seventy-five yards separated the mob and the mob's prospective victims. From the advancing mass a growling of many voices rose. Rampant, unloosed mischief was in the sound.

Somebody who was drunk yelled out shrill profanity and then laughed a maudlin laugh. The group against the bank kept silent. Theirs was the silence of a grim and desperate resolution. Their only shelter had been fired over their heads; they were beleaguered and ringed about with enemies; they had nowhere to run for safety, even had they been minded to run. So they would fight. They made ready with their weapons of defence—such weapons as they had.

A man who appeared to hold some manner of leadership over the rest advanced a step from the front row of them. In his hand he held an old-fashioned cap-and-ball pistol at full cock. He raised his right arm and sighted along the levelled barrel at a spot midway between him and the oncoming crowd. Plainly he meant to fire when the first of his foes crossed an imaginary line. He squinted up his eye, taking a careful aim; and he let his trigger finger slip gently inside the trigger guard—but he never fired.

On top of the hill, almost above his head, a bugle blared out. A fife and a drum cut in, playing something jiggy and brisk; and over the crest and down into the flat, two by two, marched a little column of old men, following after a small silken flag which flicked and whispered in the wind, and led by a short, round-bodied commander, who held by the hand a little briskly trotting figure of a child. Tony Wolfe Tone had grown too heavy for the judge to carry him all the way.

Out across the narrow space between the closing-in mob and the closed-in foreigners the marchers passed, their feet sinking ankle-deep into the crusted snow. Their leader gave a command; the music broke off and they spread out in single file, taking station, five feet apart from one another, so that between the two hostile groups a living hedge was interposed. And so they stood, with their hands down at their sides, some facing to the west, where the Italians were herded together, some facing toward the east, where the would-be lynchers, stricken with a great amazement, had come to a dead stand.

Judge Priest, still holding little Tony Wolfe Tone's small mittened hand fast in his, spoke up, addressing the mob. His familiar figure was outlined against the burning barracks beyond him and behind him. His familiar whiny voice he lifted to so high a pitch that every man and boy there heard him.

"Feller citizens," he stated, "this is part of Forrest's Cavalry you see here. We done soldierin' oncet and we've turned soldiers ag'in; but we ain't armed—none of us. We've only got our bare hands. Ef you come on we can't stop you with guns; but we ain't agoin' to budge, and ef you start shootin' you'll shorely git some of us. So ez a personal favour to me and these other gentlemen, I'd like to ast you jest to stand still where you are and not to shoot till after you see what we're fixin' to try to do. That's agreeable to you-all, ain't it? You've got the whole night ahead of you—there's no hurry, is there, boys?"

He did not wait for any answer from anyone. By name he knew a good half of them; by sight he knew the other half. And they all knew him; and they knew Tony Palassi's boy; and they knew Father Minor, who stood at his right hand; and they knew the lame blacksmith and the little bench-legged Jewish merchant, and the rich banker and the poor carpenter, and the leading wholesaler, and all the other old men who stretched away from the judge in an uneven line, like fence posts for a fence that had not been built. They would not shoot yet; and, as though fully convinced in his own mind they would bide where they were until he was done, and relying completely on them to keep their unspoken promise, Judge Priest half-turned his back on the members of the mob and bent over little Tony.

"Little feller," he said, "you ain't skeered, are you?"

Tony looked up at his friend and shook his head stoutly. Tony was not scared. It was as good as play to Tony—all this was.

"That's my sandy little pardner," said Judge Priest; and he put his hands under Tony's arms and heaved the child back up on his shoulders, and swung himself about so that he and Tony faced the huddle of silent figures in the shadow of the bank.

"You see all them men yonder, don't you, boy?" he prompted. "Well, now you speak up ez loud ez you can, and you tell 'em whut I've been tellin' you to say all the way down the street ever since we left your mammy. You tell 'em I'm the big judge of the big court. Tell 'em there's one man among 'em who must come on and go with me. He'll know and they'll know which man I mean. Tell 'em that man ain't goin' to be hurt ef he comes now. Tell 'em that they ain't none of 'em goin' to be hurt ef they all do what I say. Tell 'em Father Minor is here to show 'em to a safe, warm place where they kin spend the night. Kin you re-member all that, sonny-boy? Then tell 'em in Eyetalian—quick and loud."

And Tony Wolfe Tone told them. Unmindful of the hundreds of eyes that were upon him—

even forgetting for a minute to watch the fire—
Tony opened wide his small mouth and in the
tongue of his father's people, richened perhaps
by the sweet brogue of his mother's land, and
spiced here and there with a word or two of
savoury good American slang, he gave the message a piping utterance.

They hearkened and they understood. This
baby, this *bambino*, speaking to them in a poly-
glot tongue they, nevertheless, could make out—
surely he did not lie to them! And the priest of
their own faith, standing in the snow close by
the child, would not betray them. They knew
better than that. Perhaps to them the flag, the
drum, the fife, the bugle, the faint semblance of
military formation maintained by these volunteer rescuers who had appeared so opportunely,
promising succour and security and a habitation
for the night—perhaps all this symbolised to them
organised authority and organised protection,
just as Judge Priest, in a flash of inspiration back
in Kamleiter's Hall, had guessed that it might.

Their leader, the man who held the pistol,
advanced a pace or two and called out something; and when Tony Wolfe Tone, from his
perch on the old judge's shoulders, had answered
back, the man, as though satisfied, turned and
might be seen busily confabbing with certain of
his mates who clustered about him, gesticu-
lating.

"Whut did he say, boy?" asked Judge Priest,
craning his neck to look up.

"He say, Mister Judge, they wants to talk it over," replied Tony, craning his neck to look down.

"And whut did you say to him then?"

"I say to him: 'Go to it, kiddo!'"

In the sheltering crotch of little Tony's two plump bestraddling legs, which encircled his neck, the old judge chuckled to himself. A wave of laughter ran through the ranks of the halted mob—Tony's voice had carried so far as that, and Tony's mode of speech apparently had met with favour. Mob psychology, according to some students, is hard to fathom; according to others, easy.

From the midst of the knot of Sicilians a man stepped forth—not the tall man with the gun, but a little stumpy man who moved with a limp. Alone, he walked through the crispened snow until he came up to where the veterans stood, waiting and watching. The mob, all intently quiet once more, waited and watched too.

With a touch of the dramatic instinct that belongs to his race, he flung down a dirk knife at Judge Priest's feet and held out both his hands in token of surrender. To the men who came there to take his life he gave no heed—not so much as a sidewise glance over his shoulder did he give them. He looked into the judge's face and into the face of little Tony, and into the earnest face of the old priest alongside these two.

"Boys"—the judge lifted Tony down and, with a gesture, was invoking the attention of his townsmen—"boys, here's the man who did the knifin' this mornin', givin' himself up to my pertection—and yours. He's goin' along with me now to the county jail, to be locked up ez a prisoner. I've passed my word and the word of this whole town that he shan't be teched nor molested whilst he's on his way there, nor after he gits there. I know there ain't a single one of you but stands ready to help me keep that promise. I'm right, ain't I, boys?"

"Oh, hell, judge—you win!" sang out a member of the mob, afterward identified as one of Beaver Yancy's close friends, in a humorously creditable imitation of the judge's own earnest whine. And at that everybody laughed again and somebody started a cheer.

"I thought so," replied the judge. "And now, boys, I've got an idea. I reckin, after trampin' all the way down here in the snow, none of us want to tramp back home ag'in without doin' somethin'—we don't feel like ez ef we want to waste the whole evenin', do we? See that shack burnin' down? Well, it's railroad property; and we don't want the railroad to suffer. Let's put her out—let's put her out with snowballs!"

Illustrating his suggestion, he stooped, scooped up a double handful of snow, squeezed it into a pellet and awkwardly tossed it in the general direction of the blazing barracks. It flew wide of the mark and fell short of it; but his

intention was good, that being conceded.
Whooping joyously, four hundred men and half-
grown boys, or thereabouts such a number,
pouched their weapons and dug into the drifted
whiteness.

"Hold on a minute—we'll do it to soldier
music!" shouted the judge, and he gave a signal.
The drum beat then; and old Mr. Harrison Treese
buried the fife in his white whiskers and ripped
loose on the air the first bars of Yankee Doodle.
The judge molded another snowball for himself.

"All set? Then, ready!—aim!—fire!"

Approximately two hundred snowballs battered and splashed the flaming red target. A
great sizzling sound rose.

Just after this first volley the only gun-powder
shot of the evening was fired. It came out afterward that as a man named Ike Bowers stooped
over to gather up some snow his pistol, which he
had forgotten to uncock, slipped out of his
pocket and fell on a broken bit of planking.
There was a darting needle of fire and a smart
crack. The Sicilians wavered for a minute,
swaying back and forth, then steadied themselves as Father Minor stepped in among them
with his arms uplifted; but Sergeant Jimmy
Bagby put his hand to his head in a puzzled sort
of way, spun round, and laid himself down full
length in the snow.

It was nearly midnight. The half-burned hull
of the barracks in the deserted bottom below the

Old Fort still smoked a little, but it no longer blazed. Its late occupants—all save one—slept in the P. A. & O. V. roundhouse, half a mile away, under police and clerical protection; this one was in a cell in the county jail, safe and sound, and it is probable that he slept also. That linguistic prodigy, Master Tony Wolfe Tone Palassi, being excessively awearied, snored in soft, little-boy snores at his mother's side; and over him she cried tears of pride and visited soft kisses on his flushed, upturned face. To the family of the Palassis much honour had accrued—not forgetting the Callahans. At eleven o'clock the local correspondent of the *Courier-Journal* and other city papers had called up to know where he might get copies of her son's latest photograph for widespread publication abroad.

The rest of the town, generally speaking, was at this late hour of midnight, also abed; but in the windows of Doctor Lake's office, on the second floor of the Planters' Bank building, lights burned, and on the leather couch in Doctor Lake's inner room a pudgy figure, which breathed heavily, was stretched at full length, its hands passively flat on its breast, its head done up in many windings of cotton batting and surgical bandages. Above this figure stood old Doctor Lake, holding in the open palm of his left hand a small, black, flattened object. The door leading to the outer office opened a foot and the woe-begone face and dripping eyes of Judge Priest appeared through the slit.

"Get out!" snapped Doctor Lake without turning his head.

"Lew, it's me!" said Judge Priest in the whisper that any civilised being other than a physician or a trained nurse instinctively assumes in the presence of a certain dread visitation. "I jest natchelly couldn't wait no longer —not another minute! I wouldn't 'a' traded one hair off of Jimmy Bagby's old grey head fur all the Beaver Yancys that ever was whelped. Lew, is there a chance?"

"Billy Priest," said Doctor Lake severely, "the main trouble with you is that you're so liable to go off half-cocked. Beaver Yancy's not going to die—you couldn't kill him with an ax. I don't know how that story got round to-night. And Jim Bagby's all right too, except he's going to have one whale of a headache to-morrow. The bullet glanced round his skull and stopped under the scalp. Here 'tis—I just got it out. . . . Oh, Lord! Now look what you've done, bursting in here and blubbering all around the place!"

The swathed form on the couch sat up and cocked an eye out from beneath a low-drawn fold of cheesecloth.

"Is that you, Judge?" demanded Sergeant Bagby in his usual voice and in almost his usual manner.

"Yes, Jimmy; it's me."

Judge Priest projected himself across the room toward his friend. He didn't run; he didn't jump; he didn't waddle—he projected himself.

"Yes, Jimmy, it's me."

"Are any of the other boys out there in the other room?"

"Yes, Jimmy; they're all out there, waitin'."

"Well, quit snifflin' and call 'em right in!" said Sergeant Bagby crisply. "I've been tryin' fur years to git somebody to set still long enough fur me to tell 'em that there story about Gin'ral John C. Breckenridge and Gin'ral Simon Bolivar Buckner; and it seems like somethin' always comes up to interrupt me. This looks like my chance to finish it, fur oncet. Call them boys all in!"

VIII

DOUBLE-BARRELLED
JUSTICE

A LONG and limber man leaned against a doorjamb of the Blue Jug Saloon and Short Order Restaurant, inhaling the mild clear air of the autumnal day and, with the air of a man who amply is satisfied by the aspect of things, contemplating creation at large as it revealed itself along Franklin Street. In such posture he suggested more than anything else a pair of callipers endowed with reason. For this, our disesteemed fellow citizen of the good old days which are gone, was probably the shortest-waisted man in the known world. In my time I have seen other men who might be deemed to be excessively short waisted, but never one to equal in this unique regard Old King Highpockets. A short span less of torso, and a dime museum would have claimed him, sure.

You would think me a gross exaggerator did I attempt to tell you how high up his legs forked;

suffice it to say that, as to his suspenders, they crossed the spine just below his back collar button. Wherefore, although born a Magee and baptised an Elmer, it was inevitable in this community that from the days of his youth onward he should have been called what they did call him. To his six feet five and a half inches of lank structural design he owed the more descriptive part of his customary title. The rest of it—the regal-sounding part of it— had been bestowed upon him in his ripened maturity after he achieved for himself local dominance in an unhallowed but a lucrative calling.

Sitting down the above-named seemed a person of no more than ordinary height, this being by reason of the architectural peculiarities just referred to. But standing up, as at the present moment, he reared head and gander neck above the run of humanity. From this personal eminence he now looked about him and below him as he took the sun. There was not a cloud in the general sky; none in his private and individual sky either. He had done well the night before and likewise the night before that; he expected to do as well or better the coming night. Upstairs over the Blue Jug King Highpockets took in gambling —both plain and fancy gambling.

There passed upon the opposite side of the street one Beck Giltner. With him the tall man in the doorway exchanged a distant and formal greeting expressed in short nods. Between these two no great amount of friendliness was lost. Professionally speaking they were opponents. Beck Giltner was by way of being in the card and dicing line himself, but he was known as a square gambler, meaning by that, to most of mankind he presented a plane surface of ostensible honesty and fair dealing, whereas within an initiated circle rumour had it that his rival of the Blue Jug was so crooked he threw a shadow like a brace and bit. Beck Giltner made it a rule of business to strip only those who could afford to lose their pecuniary peltries. Minors, drunkards, half-wits and chronic losers were barred from his tables. But all was fish—I use the word advisedly—all was fish that came to the net of Highpockets.

Beck Giltner passed upon his business. So did other and more reputable members of society. A short straggling procession of gentlemen went by, all headed westward, and each followed at a suitable interval by his negro "boy," who might be anywhere between seventeen and seventy years of age. An hour or two later these travellers would return, bound for their offices downtown. Going back they would mainly travel in pairs, and their trailing black servitors would be burdened, front and back, with "samples"—sheafs of tobacco bound together and sealed with blobs of red sealing wax and tagged. For this was in the time before the Trust and the Night Riders had between them disrupted the trade down in the historic Black Patch, and the mode of marketing the weed by loose leaf was a thing as yet undreamed of. They would be prizing on the breaks in Key & Buckner's long warehouse pretty soon. The official auctioneer had already reported himself, and to the ear for blocks round came distantly a sharp rifle-fire clatter as the warehouse hands knocked the hoops off the big hogsheads and the freed staves rattled down in windrows upon the uneven floor.

A locomotive whistled at the crossing two squares up the street, and the King smiled a little smile and rasped a lean and avaricious chin with a fabulously bony hand. He opined that locomotive would be drawing the monthly pay car which was due. The coming of the pay car meant many sportive railroad men— shopmen, yardmen, trainmen—abroad that evening with the good new money burning holes in the linings of their pockets.

Close by him, just behind him, a voice spoke his name—his proper name which he seldom heard—and the sound of it rubbed the smile off his face and turned it on the instant into a grim, long war-mask of a face.

"Mister Magee—Elmer—just a minute, please!"

Without shifting his body he turned his head and over the peak of one shoulder he regarded her dourly. She was a small woman and she was verging on middle age, and she was an exceedingly shabby little woman. Whatever of comeliness she might ever have had was now and forever gone from her. Hard years and the strain of them had ground the colour in and rubbed the plumpness out of her face, leaving in payment therefor deep lines and a loose skin-sac under the chin and hollows in the cheeks. The shapeless, sleazy black garments that she wore effectually concealed any remnant of grace that might yet abide in her body. Only her eyes testified she had ever been anything except a forlorn and drooping slattern. They were big bright black eyes.

This briefly was the aspect of the woman who stood alongside him, speaking his name. She had come up so quietly that he never heard her. But then her shoes were old and worn and had lasted long past the age when shoes will squeak.

He made no move to raise his hat. Slantwise across the high ridge of his twisted shoulder he looked at her long and contemptuously.

"Well," he said at length, "back ag'in, huh? Well, whut is it now, huh?"

She put up a little work-gnarled hand to a tight skew of brown hair streaked thickly with grey. In the gesture was something essentially feminine—something pathetic too.

"I reckon you know already what it is, Elmer," she said. "It's about my boy—it's about Eddie."

"I told you before and I tell you ag'in I ain't your boy's guardeen," he answered her.

"How comes you keep on pesterin' me—I ain't got that boy of yourn?"

"Yes, you have got him," she said, her voice shaking and threatening to break. "You've got him body and soul. And I want him—me, his mother. I want you to give him back to me."

His gaze lifted until he considered empty space a foot above her head. Slowly he reached an angular arm back under his right shoulder blade and fished about there until he had extracted from a hip pocket a long, black rectangle of navy chewing tobacco that was like a shingle newly dipped in creosote. It was a virgin plug —he bought a fresh one every morning and by night would make a ragged remnant of it. With the deliberation of a man who has plenty of time to spare, he set his stained front teeth in a corner of it and gnawed off a big scallop of the rank stuff. His tongue herded it back into his jaw, where it made a lump. He put the plug away. She stood silently through this, kneading her hands together, a most humble suppliant awaiting this monarch's pleasure.

"You told me all that there foolishness the other time," he said. "Ain't you got no new song to sing this time? Ef you have I'll listen, mebbe. Ef you ain't I'll tell you good-by."

"Elmer," she said, "what kind of a man are you? Haven't you got any compassions at all? Why, Elmer, your pa and my pa were soldiers together in the same regiment. You and me

were raised together right here in this town.
We went to the same schoolhouse together as
children—don't you remember? You weren't
a mean boy then. Why, I used to think you
was right good-hearted. For the sake of those
old days won't you do something about Eddie?
It's wrong and it's sinful—what you're doing
to him and the rest of the young boys in this
town."

"Ef you think that why come to me?" he
demanded. "Why not go to the police with
your troubles?" He split his lips back, and a
double row of discoloured snags that projected
from the gums like little chisels showed between
them.

"And have 'em laugh in my face, same as
you're doing now? Have 'em tell me to go and
get the evidence? Oh, I know you're safe
enough there. I reckon you know who your
friends are. You shut up when the Grand
Jury meets; and once in a while when things
get hot for you, like they did when that Law
and Order League was so busy, you close up
your place; and once in a while you go up to
court and pay a fine and then you keep right
on. But it's not you that's paying the fine—
I know that mighty good and well. The money
to pay it comes out of the pockets of poor
women in this town—wives and mothers and
sisters.

"Oh, there's others besides me that are suffering this minute. There's that poor, little,

broken-hearted Mrs. Shetler, out there on Wheelis Street—the one whose husband had to run away because he fell short in his accounts with the brickyard. And there's that poor, old Mrs. Postelwaite, that's about to lose the home that she's worked her fingers to the bone, mighty near, to help pay for, and she'll be left without a roof over her head in her old age because her husband's went and lost every cent he can get his hands on playing cards in your place, and so now they can't meet their mortgage payments. And there's plenty of others if the truth was only known. And oh, there's me and my boy—the only boy I've got. Elmer Magee, how you can sleep nights I don't see!"

"I don't," he said. "I work nights." His wit appealed to him, for he grinned again. "Say, listen here!" His mood had changed and he spat the next words out. "Ef you think I ain't good company for that son of yourn, why don't you make him stay away from me? I ain't hankerin' none fur his society."

"I've tried to, Elmer—God knows I've tried to, time and time again. That's why I've come back to you once more to ask you if you won't help me. I've gone down on my knees alone and prayed for help and I've prayed with Eddie, too, and I've pleaded with him. He don't run round town carousing like some boys his age do. He don't drink and he's not wild, except it just seems like he can't leave gambling alone. Oh, he's promised me and promised

me he'd quit, but he's weak—and he's only a
boy. I've kept track of his losings as well as
I could, and I know that first and last he's lost
nearly two hundred dollars playing cards with
you and your crowd. That may not be much
to you, Elmer—I reckon you're rich—but it's
a lot to a lone woman like me. It means bread
and meat and house rent and clothes to go on
my back—that's what it means to me. My feet
are mighty near out of these shoes I've got on,
and right this minute there's not a cent in the
house. I don't say you cheated him, but the
money's gone and you got it. And it's ruining
my boy. He's only a boy—he won't be twenty-
one till the twelfth day of next April. If only
you wouldn't let him come inside your place
he'd behave himself—I know he would.

"So you see, Elmer, you're the only one that
can make him go straight—that's why I've
come back to you this second time. I reckon
he ain't so much to blame. You know—yes,
you've got reason to know better than anybody
else—that his father before him couldn't leave
playing cards alone. I hoped I could raise
Eddie different. As a little thing I used to tell
him playing cards were the devil's own play-
things. But it seems like he can't just help
it. I reckon it's in his blood."

"Whut you need then is a blood purifier,"
mocked the gamester. He pointed a long forefinger toward the drug store across the street.
"You'd better go on over yonder to Hinkle's

and git him some. I see they're advertisin' a new brand in their window—a dollar a bottle and a cure guaranteed or else you gits your money back. Better invest!"

He showed her his back as he turned to enter the Blue Jug. Pausing halfway through the swinging doors he spoke again, and since he still looked over her head perhaps he did not see the look that had come into her eyes or mark how her hands were clenching and unclenching. Or if he did see these things perhaps he did not care.

"That's all I've got to say to you," he added, "exceptin' this—I want this here to be the last time you come pesterin' me on the street."

"It will be," she said slowly, and her voice was steady although her meagre frame shook. "It's the last time I'm coming to you on the street, Elmer, for what's mine by rights."

"Then good-day to you." He disappeared.

She turned and went away, walking fast. Her name was Norfleet and she was a widow and alone in the world. Except for her son, who worked at Kattersmith Brothers' brick-yards as a helper for twelve dollars and a half a week, she had no kith or kin. She lived mainly by her needle, being a seamstress of sorts.

King Highpockets' establishment was the nearest approach to a gilded gambling hell— to quote a phrase current—that we had. But certainly it was not gilded, although possibly by some it might have been likened to a hell. Under the friendly cover of darkness you ascended a steep flight of creaky wooden steps and when you had reached the first landing you knocked at a locked wooden door. The lock slid back and the door opened a cautious inch or two and a little grinning negro, whose name was Babe Givens, peeped out at you through the opening. If you were the right person, or if you looked as though you might be the right person, Babe Givens opened the door wider and made way for you to enter.

Entering then, you found yourself in a big room furnished most simply with two tables and some chairs and several spittoons upon the floor, and a portable rack for poker checks and a dumbwaiter in a corner—and that was all. There was no safe, the proprietor deeming it the part of safety to carry his cash capital on his person. There was no white-uniformed attendant to bring you wine, should you thirst, and turkey sandwiches, if you hungered while at play. I have read that such as these are provided in all properly conducted gambling hells in the great city, but King Highpockets ran a sure-thing shop, not a restaurant. Drinks, when desired, were paid for in advance, and came from the bar below on the shelf of the creaking dumbwaiter, after Babe Givens had called the order down a tin speaking tube. There were no rugs upon the floor, no pictures against the walls. Except for the decks of cards, opened fresh at each sitting, there was nothing new or bright about the place. The King might move his entire outfit in one two-horse wagon and put no great strain upon the team. He might lose it altogether and be out of pocket not more than seventy-five dollars. In him the utilitarian triumphed above the purely artistic; himself, he was not pretty to look upon.

Of the two tables, one ordinarily was for poker and the other was for craps. The King banked both games, and sometimes took a hand in the poker game if conditions seemed propitious. Whether he played though or whether he didn't, he stood by always to lift a white chip out of each jackpot for a greedy and omnivorous kitty, whose mouth showed as a brassbound slot in the middle of the circular cover of dirty green baize. Trust him to minister to his kitty every pop. She was his pet and he loved her, and he never forgot her and her needs.

This night, though, the poker table lacked for tenants. The pay car had come and had dispensed of its delectable contents and had gone on south, and on this particular night most of the King's guests were railroad men. Railroad men being proverbially fond of quick action and plenty of it, the crap table had been drawn out into the middle of the room and here all activities centred. Here, too, the King presided, making change as occasion demanded from a mound of specie and a sheaf of currency in front of him—for all transactions were cash transactions and no chips used. While he did this his assistant, an alert individual called Grimes—or Jay Bird Grimes, for short—kept track of the swift-travelling dice and of the betting, which like the dice moved from left to right, round and round and round again.

Jay Bird had need to keep both his eyes wide open, for present players and prospective players were ringed four deep about the table. The smoke of their cigars and their cigarettes went upward to add stratified richness to the thick blue clouds that crawled in layers against the ceiling, and the sweat of their brows ran down their faces to drip in drops upon the table as one after another they claimed the dotted cubes and shook, rattled and rolled 'em, and snapped their finger in importunity, calling upon Big Dick or Phœbe Dice to come and to come right away. And then this one would fail to make his point and would lose his turn, and the overworked ivories would go into the snatching eager hand of that one who stood next him, and all the rest, waiting for their chance, would breathe hard, grunting in fancied imitation of negroes, and shouting out in a semi-hysterical fashion as the player passed or didn't pass.

A young freight conductor laid down a ten-dollar bill and the King covered it with another. The freight conductor ran that ten up to one

hundred and eighty dollars, ten or twenty at a
clip, then shot the whole amount and lost it;
then lost ninety more on top of that, and with
a white face and a quite empty pay envelope,
still held fast in a shaking left hand, fell back
out of the hunched-in, scrouging circle. But he
didn't go away; he stayed to watch the others,
envious of those who temporarily beat the game,
dismally sympathetic, with an unspoken fellow feeling, for those who, like him, went broke.
Josh Herron, the roundhouse foreman, dropped
half his month's wages before he decided that,
since luck plainly was not with him, he had had
about enough. A clerk from the timekeeper's
office shoved in, taking his place.

When he wasn't answering knocks at the
door Babe Givens circulated about the out-
skirts of the tightened group like a small, black
rabbit dog about a brush pile harbouring hares,
his eyes all china and his mouth all ivory. The
sound of those small squared bones clashing
together in their worn leather cup was music
to his Afric ears. The white man in the first
place stole this game from Babe's race, you know.

Babe had to answer knocks a good many
times. Newcomers kept on climbing the stair
and knuckling the door.

"Game's mighty full, genelmens—but they's
always room fur one mo'. Step right in and
wait yo' turn," Babe would say, ushering in the
latest arrival. Babe was almost as happy as
if he had been shooting himself.

As I say, they kept coming. At length, a few minutes before midnight, when the pile of silver under the King's hands had grown from a molehill to a mountain and the wadded paper money made a small shock of yellow-and-green fodder upon the green pasture of the table-top, came still another, and this one most strangely burdened. Very mousily indeed this eleventh-hour visitor ascended the steps, and first trying the doorknob, knocked with a fumbling knock against the pine panels.

Babe drew back the bolt and peered out into the darkness at the solitary figure dimly seen.

"Game's mighty full, genelmen," he began the formula of greeting, "but you kin——"

Babe began it but he never finished it. Something long and black, something slim and fearsome—yes, most fearsome—slid through the opening, and grazed his nose so that the little darky, stricken limp, fell back.

"Please, suh, boss," he begged, "fur Gawd's sake don't shoot—don't shoot!"

Babe started his prayer in a babble but he ended it with a shriek—a shriek so imploringly loud that all there, however intent they might be, were bound to hear and take notice. Over the heads of his patrons Highpockets looked, and he stiffened where he stood. They all looked; they all stiffened.

There was just cause. Inside the door opening was a masked figure levelling down a double-barrelled shotgun upon them. Lacking the

mask and the shotgun, and lacking, too, a
certain rigid and purposeful pose which was
most clearly defined in all its lines, the figure
would have lacked all menace, indeed would
have seemed to the casual eye a most impotent
and grotesque figure. For it was but little
better than five feet in stature and not overly
broad. It wore garments too loose for it by
many inches. The sleeve ends covered the
small hands to the finger ends, and the trousers
wrinkled, accordion fashion, to the tips of the
absurdly small toes. An old slouch hat threatened to slip all the way down over the wearer's
face. The mask was a flimsy thing of black
cambric, but the eyeholes, strange to say, were
neatly worked with buttonhole stitching. From
beneath the hatbrim at the back a hank of
longish hair escaped. On the floor, a yard or
so before the apparition where it had been
dropped, rested an ancient black handbag un-
latched and agape.

I am not meaning to claim that at the first
instant of looking the several astonished eyes
of the gathering in King Highpockets' place
comprehended all these details; it was the
general effect that they got; and it was that
shotgun which mainly made the difference in
their point of view. What they did note most
clearly—every man of them—was that the two
hammers of the gun stood erect, ready to drop,
and that a slim trigger finger played nervously
inside the trigger guard, and that the twin

muzzles, shifting and wavering like a pair of round hard eyes gazing every way at once, seemed to fix a threatening stare upon all of them and upon each of them. If the heavy gun shook a bit in the grip of its holder that but added to the common peril. Anyone there would have taken his dying oath that the thing aimed for his shrinking vitals and none other's.

"Hands up—up high! And keep 'em up!"

The command, given in a high-pitched key, was practically unnecessary. Automatically, as it were, all arms there had risen to full stretch, so that the clump of their motionless bodies was fronded at the top with open palms and tremulous outstretched fingers. But the arms of old King Highpockets rose above all the rest and his fingers shook the shakiest.

"If anybody moves an inch I'll shoot."

"That don't go for me—I ain't aimin' to move," murmured Josh Herron. Josh was scared all right, but he chuckled as he said it.

"Now—boy—you!"

The gun barrels dipped to the right an instant, including the detached form of Babe Givens in their swing.

"Yas, suh, boss, yas!"

"You put all that money in this grip sack here at my feet."

"W-w-which money, boss?"

"All the money that's there on that table yonder—every cent of it."

The little darky feared the man who paid

him his wages, but there were things in this world he feared more—masked faces and shot-guns, for example. His knees smote together and his teeth became as castanets which played in his jaws, as with rolling eyes and a skin like wet ashes he moved shudderingly to obey. Between the table and the valise he made two round trips, carrying the first time silver, the second time paper, and then, his task accomplished, he collapsed against the wall because his legs would no longer hold him up. For there was water in his knee joints and his feet were very cold.

Through this nobody spoke; only the eyes of the armed one watched vigilantly everywhere and the shotgun ranged the assemblage across its front and back again. Under his breath some one made moan, as the heaping double handful of green-and-yellow stuff was crumpled down into the open-mawed bag. It might have been Highpockets who moaned.

"Now then," bade the robber, when the paper had gone to join the silver, "anybody here who's lost his money to-night or any other night can come and get it back. But come one at a time—and come mighty slow and careful."

Curiously enough only two came—the young freight conductor and the youth who was a clerk in the time-keeper's office at the yards.

Shamefacedly the freight conductor stooped, flinching away from the gun muzzles which

pointed almost in his right ear, and picked out
certain bills.

"I lost an even hundred—more'n I can afford
to lose," he mumbled. "I'm takin' just my
own hundred." He retired rearward after the
manner of a crab.

The boy wore an apologetic air as he salvaged
twenty-two dollars from the cache. After he
had crawfished back to the table where the
others were, none else offered to stir.

"Anybody else?" inquired the collector of loot.

"Well, I squandered a little coin here this
evenin', but I'm satisfied," spoke Josh Herron,
now grinning openly. "I'm gittin' my money's
worth." He glanced sidewise toward the suffering proprietor.

"All done?"

Nobody answered.

"Here, boy, come here then!"

Babe Givens came—upon his knees.

"Close that bag."

Babe fumbled the rusted claps shut.

"Now, shove it up close to me along the
floor."

Babe, he shoved it.

"Now get back yonder where you were."

I leave it to you whether Babe got back yonder.

The figure swooped downward briskly, and
two fingers of the hand which gripped the fore-
arm of the gun caught in the looped handles
of the black bag and brought it up dangling
and heavy laden.

And now the custodian of these delectable spoils was backing toward the door, but still with weapon poised and ready.

"Stay right where you are for five minutes," was the final warning from behind the cambric mask. "Five minutes, remember! Anybody who tries to come down those steps before that five minutes is up is going to get shot."

The door slammed. Through the closed door the crap-shooters, each in his place and all listening as intently as devout worshippers in a church, heard the swift footsteps dying away. Josh Herron brought down his arms and took two steps forward.

"Wait, Josh, the time limit ain't up yit," counselled a well-wisher.

"Oh, I ain't goin' nowheres jest yit—I'm very comfortable here," said Josh. He stooped and seemed to pick up some small object from the bare planks.

Five minutes later—or perhaps six—a procession moving cautiously, silently and in single file passed down the creaky stairs. It was noted—and commented upon—that the owner of the raided place, heaviest loser and chief mourner though he was, tagged away back at the tail of the line. Only Babe Givens was behind him, and Babe was well behind him too. At the foot of the stairs the frontmost man projected his head forth into the night, an inch at a time, ready to jerk it back again. But to his inquiring vision Franklin Street under its gas lamps yawned as empty as a new made grave.

For some unuttered and indefinable reason practically all of the present company felt in a mood promptly to betake themselves home. On his homeward way Josh Herron travelled in the company of a sorely shaken grocery clerk, and between them they, going up the street, discussed the startling episode in which they had just figured.

"Lookin' down that pair of barrels certainly made a true believer out of old Highpockets, didn't it?" said the grocer's clerk, when the event had been gone over verbally from its beginning to its end. "Did you happen to see, Josh, how slow he poked his old head out past them doorjambs even after Jasper Waller told him the coast was clear? Put me in mind of one of these here old snappin'-turtles comin' out of his shell after a skeer. Well, I had a little touch of the buck-ager myself," he confessed.

"It was sorter up to our long-laiged friend to be a little bit careful," said Josh Herron. "Coupled up the way he is, one buckshot would be liable to go through his gizzard and his lights at the same time."

A little later the grocery clerk spoke, in reference to a certain quite natural curiosity which seemingly lay at the top of his thoughts, since he had voiced it at least three times within the short space of one city block:

"I wonder who that there runty hold-up could 'a' been?"

"Yes, I wonder?" repeated Josh Herron in a peculiar voice.

"He certainly took a long chance, whoever he was—doin' the whole job single handed," continued the grocery clerk. "Well, I ain't begrudgin' him the eight dollars of mine that he packed off with him, seein' as how he stripped old Highpockets as clean as a whistle. And he couldn't 'a' been nothin' but a half-grown boy neither, judgin' from his build."

"Boy—hell! Say, Oscar, are you as blind as the rest of that crowd?" asked Josh Herron, coming to a halt beneath a corner gas lamp. "Was you so skeered, too, you couldn't see a thing that was right there before your eyes as plain as day?"

"What you talkin' about?" demanded the other. "If it wasn't a boy, what was it—a dwarf?"

"Oscar, kin you keep a secret?" asked Josh Herron, grinning happily. "Yes? Then look here."

He opened his right hand. Across the palm of it lay a bent wire hairpin.

It is possible that Oscar, the grocer's clerk, did know how to keep a secret. As to that I would not presume to speak. Conceding that he did, it is equally certain that some persons did not possess the same gift of reticence. By noon of the following day, practically all who had ears to hear with had heard in one guise or another the story of those midnight proceedings upstairs over the Blue Jug. It was inevitable that the editor of the *Daily Evening News* should hear it, too, which he did—from a dozen different sources and by a dozen differing versions. For publication at least the distressed Highpockets had nothing to say. All things being considered, this was but natural, as you will concede.

Naturally, also, none might be found in all the width and breadth of the municipality who would confess to having been an eye witness to the despoiling operations, because if you admitted so much it followed in the same breath you convicted yourself of being a frequenter of gaming establishments, and, moreover, of being one of a considerable number of large, strong men who had suffered themselves to be coerced by one diminutive bandit. So, lacking authoritative facts to go upon, and names of individuals with which to buttress his statements, Editor Tompkins, employing his best humorous vein, wrote and caused to be printed an account veiled and vague, but not so very heavily veiled at that and not so vague but that one who knew a thing or two might guess out the riddle of his tale.

Coincidentally, certain other things happened which might or might not bear a relationship to the main event. Old Mrs. Postelwaite received by mail, in an unmarked envelope and from an unknown donor, three hundred and odd dollars—no great fortune in itself, but a sum amply sufficient to pay off the mortgage on her small birdbox of a dwelling, and so save the place which she called home from foreclosure at the instigation of the Building & Loan Company. Since little Mrs. Shetler, who lived out on Wheelis Street, had no present source of income other than what she derived by taking subscription orders for literary works which nobody cared to read and few, except through a spirit of compassion for Mrs. Shetler, cared to buy, it seemed fair to assume that from like mysterious agencies she acquired the exact amount of her husband's shortage, then owing to Kattersmith Brothers, his recent employers. This amount being duly turned over to that firm the fugitive was enabled to return from his hiding and, rehabilitated, to assume his former place in the community. For the first time in months little Mrs. Shetler wore a smile upon her face and carried her head erect when she went abroad. Seeing that smile you would have said yourself that it was worth every cent of the money.

The Widow Norfleet, seamstress, squared up her indebtedness with divers neighbourhood tradesmen, and paid up her back house rent, and after doing all this still had enough ready cash left to provide winter time garments for herself and a new suit for her threadbare son Eddie. Finally, Mrs. Matilda Weeks, who constituted in herself an unofficial but highly efficient local charity organisation, discovered on a certain morning when she awoke that, during the night, some kindly soul had shoved under her front door a plain Manila wrapper, containing merely a line of writing on a sheet of cheap, blue-ruled notepaper: "For the poor people," and nearly three hundred dollars in bills—merely that, and nothing more. It was exactly in keeping with Mrs. Weeks' own peculiar mode of philanthropy that she should accept this anonymous gift and make use of it without asking any questions whatsoever.

"I think, by all accounts, it must be tainted money," said Mrs. Weeks, "but I don't know any better way of making dirty money clean than by doing a little good with it."

So she kept the donation intact against the coming of the Christmas, and then she devoted it to filling many Christmas dinner baskets and many Christmas stockings for the families of shanty-boaters, whose floating domiciles clustered like a flock of very disreputable water fowl down by the willows, below town, these shiftless river gypsies being included among Mrs. Weeks' favourite wards.

Meanwhile, for upward of a week after the hold-up no steps of whatsoever nature were taken by the members of the police force. For the matter of that, no steps which might be called authoritative or in strict accordance with the statutes made and provided were ever taken by them or any one of them. But one evening the acting head of the department went forth upon a private mission. Our regular chief, Gabe Henley, was laid up that fall, bedfast with inflammatory rheumatism, and the fact of his being for the time an invalid may possibly help to explain a good deal, seeing that Gabe had the name for both honesty and earnestness in the discharge of his duties, even if he did fall some degrees short of the mental stature of an intellectual giant.

So it was the acting chief—he resigned shortly thereafter, as I recall—who took it upon himself to pay a sort of domiciliary visit to the three-room cottage where the Widow Norfleet lived with her son Eddie and took in sewing. He bore no warrant qualifying him for violent entry, search of the premises or seizure of the person, and perhaps that was why he made no effort to force his way within the little house; or maybe he desired only to put a few pointed questions to the head of the house. So while he stood at the locked front door, knocking until his knuckles stung him and his patience had become quite utterly exhausted, a woman let herself out at the back of the house and ran bareheaded through an alley which opened into Clay Street, Clay Street being the next street to the west. When she returned home again at the end of perhaps half an hour a peep through a hooded and shuttered front window revealed to her that the brass-buttoned caller had departed.

It was the next morning, to follow with
chronological exactitude the sequence of this
narrative, that our efficient young commonwealth's attorney, Jerome G. Flournoy, let
himself into the chambers of the circuit judge.
Mr. Flournoy wore between his brows a little
V of perplexity. But Judge Priest, whom he
found sitting by a grate fire stoking away at
his cob pipe, appeared to have not a single care
concealed anywhere about his person. Certainly his forehead was free of those wrinkles
which are presumed to denote troublesomeness
of thought on the inside.

"Judge," began Mr. Flournoy, without any
prolonged preliminaries, "I'm afraid I'm going
to have to take up that Blue Jug affair. And
I do hate mightily to do it, seeing what the
consequences are liable to be. So I thought
I'd talk it over with you first, if you don't
mind."

"Son," whined Judge Priest, and to Mr.
Flournoy it seemed that the phantom shadow
of a wink rested for the twentieth part of a
second on the old judge's left eyelid, "speakin'
officially, it's barely possible that I don't know
whut case you have reference to."

"Well, unofficially then, you're bound to
have heard the talk that's going round town,"
said Mr. Flournoy. "Nobody's talked of
anything else much this past week, so far as
I've been able to notice. Just between you
and me, Judge, I made up my mind, right from

the first, that unless it was crowded on me I wasn't going to take cognisance of the thing at all. That's the principal reason why I haven't mentioned the subject in your presence before now. As a private citizen, it struck me that that short-waisted crook got exactly what was coming to him, especially as I never heard of bad money being put to better purposes. But aside from what he lost in cash—and I reckon he doesn't think any more of a silver dollar than you do of both your legs—it made him the laughing stock of twenty thousand people, and more particularly after the true inside facts began to circulate."

"Now that you mention it, son," remarked Judge Priest blandly, "it strikes me that I did ketch the distant sound of gigglin' here and there durin' the past few days."

"That's just it—the giggling must've got under the scoundrel's hide finally. I gather that at the beginning Magee made up his mind to keep his mouth shut and just take his medicine. But I figure him for the kind that can't stand being laughed at very long—and his own gang have just naturally been laughing him to death all week. Anyhow, he came to my house to-day right after breakfast, and called on me as the commonwealth's attorney to put the facts before the Grand Jury when it convenes next Monday for the fall term. He's even willing to testify himself, he says. And he says he can prove what went with the money that he lost

that night—or most of it—and what became
of the rest of it.

"That's not all, Judge, either. Right on
top of that, when I got down to my office I
found a letter from Mrs. Hetty Norfleet, saying she had nothing to conceal from the duly
sworn officers of the law, and that she was
perfectly willing to answer any charges that
might be made against her, and that she would
come to me and make a full statement any time
I wanted her to come. Or substantially that,"
amended Mr. Flournoy, with the lawyer's
instinct.

"Is that possible?" quoth the judge in tones
of a mild surprise. With his thumb he tamped
down the smoulder in his pipe. The job appeared
to require care; certainly it required full half
a minute of time. When next he spoke he had
entirely departed from the main line of the
topic in hand.

"I reckin, son, you never knowed little Gil
Nickolas, did you? No, 'taint in reason that
you would. He died long before your time.
Let's see—he must've died way back yonder
about eighteen-sixty-nine, or maybe 'twas
eighteen-seventy? He got hisself purty badly
shot up at Chickamauga and never did entirely git over it. Well, sir, that there little
Gil Nickolas wasn't much bigger than a cake
of lye soap after a hard day's washin', but let
me tell you, he was a mighty gallant soldier
of the late Southern Confederacy. I know he

was because we both served together in old
Company B—the first company that went out
of this town after the fussin' started. Yes,
suh, he shorely was a spunky little raskil. I
reckin he belonged to a spunky outfit—I never
knowed one of his breed yit that didn't have
more sand, when it come right down to cases,
than you could load onto a hoss and waggin."
Again he paused to minister to the spark of life
in his pipe bowl. "I recall one time, the first
year of the war, me and Gil was out on a kind
of a foragin' trip together and——"

"I beg your pardon, Judge Priest," broke
in Mr. Flournoy a trifle stiffly, "but I was
speaking of the trouble Mrs. Hetty Norfleet's
gotten herself into."

"I know you was," assented Judge Priest,
"and that's whut put me in mind of little Gil
Nickolas. He was her paw. I ain't seen much
of her here of recent years, but I reckin she's
had a purty toler'ble hard time of it. Her husband wasn't much account ez I remember him
in his lifetime."

"She has had a hard time of it—mighty
hard," assented Mr. Flournoy, "and that's one
of the things that makes my job all the harder
for me."

"How so?" inquired Judge Priest.

"Because," expounded Mr. Flournoy, "now,
I suppose, I've got to put her under arrest and
bring her to trial. In a way of speaking Magee
has got the law on his side. Certainly he's got

the right to call on me to act. On the surface
of things the police are keeping out of it—I
reckon we both know why—and so it's being
put up to me. Magee points out, very truly,
that it's a felony charge anyhow, and that even
if his dear friend, the acting chief, should start
the ball rolling, in the long run, sooner or later,
the case would be bound to land in circuit
court."

"And whut then?" asked Judge Priest.

"Oh, nothing much," said Mr. Flournoy
bitterly, "nothing much, except that if that
poor little woman confesses—and I judge by the
tone of her letter she's ready to do just that—
anyway, everybody in town knows by now
that she was the one that held up that joint of
Magee's at the point of a shotgun—why the
jurors, under their oaths, are bound to bring
in a verdict of guilty, no matter how they may
feel about it personally. Magee has about
reached the point where he'd risk a jail term for
himself to see her sentenced to the penitentiary.
Judge Priest, I'd almost rather resign my office
than be the means of seeing that poor, little,
plucky woman convicted for doing the thing
she has done."

"Wait a minute, son! Hold your hosses and
wait a minute!" put in the judge. "Mebbe it
won't be absolutely necessary fur you to up and
resign so abrupt. Your valuable services are
needed round this courthouse."

"What's that you say, Judge?" asked the

young prosecutor, straightening his body out of the despondent curve into which he had looped it.

"I says, wait a minute and don't be so proneful to jump at conclusions," repeated and amplified the older man. "You go and jump at a conclusion that-away and you're liable to skeer the poor thing half to death. I've been lettin' you purceed ahead because I wanted to git your views on this little matter before I stuck my own paddle into the kittle. But now let's you and me see ef there ain't another side to this here proposition."

"I'm listening, your Honour," said Flournoy, mystified but somehow cheered.

"Well, then!" The judge raised his right arm ready to emphasise each point he made with a wide swing of the hand which held the pipe. "Under the laws of this state gamblin' in whatsoever form ain't permitted, recognised, countenanced nor suffered. That's so, ain't it, son? To be shore, the laws as they read at present sometimes seem insufficient somehow to prevent the same, and I hope to see them corrected in that reguard, but the intent is plain enough that, in the eye of the law, public gamblin' es sech does not go on anywhere within the confines of this commonwealth. You agree with me there, don't you?"

"May it please the court, I agree with you there," said Flournoy happily, beginning, he thought, to see the light breaking through.

"All right then—so fur so good. Now then, sech bein' the situation, we may safely assume, I reckin, that within the purview and the written meanin' of the statute, gamblin'—common gamblin'—don't exist a-tall. It jest natchally ain't. Understand me, I'm speaking accordin' to a strict legal construction of the issue. And so, ef gamblin' don't exist there couldn't 'a' been no gamblin' goin' on upstairs over the Blue Jug saloon and restauraw on the night in question. In fact, ef you carry the point out to its logical endin' there couldn't 'a' been no night in question neither. In any event, ef the person Magee could by any chance prove he was there, in the said place, on the said date, at the said time, it would appear that he was present fur the purpose of evadin' and defyin' the law, and so ef somebody ostensibly and apparently seemed to happen along and did by threat and duress deprive him of somethin' of seemin' value, he still wouldn't have no standin' in court because he couldn't come with clean hands hisse'f to press the charge.

"But there ain't no need to go into that phase and aspect of the proposition because we know now that, legally, he wasn't even there. Not bein' there, of course he wasn't engaged in carryin' on a game of chance. Not bein' so engaged, it stands to reason he didn't lose nothin' of value. Ef he states otherwise we are bound to believe him to be a victim of a diseased and an overwrought mind. And so there, I take it, is the way it stands, so fur ez you are concerned, Mister Flournoy. You can't ask a Grand Jury to return an indictment ag'inst a figment of the imagination, kin you? Why, boy, they'd laugh at you."

"I certainly can't, Judge," agreed the young man blithely. "I don't know how the venerable gentlemen composing the court of last resort in this state would look upon the issue if it were carried up to them on appeal, but for my purposes you've stated the law beautifully." He was grinning broadly as he stood up and reached for his hat and his gloves. "I'm going now to break the blow to our long-legged friend."

"Whilst you're about it you mout tell him somethin' else," stated his superior. "In fact, you mout let the word seep round sort of promiscuous-like that I'm aimin' to direct the special attention of the next Grand Jury to the official conduct of certain members of the police force of our fair little city. Ez regards the suppressin' and the punishin' of common gamblers, the law appears to be sort of loopholey at present; but mebbe ef we investigated the activities, or the lack of same, on the part of divers of our sworn peace officers, we mout be able to scotch the snake a little bit even ef we can't kill it outright. Anyway, I'm willin' to try the experiment. I reckin there's quite a number would be interested in hearin' them tidin's ef you're a mind to put 'em into circulation. Personally, I'm impressed with the idea that our civic atmosphere needs clarifyin' somewhut. All graftin' is hateful but it seems to me the little cheap graftin' that goes on sometimes in a small community is about the nastiest kind of graft there is. Don't you agree with me there?"

"Judge Priest," stated Mr. Flournoy from the threshold, "I've about made up my mind that I'm always going to agree with you."

Inside of two hours the commonwealth's attorney returned from his errand, apparently much exalted of spirit.

"Say, Judge," he proclaimed as he came through the door, "I imagine it won't be necessary for you to take the steps you were mentioning a while ago."

"No?"

"No, siree. Once I'd started it I judge the news must've spread pretty fast. Outside on the Square, as I was on my way back up here from downtown, Beck Giltner waylaid me to ask me to tell you for him that he was going to close down his game and try to make a living some other way. I'm no deep admirer of the life, works and character of Beck Giltner, but I'll say this much for him—he keeps his promise once he's made it. I'd take his word before I'd take the word of a lot of people who wouldn't speak to him on the street.

"And we're going to lose our uncrowned king. Yes, sir, Highpockets the First is pre-

paring to leave us flat. After hearing what I
had to tell him, he said in a passionate sort of
way that a man might as well quit a community
where he can't get justice. I gather that he's
figuring on pulling his freight for some more
populous spot where he can enjoy a wider field
of endeavour and escape the vulgar snickers
of the multitude. He spoke of Chicago."

"Ah, hah!" said Judge Priest; and then after
a little pause: "Well, Jerome, my son, ef I
have to give up any member of this here community I reckin Mister Highpockets Elmer
Magee, Esquire, is probably the one I kin spare
the easiest. When is he aimin' to go from us?"

"Right away, I think, from what he said."

"Well," went on Judge Priest, "ef so be you
should happen to run acros't him ag'in before
he takes his departure from amongst us you
mout—in strict confidence, of course—tell him
somethin' else. He mout care to ponder on it
while he is on his way elsewhere. That there
old scattergun, which he looked down the barrels
of it the other night, wasn't loaded."

"Wasn't loaded? Whee!" chortled Mr.
Flournoy. "Well, of all the good jokes——"
He caught himself: "Say, Judge, how did you
know it wasn't loaded?"

"Why, she told me, son—the Widder Norfleet told me so last night. You see she come
runnin' over the back way from her house to
my place—I glean somethin' had happened
which made her think the time had arrived to

put herself in touch with sech of the authorities ez she felt she could trust—and she detailed the whole circumstances to me. 'Twas me suggested to her that she'd better write you that there letter. In fact, you mout say I sort of dictated its gin'ral tenor. I told her that you ez the prosecutor was the one that'd be most interested in hearin' any formal statement she mout care to make, and so——"

Mr. Flournoy slumped down into a handy chair and ran some fingers through his hair.

"Then part of the joke is on me too," he owned.

"I wouldn't go so fur ez to say that," spake Judge Priest soothingly. "Frum where I'm settin' it looks to me like the joke is mainly on quite a number of people."

"And the shotgun wasn't loaded?" Seemingly Mr. Flournoy found it hard to credit his own ears.

"It didn't have nary charge in ary barrel," reaffirmed the old man. "That little woman had the spunk to go up there all alone by herse'f and bluff a whole roomful of grown men, but she didn't dare to load up her old fusee—said she didn't know how, in the first place, and, in the second place, she was skeered it mout go off and hurt somebody. Jerome, ain't that fur all the world jest like a woman?"

IX

A BEAUTIFUL EVENING

THERE was a sound, heard in the early hours of a Sunday morning, that used to bother strangers until they got used to it. It started usually along about half past five or six o'clock and it kept up interminably—so it seemed to them—a monotonous, jarring thump-thump, thump-thump that was like the far-off beating of African tomtoms; but at breakfast, when the beaten biscuits came upon the table, throwing off a steamy hot halo of their own goodness, the aliens knew what it was that had roused them, and, unless they were dyspeptics by nature, felt amply recompensed for those lost hours of beauty sleep.

In these degenerate days I believe there is a machine that accomplishes the same purpose noiselessly by a process of rolling and crushing, which no doubt is efficacious; but it seems somehow to take the poetry out of the operation. Judge Priest, and the reigning black deity of his kitchen, would have naught of it. So long as his digestion survived and her good right arm held out to endure, there would be real beaten biscuits for the judge's Sunday morning breakfast. And so, having risen with the dawn, Aunt Dilsey, wielding a maul-headed tool of whittled wood, would pound the dough with rhythmic strokes until it was as plastic as sculptor's modelling clay and as light as eiderdown, full of tiny hills and hollows, in which small yeasty bubbles rose and spread and burst like foam globules on the flanks of gentle wavelets. Then, with her master hand, she would roll it thin and cut out the small round disks and delicately pink each one with a fork— and then, if you were listening, you could hear the stove door slam like the smacking of an iron lip.

On a Sunday morning I have in mind, Judge Priest woke with the first premonitory thud from the kitchen, and he was up and dressed in his white linens and out upon the wide front porch while the summer day was young and unblemished. The sun was not up good yet. It made a red glow, like a barn afire, through the treetops looking eastward. Lie-abed blackbirds were still talking over family matters in the maples that clustered round the house, and in the back yard Judge Priest's big red rooster hoarsely circulated gossip in regard to a certain little brown hen, first crowing out the news loudly and then listening, with his head on one side, while the rooster in the next yard took it up and repeated it to a rooster living farther along, as is the custom among male scandalisers the world over. Upon the lawn the little gossamer hammocks that the grass spiders had seamed together overnight were spangled with dew, so that each out-thrown thread was a glittering rosary and the centre of each web a silken, cushioned jewel casket. Likewise each web was outlined in white mist, for the cottonwood trees were shedding down their podded product so thickly that across open spaces the slanting lines of drifting fibre looked like snow. It would be hot enough after a while, but now the whole world was sweet and fresh and washed clean.

It impressed Judge Priest so. He lowered his bulk into a rustic chair made of hickory withes that gave to his weight, and put his thoughts upon breakfast and the goodness of the day; but presently, as he sat there, he saw something that set a frown between his eyes.

He saw, coming down Clay Street, upon the opposite side, an old man—a very feeble old man—who was tall and thin and dressed in sombre black. The man was lame—he dragged one leg along with the hitching gait of the paralytic. Travelling with painful slowness, he came on until he reached the corner above.

Then automatically he turned at right angles and left the narrow wooden sidewalk and crossed the dusty road. He passed Judge Priest's, looking neither to the right nor the left, and so kept on until he reached the corner below. Still following an invisible path in the deep-furrowed dust, he crossed again to the far side. Just as he got there his halt leg seemed to give out altogether and for a minute or two he stood holding himself up by a fumbling grip upon the slats of a tree box before he went laboriously on, a figure of pain and weakness in the early sunshine that was now beginning to slant across his path and dapple his back with checkerings of shadow and light.

This manœuvre was inexplicable—a stranger would have puzzled to make it out. The shade was as plentiful upon one side of Clay Street as upon the other; each sagged wooden sidewalk was in as bad repair as its brother over the way. The small, shabby frame house, buried in honeysuckles and balsam vines, which stood close up to the pavement line on the opposite side of Clay Street, facing Judge Priest's roomy, rambling old home, had no flag of pestilence at its door or its window. And surely to this lone pedestrian every added step must have been an added labour. A stranger would never have understood it; but Judge Priest understood it—he had seen that same thing repeated countless times in the years that stretched behind him. Always it had distressed him inwardly, but on this particular morning it distressed him more than ever. The toiling grim figure in black had seemed so feeble and so tottery and old.

Well, Judge Priest was not exactly what you would call young. With an effort he heaved himself up out of the depths of his hickory chair and stood at the edge of his porch, polishing a pink dome of forehead as though trying to make up his mind to something. Jefferson Poindexter, resplendent in starchy white jacket and white apron, came to the door.

"Breakfus' served, suh!" he said, giving to an announcement touching on food that glamour of grandeur of which his race alone enjoys the splendid secret.

"Hey?" asked the judge absently.

"Breakfus'—hit's on the table waitin', suh," stated Jeff. "Mizz Polks sent over her houseboy with a dish of fresh razberries fur yore breakfus'; and she say to tell you, with her and Mistah Polkses' compliments, they is fresh picked out of her garden—specially fur you."

The lady and gentleman to whom Jeff had reference were named Polk, but in speaking of white persons for whom he had a high regard Jeff always, wherever possible within the limitations of our speech, tacked on that final *s*. It was in the nature of a delicate verbal compliment, implying that the person referred to was worthy of enlargement and pluralisation.

Alone in the cool, high-ceiled, white-walled

dining room, Judge Priest ate his breakfast mechanically. The raspberries were pink beads of sweetness; the young fried chicken a poem in delicate and flaky browns; the spoon bread could not have been any better if it had tried; and the beaten biscuits were as light as snow-flakes and as ready to melt on the tongue; as symmetrical too as poker-chips, and like poker-chips, subject to a sudden disappearance from in front of one; but Judge Priest spoke hardly a word all through the meal. Jeff, going out to the kitchen for the last course, said to Aunt Dilsey:

"Ole boss-man seem lak he's got somethin' on his mind worryin' him this mawnin'."

When Jeff returned, with a turn of crisp waffles in one hand and a pitcher of cane sirup in the other, he stared in surprise, for the dining room was empty and he could hear his employer creaking down the hall. Jeff just naturally hated to see good hot waffles going to waste. He ate them himself, standing up; and they gave him a zest for his regular breakfast, which followed in due course of time.

From the old walnut hatrack, with its white-tipped knobs that stood just inside the front door, the judge picked up a palmleaf fan; and he held the fan slantwise as a shield for his eyes and his bare head against the sun's glare as he went down the porch steps and passed out of his own yard, traversed the empty street and strove with the stubborn gate latch of the little house that faced his own. It was a poor-looking little house, and its poorness had extended to its surroundings—as if poverty was a contagion that spread. In Judge Priest's yard, now, the grass, though uncared for, yet grew thick and lush; but here, in this small yard, there were bare, shiny spots of earth showing through the grass—as though the soil itself was out at elbows and the nap worn off its green-velvet coat; but the vines about the porch were thick enough for an ambuscade and from behind their green screen came a voice in hospitable recognition.

"Is that you, Judge? Well, suh, I'm glad to see you! Come right in; take a seat and sit down and rest yourself."

The speaker showed himself in the arched opening of the vine barrier—an old man—not quite so old, perhaps, as the judge. He was in his shirtsleeves. There was a patch upon one of the sleeves. His shoes had been newly shined, but the job was poorly done; the leather showed a dulled black upon the toes and a weathered yellow at the sides and heels. As he spoke his voice ran up and down—the voice of a deaf person who cannot hear his own words clearly, so that he pitches them in a false key. For added proof of this affliction he held a lean and slightly tremulous hand cupped behind his ear.

The other hand he extended in greeting as the old judge mounted the step of the low porch.

The visitor took one of two creaky wooden rockers that stood in the narrow space behind the balsam vines, and for a minute or two he sat without speech, fanning himself. Evidently these neighbourly calls between these two old men were not uncommon; they could enjoy the communion of silence together without embarrassment.

The town clocks struck—first the one on the city hall struck eight times sedately, and then, farther away, the one on the county courthouse. This one struck five times slowly, hesitated a moment, struck eleven times with great vigour, hesitated again, struck once with a big, final boom, and was through. No amount of repairing could cure the courthouse clock of this peculiarity. It kept the time, but kept it according to a private way of its own. Immediately after it ceased the bell on the Catholic church, first and earliest of the Sunday bells, began tolling briskly. Judge Priest waited until its clamouring had died away.

"Goin' to be good and hot after 'while," he said, raising his voice.

"What say?"

"I say it's goin' to be mighty warm a little later on in the day," repeated Judge Priest.

"Yes, suh; I reckon you're right there," assented the host. "Just a minute ago, before you came over, I was telling Liddie she'd find it middlin' close in church this morning. She's going, though—runaway horses wouldn't keep

her away from church! I'm not going myself
—seems as though I'm getting more and more
out of the church habit here lately."

Judge Priest's eyes squinted in whimsical
appreciation of this admission. He remembered
that the other man, during the lifetime of his
second wife, had been a regular attendant at
services—going twice on Sundays and to
Wednesday night prayer meetings too; but
the second wife had been dead going on four
years now—or was it five? Time sped so!

The deaf man spoke on:

"So I just thought I'd sit here and try to
keep cool and wait for that little Ledbetter boy
to come round with the Sunday paper. Did
you read last Sunday's paper, Judge? Colonel
Watterson certainly had a mighty fine piece
on those Northern money devils. It's round
here somewhere—I cut it out to keep it. I'd
like to have you read it and pass your opinion
on it. These young fellows do pretty well,
but there's none of them can write like the
colonel, in my judgment."

Judge Priest appeared not to have heard him.

"Ed Tilghman," he said abruptly in his high,
fine voice, that seemed absurdly out of place,
coming from his round frame, "you and me
have lived neighbours together a good while,
ain't we? We've been right acros't the street
frum one another all this time. It kind of jolts
me sometimes when I git to thinkin' how many
years it's really been; because we're gittin'

along right smartly in years—all us old fellows are. Ten years frum now, say, there won't be so many of us left." He glanced sidewise at the lean, firm profile of his friend. "You're younger than some of us; but, even so, you ain't exactly whut I'd call a young man yourse'f."

Avoiding the direct questioning gaze that his companion turned on him at this, the judge reached forward and touched a ripe balsam apple that dangled in front of him. Instantly it split, showing the gummed red seeds clinging to the inner walls of the sensitive pod.

"I'm listening to you, Judge," said the deaf man.

For a moment the old judge waited. There was about him almost an air of diffidence. Still considering the ruin of the balsam apple, he spoke, and it was with a sort of hurried anxiety, as though he feared he might be checked before he said what he had to say:

"Ed, I was settin' on my porch a while ago waitin' fur breakfast, and your brother came by." He shot a quick, apprehensive glance at his silent auditor. Except for a tautened flickering of the muscles about the mouth, there was no sign that the other had heard him. "Your brother Abner came by," repeated the judge, "and I set over yonder on my porch and watched him pass. Ed, Abner's gittin' mighty feeble! He jest about kin drag himself along—he's had another stroke lately, they tell me. He had to hold on to that there treebox down yonder, stiddyin' himself after he cross't back over to this side. Lord knows what he was doin' draggin' downtown on a Sunday mornin'—force of habit, I reckin. Anyway he certainly did look older and more poorly than ever I saw him before. He's a failin' man ef I'm any judge. Do you hear me plain?" he asked.

"I hear you," said his neighbour in a curiously flat voice. It was Tilghman's turn to avoid the glances of his friend. He stared straight ahead of him through a rift in the vines.

"Well, then," went on Judge Priest, "here's whut I've got to say to you, Ed Tilghman. You know as well as I do that I've never pried into your private affairs, and it goes mightily ag'inst the grain fur me to be doin' so now; but, Ed, when I think of how old we're all gittin' to be, and when the Camp meets and I see you settin' there side by side almost, and yit never seemin' to see each other—and this mornin' when I saw Abner pass, lookin' so gaunted and sick—and it sech a sweet, ca'm mornin' too, and everythin' so quiet and peaceful——" He broke off and started anew. "I don't seem to know exactly how to put my thoughts into words—and puttin' things into words is supposed to be my trade too. Anyway I couldn't go to Abner. He's not my neighbour and you are; and besides, you're the youngest of the two. So—so I came over here to you. Ed, I'd like mightily to take some word frum you to your brother Abner. I'd like to do it the best in the world! Can't I go to him with a message frum you—to-day? To-morrow might be too late!"

He laid one of his pudgy hands on the bony knee of the deaf man; but the hand slipped away as Tilghman stood up.

"Judge Priest," said Tilghman, looking down at him, "I've listened to what you've had to say; and I didn't stop you, because you are my friend and I know you mean well by it. Besides, you're my guest, under my own roof." He stumped back and forth in the narrow confines of the porch. Otherwise he gave no sign of any emotion that might be astir within him, his face being still set and his voice flat. "What's between me and my—what's between me and that man you just named always will be between us. He's satisfied to let things go on as they are. I'm satisfied to let them go on. It's in our breed, I guess. Words—just words —wouldn't help mend this thing. The reason for it would be there just the same, and neither one of us is going to be able to forget that so long as we both live. I'd just as lief you never brought this—this subject up again. If you went to him I presume he'd tell you the same thing. Let it be, Judge Priest—it's past mending. We two have gone on this way for fifty years nearly. We'll keep on going on so. I appreciate your kindness, Judge Priest; but let it be—let it be!"

There was finality miles deep and fixed as basalt in his tone. He checked his walk and called in at a shuttered window.

"Liddie," he said in his natural up-and-down voice, "before you put off for church, couldn't you mix up a couple of lemonades or something? Judge Priest is out here on the porch with me."

"No," said Judge Priest, getting slowly up, "I've got to be gittin' back before the sun's up too high. Ef I don't see you ag'in meanwhile be shore to come to the next regular meetin' of the Camp—on Friday night," he added.

"I'll be there," said Tilghman. "And I'll try to find that piece of Colonel Watterson's and send it over to you. I'd like mightily for you to read it."

He stood at the opening in the vines, with one slightly palsied hand fumbling at a loose tendril as the judge passed down the short yard-walk and out at the gate. Then he went back to his chair and sat down again. All the little muscles in his jowls were jumping.

Clay Street was no longer empty. Looking down its dusty length from beneath the shelter of his palmleaf fan, Judge Priest saw here and there groups of children—the little girls in prim and starchy white, the little boys hobbling in the Sunday torment of shoes and stockings; and all of them moving toward a common centre—Sunday school. Twice again that day would the street show life—a little later when grown-ups went their way to church, and again just after the noonday dinner, when young people and servants, carrying trays and dishes under napkins, would cross and recross from one house to another. The Sunday interchange of special dainties between neighbours amounted to a ceremonial; but after that, until the cool of the evening, the town would simmer in quiet, while everybody took a Sunday nap.

With his fan, Judge Priest made an angry sawing motion in the air, as though trying to fend off something disagreeable—a memory, perhaps, or it might have been only a persistent midge. There were plenty of gnats and midges about, for by now—even so soon—the dew was dried. The leaves of the silver poplars were turning their white under sides up like countless frog bellies, and the long, podded pendants of the Injun-cigar trees hung dangling and still. It would be a hot day, sure enough; already the judge felt wilted and worn out.

In our town we had our tragedies that endured for years and, in the small-town way, finally became institutions. There was the case of the Burnleys. For thirty-odd years old Major Burnley lived on one side of his house and his wife lived on the other, neither of them ever crossing an imaginary dividing line that ran down the middle of the hall, having for their medium of intercourse all that time a lean, spinster daughter, in whose grey and barren life churchwork and these strange home duties took the place that Nature had intended to be filled by a husband and by babies and grand-babies.

There was crazy Saul Vance, in his garb of a fantastic scarecrow, who was forever starting somewhere and never going there—because, so sure as he came to a place where two roads crossed, he could not make up his mind which turn to take. In his youth a girl had jilted him, or a bank had failed on him, or a colt had kicked him in the head—or maybe it was all three of these things that had addled his poor brains. Anyhow he went his pitiable, aimless way for years, taunted daily by small boys who were more cruel than jungle beasts. How he lived nobody knew, but when he died some of the men who as boys had jeered him turned out to be his volunteer pallbearers.

There was Mr. H. Jackman—Brother Jackman to all the town—who had been our leading hatter once and rich besides, and in the days of his affluence had given the Baptist church its bells. In his old age, when he was dog-poor, he lived on charity, only it was not known by that word, which is at once the sweetest and the bitterest word in our tongue; for Brother Jackman, always primped, always plump and well clad, would go through the market to take his pick of what was there, and to the Richland House bar for his toddies, and to Felsburg Brothers for new garments when his old ones wore shabby—and yet never paid a cent for anything; a kindly conspiracy on the part of the whole town enabling him to maintain his self-respect to the last. Strangers in our town used to take him for a retired banker—that's a fact!

And there was old man Stackpole, who had killed his man—killed him in fair fight and was acquitted—and yet walked quiet back streets at all hours, a grey, silent shadow, and never slept except with a bright light burning in his room.

The tragedy of Mr. Edward Tilghman, though, and of Captain Abner G. Tilghman, his elder brother, was both a tragedy and a mystery—the biggest tragedy and the deepest mystery the town had ever known or ever would know probably. All that anybody knew for certain was that for upward of fifty years neither of them had spoken to the other, nor by deed or look had given heed to the other. As boys, back in sixty-one, they had gone out together. Side by side, each with his arm over the other's shoulder, they had stood up with more than a hundred others to be sworn into the service of the Confederate States of America; and on the morning they went away Miss Sally May Ghoulson had given the older brother her silk scarf off her shoulders to wear for a sash. Both the brothers had liked her; but by this public act she made it plain which of them was her choice.

Then the company had marched off to the camp below the Tennessee border, where the

new troops were drilling; and as they marched
some watchers wept and others cheered—but
the cheering predominated, for it was to be only
a sort of picnic anyhow—so everybody agreed.
As the orators—who mainly stayed behind—
pointed out, the Northern people would not
fight. And even if they should fight could not
one Southerner whip four Yankees? Certainly
he could; any fool knew that much. In a
month or two months, or at most three months,
they would all be tramping home again, covered
with glory and the spoils of war, and then—
this by common report and understanding—
Miss Sally May Ghoulson and Abner Tilghman would be married, with a big church
wedding.

The Yankees, however, unaccountably fought,
and it was not a ninety-day picnic after all.
It was not any kind of a picnic. And when it
was over, after four years and a month, Miss
Sally May Ghoulson and Abner Tilghman did
not marry. It was just before the battle of
Chickamauga when the other men in the company first noticed that the two Tilghmans had
become as strangers, and worse than strangers,
to each other. They quit speaking to each
other then and there, and to any man's knowledge they never spoke again. They served
the war out, Abner rising just before the end to
a captaincy, Edward serving always as a private
in the ranks. In a dour, grim silence they took
the fortunes of those last hard, hopeless days

and after the surrender down in Mississippi
they came back with the limping handful that
was left of the company; and in age they were
all boys still—but in experience, men, and in
suffering, grandsires.

Two months after they got back Miss Sally
May Ghoulson was married to Edward, the
younger brother. Within a year she died, and
after a decent period of mourning Edward
married a second time—only to be widowed
again after many years. His second wife bore
him children and they died—all except one,
a daughter, who grew up and married badly;
and after her mother's death she came back to
live with her deaf father and to minister to him.
As for Captain Abner Tilghman, he never
married—never, so far as the watching eyes
of the town might tell, looked with favour
upon any woman. And he never spoke to
his brother or to any of his brother's family—
or his brother to him.

With years the wall of silence they had
builded up between them turned to ice and the
ice to stone. They lived on the same street,
but never did Edward enter Captain Abner's
bank, never did Captain Abner pass Edward's
house—always he crossed over to the opposite
side. They belonged to the same Veterans'
Camp—indeed there was only the one for
them to belong to; they voted the same ticket
—straight Democratic; and in the same church,
the old Independent Presbyterian, they wor-

shipped the same God by the same creed, the older brother being an elder and the younger a plain member—and yet never crossed looks.

The town had come to accept this dumb and bitter feud as unchangeable and eternal; in time people ceased even to wonder what its cause had been, and in all the long years only one man had tried, before now, to heal it up. When old Doctor Henrickson died, a young and earnest clergyman, fresh from a Virginia theological school, came out to take the vacant pulpit; and he, being filled with a high sense of his holy calling, thought it shameful that such a thing should be in the congregation. He went to see Captain Tilghman about it. He never went but once. Afterward it came out that Captain Tilghman had threatened to walk out of church and never darken its doors again if the minister ever dared to mention his brother's name in his presence. So the young minister sorrowed, but obeyed, for the captain was rich and a generous giver to the church.

And he had grown richer with the years, and as he grew richer his brother grew poorer— another man owned the drug store where Edward Tilghman had failed. They had grown from young to middle-aged men and from middle-aged men to old, infirm men; and first the grace of youth and then the solidness of maturity had gone out of them and the gnarliness of age had come upon them; one was halt of step and the other was dull of ear; and the town through half a century of schooling had accustomed itself to the situation and took it as a matter of course. So it was and so it always would be—a tragedy and a mystery. It had not been of any use when the minister interfered; it was of no use now. Judge Priest, with the gesture of a man who is beaten, dropped the fan on the porch floor, went into his darkened sitting room, stretched himself wearily on a creaking horsehide sofa and called out to Jeff to make him a mild toddy—one with plenty of ice in it.

On this same Sunday—or, anyhow, I like to fancy it was on this same Sunday—at a point distant approximately nine hundred and seventy miles in a northeasterly direction from Judge Priest's town, Corporal Jacob Speck, late of Sigel's command, sat at the kitchen window of the combined Speck and Engel apartment on East Eighty-fifth Street in the Borough of Manhattan, New York. He was in his shirtsleeves; his tender feet were incased in a pair of red-and-green carpet slippers. In the angle of his left arm he held his youngest grandchild, aged one and a half years, while his right hand carefully poised a china pipe, with a bowl like an egg-cup and a stem like a fishpole. The corporal's blue Hanoverian eyes, behind their thick-lensed glasses, were fixed upon a comprehensive vista of East Eighty-fifth Street back yards and clothespoles and fire escapes; but his thoughts were elsewhere.

Reared back there at seeming ease, the corporal none the less was distracted in his mind. It was not that he so much minded being left at home to mind the youngest baby while the rest of the family spent the afternoon amid the Teutonic splendours of Smeltzer's Harlem River Casino, with its acres of gravel walks and its whitewashed tree trunks, its straggly flower beds and its high-collared beers. He was used to that sort of thing. Since a plague of multiplying infirmities of the body had driven him out of his job in the tax office, the corporal had not done much except nurse the babies that occurred in the Speck-Engel establishment with such unerring regularity. Sometimes, it is true, he did slip down to the corner for maybe zwei glasses of beer and a game of pinocle; but then, likely as not, there would come inopportunely a towheaded descendant to tell him Mommer needed him back at the flat right away to mind the baby while she went marketing or to the movies.

He could endure that—he had to. What riled Corporal Jacob Speck on this warm and sunny Sunday was a realisation that he was not doing his share at making the history of the period. The week before had befallen the fiftieth anniversary of the marching away of his old regiment to the front; there had been articles in the papers about it. Also, in patriotic

commemoration of the great event there had
been a parade of the wrinkled survivors—
ninety-odd of them—following their tattered,
faded battle flag down Fifth Avenue past
apathetic crowds, nine-tenths of whom had
been born since the war—in foreign lands
mainly; and at least half, if one might judge
by their looks, did not know what the parading
was all about, and did not particularly care
either.

The corporal had not participated in the
march of the veterans; he had not even attended the banquet that followed it. True,
his youngest grandchild was at the moment
cutting one of her largest jaw teeth and so had
required, for the time, an extraordinary and
special amount of minding; but the young
lady's dental difficulty was not the sole reason
for his absence. Three weeks earlier the corporal had taken part in Decoration Day, and
certainly one parade a month was ample strain
upon underpinning such as he owned. He had
returned home with his game leg behaving more
gamely then usual and his sound one full of
new and painful kinks. Also, in honour of the
occasion, he had committed the error of wearing
a pair of stiff new shoes; wherefore he had
favoured carpet slippers ever since.

Missing the fiftieth anniversary was not the
main point with the corporal—that was merely
the fortune of war, to be accepted with fortitude
and with no more than a proper and natural

amount of grumbling by one who had been a good soldier and was now a good citizen; but for days before the event, and daily ever since, divers members of the old regiment had been writing pieces to the papers—the German papers and the English-printing papers too—long pieces, telling of the trip to Washington, and then on into Virginia and across to Tennessee, speaking of this campaign and that and this battle and that. And because there was just now a passing wave of interest in Civil War matters, the papers had printed these contributions, thereby reflecting much glory on the writers thereof. But Corporal Speck, reading these things, had marvelled deeply that sane men should have such disgustingly bad memories; for his own recollection of these events differed most widely from the reminiscent narration of each misguided chronicler.

It was, indeed, a shameful thing that the most important occurrences of the whole war should be so shockingly mangled and mishandled in the retelling. They were so grievously wrong, those other veterans, and he was so absolutely right. He was always right in these matters. Only the night before, during a merciful respite from nursing duties, he had, in Otto Wittenpen's back barroom, spoken across the rim of a tall stein with some bitterness regarding certain especially grievous misstatements of plain fact on the part of faulty-minded comrades. In reply Otto had said, in a rather sneering tone the corporal thought:

"Say, then, Jacob, why don't you yourself write a piece to the paper telling about this regiment of yours—the way it was?"

"I will. To-morrow I will do so without fail," he had said, the ambition of authorship suddenly stirring within him. Now, however, as he sat at the kitchen window, he gloomed in his disappointment, for he had tried and he knew he had not the gift of the written line. A good soldier he had been—ja, none better —and a good citizen, and in his day a capable and painstaking doorkeeper in the tax office; but he could not write his own story. That morning, when the youngest grandbaby slept and his daughter and his daughter's husband and the brood of his older grandchildren were all at the Lutheran church over in the next block, he sat himself down to compose his article to the paper; but the words would not come—or, at least, after the first line or two they would not come.

The mental pictures of those stirring great days when he marched off on his two good legs —both good legs then—to fight for the country whose language he could not yet speak were there in bright and living colours; but the sorry part of it was he could not clothe them in language. In the trash box under the sink a dozen crumpled sheets of paper testified to his failure, and now, alone with the youngest Miss

Engel, he brooded over it and got low in his mind and let his pipe go smack out. And right then and there, with absolutely no warning at all, there came to him, as you might say from the clear sky, a great idea—an idea so magnificent that he almost dropped little Miss Engel off his lap at the splendid shock of it.

With solicitude he glanced down at the small, moist, pink, lumpy bundle of prickly heat and sore gums. Despite the jostle the young lady slept steadily on. Very carefully he laid his pipe aside and very carefully he got upon his feet, jouncing his charge soothingly up and down, and with deftness he committed her small person to the crib that stood handily by. She stirred fretfully, but did not wake. The corporal steered his gimpy leg and his rheumatic one out of the kitchen, which was white with scouring and as clean as a new pin, into the rearmost and smallest of the three sleeping rooms that mainly made up the Speck-Engel apartment.

The bed, whereon of nights Corporal Speck reposed with a bucking bronco of an eight-year-old grandson for a bedmate, was jammed close against the plastering, under the one small window set diagonally in a jog in the wall, and opening out upon an airshaft, like a chimney. Time had been when the corporal had a room and a bed all his own; that was before the family began to grow so fast in its second generation and he still held a place of lucrative employment at the tax office.

As he got down upon his knees beside the bed the old man uttered a little groan of discomfort. He felt about in the space underneath and drew out a small tin trunk, rusted on its corners and dented in its sides. He made a laborious selection of keys from a key-ring he got out of his pocket, unlocked the trunk and lifted out a heavy top tray. The tray contained, among other things, such treasures as his naturalisation papers, his pension papers, a photograph of his dead wife, and a small bethumbed passbook of the East Side Germania Savings Bank. Underneath was a black fatigue hat with a gold cord round its crown, a neatly folded blue uniform coat, with the G. A. R. bronze showing in its uppermost lapel, and below that, in turn, the suit of neat black the corporal wore on high state occasions and would one day wear to be buried in. Pawing and digging, he worked his hands to the very bottom, and then, with a little grunt, he heaved out the thing he wanted—the one trophy, except a stiffened kneecap and an honourable record, this old man brought home from the South. It was a captured Confederate knapsack, flattened and flabby. Its leather was dry-rotted with age and the brass C. S. A. on the outer flap was gangrened and sunken in; the flap curled up stiffly, like an old shoe sole.

The crooked old fingers undid a buckle fastening and from the musty and odorous interior of the knapsack withdrew a letter, in a queer-looking yellowed envelope, with a queer-looking stamp upon the upper right-hand corner and a faint superscription upon its face. The three sheets of paper he slid out of the envelope were too old even to rustle, but the close writing upon them in a brownish, faded ink was still plainly to be made out.

Corporal Speck replaced the knapsack in its place at the very bottom, put the tray back in its place, closed the trunk and locked it and shoved it under the bed. The trunk resisted slightly and he lost one carpet slipper and considerable breath in the struggle. Limping back to the kitchen and seeing little Miss Engel still slumbered, he eased his frame into a chair and composed himself to literary composition, not in the least disturbed by the shouts of roistering sidewalk comedians that filtered up to him from down below in front of the house, or by the distant clatter of intermittent traffic over the cobbly spine of Second Avenue, half a block away. For some time he wrote, with a most scratchy pen; and this is what he wrote:

"To the Editor of the 'Sun,' City.

"*Dear Sir:* The undersigned would state that he served two years and nine months—until wounded in action—in the Fighting Two Hundred and Tenth New York Infantry, and

has been much interested to see what other
comrades wrote for the papers regarding same
in connection with the Rebellion War of North
and South respectively. I would state that
during the battle of Chickamauga I was for a
while lying near by to a Confederate soldier—
name unknown—who was dying on account
of a wound in the chest. By his request I
gave him a drink of water from my canteen,
he dying shortly thereafter. Being myself
wounded—right knee shattered by a Minie
ball—I was removed to a field hospital; but
before doing so I brought away this man's
knapsack for a keepsake of the occasion. Some
years later I found in said knapsack a letter,
which previous to then was overlooked by me.
I inclose herewith a copy of said letter, which
it may be interesting for reading purposes by
surviving comrades.

"Respectfully yours,

"JACOB SPECK,

"Late Corporal L Company,
"Fighting Two Hundred and Tenth New York, U. S. A."

With deliberation and squeaky emphasis the
pen progressed slowly across the paper, while
the corporal, with his left hand, held flat the dead
man's ancient letter before him, intent on copy-
ing it. Hard words puzzled him and long words
daunted him, and he was making a long job of it
when there were steps in the hall without. Entered breezily Miss Hortense Engel, the eldest of

all the multiplying Engels, pretty beyond question and every inch American, having the gift of wearing Lower Sixth Avenue's stock designs in a way to make them seem Upper Fifth Avenue's imported models. Miss Engel's face was pleasantly flushed; she had just parted lingeringly from her steady company, Mr. Lawrence J. McLaughlin, plumber's helper, in the lower hallway, which is the trysting place and courting place of tenement-dwelling sweethearts, and now she had come to make ready the family's cold Sunday night tea. At sight of her the corporal had another inspiration —his second within the hour. His brow smoothed and he fetched a sigh of relief.

" 'Lo, grosspops!" she said. "How's every little thing? The kiddo all right?"

She unpinned a Sunday hat that was plumed like a hearse and slipped on a long apron that covered her from high collar to hobble hem.

"Girl," said her grandfather, "would you make to-morrow for me at the office a copy of this letter on the typewriter machine?"

He spoke in German and she answered in New-Yorkese, while her nimble fingers wrestled with the task of back-buttoning her apron.

"Sure thing! It won't take hardly a minute to rattle that off. Funny-looking old thing!" she went on, taking up the creased and faded original. "Who wrote it? And whatcher goin' to do with it, grosspops?"

"That," he told her, "is mine own business!

It is for you, please, to make the copy and bring both to me to-morrow, the letter and also the copy."

So on Monday morning, when the rush of taking dictation at the offices of the Great American Hosiery Company, in Broome Street, was well abated, the competent Miss Hortense copied the letter, and that same evening her grandfather mailed it to the *Sun*, accompanied by his own introduction. The *Sun* straightway printed it without change and—what was still better—with the sender's name spelled out in capital letters; and that night, at the place down by the corner, Corporal Jacob Speck was a prophet not without honour in his own country. Much honour, in fact, accrued.

You may remember that, upon a memorable occasion, Judge Priest went on a trip to New York and while there had dealings with a Mr. J. Hayden Witherbee, a promoter of gas and other hot-air propositions; and that during the course of his stay in the metropolis he made the acquaintance of one Malley, a *Sun* reporter. This had happened some years back, but Malley was still on the staff of the *Sun*. It happened also that, going through the paper to clip out and measure up his space, Malley came upon the corporal's contribution. Glancing over it idly, he caught the name, twice or thrice repeated, of the town where Judge Priest lived. So he bundled together a couple of copies and

sent them South with a short letter; and therefore it came about in due season, through the
good offices of the United States Post-office
Department, these enclosures reached the judge
on a showery Friday afternoon as he loafed
upon his wide front porch, waiting for his supper.

First, he read Malley's letter and was glad
to hear from Malley. With a quickened interest he ran a plump thumb under the wrap-
pings of the two close-rolled papers, opened
out one of them at page ten and read the opening statement of Corporal Jacob Speck, for
whom instantly the judge conceived a long-
distance fondness. Next he came to the letter
that Miss Hortense Engel had so accurately
transcribed, and at the very first words of it he
sat up straighter, with a surprised and gratified
little grunt; for he had known them both—
the writer of that letter and its recipient.
One still lived in his memory as a red-haired
girl with a pert, malicious face, and the other
as a stripling youth in a ragged grey uniform.
And he had known most of those whose names
studded the printed lines so thickly. Indeed,
some of them he still knew—only now they
were old men and old women—faded, wrinkled
bucks and belles of a far-distant day.

As he read the first words it came back to
the judge, almost with the jolting emphasis
of a new and fresh sensation, that in the days
of his own youth he had not liked the girl
who wrote that letter nor the man who received

it. But she was dead this many and many
a year—why, she must have died soon after
she wrote this very letter—the date proved
that—and he, the man, had fallen at Chickamauga, taking his death in front like a soldier;
and surely that settled everything and made all
things right! But the letter—that was the
main thing. His old blue eyes skipped nimbly
behind the glasses that saddled the tip of his
short pink nose, and the old judge read it—
just such a letter as he himself had received
many a time; just such a wartime letter as
uncounted thousands of soldiers North and
South received from their sweethearts and read
and reread by the light of flickering campfires
and carried afterward in their knapsacks
through weary miles of marching.

It was crammed with the small-town gossip
of a small town that was but little more than
a memory now—telling how, because he would
not volunteer, a hapless youth had been waylaid by a dozen high-spirited girls and over-
powered, and dressed in a woman's skirt and
a woman's poke bonnet, so that he left town
with his shame between two suns; how, since
the Yankees had come, sundry faithless females
were friendly—actually friendly, this being
underscored—with the more personable of the
young Yankee officers; how half the town was
in mourning for a son or brother dead or
wounded; how a new and sweetly sentimental
song, called Rosalie, the Prairie Flower, was

being much sung at the time—and had it reached the army yet?—how old Mrs. Hobbs had been exiled to Canada for seditious acts and language and had departed northward between two files of bluecoats, reviling the Yankees with an unbitted tongue at every step; how So-and-So had died or married or gone refugeeing below the enemy's line into safely Southern territory; how this thing had happened and that thing had not.

The old judge read on and on, catching gladly at names that kindled a tenderly warm glow of half-forgotten memories in his soul, until he came to the last paragraph of all; and then, as he comprehended the intent of it in all its barbed and venomed malice, he stood suddenly erect, with the outspread paper shaking in his hard grip. For now, coming back to him by so strange a way across fifty years of silence and misunderstanding, he read there the answer to the town's oldest, biggest tragedy and knew what it was that all this time had festered, like buried thorns, in the flesh of those two men, his comrades and friends. He dropped the paper, and up and down the wide, empty porch he stumped on his short legs, shaking with the shock of revelation and with indignation and with pity for the blind and bitter uselessness of it all.

"Ah, hah!" he said to himself over and over again understandingly. "Ah, hah!" And then: "Next to a mean man, a mean woman is the meanest thing in this whole created world, I reckin. I ain't shore but whut she's the meanest of the two. And to think of what them two did between 'em—she writin' that hellish black lyin' tale to 'Lonzo Pike and he puttin' off hotfoot to Abner Tilghman to poison his mind with it and set him like a flint ag'inst his own flesh and blood! And wasn't it jest like Lon Pike to go and git himself killed the next day after he got that there letter! And wasn't it jest like her to up and die before the truth could be brought home to her! And wasn't it like them two stubborn, set, contrary, close-mouthed Tilghman boys to go 'long through all these years, without neither one of 'em ever offerin' to make or take an explanation!" His tone changed. "Oh, ain't it been a pitiful thing! And all so useless! But—oh, thank the Lord—it ain't too late to mend it part way anyhow! Thank God, it ain't too late fur that!"

Exulting now, he caught up the paper he had dropped, and with it crumpled in his pudgy fist was half-way down the gravel walk, bound for the little cottage snuggled in its vine ambush across Clay Street, before a better and a bigger inspiration caught up with him and halted him midway of an onward stride.

Was not this the second Friday in the month? It certainly was. And would not the Camp be meeting to-night in regular semimonthly session at Kamleiter's Hall? It certainly would. For just a moment Judge Priest considered the proposition. He slapped his linen clad flank gleefully, and his round old face, which had been knotted with resolution, broke up into a wrinkly, ample smile; he spun on his heel and hurried back into the house and to the telephone in the hall. For half an hour, more or less, Judge Priest was busy at that telephone, calling in a high, excited voice, first for one number and then for another. While he did this his supper grew cold on the table, and in the dining room Jeff, the white-clad, fidgeted and out in the kitchen Aunt Dilsey, the turbaned, fumed—but, at Kamleiter's Hall that night at eight, Judge Priest's industry was in abundant fulness rewarded.

Once upon a time Gideon K. Irons Camp claimed a full two hundred members, but that had been when it was first organised. Now there were in good standing less than twenty. Of these twenty, fifteen sat on the hard wooden chairs when Judge Priest rapped with his metal spectacle case for order, and that fifteen meant all who could travel out at nights. Doctor Lake was there, and Sergeant Jimmy Bagby, the faithful and inevitable. It was the biggest turnout the Camp had had in a year.

Far over on one side, cramped down in a chair, was Captain Abner Tilghman, feeble and worn-looking. His buggy horse stood hitched by the curb downstairs. Sergeant Jimmy Bagby had gone to his house for him and on the plea of business of vital moment

had made him come with him. Almost directly
across the middle aisle on the other side sat
Mr. Edward Tilghman. Nobody had to go for
him. He always came to a regular meeting of
the Camp, even though he heard the proceedings
only in broken bits.

The adjutant called the roll and those present
answered, each one to his name; and mainly
the voices sounded bent and sagged, like the
bodies of their owners. But a keen onlooker
might have noticed a sort of tremulous, joyous
impatience, which filled all save two of these
old, grey men, pushing the preliminaries forward with uncommon speed. They fidgeted
in their places.

Presently Judge Priest cleared his throat of
a persistent huskiness and stood up.

"Before we purceed to the regular routine,"
he piped, "I desire to present a certain matter
to a couple of our members." He came down
off the little platform, where the flags were
draped, with a step that was almost light,
and into Captain Abner Tilghman's hand he
put a copy of a city paper, turned and folded
at a certain place, where a column of printed
matter was scored about with heavy pencil
bracketings. "Cap'n," he said, "ez a personal
favour to me, suh, would you please read this
here article?—the one that's marked"—he
pointed with his finger—"not aloud—read it
to yourself, please."

It was characteristic of the paralytic to say

nothing. Without a word he adjusted his glasses and without a word he began to read. So instantly intent was he that he did not see what followed next—and that was Judge Priest crossing over to Mr. Edward Tilghman's side with another copy of the same paper in his hand.

"Ed," he bade him, "read this here article, won't you? Read it clear through to the end —it mout interest you mebbe." The deaf man looked up at him wonderingly, but took the paper in his slightly palsied hand and bent his head close above the printed sheet.

Judge Priest stood in the middle aisle, making no move to go back to his own place. He watched the two silent readers. All the others watched them too. They read on, making slow progress, for the light was poor and their eyes were poor. And the watchers could hardly contain themselves; they could hardly wait. Sergeant Jimmy Bagby kept bobbing up and down like a pudgy jack-in-the-box that is slightly stiff in its joints. A small, restrained rustle of bodies accompanied the rustle of the folded newspapers held in shaky hands.

Unconscious of all scrutiny, the brothers read on. Perhaps because he had started first —perhaps because his glasses were the more expensive and presumably therefore the more helpful—Captain Abner Tilghman came to the concluding paragraph first. He read it through—and then Judge Priest turned his head away, for a moment almost regretting he had chosen so public a place for this thing.

He looked back again in time to see Captain Abner getting upon his feet. Dragging his dead leg behind him, the paralytic crossed the bare floor to where his brother's grey head was bent to his task. And at his side he halted, making no sound or sign, but only waiting. He waited there, trembling all over, until the sitter came to the end of the column and read what was there—and lifted a face all glorified with a perfect understanding.

"Eddie!" said the older man—"Eddie!" He uttered a name of boyhood affection that none there had heard uttered for fifty years nearly; and it was as though a stone had been rolled away from a tomb—as though out of the grave of a dead past a voice had risen resurrected. "Eddie!" he said a third time, pleadingly, abjectly, humbly, craving for forgiveness.

"Brother Abner!" said the other man. "Oh, Brother Abner!" he said—and that was all he did say—all he had need to say, for he was on his feet now, reaching out with wide-spread, shaking arms.

Sergeant Jimmy Bagby tried to start a yell, but could not make it come out of his throat —only a clicking, squeaking kind of sound came. Considered as a yell it was a miserable failure.

Side by side, each with his inner arm tight gripped about the other, the brothers, bareheaded, turned their backs upon their friends and went away. Slowly they passed out through the doorway into the darkness of the stair landing, and the members of the Gideon K. Irons Camp were all up on their feet.

"Mind that top step, Abner!" they heard the younger man say. "Wait! I'll help you down."

And that was all except a scuffling sound of uncertainly placed feet, growing fainter and fainter as the two brothers passed down the long stairs of Kamleiter's Hall and out into the night together—that was all, unless you would care to take cognisance of a subdued little chorus such as might be produced by twelve or thirteen elderly men snuffling in a large bare room. As commandant of the Camp it was fitting, perhaps, that Judge Priest should speak first.

"The trouble with this here Camp is jest this," he said: "it's got a lot of snifflin' old fools in it that don't know no better than to bust out cryin' when they oughter be happy!" And then, as if to prove how deeply he felt the shame of such weakness on the part of others, Judge Priest blew his nose with great violence, and for a space of minutes industriously mopped at his indignant eyes with an enormous pocket handkerchief.

. . . . .

In accordance with a rule, Jeff Poindexter waited up for his employer. Jeff expected him by nine-thirty at the latest; but it was

actually getting along toward ten-thirty before
Jeff, who had been dozing lightly in the dim-lit
hall, oblivious to the fanged attentions of some
large mosquitoes, roused as he heard the sound
of a rambling but familiar step clunking along
the wooden sidewalk of Clay Street. The
latch on the front gate clicked, and as Jeff
poked his nose out of the front door he heard,
down the aisle of trees that bordered the gravel
walk, the voice of his master uplifted in solitary
song.

In the matter of song the judge had a peculiarity. It made no difference what the words
might be or the theme—he sang every song
and all songs to a fine, thin, tuneless little air
of his own. At this moment Judge Priest, as
Jeff gathered, showed a wide range of selection.
One second he was announcing that his name
it was Joe Bowers and he was all the way from
Pike, and the next, stating, for the benefit of
all who might care to hear these details, that
they—presumably certain horses—were bound
to run all night—bound to run all day; so you
could bet on the bobtailed nag and he'd bet
on the bay. Nearer to the porch steps it
boastingly transpired that somebody had
jumped aboard the telegraf and steered her by
the triggers, whereat the lightnin' flew and 'lectri-
fied and killed ten thousand niggers! But even
so general a catastrophe could not weigh down
the singer's spirits. As he put a fumbling foot
upon the lowermost step of the porch, he threw

[400]

his head far back and shrilly issued the following blanket invitation to ladies resident in a far-away district:

Oh, Bowery gals, won't you come out to-night?
Won't you come out to-night?
Oh, Bowery gals, won't you come out to-night,
And dance by the light of the moon?
I danced with a gal with a hole in her stockin';
And her heel it kep' a-rockin'—kep' a-rockin'!
She was the purtiest gal in the room!

Jeff pulled the front door wide open. The song stopped and Judge Priest stood in the opening, teetering a little on his heels. His face was all a blushing pink glow—pinker even than common.

"Evenin', Jedge!" greeted Jeff. "You're late, suh!"

"Jeff," said Judge Priest slowly, "it's a beautiful evenin'."

Amazed, Jeff stared at him. As a matter of fact, the drizzle of the afternoon had changed, soon after dark, to a steady downpour. The judge's limpened hat brim dripped raindrops and his shoulders were sopping wet, but Jeff had yet to knowingly and wilfully contradict a prominent white citizen.

"Yas, suh!" he said, half affirmatively, half questioningly. "Is it?"

"It is so!" said Judge Priest. "Every star in the sky shines like a diamond! Jeff, it's the most beautiful evenin' I ever remember!"